BLIND PROPHET

ARROW TACTICAL SERIES

ISABEL JOLIE

ISABEL JOLIE

 Formatted with Vellum

For my daughter and all the graduates: As one chapter ends, another begins. Don't write someone else's story—write your own. Write it boldly, write it true.

*"In every man sleeps a prophet, and when he wakes,
there is a little more evil in the world."*

EMIL CIORAN

PROLOGUE

CAROLINE

It was a day like any other September day. It might've been raining, or maybe it was sunny. It didn't matter on a day that carried such weight. It was the normalcy that sticks with me. Lights turned on and off. The occasional siren sounded on the streets outside. The sharp scent of citrusy dish soap clung to my hands. Notifications popped up on my phone, unaware of the enormity of what was happening.

My fingers trembled as I zipped the last suitcase. Fractures deep in my chest threatened to bring me to my knees, rendering me immobile. My heart didn't want to leave, but my survival instincts overrode emotion.

I stared at the door for hours. A weak voice begged to just leave a note, but I couldn't be that person. I'd like to think I sat there, sitting beside my luggage, remembering our past, but that wouldn't be true. I chanted to myself, in a near-meditative trance, wearing a crisp, ironed blouse and navy slacks that would garner Gwyneth Paltrow's approval. Make-up lightly done, hair glossy and smooth, gold Cartier bracelets on one wrist, and a gold diamond-encrusted Rolex on the other. My pale pink nails were freshly manicured. If the paparazzi lingered outside, the photographs would present a well put-together person departing her home with luggage.

My nerves churned. I hoped for luck, to exit unobserved. The last thing I wanted was to have my photograph circulate, fueling rumors of marital strife.

I imagined an unnamed source might say they've sensed issues for months. A writer would speculate that Dorian and Caroline Moore haven't been seen together since the MOMA exhibit two months prior. A body language expert might decode a photograph from two years prior to one snapped when we'd been ducking paparazzi: *See how she's changed? Her arms are wrapped around her middle; she's crouching forward like she doesn't want him touching her, and they aren't making eye contact.* I stopped reading the articles when my mind picked up the writing habit.

The lock clicked. I swallowed.

My spine stiffened. My chest ached.

The door opened.

His gaze tracked me and the two silver Rimowa suitcases—post-wedding gifts. Before, I had owned standard fare. To the average pedestrian, the replacements might appear ordinary, but to those in the know, they're among the most expensive on the market. Understated luxury. Something I hadn't picked up on right out of college but quickly came to understand to be a requirement for a Moore.

Wordlessly, Dorian closed the door, and the lock clicked.

When he faced me again, his shoulders sagged, I think. Time may have painted that flicker of emotion in the recesses of my memory. His freshly shaven jaw held no discernible emotion.

"So this is it."

It wasn't a question, but rather a statement of expectation.

"Where will you go?"

"I'll stay at my parents." In Connecticut, the paparazzi would be less present. At his urging, I quit my job after we got married. The ever-present paparazzi unnerved me, and my colleagues began to see me as a celebrity instead of a junior-level account manager. Ironically, if he'd supported me or helped me find a way to continue with my career, I might have thrived.

Although…thrived is a strong verb. It's possible I wouldn't have suffocated.

Anger surfaced with the memory of my resignation. If I recalled correctly, I'd made no attempt to conceal the emotion on that day in our townhome.

"You won't get a dollar more than the prenuptial agreement allows. You know that, right?"

His statement struck like a scalpel—deliberate and strategic. When Dorian chose to speak, he did so with intention.

"I don't want a fight."

I want my sanity. My confidence. My sense of worth.

He stood there by my suitcases. Unreadable. Silent.

I don't know what I expected or why I waited for hours for an awkward interlude. It was a marriage no one wanted, and it ran its course. My marriage failed, and there was little point in staying when my efforts weren't wanted.

When I stood, I swiped my palms against my trousers and noticed how cold my hands had grown.

Are photographers outside? The question died on my tongue. It didn't matter.

A thousand regrets weighed down my chest, and a singular hope kept it functioning. Maybe, just maybe, he does want me to stay. Maybe he'll want to make the effort.

But if he had nothing to say, neither did I.

My hand fell to the luggage handle, and his covered mine.

He cupped my cheek and forced me to look up into his glassy eyes.

Silent tears leaked from eyes that hadn't seen me in months.

And then his lips covered mine, and I splintered. His touch stemmed the tearful tide. I clung to him, leaning on his strength.

When he broke the kiss, he breathed into my ear. "One last time?"

That's what he wanted. Sex.

His last words to me.

A gut punch. But also a confirming blow, one that told me there was no point in staying. I don't remember saying anything. I only remember walking through the door.

As feared, when I exited the townhome, I faced a flash of lights.

One photographer with a long-range lens across the street. Two photographers close to my left. My good side. Almost as if he planned it.

He could have. We had a security camera in our living area accessible via his phone. He could have seen me and my suitcases and known exactly what was coming.

I held my head high.

"Where are you going, Mrs. Moore?"

"Are the rumors true?"

"Caroline, are you separating?"

I forced a cold, cordial smile. A barely there smile that straddled the line of detached model and wealthy philanthropist with a disdain for the media.

How did they know? Did he leak it?

Newspaper photographs struggle to capture nuance. The captions from that day spoke of a tear-streaked face, but my stoic expression concealed the evidence. Social media, however, was full of photos and commentary filled with vitriol. How could it be otherwise?

After all, I walked away from a golden boy, an American prince, a billionaire. *Stupid, crazy, cheating slut, ice-cold, plastic, full of filler, greedy, social climber*. They didn't know what exactly I might have done to be thrown out of the gilded castle, but one thing was certain: in the court of public opinion, I held the blame.

CHAPTER 1

CAROLINE

Seven years later

The conference room door remains closed. Smoked glass walls bar any view of what's happening inside. My job as an analyst is to read the signs splashed across newspapers and in briefings, but there are days I wish I weren't so aware.

For those of us specializing in counter-terrorism and a nuanced global news cycle, these are fragile times. This truth feels truer with every passing day. When one works for a black ops company that takes untouchable covert assignments, closed doors are unnerving.

My friend, Sophia Sullivan, encouraged me to apply for a position at Arrow Tactical, one of many companies within her father's investment portfolio, but one with personal ties for

Sophia. When she was fifteen, she was kidnapped, and the founders of Arrow Tactical rescued her. Her experience put her on the law enforcement path, and as an FBI-turned-CIA operative, she maintains close contacts with Arrow, as they do work for many intelligence agencies around the world.

There was no posted open position, but she told me they could use someone like me. I suspect she saw how miserable I was working for an ogre in a position with limited growth opportunities and asked her father for a favor.

Sophia and I met years ago at The Farm, the CIA's training program. From what I've observed, Sophia has worked closely on multiple projects with Arrow Tactical. So closely, the lines between Arrow and the CIA blur. The company takes on projects governments won't touch, or at least, they won't touch without plausible deniability.

The conference room door opens, and Sophia's gaze connects with mine, her blue eyes sharp and focused. She walks directly to me through the maze of cubicles.

Does she want to grab coffee, or does she need to speak to me about something going on in that conference room?

Banking on the former, I open my desk drawer and remove my purse.

"Come with me," she says in a low voice, the same decibel level we've all been using since threat levels rose and the cubicles filled with those who typically work remotely.

I follow my friend through the stairwell door. She stops mid-flight.

"How'd your date go last night?"

The stainless-steel banister digs into my back as I lean against it. I'm on the higher step, and the advantageous position gives me the opportunity to study my friend. Her assessing eyes are slightly bloodshot, and small wisps of hair frame her face, evading the band she's used to pull back her blonde hair. Wrinkles mar her white button-down blouse, and it's not even nine in the morning. Her lipstick is long gone. The tilt of her head, the crossed arms, her pressed lips—she didn't pull me out here to ask me about last night's dinner.

My dinner date was with a colleague, and I never would've agreed to a date with him if it weren't for Sophia's urging. Sophia and Stella, our human resources director, of all people, kept prodding me to give the tall, dark, and handsome former military man a chance. They applied all the adjectives. Pushed and prodded. *Give him a chance. You never know...*

Still, Sophia's not vested in Luke. And even if she's curious, she could just text me—without leaving the conference room.

"You didn't call me out here to ask about my date," I say, insistent we get to the reason we're in a stairwell.

"No, I didn't," she admits, stepping back until her back presses to the opposite railing. It's classic Sophia. One arm crossed over her stomach, fingers still. "You know I value your intelligence and believe you are a strong addition to Arrow based on your merits, right?"

My personal history prevented me from ever being considered for field work, so from the very get-go, I focused on becoming an analyst. Does my consistent focus make me better than other analysts? No.

"What's going on?"

She tucks an errant wisp behind her ear.

"Sophia, just say it."

"I want to bring you in on a project. Or, well, it's an investigation."

"But?"

"There's no but, it's... You have to be okay with it, and I wanted to ask you in private."

I scan the stairwell and the eaves. "There's got to be a security camera in here somewhere."

Her exhale sends a strand of hair northward. "Probably. But at least I can ask you away from the others."

"Ask me what?"

"We're investigating Dorian."

My chest squeezes. It's the only physical warning sign from the mention of my ex. I can believe Dorian broke the law. He's a man with a high disdain for regulation and billions to pay a legal team. But why would the CIA care about an American breaking the law in the US? That's not their territory. If the CIA didn't hire Arrow, who did? Arrow only takes projects with a client attached.

"Why? What did he do?"

"He's a person of interest."

So they don't have anything on him. They won't find anything either. If he broke the law, he's too smart to get caught.

Sophia's quiet, thoughtful. Purposeful.

"Why are you telling me this?"

"You were married to him. Your perspective is valuable."

"Do you want to ask me questions?" I haven't seen Dorian in seven years. "Or do you want me to join the project team? Is this a project?"

"Yes, it's a highly confidential and critical project, and we want you to join the team. But I won't mention your connection to Dorian unless you feel comfortable."

"But if I am comfortable—"

"Your input would be of high value."

"How would I even join the team without—" I wouldn't. She's not really asking. This is my heads-up so I'm not blind-sided in a room full of men.

"It's fine, Sophia. My marriage isn't a secret." Not exactly. "Let's go. Time is of the essence, right? I left hot coffee on my desk. Let me grab it, and I'll meet you there."

She smiles, visibly relaxed. She'd been tense, worried how I'd take her request. I climb the stairs, releasing a sigh.

What have you gotten yourself into, Dorian?

"And that date? Yes? No?" Sophia calls from behind me in her standard, relaxed tone.

"I swear. You and Stella need to find a new television series to entertain you."

"I half-expected Stella to be at your desk this morning."

"She texted at six."

Behind me, Sophia laughs, the sound light, airy, and out of place, given the reason we're in the stairwell. Some people hate their exes, but I'm not one of them. Our marriage failed, but I never hated my husband. A queasiness sets into the pit of my belly.

"You know, if things don't work out with Luke, Stella mentioned Ethan is overdue for leave."

Stella's son is in Special Forces, following in Trevor's steps. Trevor, Stella's husband, is also one of the Arrow Tactical founders and a former SEAL. Based on the photos in her office, Ethan's handsome. "Isn't Ethan younger than me?"

"As if that would matter to Stella."

Fair. Stella jokes about being a cougar, but you'd never know she's the older spouse when looking at her and Trevor. She's aged well, and while he's physically fit and hot as hell, he's got a lot of gray, especially in his beard. And he adores his wife.

"Ethan's actually a couple of years older than us."

"Huh." If I'm thirty-one, and her son is older than me, how old is Stella?

I pull open the stairwell door, and our conversation stops as several people seated in cubicles, headphones or earbuds in place, look our way.

With one quick detour to grab my coffee and laptop, I catch up to Sophia before she steps inside the conference room.

Trevor sits beside Ryan Wolfgang, who is also a founding partner, and I'm his direct report. Ryan oversees mission strategy and client management, and Trevor functions as a coach and trainer to the operatives Arrow hires. All of the founders are long-time friends.

"Caroline, the CIA, NSA, and Homeland Security have granted security clearance for you to join our team," Ryan says.

Wow. Three US intelligence agencies. What the hell have you done, Dorian?

"Welcome to Project Unity," Ryan continues. "Later, Sophia will provide a complete briefing. Over the last several weeks, allied intelligence services have gathered evidence that a multi-pronged attack is in the works. Planned timing remains unknown, as does the architect. Small-scale attacks have been occurring across Europe over the last six weeks, and we believe those are designed as tests and point to a larger, coordinated attack."

I'm familiar with the attacks Ryan is referencing. I keep up with the news.

How would global attacks relate to Dorian? I read in an article recently that Zenith, the company he founded the last year we lived together, has the most extensive satellite network in the world. Governments are Zenith's clients. Dorian wouldn't attack his clients.

Ryan continues with the update in a staid monotone. "Chemical weapons were stolen from a factory in North Korea. We've located the ship carrying the weapons and are tracking it via satellite to gain a better understanding of its intent before we disarm it. Transcontinental wires on the Atlantic Ocean floor were tampered with and damaged. Sources are telling us an EMP attack is likely. Plans to disable GPS across the United States are being circulated online."

An electromagnetic pulse, or EMP, attack is a high-intensity burst of electromagnetic energy that can disable or destroy electronic devices and electrical infrastructure. It would cause widespread power grid failure and halt communications. Coupled with plans to disable GPS, mass hysteria might be the goal. These days, everyone, from ambulances to delivery services, relies on GPS. But GPS goes beyond getting around. Military operations, telecommunications, and financial systems would be impacted. They're talking a black swan event.

"That would be next to impossible to accomplish." I can't stop myself from interrupting. "The US government has measures in place to protect GPS infrastructure and can selectively deny or degrade signals if needed."

"We didn't consider the threat to be high risk either, but two days ago, security at a ground control station in Nebraska was taken out by a sniper. Again, it appears these are tests to prepare for a full-scale attack," Ryan says.

"Chat boards have been whispering about EMP attacks for years," I say, skeptical that this is any more than fear-mongering propaganda.

Homeland Security monitors the threat. At the CIA, we worked with Homeland Security on threat assessment, as an EMP attack would have a global impact.

"True," Ryan agrees. "Our assignment is to determine who is behind the recent attacks. Global tensions and concerns are rising. Russia and China are obvious suspects, but they deny culpability."

They always deny culpability.

Last night, during dinner with Luke, our discussion circled world events and risks. *All roads lead to Russia.* That's what Luke said.

I'm fairly certain he's working on this project. I've seen him enter and exit the conference room. Is that why he kept talking about world news last night? He couldn't get his mind off work. I can commiserate.

"Intelligence services across the world, the CIA included, are analyzing involvement from an opposing country. Project Unity has tasked Arrow with gaining intel on alternate possibilities.

"We have intercepted messages and threats from someone identifying as Prophet. There are no known groups or countries that identify as that name, and that has fostered a belief in the intelligence community that we might be dealing with one person or a small group," Ryan concludes.

The screen on the back wall lights up, and a list of names in black font on a white background show. I fumble for my glasses.

With my glasses on, I scan the list, and my breathing slows and skin cools. Sophia pulling me aside before bringing me in here makes more sense now.

Amir Nooyi
Geoff Mansueto
Jiang Tu
Paola Droga
William Pearson
Halston Moore
Dorian Moore

I blink rapidly, zeroing in on the last two listed names. They're all well-connected multibillionaires. An investigation into any of these men would require a covert approach. Dorian and Halston, his father, are the only two Americans on the list.

Rumors about a cabal of powerful men pulling strings have existed for decades. We'd be better off if such a cabal existed, as the truth is worse—no one is in control.

I recently debriefed an asset Arrow helped secure overseas. He'd been working deep undercover, investigating the syndicate, an alliance of powerful men—the men listed on the screen.

"Those listed are all part of a global alliance that has recently fractured and, as such, are persons of interest," Ryan continues. "One theory is that one, or several, of these men is behind the plan and, possibly, identifying as Prophet.

"MI5, the British secret service, is investigating Amir Nooyi.

"Geoff Mansueto is a biotech engineer and a high-profile owner of Streamline Media. He resides in Australia, and ASIO, the Australian secret service, is monitoring him.

"Jiang Tu, a Chinese business magnate, went missing about two months ago. Sources say he's being held by Xi against his will. If this is correct, he's not a party to this.

"William Pearson, the CEO of Brookline, is Canadian. We're working jointly with CSIS, Canadian intelligence, to assess the likelihood of his involvement.

"Halston and Dorian Moore are Americans. They currently reside in a compound in Colorado." The black screen on the wall flickers to display satellite imagery of wooded mountains. "This is Halston Moore's compound in Colorado. He's a founding member of the fractured alliance. His compound includes eight hundred acres of heavily wooded land. He's steadily increased security over the years."

Haltson Moore, Dorian's father, is an eccentric billionaire and possesses agoraphobic tendencies. He's not on the CIA watch list, or at least he wasn't the last time I checked.

"The Moores have the contacts and the means to orchestrate the multipronged threat we are witnessing." Ryan pointedly looks at me. "Dorian Moore's name is also being floated as a replacement for chief of staff."

Halston always wanted his son to enter politics. "Conklin is stepping down?"

"Those are the rumors. It gives our investigation into the Moore men more weight, and a greater requirement for secrecy."

"If an official government body investigates, it could be seen as playing politics," I state.

"Precisely," Ryan confirms.

"Caroline, you were married to Dorian Moore. What can you tell us about him?" Sophia asks, voice low, as if utilizing a low volume makes the question less intrusive.

When we went through The Farm together, I wasn't the only candidate with a failed marriage, but I was the only well-known person in our class. I entered the class with my maiden name and never spoke of Dorian Moore, but reverting my name did nothing to diminish the class's awareness. It took years before second glances and whispers became rare occurrences.

Giving me a heads-up was the right thing for Sophia to do. Otherwise, my reaction might have been overwhelmingly defensive.

But she did give me a heads-up, and this isn't personal. I clear my throat and address the question. "Halston Moore doesn't have a military background, and while he's politically engaged, he's a both-sideser, meaning he donates to any party that can benefit his businesses. In most elections, he donates to both candidates to ensure he has a seat at the table, no matter who wins, and he has done this for decades. He's invested in the government as it exists today. In his early nineties, Halston Moore doesn't fit the profile of a terrorist." The temptation to shrink beneath Ryan's stern gaze threatens to unnerve me, but I sit straighter in my seat. The intel I possess is only valuable if I share it. "If you are asking my opinion, he strikes me as a highly unlikely participant in a plan against the United States."

"And his son?" Ryan asks.

Brown eyes rimmed in gold flash, dark wavy hair, and a distinct jaw line set with determination and drive flicker.

"A reliable source claims Dorian Moore is the mastermind. His travel records support the claim," Sophia says.

Dorian is many things, but a terrorist isn't one of them. That wouldn't change over time. The source is wrong.

"He's a pacifist," I say. "Is there any evidence, other than this one source, that ties…" I can't continue. The accusation is ludicrous.

"He has motive," Ryan says. "If you buy into uncertainty leading to additional government contracts for his company."

That's weak. They're off. Dorian inherited wealth. Money doesn't motivate him.

"A member of the Five Eyes located a detailed plan to disable GPS systems," Sophia says.

Formed after World War II, the Five Eyes is an intelligence alliance comprising Australia, Canada, New Zealand, the United Kingdom, and the United States.

"The plan includes broadcasting powerful signals to overwhelm GPS receivers and transmit false GPS signals to deceive receivers. When we reviewed who within the United States possessed those resources and technological capabilities... well, it's a short list."

I reread the list of names.

"Dorian Moore owns a satellite business," I say, trying to remember the details. He'd been excited about the concept when we were together. Given his wealth, his businesses grew quickly.

"They own more satellites than any country in the world," Ryan says, which corroborates the business article I read.

"Leasing satellites to countries is a significant source of revenue. All the more reason Dorian wouldn't be a part of an EMP attack that destroys satellites." My gaze falls on Sophia. She must see that this is a preposterous theory. Is that why she asked me in here? To back her position?

"They stand to profit handsomely if the US is forced to lease satellites post-attack," Ryan says.

Trevor taps the table and shifts in his seat. His expression is grim. "We've analyzed the compound. If we could find a way in, we could set up surveillance and determine if he's a threat."

"That would be against the law," I say, stating the obvious.

"That's why they hired us," Trevor answers matter-of-factly. His tone isn't mean, but his comment puts me in my place. "If I'm hearing you correctly, you don't believe it's him. Unfortunately, we need proof of his innocence or guilt. That's our assignment. How familiar are you with the compound?"

"Not very," I admit. "It's been years."

They're calling it a compound, but I remember a luxurious mountain home near Telluride.

"Do you remember if they outsource security? We considered creating an electrical issue and sending in our utility men, but they've got backup generators. It's not an ideal plan."

"Mr. Moore, Dorian's father, Halston, is a highly suspicious individual. Even if you could get a utility worker on the property, they wouldn't be left alone. He did deep background checks on his cleaning service. Mr. Moore has friends on the intelligence committee, and he's heard stories. It's something he used to talk about. He employs former Secret Service on his security team, and no, he doesn't outsource."

Ryan nods, satisfied with my answer.

"What kind of surveillance are you planning?" I ask Trevor. "Physical? Electronic? Computer?" Social media surveillance would be pointless. If he has a presence, a PR agency is behind it.

"All of the above. We'd like to get someone into his office, or offices, to plant cameras, or at the very least, microphones. Nothing we obtain could be used in court, but if he's involved—"

"You'll know better where to look to gain evidence," I say before he can finish his thought. "And I assume you can't tap his phones?"

"On a typical American citizen, it could be easily done. But with the Moores, any communication we access on one of their phones can safely be assumed they're okay with being public," Sophia says.

She's probably right. They're hyperaware of taps.

"We aren't looking to build a case for prosecution," Trevor says. "We're looking to stop them."

"Our aim is to dismantle the attack, and if we can't do that, to mount a multipronged defense that prevents the attack from doing any damage," Ryan says. "And to ensure we have evidence that prevents the wrong party, or in this case, countries, from being blamed."

I exhale, understanding the situation.

"If we're wrong, we exonerate the Moore men. Remove them from the persons of interest list," Sophia says, her direct eye contact communicating volumes. She's looking to me for a solution.

"If you want to get someone into his compound, then I'm your best bet." I eye Sophia, wondering if this was her objective all along. "For the record, I don't believe Dorian would do this. But I can access his home. He won't turn me away."

"You're not trained to be in the field," Sophia interjects. "What if I come with you, as your friend? We'll say we were in the area."

I haven't seen him in seven years, and I'm coming by to say hello with my friend tagging along?

"It's best if I go alone."

Dorian Moore is an all-consuming alpha male, and I left him to preserve my sanity and dignity, but they're off on this. The Moores have the means, but not the motive.

As a counter-terrorist analyst, I have the expertise and knowledge to confirm the Moore men do not match a terrorist profile. But based on recent intel, a threat looms. As Americans, we prefer to believe the threat is abroad. Before a world war commences, we need confirmation.

I understand the logic. And the truth is, I have unfinished business that I've been putting off. Perhaps this is fate's way of telling me it's time I face my past and bury it once and for all.

CHAPTER 2

CAROLINE

"You ready?" Sophia asks.

I spent the day prepping with the team and being instructed on the surveillance devices. Yes, I'm Langley-trained, but I've never served in the field.

"You sound worried."

Her doe-eyed expression says she's definitely worried. I understand. If anything were to happen to me, she'd bear the guilt.

"He might not be the man you remember." She twists a pen top in her fingers, and I release an exhausted sigh.

There are two sides to Dorian. The side I fell in love with, and the emotionless, egocentric, cold individual I left. Neither of those sides are dangerous.

"Dorian won't hurt me. Even if he's behind this, he won't

hurt me." Dorian can be emotionally distant and cruel, but he'd never physically hurt me.

For a time there, Dorian Moore was a media darling. The nephew of an American president and the son of a multibillionaire, he is American royalty. But after our split, he shunned publicity. Perhaps his fall from press pet status contributed to his placement on the persons of interest list. He's wealthy and shrouded in mystery, after all.

When I noticed his presence on tabloid covers diminished, I assumed he'd found someone, and she convinced him to step away from the limelight. I assumed she achieved what I hadn't. My assumption could still be correct.

Arrow Tactical, and apparently, intelligence agencies the world over, are placing trust in this informant who holds the Moore men accountable. But tipsters are notoriously unreliable. An unnamed insider could be anyone from the hotdog vendor on a street to a senator with a vendetta. I asked for information on the contact but was told that, for the source's safety, they were not disclosing the information.

Sophia's decision to bring me in and leverage my connection is wise. If there's a planned attack, there's an undeniable benefit to shortening the suspect list. My connection has value.

"There are other ways we can get what we need," Sophia says.

"Would you stop? It's fine. It's a chance to work in the field."

CIA candidates technically don't know what they'll be assigned to after going through training, but I never stood a chance of a coveted spy role, thanks to my marriage. Facial recognition will almost always recognize me even if hardly anyone recognizes me on the street these days.

Stella joins us. She's juggling a bottle of wine, three hard plastic wineglasses, and a corkscrew.

"Got your flight booked," Stella announces. "Let's head to the rooftop. We can watch the sunset and hear all about your date with Mr. Sexy."

"Oh, yes. Luke." Sophia's devilish grin says she's aware I'd rather not chat about my date.

I wish I'd never mentioned Luke to these two. It's not until I push open the heavy door to the roof and suck in the salty air do I find calm. I've been jittery all day, and while I'd like to lie to myself and claim it's due to the unexpected turn of events at work, I'm well aware of the truth.

Stella starts unscrewing the cork, and Sophia sets the glasses down on one of the small tables. The setting sun colors the horizon salmon pink with flecks of gold, crossing the Pacific in the distance. I've always loved the view from the rooftop of Arrow's offices. Sitting up here, seeing the tops of palm trees and cyclists in the street, you'd never know it's December. At street level, it's a different story, full of reminders, with decorations adorning the light poles and every business featuring a holiday window display.

"So, Luke…" Sophia says.

"We had one dinner," I say. We also had a lunch date, but I don't need to remind these two. "I enjoy talking with him. He keeps up with current events." I keep my voice flat to set expectations.

"I may have screwed things up," Sophia says with a scrunch of her nose. "Don't be mad."

What could she do? "Oh, my god." *I can't believe her.* "Do not tell me you planned a double date."

"What? No. Double dates aren't Fisher's thing."

That's good to know, and one more reason to like Fisher. She got together with her husband on her first assignment in the field. I was one of the few within the CIA who knew they were dating back then. They've been married for years.

"Luke's on the ground support team. He asked why you were selected to go on-site." Sophia's hands flutter, a defensive motion of hers when she thinks she needs to explain herself, which means she told him everything. "He's on the team. It's not information we keep secret."

"You didn't tell him you'd been married before?" Stella asks, picking up on the issue.

"We didn't discuss prior relationships." They both look at me like I've got a bloody nose. "One dinner," I remind them. "I wasn't keeping it a secret. It's fine."

"I get that," Stella says. "I was married before Trevor, and I rarely talk about that asshole."

"I didn't know that," I say.

Stella's never mentioned a prior marriage, but why would she? That's exactly the point I was making.

Stella passes me a glass of wine, and I gladly take it.

"Was it a bad divorce?" Stella asks.

"Nooo." I draw the word out, remembering that painful time. But, I mean, are there any good divorces?

"He's richer than Jack Sullivan, isn't he?" Stella asks. "You must've walked away with a mint."

I sip my wine rather than dignify that with a response.

"And no," Stella says, "we didn't do a detailed background report on you when you were hired. Since you were coming from the CIA and were referred by Sophia, we did the minimum. I just know you don't have debt."

"That's where I'm not feeling good about this plan," Sophia says. "Are you certain he doesn't know what you do?"

"Like I told the team, he has no knowledge that I ever worked for the CIA. I applied to Langley after we separated."

"But couldn't a friend in common have told him?"

"If you have these concerns, why didn't you speak up at the meeting?"

She licks her upper lip. Hesitant. "Because I didn't want to cast doubt on your ability to do this."

"You recommended me as a hire and didn't want to look bad."

"That's not it at all," Sophia says, a tad too defensively to be believable.

"All right. I'm a little lost here," Stella says. "I think we got off track."

I close my eyes and tilt my head back, stretching my throat. Sophia is not my enemy. She's one of my closest friends.

"It's been years since he's contacted me," I say, swirling the wine. "As far as my friends know, I work for a bank. It's the easy answer to give, since no one asks about a boring corporate job."

When I walked away from Dorian, I walked away from our mutual friends, too. I exited his world, or more like fled. "If he ever ran into a mutual acquaintance, which is doubtful, that's what he'd hear."

"You're lucky you didn't have kids with him," Stella says. Her eyes widen. "Do you have kids?"

I half-chuckle. "A child would've shown on my health insurance forms, Stella."

"Unless they were on his. Someone that wealthy probably has an executive health care plan and doesn't need health insurance. His net worth is what? Over two hundred billion?"

Hmm. That's true. I don't remember what he did for health insurance. We had private doctors from a concierge healthcare practice. The best of the best. I'd walk into a medical practice, and they knew me. I never showed a card or paid for anything.

"How do you think he'll react when you knock on his door?" Stella asks.

"You mean show up at his gate," I correct. Is this impromptu cocktail hour more of a second prep meeting than curiosity about my dinner date?

I glance between the two women. There's no reason for me to bottle this inside. If Stella ran a full background report on me, she'd pick up on it quickly.

"He's expecting me. Either me or a lawyer. I'm sure he's wondering what's taken me so long."

Sophia cuts her eyes to me. She's quick. Always has been.

"Your divorce still isn't settled? I've heard of divorces taking years...my parents, for one," she says, clearly doing math in her head. "I told you if you needed money, I'd give it to you."

Her exasperation is almost endearing. As if borrowing money from a friend, or my parents, is an easy choice.

"I know it sounds crazy."

Stella's mouth forms a circle. "Honey, how many years have you been dealing with lawyers?" she asks.

"I moved out when I was twenty-four. I'm thirty-one now."

"Honey."

I let out a sigh. "I haven't fought him because he could easily out-lawyer me."

"So what's..." Stella's confused expression is almost comical. At least, it would be if the joke wasn't on me.

"After I left, I thought he'd send divorce papers. He didn't. I eventually found a website, you know, one of those that still cost money, but it's way cheaper than a lawyer?" They both nod. "Let's call it GetADivorce.com. I don't really know what it was, but I mailed him the papers. I figured his lawyers would take one look at it and they'd mark it up or whatever, and I'd sign whatever he sent back."

"But?"

"He sent an email stating that I owed him half of this land I inherited. It pissed me off." I meet Sophia's gaze. She remembers this. She has to. I fumed to her for hours.

"You're still fighting over that land?"

"Not exactly."

"What do you mean?"

"I told him I disagreed. Via email. I clarified that by waiving my rights to the amount stipulated in the prenup, he should waive any claim on the land I inherited during our marriage."

"And?"

"Nothing. I never heard from him."

They're both staring at me like I'm a fool, and I get it—I'd give them the same treatment if the situation were reversed.

"I should've followed up. I understand. I probably should've hired a lawyer, but I figured there was no need. I thought he would meet someone and need the divorce. He'd send me papers to sign, and it would be over."

"What about taxes?" Sophia asks.

"Filing single." I shrug. You're not required by law to claim a marital deduction.

"Did he?" Sophia asks.

"I assume so. I doubt he cares about the marital deduction on his taxes. What do you save? Fifteen hundred bucks?" I haven't looked in ages, but for someone like Dorian, the amount is less than what he carries in cash in his wallet.

"What land?" Sophia asks.

"A small tract in Georgia he's never even visited." I grit my teeth, thinking about the nerve he possessed to claim he had a right to what I came into during our two-year marriage, whereas I signed a prenup limiting my claims.

"You never had a lawyer look at the prenup, did you?" Stella slaps her palm against her forehead. "Girlfriend. What were you thinking?"

I open my mouth.

"Don't tell me. You were in love. And you thought you'd be married forever."

I shrug. I don't know what the hell I was thinking. I was twenty-fucking-two.

Stella snaps her fingers. "Maybe he's trying to hold on to you. Maybe that's why he never followed up with a revised agreement or signed the one you gave him."

"No." I set the glass down, having lost my appetite. "He moved on within days of me walking out." I see the questions in Stella's eyes. "Lots of salacious photos of him with models. Our separation was publicized and promptly forgotten. Page Six news for a day. He and his flavor of the hour garnered publicity for weeks." I slap my hand on the table. "Anyway, that's why he'll see me when I arrive. My visit won't surprise him. And it's overdue."

"Is he the angry type?"

At Stella's serious tone, I put a reassuring hand over hers. "No. It was never like that. I promise. And…" I look to Sophia. "I understand why he's a person of interest. I do. But you're off. I'll do this so the team can zero in on the correct target more quickly."

"You keep saying he's innocent, but you haven't spoken to

him in years. People change," Sophia says.

"There's a limit to how much a man can change." The thing about Dorian is that there's the business alphahole who's a condescending jerk, but then there's the sweats and tee guy who flew from London to Boston to take care of me when I had the flu. "He's not behind this."

"He's spent years outside the country."

I understand Sophia's skepticism.

"I'm going in prepared. Chances are, he'll take one look at me, go to his computer, and print out a divorce agreement he probably didn't even realize I never received and signed, and then he'll whisk me out of his office so he can jump on his next call. He'll tell me I'm welcome to hang around until the driver can come and get me. He might even ask me to stay for dinner. Maybe. Unless he's in a relationship. Which is very possible." Envisioning the meeting cuts, but it shouldn't—not after all this time. I avoid my friends' gazes and keep it all cut and dry, as it should be. "I'll be escorted to his office. We'll have an awkward conversation. With luck, I'll have a chance to deposit a listening device. When he excuses me, I'll walk around the house and see what else I can do. Maybe ask if I can say hello to his father. I'll take photos. Leave behind what I can while claiming the driver is delayed in picking me up. I'll be back by the weekend."

"This sounds to me like a two birds, one stone situation," Stella pipes in. "Fate stepping in to wrap up the past and set you on a new path for the future. Trust me, you're gonna feel so much better once you have the divorce finalized and you never have to speak to the douche canoe again."

"It is behind me." I never think about the marriage. Or, I should say, I rarely think about that part of my life. "It's a technicality. That's all." He's not a douche, or at least, I never thought of him that way. But I do love how Stella leaps to my side, no questions asked.

"If he thinks you're there to get his money… You've got ways to get in touch with us, right?" Stella looks at Sophia. "I only booked a flight for her. Why isn't a team going?"

"She assured us it wasn't necessary, so we nixed a team," Sophia says. "Although Luke disagreed strongly. He's campaigning to set up in Denver so we'll have resources nearby."

Stella pats my hand. "This is good. Get this buttoned up and behind you so you can move on. I like that Luke is concerned. There's nothing hotter than a protective military guy." She grins.

"Stella, curb your enthusiasm. Luke is nice, but nothing is going to happen with us."

"Did you not have a good time?"

"He's nice."

"Well, that's the kiss of death," Stella says, and Sophia laughs. "What was his out?"

"Come again?"

Stella looks back and forth between Sophia and me. "Oh, come on, you know. The ins and outs. Singles these days have a list."

"I've never heard of this."

Sophia shakes her head and lifts her eyebrows, gesturing that she's never heard it either.

The look Stella gives me says that this is why I'm still single; she might be on to something.

"What did he do that turned you off? Whatever it was, that's on your out list. Something that gives you the ick. Like, for some women, it's a velcro wallet. Boom. Out." She gestures with her thumb over her shoulder.

I shake my head, half-laughing. A list? Really?

"Oh, come on," Stella pleads. "I need to know. I have to prep Ethan."

"I'm sure Ethan would love for his mom to set him up on a date," Sophia says.

"If I don't, he'll stay single forever," Stella retorts.

The door creaks open, and Trevor holds out a cell. "Ethan's on the line."

Stella jumps and runs for the phone. They exit together, and I look to Sophia for an explanation.

"He's been on a mission and couldn't contact them."

"A mission like disabling the ship with the chemical weapons?" Ethan's Special Forces, but they've been tight-lipped with specifics.

"It's possible." Sophia shrugs. "I can't believe you're still married. I could've gotten you lawyers. Good lawyers. He's not unbeatable."

Perhaps. But our legal system favors the wealthy. And Dorian's wealth is unfathomable to someone like me. Dorian is Halston Moore's only child. When, at fifty-two, Halston became a single father, he steered his only son into the family business. Halston Moore Sr., Dorian's grandfather, was one of the original founders of Bedrock Advisory, one of the world's leading providers of investment, advisory, and risk management solutions. On top of generational wealth, Dorian stands to inherit an inordinate sum. Plus, from what I've read, Zenith, the company he founded and hasn't taken public, is considered to be one of the most valuable privately held companies in the world.

When I met Dorian at a pub during my study abroad, I was

oblivious. He'd been a good-looking grad student with a lopsided smile, unruly curly hair, and a dimple. Our gazes locked, and well…he had me before hello.

"I don't like this," Sophia says, her tone somber.

"Ryan expects me to do it." My tone is a little colder than I intend, but he's my boss. She's not. And if she were completely against it, she would've never brought me in.

"Doesn't mean I like it."

In the CIA, we learn to do plenty that we don't like.

"He has on-site security. This isn't a risk-free op." Sophia's doubling down, but I can, too.

"He won't hurt me." I understand her fear, but he won't.

"If he did, he'd never be caught. Not with his wealth. That kind of awareness can go to a man's head. Promise me you'll be careful."

I nod at Sophia, knowing her concern comes from a place of professional assessment and friendship. "I'll be careful," I promise, but there's a part of me that knows entering Dorian's world again is like stepping into quicksand—familiar and dangerous all at once. But there's another voice, too, quieter but just as insistent, reminding me of that lopsided smile in an Oxford pub, and wondering if I'm really going there to investigate him… or to face what I left behind. Either way, I'm already crossing a threshold I swore I never would again.

CHAPTER 3

DORIAN MOORE

A fog clouds my sleep-deprived mind, blurring the numbers before me. Outside, a white contrail mocks me as it bisects the crisp blue Denver sky high above the Rocky Mountains. What I wouldn't give to be the pilot of that jet. No phone calls, no reports, no meetings. Solitude and clear blue skies.

"Mr. Moore?"

My assistant stands three feet from my desk. His blue-and-black-striped tie hangs too far left, exposing the line of buttons on his Oxford. My gaze locks on the one undone button.

"What is it, Jay?"

"Mr. Cromwell would like to see you if you have a minute. I know you reserved this time, but I told him I'd check."

Geoffrey Cromwell, my father's personal financial advisor, strides in, pretending to be unaware that my assistant planned to ask for permission to meet.

"I'd like a coffee. Black," he says as he takes a seat, discreetly adjusting his silver tie and smoothing the material on his navy pinstripe trousers. He recently stopped coloring his hair black, and the overabundance of white gives the appearance of thinning. Once I adjust to the shock of white, I probably won't notice anymore.

Why am I even registering the man's hair?

"I'd like a fresh cup, too," I say, breathing deeply in an attempt to ignore the dull pain emanating behind my temples. "Thank you, Jay."

"Did you see the portfolio adjustments I'm making?"

With a push, I roll my office chair to the right for a better view around my monitors.

"Interesting shifts."

I don't particularly care what Geoffrey does with the portfolios he manages for my father, but his moves intrigue me.

"Heavy on gold, oil, and gas." Years ago, Geoffrey bought heavily into crypto. I doubted him, but that move paid off. "And now you're sitting here. Something you want to share?"

As a board member of Bedrock Advisory, I have reams of reports from the industry's brightest. I'm not a trader, but speculation interests me. Geoffrey Cromwell's speculative record speaks of someone with insider knowledge, the kind that would land him in jail if he ever slips. It's fitting that Dad plucked him out of obscurity and claimed him.

"At your next board meeting, encourage your team to follow my strategy."

I meet his gaze head-on. The man has twenty years on me, but he can fuck all the way off.

"Surely you're up on the news," he says, adjusting his position in the seat and smoothing his dress shirt, before crossing an ankle over his knee. It's a casual position, but he's never relaxed. Always fidgeting. That's probably why I always expect him to come in with news that he lost a lot of Dad's money, but he consistently outperforms my personal team.

Jay hustles in with steaming black porcelain coffee mugs. I wait until he sets my new mug down, removes the old one, and exits before responding.

"Enlighten me," I say, wondering which lobbyist or politician has shared information that recommends a conservative exposure.

"Something's afoot. Bets are that China is moving in on Taiwan, Russia into Poland. Are you in touch with Nick Ivanov?"

"What does Ivanov have to do with it?"

Nick's my friend from university, lives in Great Britain, and I don't recall him ever meeting Geoffrey Cromwell. But, then again, our world is incestuous.

"Figured he'd keep you up to speed."

I steeple my fingers. "You shift into a conservative stance too early, and you miss opportunities. With a portfolio of Dad's size, the balance strikes me as unwise."

"Remind me. How did your portfolio perform last year compared to your father's?"

"If this is you pitching me on your management services, try again." I shift my mouse to bring my monitor to life and check the time and my calendar. *Fuck, my head hurts.* "Why are you here, Geoffrey?"

"Your father asked me to keep you informed. I'm simply executing his wishes."

I'm on the board of a firm with over half of the United States's wealth under management, and I founded and run an aerospace company. But yes, Dad would believe I need counsel for the rest of my life.

"How is Zenith doing?" Geoffrey's question confirms he's a sixty-something kiss-ass putz.

A voice in my head counters that that's not fair, that while he works for Dad, he's also one of his closest friends.

Hot coffee coats my throat, and I close my burning eyes. I'm so fucking tired. The run this morning didn't wake me enough to deal with my father, and Geoffrey represents him.

Zenith is my company, one I conceptualized and created. Founded for global high-speed internet, I now own more satellites than any government on Earth. It's privately held, so unfortunately for my father, there's no earnings call for him to receive a concise update.

"Why?"

The overhead light reflects off Geoffrey's silver-rimmed spectacles, but I'd bet beneath the reflection, he's glaring, annoyed with my evasiveness.

The dull pain intensifies, and I close my eyelids, breathing in.

"Everything's fine. Exceeding forecast." The sigh that escapes is borderline unprofessional, but he can deal. "I have a meeting in two minutes. Did you need something?"

A flash of indignation crosses Geoffrey's features.

He pushes up and sets his coffee on my desk. "As always, a pleasure."

Sarcasm at its finest.

I watch as he leaves.

"Close the door, please," I call after him.

He doesn't. Of course, he doesn't. He's an ass. Why the hell did he come in person?

The man's one positive attribute is that he keeps Dad occupied during the day. He's one of the satellites that orbit Dad, telling him everything he wants to hear and letting him win at golf. Well, it used to be golf. These days, it's chess, or maybe checkers.

If he'd stay away from me, I wouldn't find him so annoying.

Jay appears. "Do you need anything, sir?"

"Clear my calendar for the day. Keep the door closed."

"Sir? You're scheduled to take a call with the president at two."

Fuck.

"Can you request an in-person meeting? Tell him I'll be in Washington next week, and I believe an in-person meeting will be a better use of our time."

"He should be happy with that. That's what he requested initially."

I'm aware.

"Do you need aspirin, sir?" Jay knows me well.

"Yes. Please." Jay gives a polite nod, and I clarify, "The strong stuff."

"Yes, sir."

He leaves the door cracked, and when he returns, he deposits my Vicodin prescription on my desk and removes Geoffrey's coffee.

"Thank you, Jay."

I pop my pills and open a drawer, remove a secure satellite phone, and dial a number I've memorized.

It rings continually until the voicemail answers.

Realization dawns in my fogged brain, and I don't bother leaving a message. If he had any relevant information, Nick would share it.

Damn the fog in my brain. I need a stronger sleep aid. I can't go on like this.

ME TO UNKNOWN NUMBER
Are you available to meet?

I'm about to set the phone down when a text comes through.

HALSTON MOORE, JR.
Has the plan been executed?

I squint to read the message. I do not wish to speak to my father, so take the easy route.

ME TO HALSTON MOORE, JR:
Yes. Per your instructions.

UNKNOWN NUMBER
Tell me where.

I pause, weighing options that offer a discreet location without eavesdroppers.

My desk phone rings. I press the speaker button. "Yes, Jay?"

"Lewis Weston is on the line."

The name is familiar, but I can't place it.

"He's stationed at the guardhouse today. He'd like to talk to you. I told him you cleared your day, but he said this is important."

Fuck.

"Put him through."

What the hell is my father up to now?

"Mr. Moore?" a male voice asks.

"This is he." I close my eyes and exhale. "Everything okay?"

Clearly, it's not. He's calling.

"Hi, ah, sorry to bother you at work, sir, but you have a visitor. She says she's not leaving until she sees you. It's a Ms. Caroline Scott."

Her name strikes directly to my solar plexus. I rub the pain point and stretch, then crack my jaw.

She's here.

No call.

And you know why she's here.

"Tell her I'll be there in thirty minutes."

A slight tremor affects my fingers. I stretch them, spreading them wide to gain control.

With a deep breath, the tremor subsides.

I delete the incomplete text and shoot off a different one.

ME TO JAY:

Prep my helicopter. Need to get home ASAP.

"Lewis?" I ask the speakerphone.

"Yes, sir?"

"Don't let her leave. Understand? Under no circumstances are you to let her leave."

"Ah, she's not on our list, sir. If she's a threat, it's best you—"

"She's not a threat." *Jesus fucking Christ.* "Keep her there."

"Yes, sir. Will do."

A memory surfaces, and my gut cramps.

"Lewis?"

"Yes, sir?"

"Don't let my father know she's there. Keep her out of the way, but don't let her leave. I'm on my way."

"Certainly."

I slam the receiver down and charge out the door, cell phone in hand. I don't bother with my unpacked briefcase.

The room sways. *Dammit.*

"Jay? Is it ready?"

He's at the elevator, holding the door for me.

Good man.

"Yes, sir."

"With a pilot?" I often fly myself, but Jay knows I'm medicated.

"Yes, sir. There's no meeting on your calendar, sir. Did I overlook—"

"No."

The doors slide closed on my disconcerted assistant.

Don't worry, Jay. This isn't on you. It's all on me.

CHAPTER 4

CAROLINE

A small guardhouse sits to the left of the gate, just large enough to shelter the attendant. Movable security cameras hang below the roof's edge on each corner. To the right of the gate, there's a small two-story stone house. The road into the compound is wide enough to accommodate two lanes of traffic, but if the process remains the same, vehicles enter here and exit about a half-mile down the road.

When Dorian first brought me here, I thought he'd taken me to a resort. I couldn't quite grasp that this was his family home, with staff, guesthouses, tennis courts, and an indoor lap pool in the mountains. I'd been awestruck as we weaved our way up the mountain to his father's mansion.

"Ma'am?"

"Yes?" My lips curl into my friendliest smile.

The guard hadn't been pleased when the Uber driver pulled

away. My fingers grip the suitcase handle, and I can't seem to look away from the gate, my heart palpitating as if I've traveled back in time and am about to meet my boyfriend's father.

"Please come in. Mr. Moore is on his way."

I look through the bars, expecting to see a golf cart or an ATV powering down the road.

Will he send staff for me?

What am I thinking? Of course, he'll send a staff member to fetch me.

"He's asked that you wait here. He should be landing shortly."

"Helicopter?" Understanding dawns. "He's at the Denver office."

We'd known that was a possibility. And it's the best-case scenario. I'll have time to scout the grounds.

"This way, please."

The uniformed guard opens a wrought iron door to the side of the gate. As I approach, he reaches for my suitcase.

"That's okay. I've got it."

It's an automatic response that lets him know I'm like him, a normal person living an ordinary life. I don't need others to handle my baggage. My staff comprises me, myself, and I.

"It's no problem, ma'am."

He reaches for the bag again, and this time, I step past him, grip firm on the handle.

The winding asphalt road leads up to the main house that sits atop a crest with stunning views of the San Juan Mountains. Here at the gate, we're much lower, and the view is a mix of mostly barren trees and evergreens.

It's too late in the season for fall foliage. Brown, dried leaves cling to limbs here and there. Mounds of curled dead leaves line the sides of the woods. The grounds crew must blow the leaves from the road and the paths on a regular basis.

The uniformed guard swings a door open to the two-story stone house, and I read his gold-plated name tag. *Lewis Weston.*

"Please, he asked that you wait inside."

I narrow my eyes, wondering why he has me waiting here at the entrance. Is he hiding me? From whom? A girlfriend? If that's the case, I can't blame him for keeping me out of her path. It will be challenging to explain. Luke's terse, *"You're married?"* still stings, even though Dorian and I are nothing to each other. I argued that we were legally separated, and he asked, *"Were you going to tell me?"*

What a mess.

The truth is, I wasn't going to tell Luke, because I didn't plan on going out with him again. But when put on the spot, I said, *"Yes, of course."*

I told Luke we needed to focus on the project. I'd been annoyed that he had any expectations of me. And we do need to focus on Project Unity.

Here I am, in Colorado, and I need to focus.

The scent of paint fills the air, and the rumble of the suitcase wheels over the polished concrete floor mixes with the sound of air flowing from a nearby vent. Along the hallway, rifles hang in neatly lined racks along the wall.

"Is this building new?"

I remember the gate and the guardhouse. My memory is hazy on what was on this side of the road when I visited before.

"Yes, ma'am. This building replaced a much smaller one. All before my time, though."

"Are you new?"

Lewis slows by a room with a single bed and a window with a view of the woods.

"Been here a little less than two years," Lewis says. "If you wouldn't mind waiting here."

I scan the corners of the room for cameras. If Dorian's plan is to meet me here and then send me on my way, I won't get any valuable information for the team.

"In the past, I've waited in the main house. Is that possible? I don't need to be in your way."

"You've been here before?" I read his tone and the tilt of his head. He's skeptical.

"It's been years," I say, since I obviously haven't been here since he's been employed. "But I love the library. It's my favorite room, and the view is spectacular." I look out the window wistfully, envisioning the view from the main house high above. "It's like a fortress tucked away in a mountainside."

"The mountain house is spectacular," he agrees.

"Do you mind if I walk around until Dorian arrives? It's been so long since I've wandered through the trails." His lips squeeze into a flat line. "I'll leave my suitcase here."

"Sorry, ma'am. I can't let you do that. Mr. Moore gave specific instructions."

"Oh?" I take in the sterile room one more time, Lewis's stiff posture, and his hand on the doorknob. "Are you sure I can't just...take a walk outside?"

"No, I just...this is the best space for you to wait. It's where we rest between shifts sometimes. Upstairs, we have a break room, but there are other guys up there. Mr. Moore won't be long."

Unease settles in my gut. This room feels a little too much like a cell.

"You know what? I changed my mind." I pull out my phone. "I'm going to schedule an Uber and go back into town. I'll check in at my hotel, and then I'll come back later when he's here." I force a smile and open the Uber app.

"I can't let you do that, ma'am."

I narrow my eyes and take a sharp breath. I flew commercial and therefore didn't carry a gun. Not that I would normally carry a gun. But Luke's insistence that this is a bad idea replays in my head. And what did Sophia say? A man like Dorian can do whatever he wants and get away with it.

"I'm going to need to insist," I say. "I'll return at a better time."

"I'm sorry, ma'am. He's going to be here any minute." He checks his watch. "He gave specific instructions."

"Do you always do what he says? Are you willing to hold someone against her will?" Halston Moore hired former Secret Service for his security, but this man is too young to have that pedigree.

"Ma'am. Please. Can I get you something to drink? He's going to be here in fifteen minutes. It would be a shame for you to leave after you've come so far."

That's true. I need to see Dorian. If he never takes me to the main house, I'll fail at planting surveillance and scouting the grounds, but I need Dorian to sign a divorce agreement. If he won't sign mine, he needs to draft one for me to sign.

But still...Lewis is young. Malleable. "I will not wait in this room. I will not be treated like a prisoner."

"Ma'am, I'm not trying to make you feel—"

Footsteps fall along the hall outside. A man in a matching uniform comes up behind Lewis.

"Lewis, head on out to cover the gate. I'll stay with our guest."

"I'd like to leave."

"Can I get you a drink? We also have crackers and protein bars if you're hungry."

What have I walked into?

This man is older, with silver wisps and crow's feet. He's stern, formidable even. This man might be former Secret Service.

Lewis obediently departs for his command post.

I scan the walls and ceiling, searching for a lens. Is there a security team on the grounds, watching us? Is that why this older man arrived?

"Ma'am, can I get you a drink?"

"I'd prefer to wait in the main house."

"I'll be back shortly."

The door closes and clicks.

I go to the door and twist the knob. He locked me in.

What the hell?

I pull out my phone and debate. Call Sophia? No. This hasn't gone exactly according to plan, but I'm not in danger—I don't think. I have cell signal and a tracker in my suitcase. They left my suitcase with me and didn't ask for my phone.

Do they plan on keeping me in this room all day? Dorian's thirty minutes equals hours.

I pace the room.

Check the window. It's a double-hung window. I unlock it and lift from the bottom. It doesn't budge. It's stuck. Most likely from lack of use, not from any nefarious purpose. If necessary, I can break the glass.

This is ridiculous. I should try harder. I should insist on being taken to the house.

I knock on the door. "Hello?"

Nothing. I pound with the butt of my hand.

Nothing.

What is Dorian trying to prove? Why not let me wait in the house?

I sit on the edge of the bed and flick between news articles, debating my next move. How long do I wait before I break the window? I won't call Sophia until I'm in danger. Calling on the team is a last resort.

The tree tops off in the distance sway. And then I hear it. A helicopter.

The door clicks open.

"That'll be Mr. Moore. He won't be long now."

The older guard stands in the doorway, arms behind his back, gaze just above my head, black leather gun holster around his waist.

There's nothing to do but wait.

CHAPTER 5

DORIAN

The Airbus H160 lands with a smoothness derived from exquisite engineering. An employee heads over as I exit the helicopter. The rotor slows to a drumbeat.

"Mr. Moore. Will you be needing her again today?"

"Possibly. Keep her ready."

"Aye aye, sir."

The pilot's an older, fit man with a shock of white tufts past a receding hairline and deep wrinkles around his eyes and mouth. I interviewed him. Spent his career in Naval Aviation. Retired in Colorado because his kids live in the state.

"Thank you, Rex."

"No problem, sir."

"I'll let you know when you can put her away."

"Yes, sir."

It's a long walk to the guardhouse, so I head to one of the

golf carts we keep on the property. The key's in the ignition, as expected, and I twist it and take off as my phone vibrates. It always vibrates.

Jay will access the messages. Flag the important ones. It's the same with my emails. And around two or three in the morning, when the rest of the world sleeps, I'll go through it all and respond.

My pressure on the accelerator lessens the closer I get to the guardhouse.

What does she want?

A divorce. Obviously.

But why now?

Has she met someone?

We've been separated for years. In all that time, she never filed for divorce.

Of course, neither did I.

She handed me a divorce agreement that she printed from a website.

I told her I'd have my lawyers draft an agreement, but I never did.

I lied to my father about it to get him off my back. My chief legal counsel is aware and understands my marital situation isn't his concern until I make it his concern.

A feminine shadow captures my attention.

The light reflects on the panes, blocking the details of the silhouette. But certainty resonates through my being. *It's her.*

Why now?

Why not years ago?

Why didn't I deal with this years ago?

My temples pulse, and I twist the top on the Vicodin and pop another one.

Two were never going to get me through this day.

I leave the cart on a patch of grass beside the stone path leading up to the guardhouse.

For December, the day is unseasonably warm. Little to no wind. A cold front is blowing in tomorrow. The grass, in areas not covered by leaves, is a mix of brown and green. Soon enough, it'll be covered in white.

When I first brought Caroline to our property here, she'd been blown away by the foliage, the mix of golds and reds. It must've been October. She thought I'd taken her to a resort.

"This is yours?" she'd asked, amazed. Flabbergasted, even. And my stomach had churned. If only I could've hidden my background from her... It's a pointless mental exercise. Things changed. She left.

A uniformed guard exits the guardhouse. Mid-to-late twenties, clean-cut, amenable, impossibly eager. I read his name tag.

"Lewis. She's here?"

"In the bunkroom."

"Why'd you put her there?"

A vision of bunks lined up along walls comes to mind.

Jesus.

"Don't really have a place to keep visitors, sir."

The house? He didn't bring her up to my house?

I grit my teeth so hard my molars ache.

He fidgets.

Ripping into this guy will serve no purpose.

"Take me to her."

Lewis turns, eager to comply.

The hallway blurs. The ache behind my temples dulls. I force my limbs forward. There's no point in hiding from the end.

The end is the price we pay for love.

God, I'm such a fucking tool.

A uniformed man stands in front of a closed door. He swings wide to face us.

Did they lock her in the room? What the fuck did I say to these guys on the phone?

"Mr. Moore," he says, shoulders back, arms straight along his sides.

Christ, you'd think I'm a squadron leader.

My throat tightens, and saliva pools in my mouth. I force myself to swallow and stand tall.

If he speaks, I don't hear him. A whooshing sound fills my ears. My peripheral vision remains a blur.

I brush his hand away from the knob and twist.

She's a silhouette, only this time, I'm with her, on the same side of the window.

I fumble on the wall for a light switch.

Golden light fills in the details.

Light blonde hair falls below her shoulders, skimming her breasts. When I met her, it reached the curve of her lower back.

Her elegant black pantsuit and white silk blouse fit her perfectly. Strictly professional. The black, square, no-nonsense pumps round out the outfit.

I expected nothing less. This is a business call, after all. A long-overdue meeting to settle affairs from the past.

My gaze drifts from her short, pale pink nails to the prominent gold decorative band on her right index finger, to her left, ringless hand.

My chest quivers with the hit of the Vicodin.

The solitary diamond pendant hanging demurely above the singular unfastened button catches my attention. I zero in on the diamond for confirmation. It's the necklace her parents gave her for college graduation.

Red splotches dot her neck and chest, marring her unblemished pale skin.

Is she nervous?

With a deep inhale, I lift my gaze to her pale pink lips, over the nose that she believes is too long, but that is refined and fitting on her heart-shaped face, and I meet her light blue eyes head-on, brushing aside the constriction in my chest.

"Caroline," I say.

That's a weak greeting.

The gold ring glimmers in the light when she rests her hand on the extended suitcase handle.

Her thumb strokes the plastic.

She looks behind me, over my shoulder. I follow her gaze.

Lewis and the other employee fill the doorway.

"Thank you," I say to them. "We're fine now."

They take the hint and leave.

I scan the functional, drab room and look past her to the bare aspens and birches.

"Is there somewhere we can talk?"

She sounds determined. Strong.

"Yes, of course. I need some coffee. You?"

"It's almost eleven."

"Do you no longer drink coffee?"

She almost smiles.

"I still drink coffee. I was up early for my flight. Let's get some."

I reach for her suitcase, and my skin brushes hers.

Heat emanates from the point of contact.

She pulls away like I shocked her.

The heat works its way up the side of my hand and my arm.

"How long are you here for?" I hold an arm out for her to proceed. "There's a cart parked right outside the door," I tell her, as much to fill the quiet as to explain where I'm gesturing for her to go.

"Just for the night," she answers.

"Where are you staying?"

"In Denver."

"With whom?"

"A hotel. A Hyatt. Nothing fancy."

She means the comment as a dig. She also skirted my question.

We exit the guardhouse, and I set her suitcase on the back of the golf cart.

Those pale blue eyes sear me. With so much time lapsed, you wouldn't think that would happen. She shouldn't still have a hold on me.

She shouldn't be here. You should've mailed her the agreement years ago.

You're the asshole.

I reach for the golf cart hood to steady myself. My damn inner voice needs to shut the hell up.

"Are you okay?"

She's concerned. *Always has been.*

"I'm fine."

"Are you sure?"

She's not here to talk about your health, Dorian.

"I just need coffee."

She's dressed professionally. Here to do what you should've done. There's someone else. That's what's forced her to finish this. You always knew this day would come. And here it is.

CHAPTER 6

CAROLINE

Dorian's presence diminishes the surroundings, blurring the periphery and depleting the oxygen.

At six-one, he shouldn't have that effect, but with his broad shoulders and dark, wavy hair, he's quite possibly the most charismatic man that ever lived. *People Magazine* named him "Sexiest Man Alive," and he's not an actor. That alone should've served as a warning. I had no business being with this man.

Today, he's paired a crewneck sweater with casual midnight navy trousers and brown Chelsea boots. The tweed sports jacket gives his shoulders substantial breadth.

Years ago, he lived in suits, ties, and buffed dress shoes.

The lines around Dorian's deep-set eyes remind me that time has passed, as does the sprinkling of gray near his temples. He's never been one to take care of his skin, eschewing moisturizer and sunscreen, but the marks of age have served to distinguish him. If possible, he's grown more handsome. It's the hallowed, shadowy complexion beneath his doleful dark eyes that is disconcerting.

He wasted no time escorting me out of the guardhouse. Based on his dismissive treatment of his staff, I imagine he has little interaction with them. His house manager probably handles his staff.

He didn't lead me to the road and turn me away at the gate. That's good. But why would he turn me away? We aren't one of those couples who spent years duking it out over money. No, we're the rare breed who avoided the fight altogether.

It's good I'm here. We're overdue for resolution. And I'll prove his innocence.

He brushes his hands against each other after depositing my luggage on the back of the golf cart, and for a second, our eyes connect. The familiar deep brown of his eyes draws me in, but something's off—his pupils? He looks away before I assess.

My heart aches to know what's bothering him, but I bite back the question. It's not my business, but the concern still flows.

There's no point in asking, because he won't tell. That's the way he operates, and that's a reason you left. If he says he needs coffee, just accept the answer.

The sun shines onto the path, casting shadows between the trees. It's the end of the season, and many limbs are bare, but some leaves don't give up easily, reminders of a vibrant season. And then there are the evergreens. Beautiful in their perpetual might, limbs bowing gracefully as if eagerly awaiting a dusting of snow.

"It's always been so beautiful here," I say. "Peaceful. They wouldn't let me walk around. Insisted I remain inside." I tilt my head, letting the words land however they may.

"My apologies."

Always so formal.

"I didn't want you to leave."

His statement actually feels honest.

"Did you think I'd drive so far out of my way and then leave once I had confirmation you'd be arriving in thirty minutes?"

A familiar expression forms on his face—narrowed, thoughtful eyes and a frown. There's a response passing through his head, but he won't verbalize his thoughts.

I scan the area, searching for cameras. Is his security team listening? He's always on display. A heavily staffed home equals observant parties at all times.

He rests his hand on the top of the golf cart. There's no ring. No indentation in the skin of a ring. Same as mine. As expected, he removed his ring. What's not expected is for me to be drawn to his ring finger, or for residual pain to surface.

"If you'd like, we can walk the trail." He glances down, probably noting my two-inch pumps. A reasonable selection for a business meeting, but not for traversing a trail covered in slippery pine needles and leaves. "Or we can ride it."

He taps the top of the golf cart.

"Will it make it?" I ask.

We used to ride ATVs on the trail. The golf carts do better on the paved pathways, but at the top, where it's steep, the wheels can spin.

"Still doubt me?"

Beneath the frown, there's a hint of a smile. If I didn't know him better, I'd miss it, given how quickly it passes.

"I'm the unannounced guest. You pick."

"Would you care to drive?"

"What a gracious offer," I say, smiling at the memory of us racing to the front seat.

I loved to drive, and he always said I was the worst driver he'd ever met. He didn't mean it; it was just how he teased. He let me win most races when we found ourselves in separate carts. It was fun, but I'm not here for fun.

"It's best an expert sits behind the wheel," I say, slinging myself into the front passenger seat.

There's a steel-gray Yeti with condensation beneath the clear lid in the cupholder.

"Looks like you already have coffee," I say.

"But you don't," he says, flicking the key to start.

I inhale, breathing in cedar and balsam. I've purchased hundreds of candles seeking this scent, but I've yet to find one that matches the splendor of the woods.

"It's unseasonably warm," I comment.

Leaves scatter on the ground, and yes, there are bare tree limbs, but there's still color and life dotting the landscape, and while the air is crisp, I don't require a coat.

"It is," he says.

"I imagine the holiday ski crowd's getting concerned."

"Holiday skiing is always dicey."

That's what he used to say when I'd comment on the lack of snow in the nearby ski resorts this time of year. Our exchange is too familiar.

"A cold front arrives tomorrow," he says, seemingly oblivious that we just repeated a conversation we had years ago.

"First snow of the season?"

"Third."

There's a distinct absence of snow between the trees. If anything, the ground looks dry.

"It all melted," he explains. "Wasn't substantial. Maybe next week, as I'm sure you know, given your love for weather forecasts. Unless you've changed and there's a winter coat crammed in your suitcase."

"I don't cram items into my suitcase."

One corner of his lip turns up.

Yes, he's biting back his response.

"It's good to see you."

Now that's something I didn't expect him to say. I shift to better see him, but he stares straight ahead.

"How have you been?"

He's always been cordial. That was one of our problems.

"I'm good," I say.

The incline increases, and my back flattens against the seat. I press my heels against the front of the cart and hold on to the handrail.

"I moved to Santa Barbara."

His lips scrunch.

"What?"

I hate when he does that. He's clearly thinking something but won't say it.

Seconds pass, and tension wraps around my chest, forcing me to use effort to breathe. It might not be tension. It could be the altitude.

"I'm aware you moved," he says.

The invisible pulse between us pulls me in his direction, and I cling to the rail on the side of the seat, holding me in place. His focus remains ahead, and I study his profile. He's fit, but has he lost weight?

He turns slightly, catching me staring.

"Who told you I moved?"

"Did you think I wouldn't keep up with you?"

How well did he keep up with me? Sophia's caution comes to mind, but what am I thinking? This is Dorian.

The cart meanders slowly along the weaving path. In the thick of the trees, there's no sign of civilization. It would be easy to get lost in these woods.

"Banking. Finance. I didn't see that for you." He lowers a hand from the wheel, and it falls to his thigh. His pant leg rises, revealing dress socks in a muted pattern above the rim of his low leather boot. "Don't look so surprised. I only meant to look out for you."

But how did you keep up with me? Which friend told you?

The cart's wheels spin for a brief second, and there's a bump as we hit pavers. Up ahead is a building that appears to be a timbered garage.

"This is new," I say.

"Lots of things are new," he says with a sigh.

He parks in front of a closed dark-green garage door. He remains still and silent, prompting me to ask, "How have you been?"

He angles his head, and my breaths slow in anticipation. It's his turn to study me, and the effect is unnerving.

"Do you have meetings in Denver?"

A question instead of an answer.

I have no meetings, but I repeat the answer Sophia coached me to say. "I have meetings tomorrow."

"Then you should stay here tonight."

"Oh, I don't want to put you out." My cordial response is the expected one, but staying overnight is an ideal result.

He eyes my suitcase, and my gut churns. Does he think I came here hoping to stay the night?

"Stay. Let's have dinner. Besides, I suspect you have paperwork for me to sign?"

He's so casual, so breezy.

"What's his name?"

"My lawyer?" I allowed Sophia's lawyer to prepare a divorce agreement, so this time, I'm prepared with something that's not a printout from the internet. But I still expect that his lawyers will mark it up to the point they should draft whatever it is he wants me to sign.

"I meant, who is the person you're dating?"

In this lighting, beneath the shadow of the building, his eyes are so dark they're nearly pools of black.

"I don't see a ring on your finger, so I assume you're not engaged."

"There's no one." I take in his ringless finger one more time and look ahead through the windshield. "But it is time. You know that, right?" He's muted, expression unreadable, lips a flat line. "I expected papers to come. And months turned into years. Why didn't you file for divorce?"

It's the question I've attempted to bury. Less than five minutes with him, and we're tackling the elephant.

Or I am. He rests both hands on the steering wheel, his expression is pained, which makes no sense.

"I've seen photos of you with other women. It's not like—"

"We're legally separated."

Defensive.

"I'm aware. I wasn't accusing you of anything. But that's why I asked the question. Why didn't you have your legal dream team draw up papers?"

Years ago, I finally called a lawyer, determined to put this episode of my life behind me, only to find out his firm couldn't take my case because of a conflict of interest with one of Dorian's companies. I called two more firms and gave up. Told myself I'd wait for the divorce agreement his lawyers drafted, and then I'd find an attorney. The agreement never arrived.

His phone lights up on the dash. In silence, he reads the screen and exhales.

"Let's get that coffee. I'll get you situated, then I've got to take this."

Of course, he must handle the business matter.

That's fine. That's what I hoped. Expected. I'll have plenty of time to scope out the property.

"I'll get you set up in a guest room. There's a swimming pool, a steam room, a sauna, the trails, a theater…an office if you'd like."

"How's your father?" Assuming any real conversation will be postponed until after he's handled his business, it's best to proceed with cordial conversation.

He exits the golf cart and lifts my suitcase from the seat.

I get out, and he gestures with his arm to a narrow stone path.

My suitcase scratches the ground when it twists in his hand.

"Sorry about that," he mutters.

I follow behind him along the path. The opening past the trees reveals a modern framed structure with open glass exposures.

It's not at all what I remember. "Did you rebuild?"

"My father's still in the main house."

"Is that far?"

"Not by car. About a twenty-minute walk." We'd seen

multiple buildings on the satellite view, and I assumed they were guest cottages or housing for staff. I suppose it makes sense that he didn't want to live with his father.

"And he's doing well?" I ask, repeating my earlier question.

A squirrel up ahead pauses, stares us down, and darts up a tree.

"He's fine."

Relations between Dorian and his father were always strained. He opens the door, and I forget all about his father.

Floor-to-ceiling windows open into the woods, giving the sense of being outdoors. Leather furnishings, fur throws, and deep browns infuse the open space with warmth. I bet when it snows, this is stunning.

"Dorian, this is gorgeous."

"It's not as big as my father's place, but…"

"That house could double as a hotel." No one needs a place that massive.

"How are your parents?"

There's a Pinterest-worthy open kitchen that faces into the great room, and I take a moment to appreciate the Viking refrigerator and range and the dark green cabinetry and exquisite wood island.

"This is truly beautiful."

"Your parents?" he repeats.

"Fine," I say, repeating his word, but the short answer feels unnecessarily cold. "Still working."

"Really? Aren't they, what? In their mid-sixties?"

"My father loves his job. They're debating what's next. I think once they have a plan, they'll retire. Mom loves her job, too."

"Teaching?"

"No, she retired from teaching; she's a part-time librarian. She loves it. Like really loves it."

"Will they stay in Connecticut?"

"That's the debate."

"Ah. Are they considering moving to California to be closer to you?"

"No." I stare out the windows to the side of the house, taking in his breathtaking view of the mountains. "The debate is between Florida, Arizona, or another country. What about your father? Does he spend his time here or in one of his tropical locations? He's in his nineties now, right?" Our sources claim his father lives here, but knowing how many properties he owns, it's difficult to fathom he doesn't travel to warm locales.

"Ninety-two. But he likes it here."

Halston Moore was fifty-two when Dorian was born. When his mother divorced his father, she left him behind to be raised by an absent father and a nanny.

"How's Gloria?"

"She's good." His face softens, and he exhales, shaking his head like he's waking up. He enters the kitchen and pulls out a drawer of pods. "What kind of coffee do you want? Or tea? I have that, too."

I step up and review his selection, seeking a decaf tea option.

"What's she up to these days?" Gloria is, in my opinion, the parent who actually raised Dorian.

"She prefers California. She oversees the Montecito property." I eye him curiously. I would've thought she'd want to be near him. "She has one son in LA and a daughter outside of San Francisco."

"Ah. Perfect location."

"It is. And I spend a fair amount of time there."

I skim the drawer. I only agreed to coffee to talk with him, and he's about to dismiss me.

"You know, I think I'll take water. I'm dehydrated from the flight. If you need to get to business, I'll be fine."

"Right."

Once again, he squeezes his eyes closed and shakes his head quickly, like he's waking up.

"Are you okay?"

"Didn't sleep well last night," he says. "Here, let me show you the guest room. Make yourself at home. I won't work late."

That's something I've heard before.

"I promise."

A younger me would've expressed incredulity at his statement, but today, it doesn't matter if he hides in his office. The longer he's away, the longer I can explore. Tonight, once he's asleep, I'll pop into his office.

Before I leave tomorrow, I'll ask that he sign the divorce agreement so that I return to California to assist with issues of far more importance.

Dorian leads me to a stylish guest suite that's close to the kitchen and great room. I assume the primary suite is upstairs.

Out the window, I spy a covered, windowed pathway that leads to another building.

"What's that?"

"My home office," he answers.

"Ah."

Connected by a glass breezeway, it's stunning architecture.

"Do you need anything?"

"I'm good," I say, forcing a false brightness.

"Feel free to roam. The temperature might drop, but you can

use any of the coats hanging in the entry near the garage. If you need shoes, there are muck boots and snow boots. I'm told it's well stocked. You should be able to find whatever you need."

"Do you still have the library?"

"In the main house?" he asks.

"I always loved that room."

"I'll take you there after dinner," he says. "It's best if you don't visit the mountain house without me."

That's curious. But I suppose it makes sense. His father probably has a full staff who wouldn't recognize me.

"I need to go." He withdraws his phone from his sports jacket. The screen, as always, is lit. "Make yourself at home."

I stand by the window, watching until he strides through the glass breezeway, phone held in front, speaking into it. He might be dictating, or he might be speaking to someone. But he's no longer in this section of the house.

I dial Sophia.

"I landed safely," I say, purposefully nondescript on the off-chance I might be overheard. We didn't come across any staff, but that doesn't mean they aren't on-site.

"Have you spoken to him?"

"Yes."

"How'd it go?"

"Fine. He's working from home today. I'll stay here tonight and return to Denver in the morning."

"Was he surprised to see you?"

I reflect on his reaction. "Honestly, I think he expected it."

"Be careful," Sophia says.

I understand her concern, but I believe he expected me for reasons entirely unrelated to our plans. After all, we've both put this off for far too long.

"What're your plans?"

"I'm going to explore."

"Be careful," she reiterates.

I understand they believe Dorian is dangerous, but they're wrong. He's closed off, uncommunicative, and ambitious, but at his heart, he's a good person. We weren't a good match, but he's not evil or dangerous.

I step into the en suite bathroom, change into jeans, running shoes, and a lightweight sweater, grab my phone and the water bottle Dorian gave me, and head off to explore.

CHAPTER 7

DORIAN

My temples throb with such intensity that my vision blurs at the edges. I reach for my collar to loosen my tie, but there is no tie. I'm not wearing one.

I pace the room, the world outside a blur. I could grab my glasses, which might help my headache.

Where's the Vicodin?

My fingers pause on the drawer pull. *I don't need to pop more pills.*

The voice is my father's. His curmudgeonly tone almost has me smiling. Almost. His doctors have him popping a pharmacy.

Caroline's here. In Colorado. On the property.

Without enough consideration, I dial my one friend who knows her well.

Clicks sound.

Ring.

Ring.

Ring.

My thumb hovers over the red circle when I hear, "What the bloody hell? You can't leave well enough alone? Got a pressing need to gloat?"

I press the speaker phone option but keep the phone in my hand.

"What have I done that deserves a boast?"

"Well, my house is blown to bits."

He was pissy the last time we spoke. "Already told you. I'm not responsible."

His country home was blown to smithereens a week ago. Images all over the BBC. Didn't hit the wire in the States, but not much international news does.

"You took out a bloody two hundred and fifty million bounty on me, you bastard!"

"Not me. We've been over this. Can't believe you're still going on about it."

Like Nick, I have a team of cyber analysts tracking the source. But I'm told whoever did it is good. That's code for *it's unlikely the brainiacs I employ will solve the puzzle.*

"I threatened you with a counter bounty, and the bloody bounty mysteriously lifted. Don't go playing tickle fuck with me."

I open my mouth and half-chuckle. Tickle fuck. Always liked that phrase.

"Are you serious?" My best guess is Nick pissed off a powerful someone. He pissed me off, too, bringing the syndicate into some mafia nonsense.

"You absolute bastard." Raw fury slices his tone.

"Wait. You genuinely believe I'd put a price on your head? You don't trust me? After everything?"

"You threatened me."

"Well, Christ! Yes. I threatened you. You pissed us off. But I wouldn't…"

I'm about to say I wouldn't know how to set a bounty, but with one phone call… "I wouldn't do that to you."

"Is that so? And you didn't convene an alliance meeting recently? A vote?"

"The vote was to excommunicate you. Kick out. Buh-bye. Not burn you at the stake."

"A drone strike. On my estate. Blasted the place to bits. You really mean to tell me that wasn't your plan? You have no idea about it?"

He was targeted. Not exactly surprising given he'd been fucking with the Italian mafia for the past two years.

"You survived. That's the bit I paid attention to. And you've been playing the Italian mafia for years. What'd you expect?"

"Denial. That's what you're going with?"

"I swear to god, I had no part in it. I can't believe you're still going on about this. Think about it. Is a bounty my style?"

When he accused me before, I'd set about learning what I could. Before I learned much, the crisis was over.

The line goes silent.

He has to know that me being the poster is illogical.

"The alliance is far more refined than to sic randoms on you."

"Refined. Right. Moscow rules and all."

"If by Moscow you mean your death would appear natural, yes. There's nothing about a drone strike that's natural. It's still in the news, and that's with you presumably doing damage control."

Silence.

"Think about it." I can't believe I'm having to do his thinking for him. "You're the king of the hackers." Nick's not an active hacker himself, but he owns a few small outfits that do damage.

"What's that got to do with it?"

"Did you piss one of them off? Seems more likely to me a pissed hacker would be comfortable enough on the dark web to post a kill. I've got people looking into it. I'm told it was exceptional work."

"You truly didn't post it? Because I swear, within minutes of our call, the bounty got called off."

"Scout's honor."

"You were never a Scout."

"But I've always been a friend. Always."

He grumbles.

"What do your people say? Could they find anything? Any payments? Surely, any mercenary pursuing a bounty would want verification that a payment can be made." This isn't rocket science. His people had more time to research while the post was live. Mine are hunting ghosts.

"If you go far enough in the process, there's verification."

"And?"

"I'm working on it. It's set up well."

"I expect an apology when you figure it out."

There's a loud huff through the line. "If you're not calling to gloat, why are you calling? Two times in one day."

The first time he didn't answer, but…"Caroline's here."

"Scott? She's where? Where are you?"

"In Colorado."

"Ah. The place you built."

"That you haven't visited."

"A bitch to get to. Besides, there was a time when you showed up on the reg at my doorstep. Funny how you haven't shown up since the doorstep met its maker."

"Over a week ago. I checked on you. My source said you'd gone off grid."

"Yet you just called."

"Habit. I called earlier, and you didn't pick up. You've got to get off this. You seriously think I'd blow up your home? We shared a flat for years. You're one of the few friends I have."

I rub a hand over my face. I sound pathetic. But it's the same for Nick. It's rare we let someone in.

"You? Few friends? That, I believe."

"Asshole."

"Fair."

"You believe me?"

"Not sure." He sniffs, and if he could see me, I'd flip him off. "So, Scott's at your place. How is she?"

"I'm not sure."

"But she's there?"

"Yep." I step up to the window, peering over at the section of the house I left her in. From this angle, I can't see much of the house. Definitely can't see the guest room.

"And you're on the line with me?"

I grunt.

"What was that?"

"I have work to do."

"Clearly."

"Fuck you."

He chuckles. Because, of course, he does. "When was the last time you saw her?"

I get monthly reports, and sometimes they include photos and videos. But in person... "Six years ago."

Six years and two months, but adding the months sounds pathetic.

What's worse is I saw her, but she didn't see me.

"How's she look?"

"What do you mean?"

"It's been six years. Has she gained weight? Wrinkled? Gone gray? What is she now? Mid-thirties? Probably not gray, and she's American, so she'd cover it."

She's thirty-one. "She looks the same." *Elegant. Beautiful. Perfect.*

"So you've buggered off to your study, and she's...what? Hanging with your pops?"

"God, no." The response is immediate. Dad doesn't need to know she's here. He especially doesn't need to know I never filed for divorce.

Are you a fucking imbecile?

It's a question I've asked myself countless times in my father's booming roar.

"I always liked Caroline."

Me too.

"When I think of her...you know what I remember?"

"What?" I press my shoulder against the glass and crane my neck to see more of the house in case she's near a window.

"Those tiny pearl earrings she always wore and her properly fitting tops—"

"Do not go there." If he's about to talk about her breasts...

He chuckles.

Yes, that's where he was going.

"A right cool bird. Too fucking elegant and poised. Made getting her tossed a load of fun. Remember that night we had to carry her home, and she was singing…what's the bloke's name?"

"Neil Diamond."

"Yeah. She had a playlist filled with Neil Diamond…god awful taste in music. Played songs from a cover band of that shite. Super Diamond, right? Like…what nut listens to cover bands on their iPod? Of course, that was back before Spotify dominated."

When things were simpler. My breath fogs the glass in a nearly perfect circle.

"And now you're hiding from her?"

"I'm not hiding."

"You're not working."

Fucker.

"I am working, so…"

"Liar."

On this point, he's not wrong. "I'm going to tell you something I've told no one."

"Go on."

"Don't laugh."

"Aye, won't promise that."

"We're still married."

"No shit? Huh. So she's there to get papers signed or something or another. I'd say to cash in, but that's not Caroline. She's there to wrap it up, and you're playing the pansy and hiding."

"I'm not hiding. Work's insane."

"You still love her."

I flatten my forehead against the cool glass.

"Can't help you there, mate. But I will say that this call clears you from my list of suspects."

I still love her. He's right.

He goes on, rambling with his colloquial Brit humor while asking me questions about who I spoke to and the chatter about him, but my brain snags on that one true bit.

"What are you going to do?" Of course, he comes back to that question because he knows I've been half-listening, half-participating during his interrogative ramble.

What am I going to do? Shake her hand goodbye? Give her a goodbye hug? Repeat history? Watch her leave?

"Dorian? You there, mate?"

"Yeah, I'm here. Sorry."

I pinch the bridge of my nose and stare at the minute counter on the phone.

"Want some advice?"

"Shoot."

"Get the fuck out of your office and go talk to her."

I nod, not that he can see me.

"And if she has papers, tell her you'll sign them after a lawyer looks them over. Then talk to her."

"What's with you giving me advice?"

"That's why you called, isn't it?"

Hmm. Yes. Maybe.

"I'm glad you called."

"Yeah?"

"Because I didn't think I'd have a best mate at my wedding. Now I know I will."

"Best... You're getting married?"

"Eventually. She's not big on the marriage thing."

"Is this...the redhead?"

"Scarlet."

"Right. Wow. You're serious?"

"Deadly."

Huh. She wasn't just a lay. Guess that's why he wouldn't send her back to her family as requested.

"And here I thought you were using her to screw that mafia family."

"For best mates, we think a lot of each other, don't we?"

"Truthfully, you're one of the few people I know who's as horrible as me. That's why I like hanging out with you."

"Horrible as in...judgy and shit? That's what you mean, right? Not horrible in like use a woman and toss her?"

"Truthfully, I can't recall you dating. Ever."

"You know, I remember the day you met Caroline."

So do I.

"Love at first sight," he says.

"That's a stretch."

"No. 'Twas."

Probably.

"How'd you fuck it up? You never did say."

She left.

"Right, then," he says. "You don't want to tell me, that's fine. But it's on you if you don't want to talk about it with her."

"There's no point."

"Get your ugly arse out of your cave and go spend time with her! No one in their right mind makes that trip without wanting something. Maybe it's you."

He has a point. I expect she met someone and needs a divorce, even though she denied it.

"Let me know how it goes. I'll be on the lam."

"On the... Where are you?"

"Not telling. Tracing the call will be a waste of your time."

"Bounty's off, right?"

"Doesn't mean I'm not someone's target. Can you think of anyone with a quarter billion to burn?"

"Who wants you dead?" What he did to the Italian mafia didn't win him friends.

"Your old man?"

"My father likes you."

"Bullshit."

"He's the old generation. He'd be judicial with his money, hire the best, and spend less." That rationale should clear my father's name without my having to share the truth.

"Your father hasn't texted me since the explosion."

"How often does he text you?"

"More than you'd think."

Fuck. My gaze rises to the heavens.

"If it wasn't you, who the bloody hell did it?"

"I'll ask around." I'll follow up with my team, but if they had something, I would've heard. "If you need anything, let me know. You can come on out here, you know."

"Cause the States are safe."

"They are." Of course, so is Great Britain. "Seriously. Need anything, let me know. I've been remiss... I should've followed up, but when I found out you were all right, I just kind of..." Forgot. Lapsed. What the hell is wrong with me?

"Are you high?"

"No."

A beep sounds. I read the screen. *Geoffrey Cromwell.*

Fuck.

"I'd better take this call."

"Fine. Then turn the mobile off and go talk to her. Christ.

You've got her in that creepy mountain house in the middle of nowhere by herself. She's going to think you're plotting a murder."

My house isn't creepy. My father's…those big game trophy heads… Hmm, yeah.

I click over to take Geoffrey's call.

What does Dad want now?

"Geoffrey."

"You've got a guest?"

What the hell? "Yes."

"Security picked her up on the perimeter sensors."

"And?" Why am I even talking to Geoffrey? Why didn't security call? "What's her current position?"

"I'm not sure."

"What do you mean?"

"You aren't getting the texts? They sent texts to both you and your father." That's why Geoffrey got it.

I'm already moving through the corridor to the main house, pulling up the compound's security feed on my phone. The tactical response team would be running standard containment protocols—retired former Special Forces operators with enough firepower to defend against a small army. She must think I've lost my mind if she's spotted them tracking her movements.

I open my custom security app.

The Security Operations Center's feed appears on my screen, showing thermal imaging of Caroline moving along the property's eastern perimeter. Multiple guards maintain distance, running parallel tracks to her position.

"Odd behavior. I don't believe they've apprehended your

guest. They need confirmation that they should allow her to continue. You didn't respond."

"I was in a meeting."

Jesus.

"There. Sent a text confirming she may continue. Although, you may want to look at the footage."

"Why?" I swing open the door to the main house while keeping an eye on the live SOC feed.

"Because security believes she's behaving suspiciously. If you don't care, don't review it. I don't know why I bother."

CHAPTER 8

CAROLINE

Shadows blur the details of the roofline. I enlarge the image with my fingers, mentally noting the blind spots in the security coverage—two in particular, where the roof meets the façade. Our imagery enhancement software could clean up these shots, but the resolution might not be sufficient for full structural analysis. I take three more rapid shots at different exposures, a technique I learned during technical surveillance training.

The modern farmhouse aesthetic, expansive windows, and black-stained wood are reminiscent of homes I captured on Pinterest boards years ago. Dorian's design aesthetic has always matched mine. He likely hired a sought-after, talented designer with a Scandinavian sensibility, hence the reason the interior is breathtaking, with a balanced mix of simplicity and scaled grandeur.

Halston's massive mountain home is plenty big enough for

the two men. Perhaps his father has a new woman in his life, and Dorian desired his own space.

There was a time when it would have been impossible to be unaware of Halston Moore's relationship status. Any marriage received a press blitz. But like his son, he's drifted from the limelight. I can't remember the last time I saw a photograph of him in a newspaper or magazine. At ninety-two, I imagine he's ripe for the dead or alive celebrity game.

If Halston had remarried, we'd have a file on his wife with a detailed background and connections. Come to think of it, I'm sure Project Unity has a file on me as Dorian's legal wife.

The crinkling of leaves steals my attention from the eaves of the home. My hand instinctively moves to check my transmitter, disguised as a Cartier bracelet. I scan the woods in a grid pattern, the way we were trained—quadrant by quadrant, identifying and cataloging movement patterns. The sound's distinct rhythm and weight suggest bipedal, human, rather than animal origin, approximately 100 feet out.

While the compound encompasses over one thousand acres, I've stayed within the perimeters of the homes, and the Moores have a full staff. Where is the staff located?

I slip my phone into my jeans's back pocket and push up my sleeves, prepared to greet the approaching person. Security, perhaps?

It's definitely a human. Deer and other animals evoke a lighter sound with a more spontaneous pace.

The crinkling grows louder.

"Hello?"

A deer's head emerges.

We both still. Watching each other.

The female deer with big black orbs munches on her leaf.

She decides I'm not a predator and lowers her head and continues foraging. A younger deer with a smaller frame presses further into the woods, giving me little attention.

Deer. I don't see many of those in Santa Barbara, not where I've chosen to live.

I inhale deeply, breathing in the clean air, loaded with hints of earth and cedar.

But that sound? The crinkling of leaves. The snapping stick. It wasn't the deer. Someone else is in these woods.

Light reflects on the windows of the section of the house Dorian entered, yielding a black, impermeable screen.

Is he watching me from his office?

When I see Dorian, I'll tell him I love the house. He'll believe me. When I quit work, studying architecture became a passive hobby.

Of course, he's probably not watching me. He's lost in video conference calls and juggling a day packed with meetings of thirty-minute increments. A full hour wastes his time. He can cover more by entering meetings in the last half-hour, a trick he learned long ago from a time management consultant.

Tonight, I'll explore the extension of the home that holds his office. I've already planted three NightHawk minis—the latest gen surveillance tech with adaptive frequency to avoid detection. Kitchen, great room, entryway. But those locations are too public for real intel. Anyone trained in countersurveillance would avoid sensitive conversations there. The office is the target—assuming he hasn't upgraded to the latest Israeli white noise systems the agency uses.

Perhaps I should place a device in his bedroom. Although the bedroom crosses a line I don't believe is necessary. When we were together, he kept work out of the bedroom, choosing instead to split his eighteen-hour workdays between his offices.

The memory dredges up loneliness and abandonment, feelings long since smothered with an active life. I close my eyes and face the sun, partially hidden by the trees. When I leave this time, I won't return. A chapter of my life will close, never to be reread. An unwieldy wound, the source of which healed long ago, resurfaces like an unsightly varicose vein that only surfaces with movement.

"You must have had a busy day."

"Back-to-back meetings."

"I figured. You didn't respond to any of my texts."

"Hmm. I'm tanked. Going to bed."

"The texts showed as read. Did you read my texts?"

"Lorelei probably did."

"Your assistant?"

"One of them." He loosened his tie and slowed his steps. *"Did you need something?"*

I'd spent the day holed up in our apartment, avoiding the paparazzi. When photographed, journalists analyzed my outfit for confirmation of the quiet elegance *New York* magazine declared I possessed. Maybe I could've survived if he hadn't reduced us to an agenda item on his calendar. If I'm honest, I didn't get a thirty-minute slot. No, I received resentment for asking for his time, for not playing my supportive role and appreciating the coveted lifestyle.

My throat tightens with emotion. I've hours to kill before he emerges from his office, longer before I can complete my mission and escape in the morning. He's once again set me aside, and his action stirs up memories. At least this time around, I have a purpose. And there are no intrusive, blinding, camera flashes.

I turn the corner of the house and smash into a hard body. Thrown, my focus falls on a navy sweater and the strong hand gripping my forearm for support.

"Dorian?"

His arms fall to his side. "I didn't mean to startle you."

"Where'd you come from?"

"Just indoors." He gestures behind him.

"What're you doing—"

"I got a call that a guest was roaming the grounds. Wanted to be sure you were okay."

"You wanted to be certain an overzealous security team member didn't have me locked in a cell back at the guard-house?" I give free rein to the sarcasm, not to spark an argument, but because it's ludicrous he forced me to wait at the guardhouse.

"That wasn't a cell." He shoves his hands into his trouser pockets, defensive yet slightly remorseful. "What have you been doing?"

"Checking things out." I release a sigh, and along with it, the temptation to argue. "I love the house. It's beautiful. Impressive."

He's thoughtful. His gaze briefly falls on me, then out into the woods. "Want to go on a hike?"

He's in trousers and dress boots.

"Already went. Walked up to your father's house. It hasn't changed."

"No, it hasn't." His gaze remains on the woods. He's circumspect.

"Someone's out there. I'm guessing it's your security."

"As usual, you are correct." The hint of a smile softens what might have been reproach years ago. "Can I interest you in a drink? Coffee? Tea? What is it you drink these days?"

"Do you have mint tea?"

"We can check."

He has no idea what's stocked in the house; that's what he's saying.

"That sounds nice."

I follow him inside and can't stop myself from asking, "You aren't needed at the office?"

He exhales.

I probably shouldn't have said anything, given that work was a sore point between us. A therapist helped me see it was symptomatic of larger issues, namely an inability to communicate.

"Spoke to Nick."

I pause, one hand on the stairwell as my mind runs through my mental Rolodex.

"Ivanov?"

"The one and only."

"How's he doing?"

"He's not my biggest fan these days."

"He's never been a fan."

That earns a chuckle.

"Always been one of yours."

Realization dawns. "Nick told you to get out of the office and spend time with me."

He's at the top of the stairs, whereas I'm still on the first step. He doesn't confirm or deny.

"You want honey with your tea?"

"Sure," I call.

"How is Nick these days?" I ask.

"Same Nick."

"How so?"

"Making enemies with the wrong people."

I stand in the kitchen, watching as Dorian opens the kitchen cabinet doors with a methodical, one-at-a-time approach.

"Funny, I don't recall that about him."

"No?"

"If my memory serves, everyone loved Nick."

"Women."

"Well, that too." He opens a drawer.

"Why don't you just ask your chef to make you tea?" It's a bit of a dig, but it's also the truth. He doesn't know where anything is, which means he's never in the kitchen.

I step past him into the butler's pantry. There's a coffee machine on the counter, and I open one cabinet to reveal coffee mugs. When I open the adjacent door, I discover a tightly sealed glass jar full of wrapped tea bags. I lift a panel beside the coffee machine, find a teapot on a warmer, and lift it to fill it with water.

"Do you want any?" I ask.

"I don't drink tea."

"Who makes your coffee in the morning?"

"I make my own."

I slow and tilt my head, remembering the pods from earlier.

"Someone comes along and cleans after me. But yes, I make my coffee, just like before."

"I made the coffee."

"I meant before you."

I slide the teapot onto the burner and lift the glass jar off the shelf so I can better rummage through the tea selection.

Dorian's gaze locks on me, wrapping around me as if he's searching for a fissure to infiltrate. The warm tendrils unnerve me.

Knock. Knock.

"Sounds like someone's at the door. Will the butler get it?"

He narrows his eyes, but his lips curve into an amused smirk. It's one of my favorite looks of his, and given he's gone to answer the door, I don't bite back my smile.

"Geoffrey." Dorian's tone is one he uses when he's greeting someone he doesn't like.

I snag a green packet of mint tea while trying to recall a Geoffrey. When we were married, I met dozens of colleagues. Most of whom, if I'm honest, Dorian didn't like.

Nick Ivanov had been one of the few he genuinely held as a friend, and I always presumed that was because they met during college. When we were together, his only close friends were those who knew him as a child or those who met him abroad and saw him as a regular guy.

"Here's an NDA for your guest to sign."

"She won't need that."

"Don't be dimwitted—"

"She's already signed one."

Dorian's right, of course. I signed a lengthy NDA on the day he brought me home to meet his father. An all-encompassing, lengthy agreement that I'm ashamed to admit I never read.

"Very well, then. There's a pilot on standby, if you need him."

I cock my head, listening. Geoffrey. The name is familiar. Head of security? Is he here because they watched me taking photographs?

"That's unnecessary."

"Dorian—" *Not Mr. Moore.*

"I'll fly her back."

"As you wish."

The door closes, and Dorian's footsteps grow louder until he appears in the doorway.

"Who was that?" I ask, maintaining a casual posture, though my pulse quickens as I catalog his microexpressions. The slight tension in his jaw. The weight shift to his back foot. Classic indicators of suspicion I clocked countless times in surveillance footage when working for the CIA.

"Who are you working for these days?" he counters.

My mind races through my cover story's contingencies, the nested layers of truth and fiction we constructed. At the agency, I built profiles of people like Dorian—brilliant, paranoid, three steps ahead. Now the stakes feel exponentially higher.

I drop the tea packets into the top of the teapot, close the lid, and press the boil button. If I tell him, he'll search the house for listening devices after I'm gone.

"You're not with the CIA anymore."

I twist the lid, avoiding his gaze in an attempt to conceal my surprise that he has that information.

"Did you really think I wouldn't keep track of you?"

CHAPTER 9

DORIAN

What are you up to, Caroline?

Her cheeks flush, and her astute nose tilts upwards slightly. I ache to pull her against me, to push my nose into her hair and learn if she's changed her shampoo or perfume—the hell with her scent. I want to hold her again.

Don't be a loser.

Is that my father's voice, or mine? After forty years of Halston Moore's particular brand of tough love, sometimes it's hard to tell where his ruthless pragmatism ends and mine begins. The old man would say I'm being weak, letting her affect me like this.

"You're my wife. You had to know I'd keep up with you."

"Have an employee on it, do you? An assistant? A team?"

The sharp tone is new. She's stronger. More demanding.

She's become a better person without me in her life. Healthier. "Who was that man at the door?"

Who is this determined woman? What's driving her? In our world of calculated moves and strategic plays, nobody shows up without an agenda. She left me—walked away from the wealth, the influence, all of it. That kind of conviction always gave her power. Made her different from the others. Independent.

"Jesus, Dorian, are you going to answer any of my questions?"

"Sorry." I blink, snapping myself out of my head. "One of my father's employees."

"Security?"

"No."

Geoffrey's definitely not security. I wonder how long it will be before facial recognition identifies Caroline, and Geoffrey figures out who she is. Perhaps security already identified her, and that's why Geoffrey showed up at my door, eager to send her on her way.

Didn't he meet her? Maybe not. She met with *my* financial advisor, not Geoffrey. The sixty-something-year-old man doesn't strike me as the type to read Page Six and the like. He's the guy you want on your team when making stock picks, not on a pop culture trivia night.

I don't remember exactly when Geoffrey became an integral part of my father's life. By the time Dad introduced me to Geoffrey, he'd been working with him for a long time, and I hadn't yet entered the family business. I was busy rebelling against the Moore legacy, building satellite prototypes in Oxford's engineering lab while my father's empire waited. Geoffrey was already there when I finally stepped into

Bedrock, wearing suits that cost more than my first research grant.

I didn't expect Geoffrey to move to Colorado with us, but Dad is his only client, and he might be Dad's only true friend.

"Are you planning to fly me back to Denver?"

Caroline's annoyed. As she should be. It's too easy to get lost in my head.

"I said I would." I rub my temple, and the pain intensifies. The light brightens. *Fuck.*

"That man mentioned me leaving today."

She listened, did she?

"Tomorrow morning." She avoids my gaze. "As planned. We have things to discuss. Don't you think?" The words come out with the same careful neutrality I use in hostile takeover negotiations. Ironic—that's essentially what this is. A corporate restructuring of the heart.

Those unforgettable blue eyes widen. Incredulous. And angry.

What is this anger? Time mellowed my anger. Why hasn't it done the same to hers?

"We can't fly back this afternoon. Winds are picking up. It's inadvisable." It's a lie. A cold front is moving in, but the expected winds wouldn't prevent the helicopter from flying. But she won't push it. She's a nervous flier.

"I see."

Does she doubt me? Does she want to fight?

"I'll fly you back in the morning. As planned," I reiterate.

The teapot boils, and she goes to it. I rest my palms against the island, watching her closely. Her jeans are loose along the length of her legs, up to her shapely ass. Her light sweater hangs loose, skimming above her hips, mostly concealing her curves.

Even in casual attire, she's professional and polished because she's here for business. I should follow her lead. God knows I've spent enough time in boardrooms to recognize when someone's building up to a proposal. The Moore method: let them reveal their position first. Never show your hand until you have to.

She hasn't asked about the divorce agreement, and I won't be the one to broach the subject.

"Do you live here full-time?"

"These days, yes."

"I would've never expected you to move to Colorado."

That's not a topic to discuss with her. *Talk about her family.*

"How are your parents?"

"You've already asked about them."

So I have. But there is a question I haven't yet asked.

"Are you seeing anyone?"

"That's not your business."

That's not a yes. Which means she's not. That's good. Don't be a jackass. She's not here to pick up where we left off.

My vision blurs, and I squeeze my eyes shut while kneading my temple. The migraine's timing couldn't be worse; I have a video call with the European Space Agency in six hours about orbital patterns for the new constellation launch.

Nausea circulates. The swift onslaught of symptoms is ominous.

"You're still getting migraines?"

She remembers.

"Not the kind of thing to go away."

"Are you eating gluten?"

My brow aches, and I press into the bone with my fingers,

soothing the tight muscles with a circular motion. Shit. I'm probably overdue for Botox injections.

"Dorian? If you don't take care—"

"The gluten-free diet didn't help."

She'd been adamant it would. She'd been wrong.

"How long did you give it?"

"Years."

"It's hard to stay on a gluten-free diet."

I exhale frustration. Of course, she believes it's my fault. "I hired chefs. It wasn't that hard. Simply didn't help."

Is it so hard to believe that all her new-age crap didn't work?

"I hired some of the best doctors—" Pain sears behind my eyes.

"You are so stubborn."

"Projecting?"

Pressure on my arm has me squeezing my eyelids open into slits, confirming she is indeed touching me.

"What's a good room to lie down in? One we can darken?"

I squeeze my eyes closed, breathing deeply to control the nausea.

"Dorian?"

"My bedroom."

One eyelid cracks open, watching her. The answer wasn't intended to be sexual, but we once shared a bedroom, and having her in mine again dredges up memories. The desire roared back the moment I saw her silhouette. But not now. She could be naked in front of me, and I couldn't touch her.

My employees would have a fit seeing someone lead me anywhere—the moody boss helpless, being guided through his own house. The irony isn't lost on me. The pressure on my arm intensifies.

"What?" Jesus, I'm growling at her.

"Let's go."

Funny how she can still command my compliance when my board of directors can't.

"Keep walking."

Poetic. She's forcing me into a bedroom, and I'm too incapacitated to do anything about it.

Through a squinted lid, I stumble to the stairs and press the master dimmer switch. The house's environmental system automatically dims the lights to 30 percent—a feature I had custom-designed after the migraines started getting worse. The Italian marble underfoot cost more than most homes, but right now, it's just another hard surface to navigate.

Her hand never leaves my arm, letting me know she's right there.

"I'm surprised you didn't choose a bedroom next to your office."

How does she know where my office is?

"I saw you walking to the adjacent building. You said that's your office, right?"

"Home office," I answer.

Fuck, my head hurts.

"I'm surprised you didn't put your bedroom next to your home office," she repeats.

We finally reach my bedroom, and I toe off my shoes and collapse onto the bed, resting an arm over my eyes. She leaves my side, and once again, I force an eyelid open to see.

"There's a button. A remote. On the dresser."

She finds it, and the shade falls from the ceiling, draping the room in blissful darkness.

I listen as she steps into the bathroom. "Is your medicine in here?"

"Press on the floor-length mirror. It opens to a medicine cabinet."

"Jesus, Dorian. How much medicine are you taking?"

"A lot is probably expired."

She might not hear me. I have the house manager handle most things, but my medicine cabinet is private.

"What do you want to take?" she calls.

Dammit. I'm going to have to get up and get it.

I push off—

"No."

I freeze at the sharpness.

Water runs from a faucet in the bathroom.

"Lie back. I've got it." Her voice echoes slightly in the marble bath.

Steps sound against the marble, then stop. She's near.

Pills rattle in a bottle.

"Why do you have so many bottles of Vicodin?"

"It works." Unlike the experimental treatments from that neurologist in Switzerland or the cutting-edge therapy my medical team insisted would be revolutionary.

"That can't be good for you."

For the first time since she walked out the door so many years ago, I feel a measure of gratitude that she left.

She raps my chest. "Take these."

I pop the pills, swallowing them together.

"You don't want water? I have water."

"I'm fine."

"Are you drinking enough water? Drink this"

"Just leave. I'll be fine."

How many times has this scene played out?

"No. You need water."

"I can't keep it down."

"You don't have to drink the whole glass. Wet your tongue."

Her hand slips behind my head, lifting me slightly, and the cool glass presses on my lips.

It's awkward. But I sip. My mouth is dry, so I drink more.

She pulls on my sweater. "Sit up."

"What?"

"I'm going to try something."

Dizziness and nausea swirl.

The bed sinks, and she says, "Lie back."

Confused, I crack an eye open. She's sitting on my bed. Her back to the headboard.

"Lay your head down here." She pats her denim-clad thigh.

She's kicked off her running shoes, and her multicolored socks blur.

I lie back until my head rests on her thigh. She reaches for a pillow, tells me to lift, then recline.

"Better?"

"Yes."

"Close your eyes." And her fingers take over.

Magic. It's the only word for her touch. She soothes the pain. Comfort and warmth permeate my chest. My neck muscles strain, but those magical fingers ease the muscles. I want to lie like this forever.

"You've never done this before."

"You always told me to leave you alone."

"Did I say that out loud?"

"Yes." Amusement laces her answer.

"Damn." What pills did she give me?

"These pills are going to knock you out, aren't they?"

"I hope not. This feels like heaven."

"You don't take care of yourself."

"I have an entire staff that takes care of everything." It's true —a machine of efficiency that runs my life while I run a company that tracks everything from weather patterns to global security threats. Twenty thousand employees worldwide.

"Yet you get migraines."

"Why are you here?" My tone is purposefully soft. I don't want an argument.

"You know why."

I let my neck turn, face against her thigh, ending the conversation. She's here for the divorce agreement. Another contract to negotiate, another asset to divide. The irony never escapes me—I can orchestrate a satellite launch from my phone, but I couldn't keep my marriage in orbit. Father would say that's the price of empire-building, and he would know.

We can't negotiate when I'm incapacitated. I need sleep.

CHAPTER 10

CAROLINE

"Don't leave."

The barely audible words circulate slowly, gradually depleting the surrounding oxygen. His breathing slows, and the muscle tension relaxes as he slips into sleep. The weight of his head on my thigh increases, and I take him in, so unexpectedly vulnerable.

A torrent of conflicting emotions erupts.

Sadness. Grief. Guilt.

I shouldn't let my personal history interfere with mission objectives. Yet here I am, my fingers still working through his hair like we're back in Oxford, before I understood what it meant to marry into a powerful, enigmatic family.

Why should I feel guilty? He didn't fight for our marriage. He did nothing to stop me. No, he wanted me to leave.

Back then, all I wanted was to hear those words…*Don't leave.*

My head rests on the cushioned headboard, and his rests in my lap. My fingers fall from his temples. Asleep, he's peaceful. The tiny lines around the corners of his eyes smooth, and his jaw and lips relax.

"Don't go. Stay. Please."

Words from so long ago come back to me, pulling me into a memory of the first time I spent the night. Back then, to me, Dorian Moore was a slightly nerdy American studying abroad. His elusive dimple, unruly wavy hair, and wrinkled appearance set my heart into a spin.

I had no idea older Americans had watched him grow up in the pages of *People Magazine*. Perhaps I should have. But the celebrities I paid attention to attended premieres and rock concerts. I had never opened an issue of *Forbes* or the *Wall Street Journal*, and even if I had, I wouldn't have recognized his father or put two and two together with the name. If he'd been involved in an *Esquire*-worthy scandal, perhaps I would've recognized him. Or if his father or he had ever been in an HGTV episode or a season of *The Bachelor* or *Undercover CEO*.

That summer, to me, he was a grad student. Brilliant, obviously, as is required to attend Oxford. My semester abroad only required signing up and paying the fee, but he was registered in a PhD program.

My campus roommate told me the key to a carefree fling abroad was to never stay the night. Feelings hatch if you stay over, she said. And I'd been so freaking clueless. I thought I could carry on like a wild girl. See a handsome guy, party, and move on, heart intact.

Like so many others, our love story was mundane. We met in a pub. Our gazes caught across the bar, and it was as if a string instantly connected us. The perimeter dimmed, and he became everything.

He approached. We talked for hours. He invited me to a party at his place that weekend. I agreed. For days, we spoke on the phone. Casual and polite. Nothing wild or reckless. But I grinned constantly, and my roommate teased me.

The second I entered the privacy of his flat, we were on each other. Couldn't get our clothes off fast enough. It was as if the moment we were out of the public eye, all restraints snapped. Fitting, in retrospect.

After we got around to eating, I gathered my things, put on my shoes, intent on the casual pretense. He didn't ask. No, he told me to stay.

And I did not obey. I stayed strong. I left.

Until the second time.

I breathe out the memory. Release the self-contempt. I couldn't have known what would happen or how he would gut me. In those early years, we felt like a modern fairy tale.

He rolls onto his side, his nose angling into my hip. I run my fingers through his soft strands, trimmed so short that the waves are gone. He releases a subtle groan that reverberates up my thighs and awakens a need that has no place in this moment.

What I need is to focus.

With luck, he'll sleep for hours. The medicine he took should knock him out. I ease his head up and slide out from under him. He grunts, and I freeze, holding my breath, waiting. He rolls further onto his side. I tiptoe, searching for a blanket. In his walk-in closet, I find several folded neatly on the top shelf.

Glancing around the closet, it's clear that an employee organized this space. He'd never take the time. White oxford button-down shirts hang in a row before a series of colored shirts from light to dark. Thin cashmere sweaters and thick wool sweaters are folded in color-coordinated stacks from light to dark. I open a walnut drawer to find neatly folded T-shirts in white, shades of gray, and black. Narrow drawers with custom inserts hold sunglasses and watches. Rows of jeans hang with trousers. On the back wall hang suits and overcoats. Slanted shelves with a bar on the end hold dress shoes, while dress boots can be seen behind glass horizontal doors. I'm sure ties, belts, socks, and briefs are neatly stored in drawers or behind a hidden panel. If I were to guess, he hired someone to design the closet and then hired someone else to fill it. Or his house manager did it all.

The freshly pressed clothes appear new. Tags dangle from several coats. I'd bet a personal shopper ordered every single item in this closet, and tags remain on items he hasn't yet worn, not to be returned, but should he decide he doesn't want to wear them, or never wears them, it makes them more desirable when he donates them to charity.

Are his personal items in another home? His old sweatshirts, crew tees, his favorite navy sweater fraying along the edges… Are they stored in the house he considers home? No, what am I thinking? He probably tossed them all. Sentimentality is absent from his DNA. With a faux fur blanket in my arms, I exit the closet and carefully place it over his feet and legs, draping it around his waist.

With one last glance, I exit the darkened room and silently tug the door closed. Then I speed walk to the guest room downstairs, mentally mapping potential camera angles and blind spots. My training screams at me to maintain a natural pace—just in case someone's watching.

I gather my pocketbook with the listening devices inside. NightHawk X7s, latest gen surveillance tech. Better than anything we had at the agency. The placement protocol must be remembered: minimum eighteen inches from any electronic devices, avoid metal surfaces, maintain line of sight to exterior walls where possible.

I casually stroll through the home, keeping my movement patterns consistent with someone exploring out of curiosity. Years of analyzing surveillance footage taught me that irregular movement patterns are the first thing that triggers security AI. I doubt he'd put security cameras inside his living quarters—he was always paranoid about his own privacy—but it's conceivable some of the outside cameras cover the glass hallway connecting the home with the office section. I catalog every potential sight line, each reflective surface that could hide a lens.

If he wakes, or anyone asks, I'll say it was too early to fall asleep, and I wandered around, curious about Dorian's life. He wouldn't suspect me of stealing.

A memory flashes of a tear-stricken maid in a black-and-white uniform. Halston required his staff to wear uniforms so they could be easily recognized. Everyone in his orbit needed recognizable status. I strain to remember if he suspected the maid of stealing a watch or his eyeglasses.

His prescription eyeglasses. That's what it was. Ludicrous. He verbally lashed out so loudly and violently that Dorian sprang into action, protecting the middle-aged woman. If Halston ever found his lost glasses, he never said. Halston Moore didn't admit when he was wrong.

If anyone watched security footage, it would be Halston. One might expect that a man with more money than god wouldn't care about minor theft. One would be wrong. Halston cares. It used to surprise me that he invested his money, as he'd be happier buying gold coins and filling rooms with them in a treasure motif.

If Halston saw me roaming the property, he'd assume I was looking for something of value to steal or assessing value for some nefarious purpose. My years of analyzing security protocols tell me the real defense isn't in the obvious cameras or guards—it's in the layers of subtle surveillance I can sense but not quite see. The well-maintained paths aren't just aesthetic; they funnel visitors through predetermined routes, probably lined with motion sensors and thermal imaging.

The paths through the woods are suspiciously well-maintained. Instead of wilderness, the acreage between the Moore men's dwellings is park-like—engineered sightlines, I realize now. Everything is designed to look natural while optimizing surveillance coverage.

What must it be like to believe every person you come across wants to steal your hard-earned wealth?

Years have passed. Perhaps Halston's mellowed. I did, after all, wander through his compound without coming across any barriers.

If someone inquires about why I'm in Dorian's home office, I'll say I was curious about Dorian's life. It's the truth, but not the whole truth.

Glass windows with black iron grids line the connector between the main house and the attached office. The floor looks like white pine laid in a herringbone pattern, but the subtle change in sound underfoot tells a different story. I didn't expect a tile floor, but given the snowy months, it's practical, and Dorian has always been practical.

A black iron-framed glass door divides the hallway to the adjacent building—again, most likely a practical addition. The glass allows light to flow between the spaces, but I imagine the door increases energy efficiency.

Will the door be locked? And if it is, will that prove the suspicions about Dorian correct? Why else would a man living alone lock a section of his home?

My hand falls on the black iron handle. A chill burns my palm, and I press down. Nothing happens.

I look through the glass into an inviting space with the feel of a living area. Fur rugs warm the floor in front of brown leather sofas and loveseats. I half-expect heads of game to hang on the wall, but instead, I see framed photography.

My breath catches, and as if motivated by an unseen force, I push harder on the handle, and it clicks. I push on the door and enter the room.

The photographs on the walls are all mine. I'm not a photographer, but I took lessons, and whenever we traveled to Colorado, I practiced. Blown up to portfolio proportions are my favorites. Shots taken from the mountain peaks and across the streams.

Behind glass, framed in walnut, my photos are stunning. Or maybe it's not the shots, but the realization he kept them and put them on display.

To the right, the view is of the main section of the house. I can see what I believe is Dorian's bedroom window with the shades drawn down. To the left are trees. At one end of the room is a fireplace, and on the opposite wall is a galley kitchen. It's easy to imagine snuggling up beneath blankets and watching it snow. Bookcases would improve the space, as would personal mementos. There's an industrial iron spiral staircase, and I climb.

The open upstairs floor holds Dorian's office. The windows are smaller upstairs with functional credenzas below them. An executive alpine desk commands the room. A small round table with chairs to one side implies he invites others to this home office, but it's hard to imagine Dorian inviting others into his home. He rarely did when we were together. This is a functional office set-up, as a decorator would recommend.

The office is exactly what you'd expect from someone running a corporation: clean lines, minimalist, designed to project power while revealing nothing. I analyze it the way I used to analyze target locations: primary work zone centered on the desk, secondary meeting area by the round table, likely locations for secure communications equipment. The credenzas below the windows could easily house signal scramblers or countersurveillance gear.

Framed photographs line the credenza closest to his desk. A lampshade hangs on his desk lamp, offering another option for placement. My fingers brush the NightHawk in my bag. The mission brief replays in my head: clean installations, undetectable footprint, focus on high-value intelligence locations.

Don't place it where the cleaning service might find it.

Luke's instructions echo as I assess the frames, calculating angles and audio capture zones. I step closer to examine the wooden frames and stop in my tracks when my gaze falls on a photo of us, bundled in winter clothes, poles in our hands with goggles and helmets covering our foreheads, smiling. The photo is from our first ski trip together. It once hung on a wall in our home, but it sits here, reframed in a rustic wood frame.

The photograph beside it is smaller, but it's me, walking along the beach, my back to him, sandals dangling from my fingers. My index finger lightly brushes over a photograph of Dorian's childhood dog, a Labrador retriever that passed during his college years. The last framed photograph is of our first home, the one where he carried me across the threshold. To a casual observer, it might appear as a New York brownstone, the nearby tree a common enough photo for New York City aficionados, but I'm not a casual observer.

He's kept me close. But he's chosen moments unrecognizable to others. He's not a man planning to disrupt the United States. He's private, wounded, and misunderstood.

He hasn't let us go.

He has held on to little, but he's held on to the memories.

Vibrations from my shoulder bag remind me of my purpose. I don't check the caller, as I assume it's Sophia reaching out for a status update. I'll return her call when it's time for the team to confirm the device's function.

The team needs to focus elsewhere. Dorian is not the madman seeking to disrupt the free world. But too much is at stake. They won't take my word for it. I withdraw the first listening device, a small silver piece. I lift one of the heavy frames and search the back.

This will work. I can secure the device behind the back fold, and if someone lifts it to dust, it shouldn't fall out or be noticed.

I don't see a similar place on the lamp. There's no dust anywhere, which tells me his cleaning service is thorough. His leather chair, though…I bend to the floor and peer up at the bottom of the throne. There's a discreet handle to the side for lowering and raising the chair. I secure the slim piece on the lever. If it were to fall, he might assume it's a mechanical piece of the chair. But it shouldn't fall, and he would never peer beneath a chair.

The dark monitors reflect my silhouette, and I pause for a minute, wondering if his password remains the same. I note the keyboard wear patterns, the slight discoloration on specific keys that might indicate frequent use. But what would I search for? Even with my background in data analysis, I'd never guess his filing nomenclature. And he's not guilty.

I scan for any signs of the advanced tech we were briefed about: quantum encryption keys, neural pattern locks, biometric scanners disguised as ordinary office equipment. The setup looks deceptively normal, but that's exactly what we'd expect from someone potentially orchestrating global disruption events. Yet those photographs...

I might have questioned if he could change, but those photographs show that, if anything, he hasn't changed enough. I've moved on, and he hasn't. A fact he keeps close to the chest and hidden.

I once had a Pinterest board filled with modern farmhouse architecture. Did he design this mountain retreat with my preferences in mind? Did he hand over my Pinterest board to the designer? Because the longer I take in the architectural details, I begin to wonder.

A sadness fills me, working its way in the way an icy wind infiltrates the thickest wool.

Did I give up too soon? Should I have stayed?

The vibrations resume, and this time, I remove my phone. Sophia's name flashes on the screen.

"Hey," I answer, voice soft, weighted with my heavy thoughts.

"Can you talk?"

"Yes. It's done. Do you want to check if they're working? He's asleep, so if there's an issue, I can adjust them."

"He's asleep? In the afternoon?"

"Migraine. He took Eletriptan." Based on the contents of his medicine cabinet, he likely took Vicodin earlier in the day. The combination would act like a sedative. "I don't know how much time we have."

"Excellent. Have you seen Halston?"

"He and his father live in separate dwellings. I hiked up to Halston's home earlier today and entered the garage. It's the main house I showed you on the satellite imagery. Placed trackers in two vehicles and listening devices beneath the front seats, but I don't know how often, if ever, his father uses those vehicles. The man's ninety-two. He may never leave the compound. I'll see if I can convince Dorian to let me say hello to his father before I leave, but I doubt I'll be left alone inside his father's home."

"We're going to send someone up to retrieve you. If you can get into his father's house before nightfall, that's great. Otherwise, let's get you out of there."

"I'm not in danger, Sophia. Dorian's going to fly me into Denver in the morning." My gaze crosses the lawn to the darkened main house. "There are still things we need to discuss." It's a painful admission, but the truth is in black and white, framed behind glass.

"Caroline, we traced the source of the calls to burner phones found near scenes of the attacks to your geographical area. There are no neighboring properties."

My brain kicks into overdrive, processing the tactical implications. Isolated location. Direct access to global satellite networks. A brilliant but reclusive billionaire with unlimited resources. It's textbook—exactly the pattern I would have flagged in my CIA days. But the personal photographs, the preserved memories...they don't fit the profile. Unless...

A cold realization hits me: What better cover than appearing to be a man still pining for his ex-wife? I, of all people, should know, sometimes the most convincing tradecraft is built on genuine emotion.

"The team has reviewed the evidence, and the decision has been made." Sophia's voice carries the crisp certainty I remember from agency briefings.

Burner phones mean planned anonymity; geographical correlation suggests either sloppy tradecraft or intentional misdirection. The analyst in me wants to request raw data, verification protocols, and pattern analysis. But there's no time for that now.

"Dorian Moore is not the man you think he is, and we need to get you out of there."

The words hit differently when you're in the field versus behind a desk. Years of analyzing threat assessments, and suddenly, I'm inside one.

CHAPTER 11

DORIAN

Gravel scatters across the asphalt drive. A red juice stains my striped shirt, and my too-long jeans drag the ground. The brick building comes into focus—my elementary school. The same prestigious prep school where three generations of Moore men learned to carry the weight of a legacy.

There are no cars in the parking lot. If I go into the building, I can tell them my driver didn't come. Do I have keys? I want to move, but inertia binds my legs. An old Honda Accord rounds the bend. Recognition dawns.

The horizon brightens.

The window rolls down, and Caroline's golden hair drapes her arm as she leans across the divide, her smile warm and true, skin flushed, reminiscent of a young Maine summer girl.

She shakes her head. Her lips turn down in disappointment.

The vehicle drives away, and I lose sight of the wheels. I reach for her, wanting to run, but I can't. My legs won't move.

I struggle until the scene shifts. I blink into darkness. Sweat coats my brow. My breaths come short and fast. My eyesight adjusts, taking in the dark room and the circular blue ceiling light triggered by my movement. Outside, it's dark.

What time is it? I swipe my hand over my damp brow. Jesus. My fucking childhood dream twisted to include Caroline. How many pills did I take?

Weak, I stumble out of bed and head to the bathroom. The bedside clock shows ten after four a.m. The meds knocked me out.

What did Caroline do? Did she find something to eat for dinner? The house manager stocks the kitchen, but I often eat dinner with Dad up at his house. I assume there was something for her to eat. I'd planned to have the chef cook for us last night.

My limbs are shaky, the weakness noticeable with the slight tremble in my hand while brushing my teeth. I need food. Something to settle my stomach. Caffeine to ward off another headache. After changing into pajama bottoms, a plain T-shirt, and slippers, I head downstairs.

Motion-activated lights trigger along my path, casting a glow beneath cabinets and along the floor.

In a dreamlike fog, I start the coffee machine and place a slice of bread in the toaster. The same mindless routine I follow during five a.m. investor calls with Europe. Of course, Caroline had to see me like this—not the polished CEO who commands boardrooms, but the version that gets migraines and drugs himself into a comatose sleep.

The house manager stocks premium bread from an artisanal bakery here in Telluride, the kind Caroline used to special order in New York. I'd planned to have the chef prepare something more impressive, another carefully orchestrated performance like the quarterly earnings calls.

Fuck migraines.

I lost time with her. Time for what? For me to promise to sign a divorce agreement?

I should've done it years ago. She made it easy to ignore. It's not like I haven't had plenty else occupying my time.

Coffee in hand, on autopilot, I head to my office, but I slow as I pass the guest room's open door. In the past, she never slept in a room with an open door. I shouldn't risk waking her. A magnetic pull drags me into the room. I shouldn't—the bed comes into view, and the temperature in the room drops several degrees. She didn't sleep here.

Did she leave? How? A driver? Is she in Denver?

I rush down the breezeway, headed to my office. The security system silently logs my movement—a habit from running a company where every satellite position is tracked, every signal monitored. I'll check the tapes. Access logs. Camera feeds. The same protocols we use to monitor orbital paths, applied to finding my wife.

Who can I call to find out where she's staying in Denver? Who can I call to search hotel bookings? Or access her credit card charges?

I push through the glass door, mentally running through my resource list, when I halt.

There she is. Asleep on the leather sofa. The gas fireplace blazes and wraps the space in a comforting glow. Golden strands cascade around her, and there's a fur throw pulled up over her waist. The light-pink silk pajama top is all Caroline. Demure, classic, and sensible. Perfect for travel. A memory of flicking the pearl-like buttons surfaces, of cupping her breast, tweaking her nipple… *Shut it down.*

Did she not like the guest room? Did she come here to read and fall asleep?

Minutes pass. Once again, inertia binds my legs and slows my thoughts. Her skin glows in the firelight. The prominent rosiness on her cheeks is absent. She washed her face, removing her makeup before falling asleep. Why sleep here?

My gaze lifts from Caroline, asleep in my home, to the landscapes hanging on the wall.

Did she recognize the shots? Did she feel more comfortable in this room?

I sink into the armchair closest to the sofa. Is it weird that I'm watching her? Maybe. But what else am I going to do? The sun won't rise for a couple of hours. I missed the call with the European Space Agency, but I'm sure my staff handled it. I could check the Asian or European markets, but I lack the incentive. If there were any unexpected fluctuations, I would've been notified. As chairman of the board of Bedrock Advisory, I don't trade. Brilliant men and women trade, keeping us at the top of the game.

I'm sure there are emails I should read. There are always emails.

Peace flows through my veins, and I settle deeper into the cushion. I set my ankles on the coffee table. My breathing slows until it matches the gentle up and down movement of Caroline's rib cage.

I wish I'd found her earlier.

If I had, would I have moved her, or sat here, watching and memorizing?

"Dorian."

The voice is distant. Familiar.

"Dorian." She's close.

I blink and squint into the golden light.

"You fell asleep and spilled your coffee."

I look down. A brown stain spreads across my abdomen. It's still damp, and the cotton clings to my skin.

"Doesn't look like you spilled much." She reaches across my lap, and light shimmers against the pink silk. "Doesn't look like there was much in it."

She holds the mug, smiling.

I rub a hand over my face, swallowing. "I must've fallen asleep. Again."

"Did you take more medicine?" She frowns. "How's your migraine?"

"It's fine."

Slightly out of it, I push up and peel the wet material away from my skin, lifting the shirt over my head.

Caroline steps back. I follow her gaze to my chest.

It's nothing she hasn't seen before. Is that stare disapproving? Or is she...

A familiar energy surges. If she's interested... Those blue eyes flicker upwards.

"Did you sleep okay?"

She nods. Her tongue licks her bottom lip.

My heart skitters like a teenage boy's.

Only her.

I reach for her, and my thumb brushes her cheek. She tilts her head into my palm, and on an inhale, I inch closer.

Her gaze locks on mine. The distance between us shrinks. I palm her hip, cloaked in silk. My fingers glide lower as my head tilts. Her light, faint floral scent has me inhaling deeper, and my skin tingles as if awakening from a long, dormant sleep.

My lips are inches from hers.

She swallows and backs away. My hands drop. She scratches her neck.

"Why don't you go get changed, and I'll pour us some coffee?"

I rub the back of my neck, forcing myself to snap out of it and wake up. Outside, the sun filters through the tops of the trees.

"What time is it?"

"Close to eight. Don't you need to leave soon for work?"

It's Friday. I cleared my calendar, but yes, it's a work day.

"Sleeping out here, I guess we both missed our alarms." My gaze falls to her darkened phone on the coffee table.

"If you need a charger—"

"I've got one," she says.

I nod, backing away, balled-up shirt in one hand. The ceramic mug sits on the armrest. I could grab it, but the staff will get it.

"Let's meet in the kitchen," she says brightly. The high pitch rings of nervousness. "I'll be ready when you are."

Right. My nails dig into my scalp, scratching furiously.

What am I doing? Caroline is preparing to leave me; only this time, I may never see her again.

"What time do you have to be in Denver?"

"Ah, this afternoon. I've got a meeting, and then my flight's at five."

"I'll clear my morning." If I were more awake, I'd laugh at the shock on her face. There was a time when I never canceled meetings. "Let's have breakfast. I'll get the—"

"We should probably get moving." Her chin juts up.

She's decided. She doesn't want to spend time with me. Wants me to agree to sign papers, and that's the end of it. Right. Makes sense.

"All right. It's a thirty- or forty-minute trip to Denver. I'll have the helicopter readied and... How long do you need to get ready?"

"Twenty—" My right eye involuntarily squints. "Thirty," she amends.

"Do you want eggs?"

She looks at me like I'm a stranger.

"I can still scramble eggs."

I sound defensive. Am I?

I'd love a Vicodin to end this discomfort in my chest, but I won't take any until I land in Denver. At least there's no sign of the migraine.

"I'm really..." Our gazes connect across the kitchen counter. Her thumb strokes the ceramic edge of her coffee mug in a mesmerizing movement. "I don't eat early in the morning. I'll grab something later."

"We could get breakfast in Denver. I know several places—"

"Maybe."

Right. Does a yes depend on how I behave in transit?

"Let's see what time it is," she clarifies.

"We might need reservations," I say, although it's Friday morning.

"We don't need to go fancy."

I bite back my disdain for that word. Toward the end, she didn't want to leave our home. She deemed every dining establishment too fancy. I didn't pick high-end locations to impress others, as she assumed. I needed locations that could ensure privacy. A small hole-in-the-wall diner isn't set up to block unwanted media attention. I tried explaining it to her, but it eventually became a silent argument, one we carried on in our heads and communicated with cold looks and physical distance.

A light on her phone flashes. She flips it to read the incoming text.

LUKE:

When will—

She clutches the phone and hurries down the hall before I can finish reading the message. *Luke.*

She said she wasn't dating anyone. But my gut says he's inquiring about her flight home. He's probably picking her up from the airport.

Is he her reason for showing up? Does she think I'm less likely to sign the divorce agreement if I believe she's got someone else in her life?

I check news alerts while drinking fresh coffee and eating another slice of toast. Bloomberg highlights Zenith's latest orbital deployment, and there's chatter about Bedrock's potential acquisition in Singapore. Asian and European markets are up, and US futures are looking stable. I should care more—the Asian markets are particularly volatile this quarter—but with Caroline here, the satellite trajectories and market indicators blur together.

Dad would say I'm getting soft, not being on three conference calls by now. Business never sleeps—there's always another deal to be made, another data stream to monitor. But for once, business can wait.

I force myself to finish the toast. I'm not hungry, but I'm physically weak, and experience taught me that my body responds poorly when I ignore it.

When I descend the stairs after showering, she's dressed, suitcase at her side, phone in hand. Her belted white cotton shirt sits above tapered black slacks that fall to yesterday's professional black heels. Her signature straight, long blonde hair reflects the light, emphasizing her natural elegance. A light pink shade adorns her lips and cheeks, but when she lifts those sky blue eyes, my periphery dims as she becomes everything.

"You look beautiful," I say, scratching my neck.

I check my phone, as much out of habit as to refocus. A text awaits. The helicopter is ready.

"Would you like a coffee to go?" I open a cabinet door, not waiting for her reply, using the same decisive efficiency I use when running board meetings, but here, it feels hollow. Strange how negotiating contracts feels easier than making coffee for my wife. Ex-wife.

I could tell her about the new communications satellite array or the emerging markets we're targeting. Instead, I'm counting the minutes until she asks for the divorce papers again. Some things even an Oxford education doesn't prepare you for.

"That'd be great."

I can feel her behind my back, watching me as I prepare our Yetis. It's hard to believe this used to be our routine every morning. I'd like to believe the stilted silence is new, but on that point, I can't lie to myself. Quiet distance was our norm at the end. She wasn't happy with me, and I'd been helpless. I hate that word. And the feeling.

"Do you think we could stop by to say hello to your father before I leave? You said he's home, right?"

"He'll be working."

I turn to give her the to-go stainless steel mug and force my most cordial and apologetic expression.

"No retirement for him, huh?" She says it with a smile, a joke.

I could respond with something trite, like there's no rest for the wicked.

"I had a lawyer draft an agreement."

It's almost cute how she drops the contentious word from that sentence, as if by not uttering the word divorce will keep the conversation light.

"I have been maintaining the land I inherited and paying taxes on it. I assume you won't fight me for it now?"

I give a short nod. I never planned on taking the land she inherited during our marriage. I'd been pissed when I demanded my share, and I suppose the tactic worked. Or, no, it delayed the inevitable. I should've put this behind me seven years ago.

"Helicopter's ready," I say, and she hesitates.

Does she want to stay longer? We said we would talk, but we haven't. Not really. "That's what you wanted, right?" Her gaze drops. My chest expands. "If you—"

"No, no," she says with far too much energy. "I need to get back."

Yes, Luke is asking.

I deflate with the weight of reality. All of this is expected. I shouldn't be reacting to anticipated events.

The ride to the helipad is quiet. She compliments me on the shower pressure and repeats that she likes the house. She's probably forgotten, but we had several conversations about the house we would eventually build here. The land is remote, far away from the hordes. Yet should we wish to go skiing, we can either have a driver take us or fly closer to the mountains. The land is largely untouched, natural, and wild. Unlike us.

She asks me about business, but my heart is not in the conversation. I prefer screaming matches to surface conversations with Caroline. Not that we had many scream fests. Silence was our weapon of choice.

In the helicopter, under Caroline's watchful eye, I perform the perfunctory routine with precision.

"You fly every day?"

"Weekdays."

"So it's no longer for pleasure? It's utilitarian?"

I grit my teeth. It's amazing, really. She can find anything, anything at all, to turn into a dig. Flying was originally a hobby, yes, but in my world, everything eventually becomes an asset. Like how my satellite company started as a fascination with space and ended up controlling most of the world's digital infrastructure. But trying to explain the intersection of passion and practicality to Caroline always ended in silence.

"Sometimes a pilot flies me. When I fly, it's because I enjoy it."

I'm defensive, but she's critical. That's the problem. With Caroline, I can do nothing right.

It's tempting to tell her the communication feature on our headphones isn't working, but she'll see through it.

I speak into the mic, "Can you hear me?"

"Yes."

The rotors come to life, whipping the air above us.

We lift, and I adjust, evening us out as we climb above the tree line.

"That's the big house, right?"

The big house. That's what she'd always called my father's mountain home.

"Yes." I circle it once. "You can see he added a screened-in porch off his bedroom. And an outdoor pool."

"Is that practical?"

"It looks more like a pond. Salt water."

"In-ground?"

"Yes. But he does things to it over the winter."

"He does things to it?"

I side-eye her, and she laughs.

"You mean he hires a pool company to take care of it?"

"Yes."

As we come around the side, Geoffrey comes into view, standing beside his sedan parked in the carport by the garage, with a phone pressed to his ear. He's got one hand over his eyes, no doubt wondering why my helicopter is circling Dad's house.

I'd wave, but he likely wouldn't see me. Instead, I head off to Denver.

"It's funny," Caroline says.

"What?"

"Your father conducts business from the wilds of Colorado, and businessmen still show up in ties and suits."

She doesn't know the half of it.

"Geoffrey always wears a suit."

"It's very New York."

"I suppose." The same cultural shorthand I learned while navigating between Oxford seminars and Brown's trading club

—how clothing becomes armor in the world of high finance. The suit is modern chainmail. "Wall Street pedigree. Goldman Sachs. He's a financial advisor. Works closely with Dad." Though "advisor" barely scratches the surface of Geoffrey's role in the Moore empire.

"Is he from New York?"

"Honestly, I'm not sure where he was born. Lived in the city for a long time. I don't remember the last time I had a casual conversation with Geoffrey. We have a professional relationship."

"Your father brings that out in people. He's ninety-two and living in the middle of nowhere, and I bet he still wears cufflinks and ties daily. The most expensive, finest custom suits, the best of everything."

"You would know, right?"

I shouldn't have said that. I sound like an asshole. She'll hear it as me criticizing her outfit or digging into an old wound. Her clothing choices are a sore subject. When we were engaged, Dad disapproved of her outfit at a charity event, and he insisted he approve her garment choices for every event leading up to our wedding. Even though the dispute was between the two of them, her outfit choice became one more land mine I stepped on more times than I can count. A sincere comment about how beautiful she looked either earned a glare or questions about whether or not she should change.

She scowls, probably remembering those disagreements.

But she's the one who brought up Dad's wardrobe, and she's dressed for business, too. "Is that why you dressed like that?"

"Like what?"

"Professionally." She's not any different than Geoffrey. She woke this morning, and instead of jeans and her running shoes, she's back in a pantsuit with low square heels.

A red light flashes on the board.

"I bet you still dress in suits to meet your father."

That's a dig. She disapproves. But, if we're going to fight, it won't be over fashion.

"Do you smell that?"

I inhale deeply. If she's implying I farted...

It's a burning odor. Oil. The smell is faint.

The master caution light illuminates. A loud alarm blares. My mind shifts instantly to the countless simulation hours, the rigorous aviation training that was as much about crisis management as actual flying. Seven figures worth of aircraft, and somehow I'm more concerned about Caroline's grip on the armrest than the hydraulic failure warnings.

"What's HYD?" Caroline asks the second the hydraulic warning light flashes on the multifunction display.

I scan the terrain with the same precision I use reviewing satellite coverage maps. The topographical features I usually observe from space are now critical landing zones. There's a break in the trees. A stream.

"What's going on, Dorian?"

"It's going to be okay. I need you to hold on. Stay calm."

I flick to contact air traffic control.

"Mayday, mayday, mayday. This is Hotel Echo One Two Three, Airbus H160 helicopter."

There's a crackle. Caroline white-knuckles the edge of the seat. This is it. She'll never fly in a helicopter again. Took me a year to convince her to go up in one.

A deep male voice responds, "Hotel Echo One Two Three, this is Telluride tower. Go ahead with your mayday."

"Tower, Hotel Echo One Two Three. We have a critical hydraulic system failure." My voice stays steady—the same tone I use while announcing disappointing quarterly results or explaining orbital trajectory modifications to investors. But this isn't about market corrections or satellite adjustments. This is Caroline's life. Our lives.

"Suspect contaminated fluid. Controls becoming unresponsive. Requesting immediate emergency landing clearance."

I scan for landing zones as if analyzing market opportunities—quickly, systematically, weighing every variable. The stream offers better visibility, but the clearing provides more control surface options. These split-second decisions feel familiar—like choosing satellite positions or timing market entries—except now, Caroline's white-knuckled grip on the seat reminds me this isn't just another business calculation.

"Unresponsive? Your controls aren't working?"

"Caroline...I need to concentrate."

The vibrations increase.

"Roger, Hotel Echo One Two Three. Understood you have hydraulic failure. What are your intentions?"

"Tower, I'm attempting to maintain control. Need to land immediately. Current position is 38.2627 North, 108.1103 West. Descending through 5,500 feet. Request any nearby clear areas for emergency landing."

"Hotel Echo One Two Three, understood. There's a clearing about two miles southeast of your position. Can you make it there?"

"Affirmative, Tower. Attempting to reach the clearing. Be advised, control is deteriorating rapidly. May not make a controlled landing."

"Roger that, Hotel Echo One Two Three. Emergency

services have been notified and are en route to the clearing. Do you have any souls on board and fuel remaining?"

"Tower, we have two souls on board and approximately"— *Fuck*—"three minutes of fuel remaining. Be advised, vibrations increasing. Situation is critical. I see a clearing. I'm taking it."

"Understood, Hotel Echo One Two Three. Keep us informed of your status."

"Wilco, Tower. Commencing final approach to clearing. Will advise on touchdown—"

"Dorian?"

The nose dives precariously.

"Oh my god."

I grit my teeth and block Caroline's cries.

Which will be a better landing pad? Boulders or water?

"Dorian!"

"Hold on!"

CHAPTER 12

CAROLINE

The rocky ground below approaches at breakneck speed, yet somehow, time slows. I mentally catalog details even as fear floods my system. The speed at which the ground approaches. The angle of the helicopter. The protruding veins on the back of Dorian's hand as he grapples with control. His blank focus: calm, collected, emotionless. I catalog the details with the same analytical process I used while reviewing surveillance footage, but now I'm clocking what might be my final moments.

This is it. I'm going to die.

I joined a black ops group after the CIA, yet I'll die in my husband's helicopter. The bitter irony isn't lost on me—I came to investigate him, and now he might accidentally kill us both.

I knew he should've never gotten his pilot's license.

I told him not to.

It's tempting fate.

The rich and famous should never get into small planes.

I told him.

His jaw flexes.

A vein in his forehead pulses.

The most handsome man I've ever met.

The most infuriating.

But if this is it...at least I'm with him.

I wouldn't want him to die alone.

I grip the seat.

The ground rushes at us.

I squeeze my eyes closed.

Bam!

Metal crunches.

Glass shatters.

The harness digs into my shoulders. We rock right, then left.

I scream.

In my head? Out loud? I'm not sure.

We still.

A low hissing noise intrudes.

I force my eyes open.

We're tilted to one side.

Unscathed evergreens stand like giants in the distance.

We landed.

"Dorian!"

He's there. In front of me, hands fumbling with my harness.

"We've got to get out of here."

Decisive. Determined.

Sweat coats his brow.

"Are you okay?"

He's calm. Commanding.

"Answer me, Cara. Is anything hurt?"

I take stock.

"Caroline." He palms my face. "Are you hurt?"

"No."

He pushes off my headphones.

Reaches past me and pushes on a door that's tilted skyward. He kicks at it.

One kick. Two. It flings open.

Ticking noises and creaks sound through the cabin.

"What's that noise?"

"Hydraulic or fuel line. I don't know which. Maybe both."

My hands and arms tremble uncontrollably—not just from shock, but from the adrenaline surge.

He climbs out and helps me, lifting me as if I'm injured.

I can't stop trembling.

I'm not sure I can walk, but we're out, beside the tilted helicopter.

Scratched. Dented.

But all things considered...it's okay.

He scoops my legs and lifts me, carrying me over the boulders.

Brown overgrown grasses mix in with the rocky terrain.

There's no smooth ground in sight.

He sets me down like an injured child and begins touching my arms, back, and legs, focus trained on me. He's looking for injuries.

"Why are you crying?" Desperation coats his words.

Am I crying?

He dabs at my cheeks, and I sniffle.

I close my eyes.

Holy shit. We almost died.

An explosion rips through the air.

I scream.

A black cloud of smoke rises from the tail of the helicopter.

The smell of burnt fuel permeates the air, and I could swear I can hear slight crackling noises, only it's not a campfire.

"Are you okay?"

He's still touching me.

We're alive.

"Hope you didn't love that helicopter."

He once professed his love for a Porsche. I'd imagine this helicopter costs a lot more.

He laughs. It's a guttural sound. I haven't heard him laugh in… He's a blur through my teary eyes.

He sits down on the boulder beside me and pulls me onto his lap.

Pink polish catches my attention. I'm missing one shoe.

I lean against his chest.

There's pressure on my head. He kissed my head.

The tears flow in heavy, quiet streams.

"I told you not to get your pilot's license."

"Wanna know something funny? I thought about that as we were going down."

"So did I." I snort, sending snot straight out of my nostrils. It's so gross. I wipe my nose, but then I catch his eye, and suddenly I'm laughing, too.

We should not be laughing, but I can't stop.

When the hysterical laughter subsides, I rest my head against his shoulder, spent.

He lets out a sigh.

During all the laughter, my butt slid off his thigh onto the mossy stone, and my legs drape his. He places an arm across my legs, and the familiarity aches.

When we were falling, I'd been afraid. Frightened. No... terrified. But I'd also been grateful to be with him. That's something I should discuss with my therapist.

"You might not believe me, but my flight instructors would be impressed with that landing."

I take in our surroundings. Much further in and we would have crashed into trees. The stream doesn't appear deep, but it might be deeper in the center. If it was spring, that stream would rush rapids. This land we're sitting on might be underwater with the snowmelt.

A deep shudder works its way through my body.

"Hey, you okay?" He's concerned again, and he pulls me back up onto his lap.

I'm obviously okay, but I don't have the strength to brush off his comfort. I burrow into him.

"I'd never let anything happen to you. You know that, right?"

I push away so I can give him an expression that calls him out on that, not to blame him but to make light of the situation, to alleviate the gravity of what we experienced. But he urges me back against his chest.

"I meant, I'd die before I let something happen to you. I wouldn't let this be the end."

His hold on me tightens, and we sit there like that, observing the mangled monstrosity before us.

"What happened?"

"I'm not sure. Hydraulic line..."

He trails off.

Unease settles into the pit of my stomach. The analytical part of my brain kicks into gear, despite the shock. Mechanical failure in a meticulously maintained aircraft. The timing, just as Sophia warned me about burner phones traced to this area.

"Do you think someone tampered with it on purpose?"

His jaw moves back and forth, considering. I read his microexpressions—the slight tension around his eyes, the controlled breathing pattern. He knows something.

The answer is in his troubled eyes. The answer is yes, this is sabotage, but he doesn't want to admit the truth.

I sit up straighter with a flash of the Arrow conference room. Sophia, Ryan, Trevor, even Luke. I told them he couldn't possibly be behind the plan, but someone tried to take him out. Why would someone try to kill him?

"Dorian, what're you involved in?"

His gaze remains locked on the helicopter.

"Why would someone try to kill you?"

He's quiet. Thoughtful. There's a full conversation going on in that head of his, and, like always, he's not letting me in.

If he's involved in a global syndicate, as the Arrow team and an unknown source claims, then it could've been anyone.

When we were together, he wouldn't let me in when he was in a bad mood. He's not going to just break down and tell me he's breaking the law.

"What happens now? Should we start walking?" I scan the area. There are no discernible trails.

"Rescue team is on the way. We sit."

I should reach out to Sophia.

"I left my phone…"

"It'll stay in there," Dorian says absentmindedly.

I force myself to nod, though every instinct screams to get the phone and my luggage—to see what survived. The tracking software, the encrypted messages, the surveillance photos—all of it potentially recoverable if my phone and laptop survived the crash.

The cabin appears intact. The explosion originated in the back, near where I presume the engine is.

"It's already exploded," I say, studying the crash. The burning scent lingers in the air, but it's lessening. I no longer hear crackling.

"Doesn't mean it won't again."

If the team's tracking me, Sophia will be worried. "The phone is likely near my seat," although, as I say it, I recognize the futility in the argument.

"I won't let you risk your life for a phone. I'll buy you a new one."

I scowl but drop it, recognizing that when the rescue team arrives, they'll retrieve what they can safely. Depending on its proximity to the explosion, it may no longer function. The explosion was a short burst and quickly fizzled. It's hard to estimate the heat level that would have penetrated the cabin.

We both stare at the wreck. One of his arms loops behind my back, and one of his hands rests on my knee, as if he needs to touch me, but his thoughts are elsewhere.

"What're you thinking?" I ask.

"Nothing."

"Why do you do that?" I push up off his chest, but he keeps his arm secured around my waist. One eyebrow arches. It's his silent way of asking what I mean. I don't know how I ever fell in love with this silent, uncommunicative man. "You're clearly thinking something. Why do you keep everything trapped in there?"

I gesture to his head as if it's a fly I need to swat.

His loud exhale resembles an amused, half-hearted chuckle. "It's learned behavior."

"You're blaming this on your dad?" I should push away, but I'm chilled, and there's nowhere else to go at the moment.

"My dad?" He sounds offended. "I meant you."

"What?" How dare he.

"If I know that what I'm going to say will upset you, we're better off if I don't speak."

I reel back, flabbergasted.

"See? We would've been better off if I hadn't said that."

"We would've been better off if you hadn't *thought* it."

He pulls me back against him, and I push back. I'd rather be cold.

"You're shivering. Come here."

He's right. I'm freezing. I relax enough that I give in to his tug and return to his chest. He rubs a hand over my arm, back and forth, generating heat.

"When we were crashing, I zoned out. Focused on what I'd learned during flying lessons."

"You saved us," I say, looking at the wreck before us. I know nothing about flying helicopters, but I fully expect that when the others get here, they'll be talking about what an excellent job he did improvising. He's a master at everything he does.

"But my first thought, after I got you out of the helicopter? After I realized you weren't injured and we survived?"

My eyes burn, and I close them. I turn my head into Dorian's chest, warming my icy nose on his shirt.

"We could've died."

No shit.

"And I would've never told you that you're the best thing that ever happened to me. There's not a lot in my life that I would do over if given the chance, but you're the one thing I'd do again a thousand times over."

His hold on me tightens ever so slightly. I swallow hard and pull back just enough to look at his face, my fingers involuntarily curling into the fabric of his shirt. The raw honesty in his eyes catches me off guard, and I force myself to take a steadying breath.

"I bet you wish I'd kept my thoughts to myself now."

CHAPTER 13

DORIAN

"You'd marry me all over again?"

I don't need to see her face to read into her quiet, uncertain tone. I'm probably her biggest regret.

"Dorian, our marriage—"

"I'm not saying there aren't things I would change." She has to know that. No one wants to endure the death of a relationship.

"Like what?"

There's no harm in telling her. It's what I've wanted to tell her for years. With an exhale, I lay it out there.

"For one, I would've never let you go."

The words come out with none of the precision I use in the boardroom. This isn't a business negotiation—it's the raw truth I've avoided for years. The kind of vulnerability that has no place in the world of high finance and global telecommunications.

She slowly lifts from my chest, those questioning blue eyes taking me in. My gaze drops to her soft, full lips.

I inch closer, eyes locked on hers.

My breath grows shallow—the world blurs.

She shakes her head, the back-and-forth motion hitting like a submerged boulder in white water rapids. I should've seen it coming by the flow of the water, yet it's a painful shock all the same.

Her fingers press on my clavicle, pushing me away.

I force myself to swallow and cover her fingers with mine.

"I did what was best for us," she pleads.

She's sincere. I see it in her expression.

"Do you really believe that?" The only way that's true is if we had continued sliding downhill into an abyss. It's only true if we had no fix.

"No." She pushes back, putting more distance between us, and the chilly air fills the divide. "I did what was best for me. I was... I lost myself."

A memory surfaces. A rolling rack of dresses.

"Your father sent these."

She'd sounded angry.

"He asked that I wear Marilyn-approved dresses when I attend public functions."

"She's his publicist."

"I think she's more than that."

I understood what she was implying, but I also didn't care. "He doesn't do single well."

She looked at the rack of dresses with disdain. I flicked through the *envelopes stacked on the counter. If she had an assistant like I requested she hire, there wouldn't be mail in the house.*

"If you don't like them, don't wear them." I didn't care what she wore, and I didn't care about pleasing my father's most recent conquest, either. What I did care about was my father questioning if I had the bandwidth to launch a new company and hold my place on the board.

"No, it's fine."

She might have said something more, she might not. But she hadn't been fine. Why hadn't I seen it? I disregarded garments as being immaterial.

But our marriage didn't end over a disagreement on attire. I heard her, but I didn't listen. I grew up with public interest in my family. With our marriage, she was thrown into the spotlight, and I expected her to deal with it. Perhaps my father steamrolled her. He handled her the way he handles everything. I saw it and did nothing. Hell, maybe I steamrolled her. I begged her to marry me within months of meeting her in a bar.

"What're you thinking?" Her voice pulls me out of the memory.

I swallow, hesitant. But why hesitate? There's nothing to lose here. I lost years ago.

"That I amend my statement from earlier. When you left, I should've followed. Moved us to another country. Become a professor somewhere or something."

"A professor." She's mocking me. That's fine. "Are you kidding?"

"You could've pursued what you wanted." It would've been a better choice. What the hell was I expecting when she quit her job because the paparazzi hounded her, making her associate-level job impossible while I was off working fifteen-hour days?

"You needed to prove yourself to your father. And you did, didn't you?"

"Did I?"

"You founded Zenith. You're chairman of the board at Bedrock Advisory."

"Nepotism flourishes." The same argument I've had in my head through every board meeting, every acquisition. Even with a global communications empire, I'm still Halston Moore's son first. The Harvard MBA and Oxford doctorate don't change that.

"Bullshit. Your father has power, but when he retired, the board could've picked someone else."

Unlikely. "Let's not talk about my father."

"Are you not getting along with him these days?"

"Depends on the day." The wind whistles through the trees, and I listen intently for sirens. Maybe the rescue team won't use sirens. It's not like there's traffic to avoid out here.

Her nails scrape across my cheek. She's tender, but insistent. With her touch, she pulls me back from my mental confines.

Her hair, understandably, is a mess, but she's still beautiful. She's the most stunning when she's raw and real. I brush some tangled strands behind her ear and see the small pearl earring. Does she still own the diamonds I gave her?

"Dorian?"

Without thinking, I lean in and press my lips to her forehead.

"If I could go back and redo that last year, I would. I closed you out. And I just... Biggest mistake of my life."

Funny how I grew a business from nothing, but I couldn't figure out how to keep my wife. Some things can't be solved with market analysis and risk management strategies.

"Oh, I think it all worked out for you."

There's a wry tone I don't get. I'm cracking my chest open and bleeding here. "What do you mean by that?"

"Supermodels. Actresses. You seemed to do just fine."

Oh. That. The carefully orchestrated public appearances that kept the papers talking about the billionaire bachelor's extracurriculars instead of his failed marriage. Every photo op was calculated to project strength, to maintain market confidence, at least until I couldn't take it anymore and lost myself in an endless succession of conference rooms around the globe.

She's tense. Avoiding my gaze. There's no reason to play games. It was a shitty ploy to begin with.

"Honestly?"

"No, lie to me." The sarcasm is definitely new. I have half a mind to spank her ass.

"I wanted you to see those photos. I hoped you'd get jealous, come back, and fight." She never even called.

"You just told me you don't say what you're thinking because you want to avoid fighting."

"That's different. Verbal sparring differs from…you coming back and telling me…" *That you want me. Jesus, is it so hard to grasp what I'm saying?*

"I stopped reading magazines. The *New York Post*. Any publication I thought might mention you, I avoided."

"That's not the reaction I desired."

"If you wanted me back, why didn't you say? Why didn't you call?"

You left.

"I wanted you to have the life you wanted." A shrill cry from a hawk overhead cuts through the sky. "Did you get it?"

She exhales in frustration. Only I haven't said anything

argumentative. I would like to know—has she been happy? Who was the guy texting her? Is he the reason she quit her job at the CIA and moved to California? How serious are they? Is it a healthy relationship? Does he give her everything I couldn't? Does he make her happy?

"Are you sure we shouldn't try to find a road?"

Classic.

Change of subject.

"They had our coordinates when we went down. There's a transponder." The same precision tracking we use for our satellites is now being used to find us. "Unless you've developed navigational skills, we're better off waiting for them as opposed to wandering in the San Juan Mountains."

"How are you always so calm? So in control?"

Stay focused. Analyze the situation. Maintain composure. The calmness she hates was the only thing keeping me from falling apart when she left.

Yes, she always hated that I stayed calm when faced with reporters. If she was alone, they scared her. I failed to take her fear seriously. I tried to keep the paparazzi away, but I felt equally frustrated that she couldn't just smile and adjust. I felt worse because I couldn't stop them. If she'd smiled more, posed, given them some money shots, they wouldn't have been so ever-present.

"You're doing it again." The accusation grabs my attention.

"What?" How can I possibly be doing anything wrong? I'm sitting still, holding her.

"You're lost in your head. There's a whole conversation going on in there."

"It's easy to get lost in what I did wrong."

"What do you believe you did wrong?"

There's no mistaking the taunt. The desire to trap me by allowing me to say the wrong thing.

"I didn't listen. I didn't take your concerns seriously. And, when you weren't happy, I felt like a failure, so I focused my energy on areas of my life where I was winning."

My fingers brush the side of her face. The smooth skin is cool to the touch. Her light blue eyes, irises the color of the sky on a crisp, clear, hopeful day, glimmer. My chest aches with the pull to her. She's the one I failed to forget, and I'll probably never get over her. Whatever pain I endure, I deserve.

"How'd I do? Did I miss anything?"

CHAPTER 14

CAROLINE

"It was a long time ago. Let's not get into this."

Avoiding his gaze, I lean against his chest, willing the frustration away.

I should take in the sky, gray and cloudy as it is, the gurgling creek, and the remaining amber and crimson aspen leaves clinging in the face of the coming winter, and be grateful.

If someone spotted us with a telephoto lens, they would see a couple, not the exes that we are. I should push away, but the deep thud of his heartbeat comforts me. And it's chilly, getting colder as the minutes tick by, and his body is a furnace.

"You said a cold front's coming through?"

"It's December in Colorado. We've had unseasonably warm weather, but this cool front coming down from Canada was forecasted a week ago. You should've packed a winter coat."

"Why do you sound offended?"

"Because."

He can't see it, but I roll my eyes at his childish response.

"You weren't planning to stay. I'm certain you checked the weather when you packed. In your mind, there was no possibility of staying through the weekend."

His heart thuds softly against my back, and the familiar rhythm reverberates through my spine and ribs.

"Why would there be a possibility? We've been legally separated for years. The divorce agreement is just a technicality. Are you egging for a fight?"

"No." He huffs and curls himself around me, shifting so he's not leaning back anymore, but leaning forward. "I'm saying the things I should've said years ago."

"Why?"

"Isn't it obvious? It's my last chance. I can't win with you, though. You're either mad at me for speaking my mind or mad when I don't."

"I'm not mad," I lie. He's right, and it pisses me off.

An ant crawls onto my bare foot, and I kick my leg up.

"You need your shoe." He taps my thigh and grunts as he pushes up off the ground, careful to leave me in place.

"You said it was too dangerous to get my phone, but you'll get my shoe?"

He shrugs, swiping dirt off his suit coat tail and ass. He's always filled out his trousers nicely, but his rear is drool-worthy in jeans. And low-slung pajama bottoms that hang just right on his hips.

"Smoke's gone. The burning smell has dissipated. And I want to see if the radio works. It feels like it's taking them a long time to get here."

It's probably only been about fifteen minutes, but I agree with him. It feels like hours have passed.

"If this is sabotage, if someone wanted to kill you, how do you know they wouldn't come after you now?"

He pauses, halfway between me and the wreck. He scans the treetops, then shakes his head.

"No. If someone purposefully did this, they expected me to die in the crash."

"They wouldn't expect you might live?"

"It'd be a gamble. But tracking my descent and sending in follow-up crews that might intersect first responders..." He shakes his head. "No. If someone tried, they're waiting for news reports to learn if they succeeded. We're in the clear. For now."

When he reaches the helicopter, he puts a hand on the side, pulling and pushing, back and forth, like he's checking stability. An unnecessary move, given that the hunk of metal isn't moving anywhere without a crane.

Satisfied, he hoists himself into the shell and drops from sight.

What if there is another explosion? Could I get him out?

When I stand, my skin tingles on my rear from sitting on the hard surface of the boulder.

A cluster of bare birch trees wedged between soaring firs stands in contrast to the aspens, their mostly leafless limbs ready to bend to the will of winter. The wind rustles the leaves along the ground.

I rub my arms as awareness sets in of how isolated we are in this valley, surrounded by wilderness. If they don't find us, we'll have to hike through a forest and hope we stumble across a road. My mouth dries, and the wind burns my eyes.

My shoe appears, then Dorian.

"Won't turn on," he announces, waving a phone in his other hand. "Most likely heat damage. I'm sure there'd be zero signal anyway."

He's right about the signal. I have no idea where our position is relative to the nearest cell towers, but unless we're close, there's a significant likelihood of signal blockage from the mountain terrain.

I scan our surroundings, noting escape routes, potential cover positions, and lines of sight. The training never really leaves you, even when you're supposedly just waiting for rescue. There's no need to take cover, as he's likely correct. If someone purposefully tampered with the hydraulic lines, it would be nearly impossible to plan where he'd choose to make a crash landing, wouldn't it?

"Here's your shoe." He throws it through the air, and it lands silently on a patch of grass near my feet. Soot covers the leather, but other than appearing like it's been near heavy smoke, the heel and sole are intact, and it's functional.

He disappears, then reappears with a rolled blanket beneath one arm and a small white box with a red first aid symbol on it.

"Comms are out. Wires got smoked in the explosion."

"How long do you think until first responders arrive?"

"Not too long. After my mayday call, air traffic control notified the Air Force Rescue Coordination Center. Activated a local search and rescue team. Given our location, it's likely the Colorado Army National Guard will deploy their High-Altitude Army National Guard Aviation Training site specialists. A scouting plane will be on its way soon. You don't need to worry. Help is on the way."

"How do you know all that?"

"I didn't buy my helicopter pilot's license. I earned it." His smug expression has me rolling my eyes, although I should be happy he studied and earned his license. I likely owe my life to his efforts.

He wiggles the white metal box. "I put some flares in here. If it gets darker and they haven't found us yet, I'll shoot them off."

"Why not now?"

"Don't want to waste them. If the fixed plane flies by, and it doesn't appear they saw us, I'll shoot one off." He scans the area. "They'd have to be blind not to see us, though." He opens the metal box and lifts a water bottle. "You thirsty?"

Given the stream, we were never in danger of dying of thirst, but I'll gladly take a bottle of water. Although looking at the yellowed label, I question the age. We might be better off emptying it and using it to collect fresh mountain water.

He spreads the blanket out on the boulder and gives a second blanket to me. "In case you get cold."

"You don't have a winter coat either." I don't mean to sound as reproachful as I do.

"I planned to land and go to the office."

"Crashing wasn't on your bingo card?"

"Emergency landing. We didn't crash."

I open my mouth and wrinkle my brow, blown away that he's going to argue this point.

"We can agree to disagree," he says at the same time I relent with the saying, "Potato potahto."

I sit on the blanket, leaving my shoes on so my toes don't freeze.

He returns to the blanket, situating himself close beside me, and I wish he would lift me onto his lap again.

"We've got nothing to do but talk. Nowhere to go." He leans

forward, untying the laces on his dress shoes. "Can we call a truce? Ask questions and get answers."

"Who are you, and what did they do with Dorian?"

"I'm being serious."

A niggling voice in my head reminds me I have questions, too. And there's a team back home expecting me to return with answers. They aren't picking up anything of value from the bugs I planted back at Dorian's home, given he's here with me.

"I'll make you a deal. You ask a question, I get a question."

He grins, and I know what he's thinking. Our third night together, we met at a pub and played guess which of the three statements is true, going back and forth for hours. Tit for tat always got us far...until it didn't.

"Truth," he says. "Let's keep it simple. One question, one answer. Back and forth."

My pulse quickens slightly. This is an opportunity for information extraction through casual conversation. The crash has given me an opening I couldn't have planned better; he's emotional, unguarded, and ready to talk. The operative in me recognizes the opportunity while guilt twists my heart at the manipulation.

A gust of wind barrels through the woods and cuts straight through my clothes.

"Let's lie down facing each other," he says, settling onto his side. "We'll drape the blanket over us. Let our body heat work to keep us warm."

I eye the space between us, envisioning the scenario. It doesn't strike me as wise. There's not a ton of space on the flat part of the boulder, and we'd need to lie close. It's not a problem, except that seconds ago, I wished he'd put me back onto his lap, and I'm emotional after the crash and prone to slipping down a familiar spiral that won't end well.

"Clothes will stay on." He's still good at reading my mind.

"Fine," I say, attempting to overlook his exasperation. This isn't a normal situation for either of us.

We settle down onto the blanket, our bottom halves aligned for warmth. We both use our arms to prop up our heads, and there's space between our top halves so we can talk.

"Too bad the chopper didn't have pillows."

"Yes, I might add a tent to the gear in my next one."

"You're going to keep flying?" He's out of his mind.

"Yes, I am. That was an easy question. Now, it's my turn."

He grins. I've always loved his boyish grins. An unrestricted curve of the lips morphs the business titan into an everyday man.

"Who is Luke?"

Whoa. Did he read my messages?

"Someone I work with. I already told you I'm not dating anyone." I narrow my eyes and scoff. "That feels like a wasted question." But his loss. Now, it's my turn.

"Are you a part of a global alliance or syndicate?"

I keep my voice casual, but I observe every microexpression, every pause, every shift in his posture. His eyes widen slightly— there it is, the tell we look for in intelligence work. Not surprise at the question, but recognition.

"I'm a member of many business associations."

Classic deflection technique—technically true but intentionally vague. He's dancing around the truth.

"To maintain global market stability."

The addendum is another beautifully crafted non-answer.

At the agency, we called these "surface truths"—statements that sound complete but leave room for darker implications.

His hand shifts underneath the blanket, and he palms my hip.

It dawns on me that Arrow's intel might be accurate. He's evading.

I'm not in danger. He'd never hurt me. But what would he do to others?

"Why'd you leave the CIA?"

"I don't believe you fully answered my question."

He smirks. This line of questioning doesn't concern him, or he'd be stone-faced.

"To expand on my answer, yes. There's a group of sector leaders who share information and resources, and I'm a part of it. They refer to themselves as a syndicate, or, depending on who you're talking to, an alliance. My father named it Obsidian, but few use the term."

"What's the objective?"

He squeezes my hip playfully. "Not so fast. My turn. The CIA? You left, right?"

His question is fair, given that employment with the CIA can be impossible to ascertain if secrecy is desired. But he needs to share more, so instead of answering, I ask, "What's the alliance's objective?"

"To maintain global market stability. My father started it decades ago. I've become more involved recently." *Is he giving me the blanket answer?* "Is Sophia Sullivan Fisher the reason you moved to California?"

"How do you—" I stop myself. Asking how he knows Sophia's full name is a wasted question. He hired someone to monitor me. He told me. There's no harm in answering his question. "Sophia doesn't live in California. She lives with her husband outside of DC." She travels frequently for work, but there's no point in confirming she works in the field. "Her father lives in San Diego. She comes to California often. She's my close friend, but no, she's not the reason I moved to California."

"Why did you move? You left the CIA, right? Why?"

"That's two questions, and it's my turn. Would the alliance benefit from an attack on the United States or allied countries?"

He shifts back like I've slapped him. His jaw shifts and cracks with the movement.

"No, it would not benefit. An attack would cripple the stock markets worldwide, and that's specifically counter to our mission." His eyes narrow into slits, and he frowns. "Who do you work for? You're asking these questions for your employer, aren't you?"

The coldness in his eyes is impossible to miss. There's no sign of flirtation. No warmth or familiarity. He's all business now. I struck a nerve.

"Yes, I left the CIA. I now work for a private security firm based in Santa Barbara. I'm an analyst. Still." I let the word hang there, studying him to see if my assumption that he knew my role in the CIA was accurate.

There's no hint of surprise. My former position isn't news to him. He probably has contacts on the Senate Intelligence Committee or within the CIA.

"When I worked at Langley, being in the field was never really an option given my past prominence in the news." I pointedly look at him because, yes, my association with him hampers my career.

"And you left because…?"

"I had an asshole for a boss at the CIA. Sophia recommended I transition. My current employer offered more money. Santa Barbara is a beautiful place with significantly less traffic than DC. Not a difficult choice. Pretty easy, actually. Why am I answering these questions more thoroughly than you are?"

"Are you here for them?"

"Arrow Tactical. That's the company. Sophia helped me get the job."

"You're here for work? That wasn't a lie? I assumed you arrived because you wanted me to sign the divorce agreement."

"You should've signed it years ago."

"The standard Divorce.com agreement you found online?"

"I expected your lawyers would draft an agreement. I simply got the ball rolling."

"That's not why you're here, though?"

"A source claims you're behind a multipronged plan to attack the United States."

"But you didn't ask questions until now. What did you do? Wire my place? That's why you were roaming the property."

He's talking to himself now, but his palm remains on my hip, a gentle and welcome source of warmth.

"What do you believe, Cara?"

He's the only one who has ever shortened my name. Well, that's not true. My grandmother tried to call me Carol, but my mother stopped that madness.

"I came here to remove you from the persons of interest list. I volunteered. I want to clear your name."

"You mentioned a source. Who?"

"It's classified."

He studies me, waiting for more.

"They didn't tell me," I offer, knowing full well that's what he wants to know.

"But you believe in me? You believe the source is wrong?"

The pads of his fingers climb my arms. My skin prickles. Golden brown, all-seeing eyes penetrate mine, and my breath catches as he seeks confirmation that I believe he's not a monster.

His vulnerability breaks through my reluctance.

With one shaky confirming nod, his lips close in on mine. I close my eyes to revel in the feel, to both remember and be present.

He nips at my lip, and his tongue presses to the seam. I open for him, returning the exploratory kiss, allowing myself to be in the moment.

What the hell am I doing?

He's always been the one who mangles my thoughts. Who robs me of reason.

But I can't. I can't do this. Not now, not with so much at stake, not when it would be way too easy to slip again.

I break the kiss and brush a finger over his lips.

"We can't," I say, ever so softly. The pain. The constant ache. I can't go through that again.

But his thoughts aren't akin to mine.

His lips curve into a tender smile, and that little dimple appears, shooting my heart well past the moon.

CHAPTER 15

DORIAN

"Don't leave today." The words rush out, uncontrolled. Her kiss confirmed there's a chance. "Please, Cara. Stay the weekend."

It's a plea. And yes, I'm purposefully using her nickname, hoping the intimacy the name implies weakens her resolve.

"I'll send you back on the corporate jet. The G650, since I know you don't like small aircraft."

The wreckage behind us is still cooling, hydraulic fluid contained by the deployed emergency barriers. We nearly died; the tail rotor failure could have sent us into an uncontrollable spin. I didn't share how close we came, how one wrong move during the autorotation landing could have meant the end. I hadn't lied when I said my flight instructors would be impressed with my landing.

We nearly died. I don't expect my nervous flier to board a small plane anytime soon, if ever. Forget helicopters.

Her fingers tangle in my hair, but she shifts, and instead of pulling me to her, she toys with my ear, then her fingers glide along my jaw. I ache to crush my mouth to hers, rip her clothes off, and rediscover every inch of a body I once knew better than my own.

But I want more than one more time. I want her back in my life. It's a truth I know with a deep, residual certainty. I've been a dead man walking for years. Lifeless.

I don't know why I couldn't get over her. Why I couldn't move on.

A range of emotions washes over her unforgettable blue irises. Lust? Uncertainty?

"If I come back with you, will you answer my questions?"

A smirk threatens.

"Not as a game," she hastens. "What I'm working on is important. I need answers. We know about your alliance. We have questions."

A small white plane whooshes above us.

Caroline's brow crinkles. "Is that plane big enough for us to ride in?"

The fear in her voice would be comical if we hadn't almost died in a crash.

"It's a Cessna. It's the scout plane I mentioned. He's assessing our location."

The Cessna circles overhead, its pilot following standard SAR protocols. I create the X signal with my arms, indicating we're mobile but need assistance. The green acknowledgment light flashes through the cockpit glass.

"What does that mean?"

"Mountain Rescue is inbound."

The small plane banks away, disappearing over the ridgeline. Its pilot will relay our exact coordinates to the ground teams.

"If there's no landing area, how would they—"

"They have specialized equipment," I interrupt, not wanting her to spiral thinking about helicopter hoists. "But we won't need it. The ATVs can reach us here."

I say that confidently, but I'm not 100 percent certain. One issue at a time.

She shivers, and I'm not sure if it's from the increasing wind or from her imagining climbing a rope ladder.

"If necessary, they'd strap you into something and hoist." Based on those wide eyes, my statement doesn't ease her concerns. "They wouldn't trust a civilian's arm strength to climb a ladder flapping in the wind. You've seen too many movies."

I sit back down beside her and pull her close to me, rubbing her arms vigorously to build heat.

"I'd never put you in a dangerous situation." The smoking helicopter we're both staring at disagrees with my oath. "Caroline, look at me." I wait until those breathtaking eyes are pointed at me and not at the wreck. "I'm not sorry this happened, if only because it's a chance to see you again. To really see you. To talk. For me to tell you how sorry I am. How much I wish I'd done differently. I never stopped loving you. I wanted to. Desperately. But you dug your way into my soul, and nothing and no one has remedied the situation. And I've tried everything."

"You mean that, don't you?"

"Give me this weekend. I love you. Always have. Always will." Saliva pools in my mouth, and I swallow it down, looking off into the dreary sky. The phrase slipped out without my putting proper thought behind it, but the lack of forethought doesn't make it less true. You can love someone and not be with them. In my case, I loved her so much that I let her walk away so she would be happy. So what am I doing now?

"They'll be here soon? The rescuers?"

And with that question, it's clear she's over me. I've been reading into things, opening up when I shouldn't have. Her fingers press down on my forearm, pulling me back to the painful present.

"Probably not long," I answer.

It's so quiet in these woods. We should hear them approach. The trees surrounding us grow closely together, but I imagine an ATV can find a path, and the first responders will likely use ATVs. Hopefully, we're not too far away from a road. And then from there…

"Will you be okay getting back into a helicopter? To get back to my house? Or would you prefer to drive?"

"How far away from your house are we?"

I try to visualize our location. It's not a route I drive, given I fly to save time. "Hour and a half. Maybe. The roads aren't a straight shot."

"If you fall off a horse, the best way to get over your fear is to get back in the saddle, right?"

Caroline rode horses growing up. Her parents have photos of her in her jodhpurs and a black velvet riding hat, beaming with crooked teeth.

"You'll seriously get into a helicopter again?"

"If it's prudent," she answers matter-of-factly, and once again, it's clear she's changed. She's stronger. But then again, she's always been strong. Maybe now, I'm finally seeing her.

An engine rumbles off in the distance.

"Do you hear that?" Excitement coats Caroline's words.

"Yeah. They aren't far away. If I were to guess..." I point an arm southward, along the creek line. "There's a cut-through in that direction that eventually ties into Route 50.

I carefully pull the extra blanket around Caroline's shoulders, press my lips to her forehead, and push up, prepared to wave my arms.

Although, if they break through the clearing, we'll be easy to spot.

A splash of white and red through the trees lets me know they're close. And with those bright colors, they aren't attempting to sneak up on us either.

"Do you see them?"

"Yeah. They'll be here soon." I look down at her, huddled in blankets, knees pulled up against her. "If you come back with me, I'll answer any questions. You might not like all of my answers, but I'll tell you anything." She twists slightly, positioning her body in the direction of the rumbling engine. "Please."

The look she gives me disagrees, and a less resilient man might give up. I should probably give up. "We were in transit returning to Denver and crashed, yet survived. Don't you think someone's trying to tell us we're not done yet? That we need to spend time together? Talk through things? I mean, that divorce agreement you brought for me to sign? It's incinerated. Don't you think that's a sign?"

She scoffs. "It's a sign someone wants you dead."

I'm not in the mood to laugh, but I do smile.

"Tell you what. Come back and spend the weekend with me. Give me one weekend. You can reprint the agreement, and I'll sign it."

She narrows her eyes. "You've given up on the Georgia land?"

I never wanted that damn land. I only wanted a reason to fight. "All yours."

"It was always mine."

"Caroline. I don't want to fight about that land. Not now. It's yours. Give me this weekend."

The front of an ATV comes into view. He's stopped about thirty yards out in front of a fallen tree. Another engine rumbles in the distance.

"Looks like our ride is here. No hoisting through the air today."

"Dorian." Her voice is sharp. "If I come back with you, we're going to talk. You're going to answer my questions."

"I'll tell you everything."

She rises and stands before me. She's assessing me. Can she see it? I'm not lying. I'll tell her what she needs to know. I have questions, too. Which government agency is investigating me? Someone hired her firm, this Arrow Tactical that she mentioned. But I don't care about that. Not really. If anything comes of her team's investigation, I have lawyers who can handle any inconveniences.

"Promise? Everything?"

"Absolutely." That's what comes out of my lips as I stare into her eyes, but what I mean is I'll tell her anything that won't hurt her.

"Okay."

I fight the urge to shove a fist into the air and shout *yes*. Instead, I wave an arm in the air, ensuring the first responder on the ATV sees us. I also study him through the trees as a precaution. He's wearing warm clothing, but it's bright, and there are no visible guns.

"Dorian, even if I stay the weekend, it doesn't mean—"

"I know," I'm quick to reassure.

But I own a property close to Santa Barbara, in Montecito. There will be challenges with leaving Denver, but nothing that's insurmountable. If I can crack the door open this weekend, there's the possibility of a workable solution.

My pulse beats furiously at the prospect of a reunion with Caroline, but of course, I'm getting ahead of myself. Our relationship wasn't perfect. We had issues. I had issues. I can't kid myself that we can resume where we left off. Nor would I want to. When she left, we were drowning in pain. Neither of us wants to return to misery. No, I want what we had before we spiraled.

The lead responder approaches in a yellow SAR jacket, his medical kit at the ready. His partner maintains perimeter security—standard procedure when dealing with a high-profile rescue.

"Mr. Moore?" He keeps a professional distance until we confirm our identities. "I'm John with Mountain Rescue. Are either of you injured?"

"Negative. The autorotation landing was successful." I gesture to the helicopter. "You'll need a HAZMAT team for the cleanup. There's hydraulic fluid contained, but the fuel system is intact."

He nods, speaking into his radio to update base. Later, I'll contact my security team and have them secure the crash site and coordinate the investigation.

"Can you walk?"

"Yes."

He turns and gives a hand signal to the other guy, I presume telling him we'll come to him. In this area, the trees are thick, and there's limited space for a path to reach us.

"We have an emergency team at the base." He clocks the wreck but doesn't step past the blankets.

"Don't know much about helicopters," he says. "I'm a medic. Since you're both mobile, let's gather your stuff and get back to the team. They're saying a fast-moving system's coming in. We had to cut a path up here. Lots of downed trees. Picked the fastest route to you. Didn't know what we'd be dealing with."

What he's saying is he didn't know what injuries we might have sustained. We got lucky as hell.

He scans both of us. "Not even a scrape, huh?"

"I'm sure we'll be sore come morning," I say.

The harnesses kept us secure in the seats, and, unlike in an automobile accident, safety bags didn't smash our faces. The windshield cracked but held. There were no loose objects in the cabin. We're good.

"Apparently, he's a master pilot," Caroline says to the man, her baby blues locked on me.

"Yeah, I'd say so," the man says. "So, like I said, I'm John. Man back there is Tito."

"Dorian. And Caroline," I respond.

"All right. Let's gather your stuff and get out of here," John says.

"I called back on the sat phone and let them know we've got you," Tito announces.

I get Caroline's suitcase, my briefcase, both salvageable, and leave everything else. I give Caroline one blanket and insist she wrap herself in it on the trip down the mountain.

The stretchers attached to the ATVs serve as a stark reminder of what could have happened.

We each sit on the back of an ATV, me behind John, Caroline behind Tito. As it turns out, we are close to a road. Still, it takes us a good two hours at the base to meet with the rescue team and to hire a lift back to my place.

We both take turns making phone calls at the base, borrowing phones from the rescue team. I deal with press issues since someone picked up that my helicopter went down. Based on Caroline's facial expressions during her phone call, her team isn't happy with her decision to stay for the weekend.

While we were given discretion for our calls, we haven't been alone since the rescue. When we finally walk through the door of the mountain house, it feels like we've been gone for days.

I've got a slew of emails and messages to return, but I don't care about any of it. By the grace of the gods, I have Caroline for two days, and she's my priority.

CHAPTER 16

CAROLINE

"And you're all right?"

Sophia's question rings through the speaker. I've already done a sweep of the bathroom for listening devices. The reflection staring back at me begs the same question, but the day's inconsistencies are of greater interest.

Thankfully, I packed a burner phone. A last-minute precaution that Luke insisted on when I packed, though I doubt he thought my phone would melt in an inferno.

"We got really lucky." It helps that Dorian learned from the best flight instructors. He's got skills.

"Has Dorian mentioned who he suspects did it?"

"Honestly, I don't think he's thought much about it." Or he has, and as is typical Dorian, he hasn't shared his thoughts. "He plans to send an investigation team to the crash site and wait for their report."

"If someone attempted to take you out, wouldn't you be concerned?"

I'm not an idiot. I hear the suspicious tone. She's wondering if my judgment is compromised.

Are attempts on his life a common occurrence? What has his life been like since I left?

"Who do you think did it? Does Arrow have any intel?"

"None. The AP release didn't mention suspicions of sabotage. Emergency landing and faulty hydraulic lines. That's all we're hearing. A full report has yet to be filed from the local authorities."

"But you believe it's sabotage?"

"It's a new helicopter, top of its class, and we assume it's well-maintained. Hydraulic lines are relatively easy to fuck with. Sabotage is the rational conclusion."

"Who do you think would do it?" Somewhere out there, there's a suspect list forming.

"I don't know," she grumbles. "Our source let us know he's not so sure Dorian is the guilty party. He's second-guessing his original conclusions. If the syndicate is no longer considering Dorian a threat, then maybe something related to Zenith would provide incentive to sabotage his helicopter. Or maybe someone isn't happy he's on the short list for chief of staff."

"The persons of interest list must be a long one."

"NSA isn't sharing. Local police in the crash vicinity are preparing for the incoming storm. The investigation into the helicopter crash isn't a priority."

The jurisdictions and authority chains are complex. Local LEOs, FAA, NTSB, possibly FBI, given Dorian's profile. The bureaucratic maze could work in someone's favor.

"For the record, I believe you should leave."

"I understand, but…Sophia, I feel like I owe him this weekend. And maybe I owe myself this, too."

"I guess a near brush with death can make you realize something like that. Are you considering getting back with him?"

"No." The answer rushes out of my mouth faster than my brain processes the words, but the memory of the kiss heats my skin in direct contradiction to my spontaneous answer. "I mean, we just…" I exhale and exit the bathroom to avoid my reflection. "It's complicated. Communication isn't our strength. It's one reason I left. I think I just want closure. Does that make sense?"

"I guess so."

"I'm going to be upfront with him. I'm going to share what's going on."

"You want to read him in? Are you sure that's a good idea?"

"Someone tried to kill him. Isn't that evidence he's not the person behind the planned attacks?"

"Why would that be evidence?"

Her annoyance comes through, and once again, I don't have the answer.

"He's not the person you're looking for," I state. "Even your source is second-guessing his information."

As certain as I am the sun will rise tomorrow, I am certain he's not the psycho orchestrating a multipronged attack on the free world. Yes, he could conceivably have a financial motive, but he has more money than he can spend in a lifetime.

Sophia's disappointment in me comes across in her audible sigh. "He could've staged the issue to appear innocent."

"Sophia, come on."

"The point is, we don't have adequate intel. You need to be careful. Emotions cloud judgment."

"Even if he's involved, he'd never hurt me. I'm absolutely positive about this."

"We have evidence that links communications from his compound to North Korea and Russia. He's in regular contact with Russia."

"That doesn't mean he's guilty. They're probably clients. He's an influential person with contacts across the globe."

"There's also his father," Sophia says it as if this fact is a piece of evidence. "Our source hasn't ruled out his father."

Mr. Moore's office in New York City had photos of him with world leaders ranging from presidents, prime ministers, and yes, I recall one photograph of him and Putin in tuxes. I didn't ask questions, but I distinctly remember the photos in silver frames on the wall where his executive assistant sat.

"His father is ninety-two. According to public flight records, the elder Moore hasn't been to New York in years." And we both know the Moores aren't the type who travel long distances by car.

"Our source claims his father is still heavily involved in syndicate matters. Caroline, I get that there's a personal component here. If I hadn't seen Fisher in years, I'm sure I'd be just like you. But remember, you left Dorian for a reason. The relationship died for a reason. And even if he's not the mastermind behind these attacks, he's involved somehow. Don't lose sight of the facts. You were with him a long time ago. People change."

"I know," I say, sufficiently scolded.

I'm not the same woman from before, either. I'm far more independent and assertive.

"Be careful."

"I will."

"And contact me every day. When are you returning?"

"Sunday. I have work on Monday, right?" There's a bite to my tone I don't intend, but I don't appreciate her lack of confidence.

"You know Ryan will give you the time off if you need it. You can take the time if you want it."

Can I? Of course, I can. Because I'm technically doing exactly what the Arrow team wants me to do. I'm learning more about a person of interest and gathering intel.

My eyes fall to the clothes Dorian must have laid out on the bed for me. I finger the old Brown University sweatshirt with the frayed edges and navy sweat bottoms. Several T-shirts are stacked on the comforter beside the sweats. The clothes in my suitcase survived, but they reek of fumes from the explosion.

I used to love wearing his clothes. More than once, I wished I hadn't left this sweatshirt behind. It's from his undergraduate days, and it's soft and worn, and well, it was always my favorite.

"I'll call you tomorrow," I say and end the call.

I'm tired and done talking with Sophia about Dorian. Project Unity consists of hundreds, if not thousands, of investigators from multiple countries, each person tasked with a role. I will perform my part and get them the intel they're seeking, but in my gut, I know Dorian's innocent, and my role is to rule out his involvement. Now his father is another story...but Halston wouldn't do something without his son's knowledge.

Dressed in Dorian's clothes and thick wool socks I found in the chest of drawers, I head into the great room. Through the picturesque windows, scattered white flakes swirl in a stunning array before the aspens and firs. Instead of getting lost in the magical scene, I find myself assessing sight lines, possible surveillance positions, and natural cover points. The snow will make tracking movement easier, but it also means we're more isolated, if that's possible. The driveway to Dorian's house is over a mile long, and it's an even longer drive to his father's place.

"Might get a couple of inches," Dorian says in greeting. "Are you in the mood for tea? Hot chocolate? Something stronger? What can I get you?"

Thick marled grey socks peek out from beneath the bottom of his jeans, and the untucked flannel shirt he's wearing brings me back to when we met in England. This was his weekend look, and I could never get enough of it. He'd wear a tee with a flannel tied around his waist when warm and over the tee, unbuttoned, when chilly. Yes, when I met him, there was nothing to indicate he was any different than the other students.

His gaze catches mine with an intensity that makes my breath hitch, and I swear I can feel the connection between us, like an invisible string, tying us together, as if years haven't separated us. The normalcy of the moment makes it hard to believe we almost died earlier in the day or that the world is on the brink of war.

It's bizarre. The far-off chaos feels surreal, like something I can ignore, and that's exactly what I want. To drink hot chocolate and watch the snow fall.

"Do you have whipped cream?"

The devilish grin that flashes heats my cheeks.

I place a hand on my waist and give him a look that says I'm serious, but I can't stop the grin.

"No, but I can fix that easily." He moves to his phone on the kitchen island.

"The grocery store delivers?"

"My house manager does."

"Don't bother. Tea is fine."

He sets about filling a kettle with filtered water, then picks up his phone and taps at it, sending a text to someone. If I were to guess, someone received an order to deliver whipped cream.

"I meant what I said about talking."

"So did I," he says. "We can watch the snow fall while we talk." He pauses, gaze flitting up and down my body. "Damn. You still look good in my clothes."

"They swallow me." I finger the frayed edge, and a flash from the past, of him peeling this off me, comes out of nowhere. Sometimes, he wouldn't even bother to remove it; he'd just remove my bottoms, and his hands would roam my skin, finding my breasts beneath the sweatshirt, tweaking my nipples—*stop*. "How old is this sweatshirt, anyway? It must be nearly twenty—"

"Cara." His voice is firm, but he's grinning enough that the dimple shows, and I love it. "Don't go there."

"I can't believe you still have it."

"I'll never get rid of it. Too many memories." He turns his back to me and places the back of his fingers on the kettle, checking the heat.

Yes, I wore this back when we were at that new stage, where all it took was one look and we'd start taking off our clothes—back when times were good.

"It's pure luck it's here at this house and not in New York."

"Do you still own our brownstone?"

"Sold it about a year after you..."

My throat squeezes.

"I couldn't stay there anymore."

"I understand." I may have been the one to physically leave

our marriage, but he emotionally abdicated months earlier, and even with him coming home at night, I found the space unbearable.

"Who were you talking on the phone with?' His question catches me off guard. "I went down the hall to check on you and heard you speaking."

"My friend. Sophia." I sit down on a bar stool, facing him.

"The friend you did not move to California for."

"Right." I narrow my eyes at him, but really, it's simply annoying how easily he takes charge of a conversation. "Are you concerned that someone sabotaged your helicopter?"

He turns his back to me, pouring boiling water into a mug. "Not particularly."

"Why?"

He opens a cabinet and closes it. Then he opens a second cabinet, then a third.

"What're you looking for?"

"Tea." He opens a deep drawer and lifts a wooden box with a lid. He slides it to me and then walks across the kitchen to another cabinet, where he retrieves honey.

He leans across the counter from me while I select mint tea.

The screen on his phone lights up with notifications, but it doesn't vibrate.

"You don't need to check those?"

"You're my priority this weekend."

It would've been nice for that to have happened just once when we were married.

"Who do you think did it?" I ask, keeping the conversation on track.

One brow rises, considering. "You mean, the helicopter?"

I nod.

"A competitor is conceivable. The simplest answer is usually correct. Disgruntled employee. Or it's not sabotage at all and someone erred and didn't do a thorough inspection."

"You seem so glib. Like it doesn't matter."

"I hire competent people. They'll figure it out and resolve the issue. Ten years from now, I won't care about the details of the crash site investigation. But decades from now, I'll remember this weekend."

"Why is that?" I stir my tea, cautious…and hopeful.

"I think you know."

"Hmm." But I don't. Not for sure.

I lift the mug, testing the heat as it nears my lips, and set it back down.

"Caroline, I've done my best to forget you. But I haven't, and I'm under no misconception that will change when you return home. I want you back in my life."

A wave of dizziness surfaces. If I'd sipped the tea, I'd suspect he drugged it. I flatten my palm on the stone counter, absorbing the chill. He's already told me he wants me back, so why am I having a physical response now?

Am I really considering this? No, we just need closure.

"We should talk." My tone is firm, but do I mean it?

"Let's sit on the sofa. Watch the snow fall."

He heads into the living area, not waiting for my agreement. He opens a cabinet, then another one, rushing around until there's a pile of throws on the sofa.

"You sit there." I point at a different sofa than the one I'm sinking into.

He smiles a slow, sexy smile, wide enough that his singular dimple pops. "You love to cuddle."

I narrow my eyes. "We need to talk."

"Who have you been cuddling with?"

His words are cold, tone stern, and once again, I'm taken aback at how quickly he transitioned from flirty and fun to icy and serious.

"That's not what we need to talk about."

"I disagree," he says, but sits where I directed.

He connects his fingers and rests his arms over his knees. Sitting forward on a leather sofa, he's not projecting his executive steel, but there's purposeful intimidation in those dark eyes and subliminal aggressive stance.

But I'm no longer easily intimidated, and there are more pressing concerns.

"Let's cover some important matters first. As I told you, I still work as an analyst." He's unreadable. "I'm here because you are a person of interest in a terrorist investigation."

Now I have his attention. The lines around his eyes deepen, and his head cocks to the side. But he's not as shocked as I would have expected.

"A terrorist cell?"

"Not exactly. We believe there may be a rogue member within the syndicate, or what you like to call an alliance."

His lips purse, and his gaze drops to a corner. "Nick told you I'm responsible." He exhales frustration. "I told him I'm innocent. He sent you on a wild goose chase. But I appreciate your vote of confidence." His tone is terse. Facial features and hands still. There's no indication he's lying.

"Nick Ivanov?"

He nods.

"There's a source. They haven't shared with me the name of the source, but he's in your syndicate?"

Again, a singular nod.

"It could be him. He could be the source." I'll definitely ask Sophia next time I speak to her. It makes sense. I should've considered Nick as the unnamed source. He's the one who was targeted by the syndicate. I guess I'd assumed, given the attack is well-documented, they wouldn't have kept his name off of reports as the source. But, Project Unity is so expansive, keeping his name off the project documentation is likely meant to prevent him from being targeted again.

"There's evidence," I say.

"If there's any evidence, it's planted." I agree, and he must recognize this in my reaction, because he visibly relaxes. "What do you have?"

"We've traced communications from this compound. I believe you're innocent, but what about your father? Would he do something like this without your involvement?"

He looks to the ceiling with an expression I haven't seen before. It's a mix of suppressed mirth and disgust. Or maybe disappointment. In me?

"Come on." He hops up.

"What?"

"Let's go."

"What?" Is he kicking me out?

"There's something you need to see." He steps forward and offers me his hand. "And no, I'm not asking you to leave. I've no intention of letting you leave until we've worked through what matters. Your investigation? I'll comply. Let's get this done so we can move on to what really matters."

I could argue that a multipronged attack aimed at destabilizing the United States and allied countries is a matter of great importance, but I hold that argument back, curious about what he plans on sharing.

We say little as he leads me to a mudroom and offers me one of his winter coats. He opens a cabinet and pulls out a pair of Hunter rain boots. Women's rain boots. "We won't be out long, but these will keep your feet dry."

"Do you entertain often?"

"Perhaps as often as you cuddle."

Nice.

It's a quiet trip on the paved path to his father's house. We're in a golf cart with closed-in sides and rugged wheels. The vehicle is essentially a battery-operated car, scaled to drive on golf cart paths.

He parks on the side of his father's mansion and sets the parking brake.

"You can't share what I'm about to show you."

"I'm on a team."

"The NDA you signed is still in effect."

I'd like to see him hold me to an NDA I signed a decade ago. *An NDA that should've been your first warning sign. Hindsight's always twenty-twenty.*

I cross my arms, scowling.

"Fine. You can tell your team back in California. I'll do what's needed to remove my father and me from your persons of interest list." He spits out the phrase as if it's poison. "But nothing in the media. Agreed?"

"Agreed." I hate the media as much as he does. Possibly more.

He opens the side door, and the silence in the stately mansion is deafening.

We quietly wander through vaguely familiar halls, our footfalls serving as the only sound. The massive traditional mountain home was built decades ago, but one of Halston's wives made this compound her personal project. From a security standpoint, it's challenging—multiple access points, too many spaces to monitor effectively. From a design perspective, it's a mishmash, but the overarching theme is of a proud hunter.

When Dorian first brought me here, he said the place tucked away, outside of Telluride, can sleep over thirty people. On one of these floors is an unforgettable library, complete with a view of snow-capped mountains and a roaring fireplace.

Dorian stops outside a door and hesitates, almost as if he's listening.

"If he's sleeping, we won't wake him." He looks to me as if asking for agreement.

I nod, but I don't recall Dorian ever being concerned in this way for his father.

Is Halston sick? Is that the secret?

The door opens, and the first thing I'm drawn to is the wall of windows and the stunning view. There's an executive desk, possibly one of the largest I've ever seen, against one wall, positioned to take in the mountain view. Near a fireplace, there are two plush leather chaise lounges, and Halston Moore is reclining on one, with a luxurious mink blanket thrown over his legs. A book is in his lap, but his eyes are closed.

He's aged since I saw him last—deeper wrinkles and a shrunken frame. The black hair dye—a single tone with unprofessional application—suggests either declining attention to detail or reduced access to his usual services.

The suit jacket crinkles around his shoulders, slightly too big for his narrow width, and his shirt collar gaps around his neck. The knot in the tie is larger, reminiscent of the 1970s style. The black sheen on his thinned hair seems unnatural, and I'm not sure if it's the deep black or the singular tone that makes the color appear so unnatural. His lips are dry and cracked, and his cheeks have hollowed.

Who is dressing him these days?

Almost as if sensing us, his head jerks, and his eyes snap open.

I brace for his greeting, fully aware that I was never his favorite.

His gaze roams the room as if remembering where he is. After taking in the windows, the fireplace, and the fur, he zeroes in on me.

"Judith." He sounds confused. "What are you doing here? All communications should go through my lawyers."

"Dad, this is Caroline. You remember Caroline, right?"

CHAPTER 17

DORIAN

Judith is one of my father's ex-wives. Caroline looks nothing like her. I'll never understand why some days he's on his game and recognizes everyone, and others, he gets confused easily.

"Dad, do you need some water?"

The glass on the side table is empty. His hand shakes slightly as he turns, following my line of sight.

"Will they serve lunch at the board meeting? Wine? Cindy. She has it under control. Is Cindy here?"

"Dad, you don't attend the board meetings anymore."

I shove my hands into my pockets and watch him absorb this news. The nursing staff prefers that we tell him lies about meetings being rescheduled.

I don't play that game. The staff's approach is kinder, but it also exacerbates his confusion.

His gaze roams the room. "Where are the straws?"

I sit on the end of the chaise lounge across from him. He does better when I'm closer and near his height.

Why is he alone? Through the discrete camera in the corner, I know the security team is monitoring, but we have a full medical staff to ensure he's got round-the-clock care. All of them—vetted, with top-level clearances and iron-clad NDAs— play the assisting-the-powerful-executive game. He shouldn't be alone, but perhaps the nurse left him to sleep.

Caroline comes forward, gingerly sitting on the end of his chaise lounge, just beyond his feet.

"Mr. Moore, it's been a long time," she says with tenderness befitting a hospital patient.

He startles, and recognition clicks behind those fading blue irises. "Oh. She's *your* ex-wife. All contact should be through lawyers."

We're not getting divorced, Dad.

That's what I want to say. But hell, he's probably right, once again. He always had a knack for predicting outcomes.

"Why is she here?" Years ago, that question would've been shouted. Today, his voice cracks, and his unfocused gaze has me wondering yet again what he sees.

"She wanted to see you."

"Is it Thanksgiving?"

"No, Dad. That was over a week ago. Remember?"

"You let the staff off. It was just us." Yes, he remembers. "We used to have a room full of people at Thanksgiving. The entire board one year. In New York. Best city in the world. Now, executives live the world over, but there's no city like New York. Sheila. She was great at spearheading events. Fantastic entertainer. The best of the best. Beautiful. A charmer. You need to find a woman like Sheila."

Dad looks down at his lap, and his expression changes—confusion, then embarrassment. I don't need to lift the blanket to know what has happened. If he'd agree to wear protective undergarments as recommended by his physicians, this wouldn't be an issue.

Where the hell is the staff?

I exit his office, noting the red light on the security keypad. The room wasn't locked. The security alarm isn't on, but this early in the day, it wouldn't be.

"Hello!"

A door opens at the end of the corridor, and a young man and woman in business casual attire exit. If Dad had his way, everyone would be in business suits, but we broke him of that policy years ago. It's too hard to find nursing staff willing to either live on-site or commute to the property. The cleaning staff doesn't wear uniforms either, but we have them avoid him so they don't cross paths.

Based on the flush of the woman's cheeks, it's clear why these two weren't with my father. I don't care about fraternization, but they need to do their fucking job.

"Mr. Moore," the young man says.

I should probably know his name. But I'm bad with the homecare staff, as we source them through an agency. It's a revolving door.

"My father had an incident."

"Is he hurt?" The woman's eyes widen, and her fingers go to her mouth.

"He soiled himself."

I hate saying those words. He's got the world's best doctors, and they've done shit to prevent his decline.

She nods.

"We'll handle it," she says, flattening her hands across her middle.

She's right to look nervous. If he had hurt himself, it would be her fault. I hire round-the-clock care for a reason.

"Are you leaving now?"

"Yes. I left a…" Friend is on the tip of my lips, but I won't diminish Caroline. "My wife is with him now. We'll get out of your way."

"Dr. Suresh is due in thirty minutes For another treatment."

Every week, my father undergoes experimental stem cell treatments. He's on Dr. Suresh's cutting-edge protocol—a combination of targeted immunotherapy and neural regeneration techniques that cost more than most companies' annual R&D budgets. The goal is to extend longevity, sharpen his mental acuity, and slow the progression of his dementia. The FDA hasn't approved it yet, but when you have the resources we do, you get first access to the most promising treatments.

I have no idea if it's helping or hurting. But Dad chose this course years ago, and he places all his trust in his treatment team.

"Is he still handling the treatments well?"

"Yes. This course is better. The nausea has abated.'

"He looks like he's lost weight."

"He has," she agrees, positioning herself next to me while the young man falls behind us. "His comprehensive annual physical is scheduled in two weeks."

"We'll know if anything is causing his weight loss then," I say, filling in what she's not saying.

"Yes, sir."

I open the door and am taken aback by the scene before me.

Caroline's hand rests over my father's. She's sitting next to him, and he's entranced.

Yes, Dad, she is beautiful.

"Mr. Moore, it's time for your next meeting." The woman's bright tone catches his attention. He breaks away from Caroline's touch and lifts his hand to point. His fingers tremble, and his forehead wrinkles in confusion.

"What meeting do I have?"

I really need to talk to his medical team. How can we expect him to keep things straight when people lie after I've corrected him?

The woman takes his hand and guides him out of the room. Physically, he's in great shape for his age. The two knee replacements and double hip replacement he endured during his seventies are still holding up.

I don't know what process she goes through to clean him up, and I don't want to know. When he comes back, he'll be disoriented. Understandably. He's a powerful man, yet he loses control of his bowel movements. His mind weaves in and out of the present. His conversation weaves. A random person might not notice, but I do. This isn't the future he wanted.

They leave the door open, and Caroline and I watch the two of them travel down the corridor, presumably to his bedroom. The man lifts the blanket he was sitting under and leaves, mumbling, "I'll be back to clean up."

"Shall we go?" I ask Caroline.

Her straight spine might appear cold to a random onlooker, but I see the sadness and concern lurking in the depths of her light blue eyes and the downward turn of her graceful lips. Her trademark poise attracted me all those years ago, when she entered a pub of tipsy men. Even now, I'm still drawn to this woman, with a softer side she shares with few.

"I'm so sorry," she says to me.

Why? I didn't bring her here to receive pity. I'm not the one suffering a loss of dignity.

"How long has he been like this?"

"How long have I suspected, or how long has he been under in-home care?" I step to the door, ready to leave.

"I saw a news alert just last week that Halston Moore backed the Homestead Act. That he met with Senator Williams." She slips her thumbnail to her teeth, thoughtful. Her eyes flash to me when she grasps the truth. "Why are you covering for him? Why not announce his retirement? Or let him drift into obscurity?"

I remain quiet. She'll figure it out.

"He retains a board seat at Bedrock. You're chairman of the board, but if he's on the board, you control his vote. Hasn't anyone gotten suspicious?"

I glance down the empty corridor, where my father disappeared.

"Dorian. You said you'd answer my questions."

"And I will," I say, the response harsher than intended. "Given his age, no one questions his reclusive nature. The existing board members are, if not friends, close associates from his early investment days. They backed my satellite ventures when everyone else thought private space infrastructure was a pipe dream. They understand I'm capable, that it's a family company, and they're content to let us handle succession quietly." I adjust my Patek Philippe watch—a habit from my post-Oxford days, when I was still learning to navigate board rooms. "The SEC filings are impeccable, Caroline. Everything's disclosed within legal parameters.

"About five years ago, the Bedrock Advisory board urged him to pass the chairman's reins to me, his son. I suspect they had suspicions back then." The accusation in her expression annoys me. "Should he retire? Yes. Absolutely. You try telling him that. What you just saw? It's a bad day. He has lucid days. He's holding on with all he has. That meeting with a senator? It probably happened. People fly out to meet with him all the time."

"You don't know if it happened?"

"Don't look at me like that."

Her eyes narrow into slits. "How, pray tell, am I looking at you?"

"Like you don't trust me."

Her hands flutter by her sides, a posture of frustration. She's seconds away from closing down and retreating.

"If I wanted to know if he met with someone, I could find out. I have full access to his calendar. His staff reports to me. But I don't care. Williams is a putz. He's the one who probably put out that press release. That Homestead bill of his is smoke and mirrors with no substance. Political showmanship. You know the game."

"How does it benefit you?"

"It doesn't."

Those liquid eyes freeze over, and our gazes lock. My body responds, like it always has with her. I want her close. The need to touch her, to put the squabbles behind us, is as strong as ever. We shouldn't be fighting...not over my father. That's why I brought her here. I have half a mind to drag her out of here and back to my bedroom, to leave these petty disagreements behind and remind her where we excel.

A door clicks, and the male staff member from earlier enters, wearing rubber gloves and carrying a cleaning bucket with supplies.

He sprays the area over the seat, wipes it, and exits. Is that really all they do to clean?

"If you don't mind, I'd like to stay to say goodbye to your father."

She's conciliatory. Is she retreating into her shell?

"He was being kind. I don't feel right about disappearing. If it's difficult for you to be around him, you can head on, and I'll walk back."

I'm about to assure her I'm fine spending time with my father when he and the nurse return.

One look at his thin, straight, pursed lips, and I register the anger.

"You didn't divorce her."

"Dad?"

"She's no good for you. She's not the right choice."

"Dad. Let's sit." I meet the nurse's gaze. "Drink some tea."

"I'll cut you from my will. You don't believe me, but I will. Don't let her make a fool of you."

That's a threat from the past. One he tossed around with regularity. Today, it's meaningless. I'm wealthy in my own right. I don't care about his will, although it's likely, as his only child, I'm his sole beneficiary.

"Geoffrey agrees. She needs to go."

Geoffrey and I agree about my father's care. We agreed long ago that Geoffrey would agree with any nonsensical rant he spews, but he would act as a prudent financial advisor and run any significant changes by me. Geoffrey encouraged me to seek a conservatorship so I would have legal standing over Dad's businesses. I have authorized our legal team to proceed down that path, but I haven't pushed them to speed it along. I have a healthcare directive, and that feels sufficient. There's a more significant legal concern regarding his board seat, but as I told Caroline, many on the board are his friends. Forcing a member off the board is distasteful and reeks of disloyalty.

"Dad." I adopt a stern, calm tone, one I've found to be effective. "Caroline is the best thing that ever happened to me." My gaze drifts from my father to the woman I aim to win back. "Letting her walk away was the biggest mistake of my life. She'll always be welcome in my home because I love her. I never stopped loving her."

There. That's what I should've said years ago.

The ice from earlier melts in Caroline's irises, shifting to shimmering pools. She and I have so much to talk through.

Dad opens his mouth to speak. Whether he loses track of his thought or needs water, I'm not sure, but I push forward, speaking for Caroline's benefit.

"You're a talented, intelligent man, but your track record for picking wives is appalling. And when it comes to Caroline, you're dead wrong."

The nurse drops a straw into a cup for my father and offers it to him. She holds it for him with a patience I do not possess.

"Thank you," I tell her.

She nods.

"We've got him," she says. "Before, he was napping. We were just down the hall."

I hold up a hand and offer a congenial smile. I'll mention the incident to the house manager. She handles the staff and can process the performance feedback through the appropriate channels.

I take Caroline's slender, chilled hand in mine, and we leave my father's office side by side. I don't glance backward, as it's best if we leave quietly. The nursing staff will manage him for the rest of the afternoon. If he gets too worked up, they'll sedate him.

We return to the electric Garia luxury cart—one of several vehicles stationed around the compound. The regular Mercedes convoy seems excessive for on-property travel, though I note Jenkins, head of security, watching from his discreet position near the garage. That's one of the problems with Dad's numerous staff. Someone's always watching or listening.

It's not until I engage the cart's reverse that Caroline speaks.

"Did you mean that?"

"I'm not one to say things I don't mean." I press the accelerator forward.

She's silent as we whip along the path.

Fuck. That sounded harsh.

"I'm not good at these things," I admit. My statement catches her attention. "But yes, I meant it."

"You said Geoffrey moved to be near your father?"

That's not where I expected her to take this conversation.

"Yes. Like I told you, he's my father's financial advisor. He's..." I take a minute to consider how best to describe Geoffrey. "He's semi-retired. Dad's his only client. They're close friends. Moving out here was partially his idea. He saw Dad struggling. Getting frustrated when his memory started slipping. Confusing words. Events. People." She witnessed that herself. "I don't know that Geoffrey loved the city. The move was probably a welcome change."

"Is he close to your father's age?"

"No. I'd say he's...mid-sixties? Met my dad in New York. They bonded over chess—both grandmasters. Now they play checkers." I navigate the cart around the winding path. "Geoffrey's not only a friend. His investment picks outperform the top funds every single year. That's why Dad trusts him."

A light dusting of snow covers the trail, but the tires easily roll through the virgin layer.

"Why the questions about Geoffrey?"

"He wears a suit to visit your father?"

"If he didn't, Dad might not recognize him. Besides, old habits die hard. Especially with their generation."

She slips her thumbnail between her teeth, thoughtful.

"What is it?"

Is she still on Geoffrey, or is she thinking about what I said back there? Does anything I say make a difference?

I pull into a garage bay and park.

"You stood up for me."

"Always." But even as I say it, I know that in the past, I didn't do it enough. Or I didn't do it well.

CHAPTER 18

CAROLINE

"Always."

The absence of truth in that one word echoes through my chest cavity.

The garage wall blurs as I'm swept back to the decisive day I stood in the dining room of our Manhattan townhome—wasted square footage—decorated by a designer his father insisted we use.

You might need to entertain, and you need to make the right impression.

Those had been his father's words, uttered on one of his first visits to our home when we first moved in together, but before we'd married.

The big rumor at the time had been that I was pregnant, and that's why Dorian proposed. I wanted to laugh it off like Dorian had, but I began to check my profile in the mirror before

leaving the house, looking for any hint that might be miscon-
strued as a baby bump.

When Halston came to visit, I attempted to assure him, but
he threw a hand up in the air, insisting it was fine. He believed
the lie, I think, even though I made it a point to always order an
alcoholic drink when dining with him, even at lunch. He didn't
seem to care about my pregnancy status, as long as we complied
with his wishes.

In retrospect, Halston's insistence on a formal dining room
was one of many warnings I ignored. Dutifully, after our
wedding, we decorated the dining room and entry to ensure we
could entertain business associates. We never used that dining
room. Not once. Halston's generation may have required enter-
taining at home to rise in the ranks, but our generation met in
restaurants. Or at least, Dorian scheduled his social business
arrangements in restaurants or clubs.

Your prenup is ironclad, right?

The question I overheard while staring at the pretentious
foyer chandelier rings through my mind. My throat tightened,
making it hard to swallow. I waited, en route to the kitchen to
fetch their drinks, to hear Dorian's response. The two men
were across the hall in our small den.

His father had observed a disagreement. We didn't yell, but
it was tense. Dorian asked me to reschedule his dinner plans
to accommodate his father, treating me like an assistant. It hit
me wrong, and I responded with a sarcastic, *"As you wish,
dear."*

Dorian picked up on it, rolled his eyes, and said, *"Don't start."*
He glowered, and the unspoken *go get us drinks now* hung in the
air. It was a side of Dorian that his father brought out. But at
that point, I was suffocating. I'd been isolated too long, made to

feel like my purpose was to assist Dorian, that what I wanted and who I was didn't matter.

Years later, a therapist helped me understand I'd been experiencing many of the symptoms of depression. Perhaps I was depressed, but I believe I was mourning our marriage and the man I fell in love with, because that man... he disappeared.

The sense of being reprimanded clings to me, the sensations of that moment wrapping around me with the full force of reliving a moment with all five senses. The sharp sting of air conditioning through crisp linen, the lingering pine scent from the polished floors, cleaned earlier in the day in preparation for dinner with Halston, the cloying sense of the walls and ceiling coming in around me, closing me into a self-made prison.

I wanted Dorian to stand up for me, for us. I needed him to tell his father that comment was uncalled for and that our young marriage was strong. I needed his response to soothe my worries that we might be facing the end of a marriage that had just begun.

Yes.

That was the one-word response he gave his father. If I close my eyes, I can hear his gravelly voice.

The same word that kicked off a new phase of life, the word I had uttered when he asked me to marry him, ended our marriage. But it wasn't just the word. It was the culmination of our relationship. The cold finality. The unspoken agreement between Dorian and his father.

Yes, the prenup is ironclad. Yes, that's all that matters.

"Caroline, are you okay?"

I flinch from the unexpected pressure on my arm, and he withdraws his hand. He pushes a button, and the garage door rolls down behind us.

Wordlessly, I push forward into the house. It's been a long time since I've thought about that day.

I pull out my phone and tap out a text while walking.

ME:

Halston Moore suffers from dementia.

I could add that this removes him as a person of interest, but there's no need. Sophia will understand.

The door closes behind me, and I focus on my breathing to clear the negative emotions. The past is the past.

"What did I say?"

His eyes are coated with concern, but the words are cautionary, a reminder that how I answer might place him on the defensive.

"You didn't say anything." The lie is automatic. There's no need to dredge up the past.

He takes my hand and leads me to one of the leather sofas in the great room. It's a stunning room, and the size exacerbates the chill infiltrating my skin.

Dorian refreshes the hearth, his back to me. I use the moment to scan the room, cataloging the cameras I've already spotted—three discrete units disguised in the canned lighting. Dorian has always valued his privacy. I expect that any interior security system is employed when he's not home. He wouldn't want someone watching him in his home. No, his security team is likely limited to using perimeter monitoring when he's home.

He joins me on the sofa and reaches for my hand.

My gaze falls to where we touch, and I fight the urge to yank my hand away.

"I didn't always defend you." He studies me, gauging if he guessed correctly. "I should have. But I was under a lot of pressure. I realize I didn't handle it well."

"Please." The smile across my face feels false bitter, and sad. "Every photo from back then showed a happy-go-lucky guy. Everybody's friend. You ate up all the attention."

"That's not fair. I smiled for the camera. I played the game."

"And it paid off." My heart is heavy, but there's no point in fighting. I didn't play the game well, and it frustrated him. It's behind us, and rehashing our actions won't change the past. "You're being considered for chief of staff." I force a brightness, wiggling my fingers in a jazz hands movement to emphasize the greatness. "A stepping stone to the White House. That's amazing."

He denied he wanted to follow in his uncle's footsteps, but clearly, he lied.

"It's an influential position. A possibility, but it's not something I'm actively seeking. I'm skeptical. I don't have the stomach to play the political game."

"Come on. You don't get considered for chief of staff without working for it."

His jaw flexes ever-so-slightly, the shift almost imperceptible.

"I probably shouldn't admit this to you, given what you do."

My spine stiffens, but at the same time, my pulse quickens at the prospect of valuable information.

"The only reason I tossed my hat in for consideration is to drum up contracts for Zenith."

"Won't you have to step aside from any conflicts of interest if you take a post in the administration?"

"Decades ago, yes. Not now."

"You mean everyone turns a blind eye?"

"If Congress had an issue with it, they could create laws preventing conflicts of interest."

"That won't happen."

Over the years, my analysis of classified contracts revealed layers of shell companies and international holdings that would take years to untangle. The kind of structure that sets off every red flag in intelligence circles, all because someone is hiding involvement. All those politicians? If you passed a law saying they couldn't serve with conflicts of interest, they'd work around the law, just like they did back when conflicts of interest were frowned upon.

"It's not a system I created. You understand that, right?"

"Couldn't you win the contracts without having to enter the political arena? Isn't that what your sales force is for?"

"Certainly. And, no matter what you are inclined to believe, I didn't actively pursue the role. When rumors started, I didn't dispel them. Me as chief of staff? It's an unlikely turn of events. But it's good for business. So, I've played along. That's different than actively pursuing it or wanting it." With tenderness, he reaches for my hand and deftly brushes his thumb over my knuckles. When my gaze lifts to his, he says, "I haven't been asked and haven't committed. It's noise."

"You tossed your hat in," I say, repeating his earlier words.

"In a manner of speaking."

Of course, what he does isn't my business. It doesn't affect me. But the intensity of his gaze and the warmth of his hand do.

"If you told me not to do it, I wouldn't."

"Why would I tell you not to do it?"

"If it's not the life you want, I won't—"

"I'm not in your life."

"But I want you to be."

"I'd never ask you to walk away from something you wanted."

His hand drops. "Like I made you do? That s what you're saying, right?"

"Don't put words in my mouth."

He hates that phrase. Any second, he'll jump on his computer, and I won't hear from him for hours.

"If I had a do-over, I'd do things differently. I wouldn't have expected your schedule to conform to mine. That was..." He huffs, the sound a mix of frustration and amusement. "You can close your mouth."

"I'm shocked. That's as close to an apology as you've ever come."

His lips curve into a smirk, but he quickly grows somber.

"I don't know why I was conforming to my father's expectations. The man's gone through eight wives. He should've been the last person I attempted to emulate."

"Eight? Is he married now?"

"No. His eighth wife died a couple of years ago."

"Oh. I missed that."

"She was about your age."

"Oh."

This time, the huff he emits is definitely akin to amusement. "Yeah. I didn't know her well, as you'd probably expect. She traveled a lot. Went to Greece with a group of friends. She drowned."

"What?"

"Dad found it embarrassing. He pulled some strings. Didn't hit the news in the US. No one really cared anyway. My father's been reclusive for years."

"I noticed that. Over the years, fewer and fewer photos of him surfaced. The same with you, after the first couple of years from our split."

"Even when you and I were together, Dad was growing more reclusive." He slides down on the cushion and rests his head against the back, and, in his position, his head is slightly lower than mine. "You asked when his dementia started. Looking back, I think the personality change might have been a symptom. Either that or he noticed issues, and he withdrew to avoid observation."

"And why did you become reclusive?"

One side of his lip rises in a crooked grin. "I wouldn't say I'm reclusive. I travel a ton. And contrary to what you believe, I didn't live for the media attention."

I narrow my eyes and give him a look that calls bullshit, but I'm teasing him.

"Seriously. And straight up?"

"No. Lie to me."

He smirks. "The only media I've ever chased was right after you left. Like I told you, I wanted pics to make you jealous. I staged a few. Hired a PR specialist and everything. Hell, I probably paid to have those photos featured."

"You did not."

"I'm not proud of it, but…" He grins.

"Look at you. You are *so* proud of it."

We both grin at each other. I hated seeing him strutting around with supermodels, but I had other diversions. I couldn't really worry about him once I joined the CIA. His grin falters, and he threads his fingers through mine.

"What about you? Any serious relationships?"

"No serious ships," I say, forcing a smile and shortening the word because it feels lighter, and some part of me doesn't really want to be having this conversation.

"Why?"

I meet his gaze head-on, reading him, sensing his mood and intention. He wants me to say he's the reason, but... "You clearly haven't tried the online dating game."

I do date. I just haven't had any luck. My dates range from not finishing my coffee before I excuse myself to suffering through a ho-hum dinner.

"No, I haven't," he admits, his cocky attitude coming through his smirk.

"What am I saying? If you created an online profile, you'd need your assistant to manage your account."

"I'm glad you haven't found anyone." He squeezes my fingers, and the sensation tightens my chest cavity.

I search his expression for any sign he's joking, but his intensity warms me from the inside out, wrapping around my heart.

"I've never gotten over you, Caroline. I don't think I ever will."

He shifts closer and caresses my cheek. Our breaths slow, and with it, time.

His dark eyes search mine, asking for permission.

I tilt my head, bending to him, granting his request. The movement is the most natural thing in the world.

His lips softly move against mine, a light stroke, testing, teasing.

The uncontrollable hammering of my heart drowns the remote part of my brain begging to push him away, to stop before I lose control.

His long fingers cup my head, positioning me as he prefers. His lips ghost over my face, his kisses lighting long-dormant needs. His groan into the shell of my ear lights through my body, shredding any control.

I slip my tongue into his greedy mouth and am momentarily awed as he seizes control, deepening the connection.

It's a reckless kiss, but beautiful. Our hands roam over each other as our mouths fuse, desire building layer by layer. I clutch his shirt, wanting it gone, but settle for reaching below the hem. He releases the softest sigh when I touch his abdomen and find my way to his chest. The thud of his heart vibrates through my fingers. My sex clenches, as if waking from a long nap, and the urge to take his hand, to put it on me, grows. *Touch me.*

He breaks the kiss and rubs his nose over mine, his mouth open, sucking in air.

"Cara, I'm going to take you right here unless you stop me."

CHAPTER 19

DORIAN

I'm faintly aware of my shallow, rapid breathing as I await her response.

Say yes. Tell me to fuck you.

Her flushed cheeks, swollen, wet lips, and shallow breaths say her body's on board, but what's going on in that brilliant mind of hers?

Those light blue irises, the color of the sky in my fantasies, flash, pupils immersive. Her fingers thread through the strands on the back of my head, and her eyelids flutter closed as she pulls me down.

Yes.

I shudder in relief.

While a part of me wants to strip her in seconds and reclaim her with one violent thrust, I shut that instinct down. I've dreamed of this for too long. We've been apart for years, but she is my recurring dream. So many times, when I've been with others, she's the one I've seen when I close my eyes.

No, I finally have her again, and I'll take my time. Ensure she remembers how good we can be together.

With her gaze locked on mine, her fingers grip the frayed edges of my sweatshirt, and she lifts the garment over her head, leaving only her bra.

She's tentative, perhaps uncertain of my reaction.

But she doesn't need to be. She's beautiful. Graceful. Seductive. The soft points of her nipples push against the lace of her bra, their pale pink a whisper through the lace. The shade will darken when sucked, and the sensitive skin peaks. She leans back, flattening her stomach, telling me to carry on.

Light reflects on two shiny diamonds in her belly button. I rub my thumb over the piercing, questioning.

"When did you do this?"

"Do you hate it?"

"Did you do it for yourself?" *Or because you thought I'd hate it?*

"I wanted it." Defiance flickers in those cerulean eyes.

I flick the side of my finger over the diamond's edge, then caress her soft, smooth skin.

Her tongue flicks over her top lip, and the corner of her lips lifts into a seductive smile.

"I love it." It's the truth. I can't wait to see her in a string bikini. But that's me, jumping ahead. There are much more important measures at hand.

I grip the rolled-up band of sweats and yank, pulling them and her panties over her bottom, thighs, and up off her legs, sending them sailing into the air.

"Wait. Do you have cameras?" Her gaze travels up the wall. Of course, she saw the security cameras.

"Internal cameras disengage when I'm home."

Her smile widens. "That's what I thought."

"Did you now?"

We grin at each other, and I have half a mind to tweak her nipple for trying to play off that she hadn't seen the cameras nesting above.

She pushes up and removes my shirt. Her touch on my skin, her active undressing of me while she's nearly nude, is enough to bring that urge to take her fast and hard roaring back.

With my shirt gone and her task accomplished, she drops her chin, looking me over appreciatively. She pushes me back until I'm reclining into the cushion and trails kisses down my chest until she arrives at a nipple and sucks, twirling her tongue.

That's my game she's playing, and the action has the desired effect.

Fuck. I'm so hard. My fingers itch to take over, but what she's doing feels too good. Just having her fingers on me, her hot mouth…

She bites playfully, then rubs the pad of her thumb over the nipped skin. She presses her body against mine, then pulls back, her expression full of questions and concern.

"What are we doing?"

Her question tells me that I've let things slow down too much, and questions are creeping in. That won't do.

"Acting on our desires."

I roll her pliant body under me, hissing as our chests meld, the first skin-on-skin contact we've had in far too many years. I find her center and press my hand over her, moving it back and forth just the way she likes it.

She releases a throaty moan that risks undoing me.

"Patience."

My directive is as much for me as for her.

She reaches for my jeans, but I tsk.

Possession. That's the goal.

My lips nibble along her slender neck, biting and sucking until she squirms. I continue to her breasts, tugging at the lace, exposing her right breast, kneading it, sucking on the nipple, swirling my tongue. Her fingers scrape my scalp, toying with me as I play with her.

She pulls away, letting me know she's almost had too much, and I repeat the actions with her left breast. With one hand, I unsnap her bra and leave it dangling off her shoulders as I descend, licking and kissing my way down.

She lifts her knees, spreading her thighs.

I touch her, lifting my gaze to meet hers as I do. Her chest rises and falls slowly.

"You're wet."

She swallows and gives a quick nod.

I drop my mouth, tasting her. She gasps and fists my hair.

I've missed this. I didn't pleasure her nearly enough when I had her.

As my mouth works her over, my finger plunders her core, stretching her tight heat, smooth as silk. I continue on and on, revelling in her moans and the slight shifts. Her hips roll, and her thighs tighten around my ears. And that's it; she comes. My fingers stop moving, and my tongue presses firmly against her clit, letting her orgasm linger.

She swipes her forehead and gulps for air.

"God, I forgot how good you are at that."

"Hmm. I didn't forget how good you taste."

She suppresses a laugh. I can tell she's holding back by the way she covers her mouth hastily with the back of her hand and the way her eyes glow with amusement.

She's the most beautiful thing. Willowy. Elegant. Long blonde strands strewn about, undone.

Can she read my mind? Does she have any idea how much I adore her? How much I still love her?

She pushes up, and the couch squeaks as she shifts lower. She palms the bulge in my jeans, and I close my eyes. *Fuck yes.*

The pressure as her hand molds to my crotch, rubbing me through my jeans, is divine.

"Jesus." The prayer slips from my soul.

My brain clouds with lust, watching as she works on my zipper and fumbles with my jeans and briefs. I roll onto my back, assisting her.

Her slender fingers wrap around me, and she bends, and as lovely as the thought is, I don't think I can wait anymore.

I squeeze her shoulder. "I need you."

Fuck, I want her so badly my dick aches and my muscles quiver.

She moves up my body, her chest inches from mine, her nipples grazing my skin, leaving a burning fire in their wake. Her lips cover mine, and I hungrily probe her mouth with my tongue, holding her in place, luxuriating in the weight of her body over mine, the pressure of her weight squeezing my erection between our bodies.

She shifts, straddling me, and captures my dick with her glistening pussy. The heat, the warmth, it's too much, and my gaze rolls upwards to the ceiling.

Light snowflakes swirl, and the fire crackles. The overhead lights gleam like stars.

She drags my tip through her slit, and my attention zeroes in on us.

"Do we need a condom?" She sounds breathless, but her hips continue to move in a mesmerizing motion.

"I'm clean."

I risk a glance up at her.

"It's been a long time for me," she says.

My gaze locks on hers.

"How long?" We've been apart seven years. There have been others, I know.

"Years."

Her answer dashes the unrealistic hope I subconsciously harbored that she'd say seven years, but I've got no rights. Only a fool would expect she's steered clear of men.

"I've been tested," I say, returning my attention to my crown, gliding across her seam, back and forth to a beat she's creating. "It's been a long time for me, too."

"I'm on the pill."

I wouldn't honestly care if she weren't. I want nothing between us. If she got pregnant, I'd be ecstatic. The thought strikes me as all kinds of wrong, but she positions me at her entrance, obliterating all additional thoughts.

"For cramps," she breathes out, and it takes several seconds before my fogged brain connects the dots.

She slowly takes me, stretching around me.

"Fuck, you're tight." *Heaven. She feels like heaven.*

"Told you it's been a while."

The vision before me is enough to make me lose control. I heave up, capturing her in my arms, forcing her mouth to mine, as deep inside her as I can be.

Our kiss is fire. The flames lap from my groin through my

spine. The urge to move builds. She tightens her hips, rocking down on me.

Instinct takes charge, and I flip her over, giving in to primal needs, slamming into her at a punishing pace. I'm so fucking close I have to slow, gather my bearings, and remember I need her quivering. I pull out, buying time, and she whimpers.

I maneuver her onto her side, lift her leg, and enter her from behind. My fingers find her mound, marked with her juices. I work her with my fingers, matching my penetrating rhythm.

The smell of sex fills the room, and I bury my nose in her neck. I scrape my teeth along the sensitive skin and nibble her earlobe; her spine curves.

"I'm close. I'm going to—"

"I know, baby."

I'm not sure who comes first. For me, it's like a dam released. I don't normally come from this angle, but fuck, it's a miracle I lasted this long. Perspiration coats our skin, and our breaths are rapid.

Minutes pass as my breathing evens, my mind clearing from the intoxicating haze of Caroline. The Italian leather sofa—a forty-thousand-dollar mistake, according to one interior designer—clings to my damp skin. The great room's temperature-controlled environment does nothing to ward off the chill of separation when she moves.

"I've got to get up," she mumbles.

I groan, my version of a complaint.

"I suppose we were bound to do that." She pushes up, and her feet hit the floor with a finality that puts me on edge. Her long blond hair cascades midway down her back, and my gaze follows the curve of her spine to the dip above her perky ass. "Needed to get that out of our systems."

"You're joking, right?"

She bends, gathering her clothes—well, my clothes that she wore—and heads down the hall, presumably to a bathroom.

"It's going to take a lot more than once on a sofa to get you out of my system," I call out after her, but she doesn't respond.

I hope she doesn't regret it. I sure as hell don't.

No, this is Caroline. It's in her nature to try to slow things down so she has time to analyze and consider. I reach for my jeans and slide them on. If I have my way, we'll have a fireside dinner with wine, and we'll take things much more slowly tonight in my bed. She can tell me more about this job of hers, and I can figure out how to make it flexible so she can join me everywhere.

In the kitchen, my phone lights up as I pass, doing a double-take at the name on the screen.

"Nick?"

"What's this about your father having Alzheimer's?"

"He doesn't have Alzheimer's."

"Dementia?"

"Yes." I rub a hand over my face. I can trust Nick and probably should've told him by now, but still... "Who told you?" I look down the hall in the direction Caroline traveled. "Are you working with a firm called Arrow?"

"Mutual contacts."

"Hmm."

I lean against the counter. Outside, night has fallen. Pure white coats the nearby surroundings in a pristine, glistening blanket, lit by the lights from the house. How many inches have we gotten?

"It's looking like I owe you an apology. My tech guys located the hit origin. Spoke to the actual human hired to set it up.

Didn't operate the way you would've handled it. You'd have used one of your own. Been smarter about it. I should've known you wouldn't aim to kill me."

"At the very least, you should've known I'd be more efficient. Two hundred and fifty million is nouveau riche territory—all flash, no sophistication. If I wanted you dead, I'd have engineered a more elegant solution."

He chuckles. But I'm quite serious. Whoever posted a two-hundred-and-fifty-million-dollar bounty might as well have walked outside and taken a blowtorch to a pile of cash. If I'm going to spend that much, I at least want a nice boat out of it. I might be a billionaire, but I have principles.

"Who posted the hit?"

"Tracing a blockchain now."

So the culprit used crypto for payment. It takes longer to track, but contrary to popular mythology, it can be traced. "Who do you suspect?"

Nick has ideas. As long as I've known him, he's always had a theory.

"An alliance member. I'd decided on your dad. He'd go about it the way this bloke did. But it doesn't sound like that's conceivable. After getting it so wrong with you and your dad, I'll wait a beat for my team to come through with answers."

"That's good of you."

"I hear Caroline's still with you."

"Did you plant listening devices in my home?" I pull up the security dashboard on my phone, scanning the latest RF sweep results. The quantum encryption system I had installed last quarter should make any surveillance attempts futile, but Nick's always been creative. "Jensen swept the place last week, but you've always enjoyed a challenge."

He chuckles.

The fucker.

"Not me, mate. Our mutual acquaintances aren't so quick to absolve you of misdeeds. Your lady reported it in. Boomeranged to me for verification."

So Caroline is his source. Should I be annoyed at that?

"Why didn't you tell me about your father?"

You didn't ask, is on the tip of my tongue, but instead, I share the truth. "Happened slowly. I was protecting him. And he still has lucid days." Although, if I'm honest, it's more lucid moments.

"Hmm."

The noise that comes across the line is loaded. "What do you mean by that?"

"If he's got his head on straight some days..."

"You already said you determined neither of us—"

"Right. Right. Still, someone's out there. Alliance member or not, these are black times. If I were you, I'd keep her there."

"From your lips to god's ear."

"I'm serious."

"So am I."

"Hey, cock twit, time to think with your bigger brain. My warning has nothing to do with the fact that you never got over your ex. If Armageddon breaks, she's in one of the safest places she can be."

"Is it that bad?" In my mind, it's all posturing. No one's really going to do something that would bring about catastrophe. All of my sources agree. Those in power have too much vested in the market.

"Someone's casting a lot of shade. Tensions between governments are rising. I'd say we're about two incidents away from escalation to a world war."

I pull up the latest satellite telemetry on my phone. Three of our birds over the Pacific reported anomalous signals last week. Could be nothing—solar flares mess with the equipment all the time—but coincidences make me uneasy. Especially when they align with Nick's networks picking up chatter.

"And you believe it's someone from the alliance?"

The unofficial consortium of tech billionaires and industry titans that meets quarterly in places like Davos and Singapore didn't believe we're in any more danger than normal, and also believed what we're seeing is more or less business as usual. But I've had moments where my concerns have risen exponentially. I turn to rational minds to calm my nerves. Reality is, it's hard to trust anyone when the global telecommunications infrastructure is a chess piece, as much as I want to trust that all is good.

"My sources claim it's not Russia," Nick says.

"How good are your sources?"

"That's always the question, isn't it?"

CHAPTER 20

CAROLINE

Beyond the guest bathroom's picture window, the floodlights cast a warm glow over a delicate blanket that has fallen over the nearby tree limbs. The soaking tub is positioned in front of the window and sits on heated tile in an open wet room shower. Thick white towels are piled on a dark wood table, and glass bottles with bath salts, matches, and candles line shelves tucked within the wall.

Weariness nips at my limbs, as does a chill.

I twist the faucet, letting steaming hot water fill the ceramic basin. My brain hasn't clicked back on entirely, but misgivings seep in all the same.

What did I do?

I did what I wanted.

Or did I?

He's always possessed an uncanny ability to weaken my walls and reshuffle my priorities.

Why open myself up?

Why risk rupturing old wounds?

At least I cleared his father's name. The senior Moore is definitely not the one causing issues or playing Prophet. And neither is Dorian.

It might be the Russians. They're experts at deception, creating doubt and discord. And they're also the country that benefits the most from the disintegration of the EU and the United States.

Dorian is allowing the world to believe his father is still functioning. Is someone taking advantage of his father's deteriorating mental capacity? Setting him up? But for what?

I drop my clothes on the floor in a messy pile and slide into the water. I whip my hair into a self-tied bun and rest my head on the back of the tub for a view into a starless sky.

There's a soft rap on the door.

"Come in."

The door cracks open, and Dorian peers in.

"The tub in my bathroom is better."

"I'm sure it is." *The master suite is always the best.*

"You should move your things to my bedroom."

"Is that so?" I smile, but he frowns.

"Why are you bathing before dinner? Do you need to wash yourself of me?"

The unexpected vulnerability catches me off guard.

"I was chilled. And this is quite the setup." He doesn't look convinced. "Care to join me?"

His expression shifts, the hard lines around his eyes softening. For a moment, he looks almost like the man I met so many years ago—less guarded, a hint of surprise in his eyes as if he hadn't expected the invitation. The corner of his mouth lifts in a half smile, erasing years of practiced stoicism.

He sets two fluffy white towels on the counter's edge near the tub and undresses.

"Which end do you want me?"

I slide forward, making room for him. Perhaps it would be best to have him across from me, at a distance, so we could talk while facing each other, but my preference is to rest against his chest.

Water sloshes over the tub as he gets in, but neither of us cares. It's a wet bathroom, designed for mess.

It takes a minute for us to get settled, for his legs to form to the sides of the tub, and for me to find a comfortable spot in front of him, but once I'm settled in his arms, the confusion from earlier dissipates, replaced by a sense of peace.

He presses his lips to the side of my head and tightens his hold.

"There's one question that keeps me up at night." His breath tickles my ear.

"What's that?" I rest my head against his shoulder, peering up for a profile view of his deep-set eyes and dark, thick eyebrows.

"I gave you everything I could. Everything I had the power to give. But it wasn't enough. You weren't happy. What did you need that I didn't give?"

"Oxygen."

The answer is painfully honest. I suffocated in his world until I reached a do-or-die juncture.

"Hmm." His response vibrates from his chest through my spine. "The attention?"

"It wasn't just that. You expected me to give up everything. For my days to circle yours, for my purpose to be you, and I know…you deserve a woman who will give up everything to be with you. But I wasn't strong enough." I'm not strong enough now. Or am I misspeaking? Is it stronger to endure an unhealthy relationship, or stronger to enact change for a better situation?

"I'd argue the opposite."

Of course, he would.

His fingers glide along my arm, dip into the water, and cup my breast. I love the ease with which he touches my body. I've missed the intimacy between us.

That's not correct. I've missed intimacy, period.

"You were a beacon of strength. Instead of falling in line with my father's expectations, you walked away. It's something I've never done."

That catches my attention. "Are you not leading the life you want?"

Of course, he is.

"Look at everything you've done. You envisioned Zenith and created it. You're chairman of the board of Bedrock, a position your father dangled like a carrot. People are floating your name as a presidential contender."

"I don't have the patience for politics."

I turn against him, my smile wide and teasing. "What exactly do you call chief of staff?"

"A limited engagement that would allow me to reset the course of the current administration and ensure defense priorities align with Zenith. Plus, it's access to the heads of state from around the world." He weaves his fingers through mine and submerges our linked fingers below the waterline. "That's all it would be. It's not a lifelong dream of mine."

"Contracts?" He's referring to coveted Department of Defense contracts. "You mentioned earlier about government contracts and conflicts of interest. What exactly would something like that be worth?"

"Over ten years, we're talking over a trillion dollars."

"And no one would care about that size of a conflict of interest?"

"Anyone in government possesses personal interest."

"You mean corruption?"

He lifts our joined hands and playfully nips at my nail. *That's not an answer.*

"Am I to take it that selling you on joining me as first lady would be a challenge?"

"I thought you just said you don't want to be president?" I twist so I can observe his facial expressions and read the truth.

"I don't." He sighs. "Is it bad that I'm grateful for my father's dementia? If he were as sharp as he was in the past, this farce would balloon out of control. He'd already be fundraising, and a strategist would've been hired. There's no doubt I'd be in the primary. Can't say I'd win, but—"

"Americans love you. You're well-spoken, photogenic, and pedigreed."

"You make me sound like a prize dog." His lips purse, and his eyes narrow. He squeezes my legs between his, the movement sending a wave of water cascading over the edge. "No, I wouldn't be a serious candidate unless I promised the right things to the right leaders."

"The oligarchs?"

"Let's skip the bashing. But if my father were of sound mind, he'd be making those deals. I'd probably have a full-time campaign advisor camped out in a DC hotel."

"Why didn't your father ever run for president?"

"Eight wives? Documented pattern of adultery. For most of his life, he assumed he'd be too scandal-prone. Left politics to his brother. By the time he realized Americans no longer cared about sex scandals, he considered himself too old and he'd pissed off too many. Plus, he'd gone too long without a boss."

"The president doesn't have a boss."

"The sitting president has a list of people he owes. Depending on what those people have on him, that can be worse than a boss."

"You've thought a lot about this."

"Not really. My priority has been Zenith. Until you showed up at my gate."

He swirls the water, and silence descends. He absentmindedly cups my breast again and brushes his thumb back and forth across my nipple. My muscles relax, and I rest my head on his shoulder once more. His heart thuds against my back, the vibration muted but recognizable and soothing.

"Oxygen, huh?" It's a matter-of-fact statement. "For years, I thought you left because I pushed for children."

"I can see why you would assume that. It's the only disagreement I stood firm on. Other than that one thing, I dressed as directed, filled my calendar as requested, and smiled at dinners and events."

"I thought you liked the access to designers."

"I did. At first. And I appreciated the gowns for events. But you were absent, and...I became this prop. A tool for a game I wasn't privy to. And I failed at it. I never met your expectations."

"That's not true."

"I definitely never met your father's. He wanted you to divorce me."

"Why do you say that?"

"I overheard you talking."

"So you left. Rather than talk to me, you said you weren't happy, and you left?"

The words strung together haul a load of anger, but his tone is more of a person who is slowly putting together all the pieces of a puzzle.

"For the record, I wanted children—one day. But we weren't happy. Children aren't the solution to an unhealthy marriage."

"We didn't have a bad marriage."

At that, I sit up so I can give him my aghast expression. "Come on now."

He's arguing in that head of his. I can see it.

"My parents, your dad, they all agreed our marriage was a mistake. You were distant. If you spoke to me, it almost always led to a fight. Mostly, you'd just look at me, silent, with god knows what going on in that head of yours. And then we'd walk out into public view, and you'd smile and pull me close and morph into this happy-go-lucky guy, and it was maddening. If I went out alone and found myself chased by photographers… you minimized my fear. Told me I wasn't handling it right. They wouldn't hurt me if I just smiled. That I was being silly." *God, I hate that word. A man is never silly. Only a woman.*

"Why didn't you give me a choice?"

"Like what? Move to a small town out of the public eye?"

"If that's what it took." He says it like it's so simple. Like any of that was on the table. "You didn't give me a chance. You didn't talk to me."

He's right, sort of. I did, but I didn't.

"I lacked the confidence. I possessed enough self-awareness to recognize I wasn't in a healthy place, but not enough to believe you would choose me, that you would even hear me. I didn't believe it mattered to you." And for that matter, I still don't. He wouldn't have walked away from his father, and it would have been selfish to ask him to.

"And when I didn't chase after you, I confirmed your beliefs."

It's not an apology, but he sounds apologetic.

"It was for the best." The automatic words flow unhindered.

He rests his chin against the side of my head. "You leaving was the worst thing to happen in my life."

My mouth forms an *O*, but before a thought coalesces, he's up, sending a tidal wave of water over the edge of the tub. He wraps a towel around his waist and then holds one for me.

The water temperature has cooled, and my skin is pruned, so I concur…it's time.

"Is there any chance I can convince you to snuggle with me?"

"Snuggle?" I can't block the incredulous smile. "Who are you, and what did you do to the business titan I married?"

Water droplets glide down his chest, and my gaze follows their trail down his fit abdomen to his towel. His work ethic clearly still extends from the office to the gym.

He smirks with cocky awareness.

"Is that a yes or a no?" he asks.

"Where do you want to snuggle?"

"My bed."

I half-laugh but quickly realize he's serious.

"Best view in the house. A fireplace."

There's a knowing look in his eye. When we first started dating, our favorite days were lazy Sundays. It's not Sunday, it's Friday, but it's the state of mind, not the day of the week.

"All right," I say. "Lead the way."

He doesn't lead, though. Instead, he slows his steps to match mine, and we walk side by side into his lair.

He tosses throw pillows to the floor and pulls back the luxurious comforter, gesturing for me to climb into his bed. I step forward, but he grips my towel.

"You don't need this."

I roll my eyes, but his comment is 100 percent expected. I let the towel drop and climb onto the bed. He drops his towel and settles beside me, pulling the comforter over both of us and me into his side.

"You're more confident now." His statement is matter-of-fact, void of judgment. "Why? Or should I ask who?"

"Langley." The word hangs between us. The CIA changed me in ways I still can't fully explain to civilians—even him. Gone is the naïve twenty-two-year-old who felt overwhelmed by his world. Intelligence work teaches you to see past the superficial power plays, to recognize that even billionaires are just people with their own vulnerabilities and tells.

I settle down on a pillow, facing him, and he turns on his side, mirroring my position.

"What are you thinking?" I ask.

"You really want to know?"

"It drives me crazy when you don't tell me." The argument is an echo of our past, but it's different, because now I'm telling him exactly how I feel.

"All right. I'm wondering what I'm going to have to do to win you back. Because I want you back."

"I'm not a possession."

"Agreed. You're the love of my life. How do I fix us?"

The irony isn't lost on me. Here's a man who can buy politicians and redirect satellites with a phone call, asking me how to fix something money can't solve. Seven years ago, this vulnerability from him would have melted my resolve. Now, I recognize it as either genuine growth or excellent artifice. The trouble is, both look the same.

It doesn't matter. You can't fix a relationship that's seven years stale. And I'm smart enough to know that for a man like Dorian, a man who has gotten literally everything he's ever wanted and can buy anything he wants, he wants me now because I'm the one thing he didn't get to keep. If I stayed, he'd fall right back into the routine where I ranked last. Maybe not at first, but eventually.

I open my mouth to tell him we've run our course, but he stops me with his lips. And soon, he does what he's always excelled at. He eradicates all thought.

CHAPTER 21

DORIAN

Caroline's head rests on my chest, and her arm stretches across my middle, asleep. The faint thump of her heartbeat reverberates through my rib cage. Her long hair cascades down her narrow back, and her soft breasts press against my side.

Outside, snowflakes glint when the light catches them right, and behind them is a wall of black. I should check the weather, see if conditions have changed.

The phone on my bedside table lights up, darkens, and lights up so regularly it might be Morse code. I should check that, too.

But I don't want to move. I don't want to leave this spot—ever. I can't remember feeling this at peace. Even when we were together before, when everything was new, I didn't feel this peaceful. I was too young; I had too many pressures, and if I'm honest, I didn't appreciate the fragility of our relationship. With marriage, an impressive diamond on her finger, and an unlimited spending black card in her wallet, I believed she'd never leave. Not unless I cheated, and cheating was never an option. Sure, my father's wives all eventually left him, but he flaunted his indiscretions. I believed if he hadn't cheated, any of his wives, even possibly my mother, would've remained, no matter how empty the marriage.

I underestimated Caroline.

The press declared she was nothing but a social climber, but she proved them wrong.

Dad told me to be prepared for an attempt to break our prenuptial agreement and for tears, begging for additional funds. She proved him wrong.

Our only disagreement, one we're still technically battling, is over a piece of land she inherited while we were married. I never wanted the land. I fought her on principle. Or that's what I told myself. In reality, I was angry. I wanted to make leaving me as difficult as possible.

I'm no longer angry. I've gone through all the emotions: anger, sadness, depression, denial, acceptance. A healthy person goes through the cycle once. Lucky guy that I am, I cycle through the emotions annually.

Nick's call from earlier comes to mind. He said she's safest here. With me in Colorado. I should check in, learn more, but that requires moving. It requires contact with the outside world and breaking this solitude.

The screen on my phone brightens an area on the bedside table, lighting up with a call, then darkening, then lighting up again. It's Friday evening. *Who the hell is so persistent?*

I don't want to move to check the phone, but given Nick's advice, instinct blended with curiosity urges me to check.

I stretch slowly, doing my best to leave Caroline undisturbed. She needs her rest because I'm not done with her. Not by a long shot. I've also realized something over these last twenty-four hours. She could be eighty and walk into a room, and I'd still want her. There's a connection between us that's hard to describe. It's as if my soul recognizes hers, even when my brain gets lost in other matters.

The question I keep coming back to is what will it take to win her back?

And what will it take to keep her? I don't think I'd survive her walking out again.

Stretched across the bed, my fingers reach the phone, and I finagle it into my hand to check the screen. Thirty-five missed calls from my assistant. The hair on the back of my neck rises.

No texts. No stock market is open. Did war break out?

Begrudgingly, I slip off the bed, pull on sweats and a thermal, and silently pad out of the room, pulling the door closed quietly. On the way through the house to my office, I press call.

A sense of dread fills me as my mind swirls with the possibilities of what could have happened. I'm barefoot, and the tile chills my feet, and a fleeting thought passes that I should've grabbed socks.

A vision of Caroline sprawled in my bed flashes, and I'm gut-punched with regret that I'm not lying in that bed with her. But no, I'm headed to the office. My command center.

"Jay," I say the second I hear him pick up. "What's going on?"

"It's your father." I halt in the glass corridor.

Flakes swirl haphazardly, lit only by the light streaming from the side of the house, twisting about in a winding, downward fall.

"What?"

"He's fine, but he had a tough afternoon."

Jay has been my executive assistant since I moved Zenith's headquarters to Denver—hand-picked from McKinsey, with the security clearances and discretion required to handle both my corporate empire and family matters. He's one of the few who know the truth about my father's health.

"He's railing. Wants to see you. The nurses aren't sure what to do. Prashi, she's the head weekend nurse, recommended we consider a sedative, but you've got in his chart—"

"He'll calm down." I'm not actually opposed to sedatives, but my father is. Although, we may have reached the stage where he's not lucid enough for his preference to matter.

"It might help if you visit him. Or call him. He's irate. He broke a lamp. Threw a glass against the wall."

I turn in the opposite direction.

"I mean, I know it's getting late. He may have calmed down by now—"

"I'll go."

"I have to warn you, sir. He doesn't sound…"

The hesitation in Jay's voice tips me off that my father is railing about me. The demons in his head are screaming that I've earned his disapproval. He spent time with Caroline today.

"Say it."

"He's been shouting about your wife. That she's going to rob you blind. That you're too weak and we need lawyers, stat. He successfully reached a lawyer, by the way. One by the name of Duncan Wallace. He's not one of ours. I'm not sure where he got the number. Possibly Google directory. I called his office and canceled the emergency meeting he requested. Prashi has his phone now. I think that's part of the reason he's so angry."

Once again, my feet have stopped. I pinch the bridge of my nose. I can't deal with my father when he's out of his mind.

Seeing Caroline set him off. He must believe no time has passed. He'd been livid with me back then because I refused to use his legal team to handle my divorce.

"Tell Prashi that she has my approval to administer a sedative."

"I'll text her. She'll want it in writing. I'll include you in the exchange."

"That's fine."

"I have a couple of other urgent items while I have you on the line."

Jay isn't one to label an item urgent unless it is.

"You've got me for five minutes." I shoot a wistful glance in the direction of my bedroom but turn on my heel to my office.

"The president doesn't want to wait until Tuesday for an in-person meeting. He's requested a time on Monday. I told him you would make yourself available."

What could he possibly want?

"Schedule it." The curt response is automatic.

"Droga sent through an email he wanted you to read."

"What's it about?"

"He has a notation that only you can read it. His assistant called before she sent it and explained that he doesn't want anyone but you to read the contents."

It's probably some news he's debating running. Drago owns a publishing network that covers most English-speaking countries in the Americas and Europe.

"I'll check it out. On my way to my computer now."

"You have calls scheduled with Australia and Japan on Sunday evening. I've left you a reminder. Do you want me to initiate the calls?"

"No, if the information is in my calendar, I'll call. Who's it with?"

"Ah, let's see. Both are for Zenith."

"Can you ask Suzette to cover?" She's my COO. She should be able to handle anything.

"She's the one who scheduled the calls, sir. These are one-off conversations."

He goes on to repeat the names of pompous, egotistical men who want to ensure I bribe them appropriately before they rubber stamp our government contracts.

I'll make the time for the meetings. These aren't just satellite contracts; they're strategic plays in the larger game of global telecommunications dominance. When you control the orbital infrastructure, every conversation with foreign officials has layers of implications.

"Fine."

"I think that's it, sir. Droga asked that you get back to him as quickly as possible."

"Is this from yesterday?"

"No, about an hour ago. I had trouble reaching you. He also called to check that you were okay. He saw the news about the crash."

"I'll check it."

"Will you be available tomorrow?"

Saturday. Movement in the doorway catches my attention. It's Caroline, wearing one of my button-down shirts, thick wool socks, and nothing else.

Fuck me, she's gorgeous.

My gaze locks with hers.

"No. If something urgent arises, text, don't call. Tell me what the issue is, and I'll respond if it's warranted."

"Yes, sir."

Jay knows to limit the content of his text, but as a precaution, I add, "Limit what you share, of course."

He'll understand. In any lawsuit, texts and emails can be subpoenaed.

I end the call and push up from my desk, but as I do, I remember Droga. If he's sending over a story as a courtesy, and I delay in responding, he might release it, and I'll lose my chance to bury it.

Unfortunately, Caroline reads me.

"Do you need some time?"

She claims I keep things in my head, but she's so good at reading me it often feels I don't have to speak. "Unfortunately. Give me ten minutes?"

I hope she can hear the apology in my tone.

"No problem. I should check in."

"Can you do me a favor?"

She pauses, waiting, and I take in her long, lean legs and the flirtatious curve of the hemline. "Keep that outfit on. Okay? No changing."

Her smile reaches her blue, blissful eyes. I take that as a win.

CHAPTER 22

CAROLINE

My cheeks flame, and it's impossible to suppress a smile. It's the way his dark eyes heat when he sees something he wants, and well, when that something is me.

My socks slide against the tile, and with one cautious glance to confirm I'm alone, I glide across the corridor like a figure skater. I'm lost in the Dorian high. I forgot what it's like to be wanted by a powerful man who can have anyone he desires.

Movement along the tree line catches my attention, and I instinctively scan the perimeter. Three visible security cameras, probably infrared coverage, and what looks like a ground-based motion detection system, which probably triggered the floodlight. Still, something feels off about those shadows.

Security wouldn't hide, especially if they noticed I observed them. There are pockets in the snow, shadowy dips that might be the shape of a shoe. It's too far on the perimeter to see from inside. I'd need to go outside to investigate, but...why? It's probably deer.

The compound is secure. I'm in one of the safest homes in America.

With one last glance across the snow-covered clearing to the wood's edge, I find my way to the guestroom.

You should move your things into my bedroom.

His words come back to me. It's tempting. If he insists, I'll acquiesce. But I won't take that step on my own. He's going to need to ask again. Or to move my suitcase himself. Most of my clothes were whisked away by his staff for cleaning.

What am I doing?

He's addictive. It's a slippery slope, and one I didn't navigate well at all years ago. The resulting fall fractured me. It took years to mend, and I bear the scars. Are the scars strong enough to prevent me from repeating past mistakes? Probably not.

But no, they are. I will return home to my job and my newfound friends and to the cute little cottage I found within walking distance of State Street. I am experiencing a momentary lapse in reason. As long as I keep my feet on the ground and my mind focused, I'm good.

Once he's chief of staff, he'll be rooted in DC. And *that* is a life I don't want. Life on a campaign trail? Definitely not.

With a sense of determination that's undercut by the cool air circulating my tush, I dial Sophia while scanning the vents, searching for a telltale red light. Of course, he claimed there's no interior surveillance when he's home, but it's best to assume I'm being recorded. Although, depending on how often Dorian entertains, maybe not. He and his father have always valued their privacy. He wouldn't want his nameless staff being aware of what happens between him and his guests.

"Caroline?"

"Yeah. It's me." I scooch on the bed, backing up to the pillows stacked along the headboard. "How are things?"

"I'm glad you called. We were debating how best to reach you."

I'm easily reachable. I also promised to keep in touch.

"Kairi and Erik's team have uncovered additional information. You need to leave. Get to the airport."

"What're you talking about?"

"Be careful what you say. There's a good chance you're being recorded."

We discussed that before I left. I haven't forgotten. Although, I doubt it's true...

"Caroline?"

I roll my eyes. Not that she can see. "I'm here."

"You said his father has dementia. Yes?"

"Yes." I cross one ankle over the other, settling in for whatever accusations the team has cooked up.

"We're sending a car to get you. Pack up your stuff, and we'll tell you when to head to the gate."

"What? No." The response is automatic and heartfelt. She's wrong. They've been stabbing in the dark and coming up with conspiracy nonsense, all because no one wants to believe the obvious.

"You still believe he won't hurt you?"

"I know he won't." Again, I feel the truth in my bones. They are off on him.

"If you saw this report, you wouldn't feel the same."

"Give me the highlights."

"We have confirmation Dorian met with arms dealers and government leaders that the CIA holds on a terrorist watch list."

"What kind of confirmation?"

"Travel records from his private jet plus commercial flights."

Dorian flies commercial? Doubtful.

"Give me a minute. I'll log into the portal so I can respond."

I locate my Arrow-issued laptop with its custom encryption suite, authenticate through three separate security protocols, and access our darknet communications portal. In the protection of my suitcase, it survived the wreck unscathed. In an abundance of caution, I position myself to avoid any possible surveillance angles.

Where I'm situated on the bed, it's impossible for a camera to have a view of my screen. The ceiling lights aren't positioned over the bed. There's a framed landscape photograph behind the bed, and I lift it, scanning to ensure there are no wires. There aren't. The frame's clear. I tap away on my laptop.

ME

At best, it's circumstantial. Zenith sells satellite capabilities to countries. Interested customers could easily make someone's watch list.

SF

An overview of his financial positions shows consistent hedging of complex derivative trades and short positions just before events.

That's interesting, but...

ME

Circumstantial.

SF

Stop. Let me relay the highlights of the report.

SF

The team identified encrypted communications sent at odd hours from his father's account. Conversations with known extremists and Russian sympathizers. EXTENSIVE conversations. And you said it can t be his father.

SF

The team tracked calls to burner phones in countries where the attacks occurred, plus calls to many of his father's known associates. Which, again, you said he's not making those phone calls, yet those calls have been increasing in frequency, not declining.

SF

Searches from the compound on infrastructure vulnerabilities. Including searches on chemical weapons and their effects.

How did they track his searches?

SF

Over the last several years, he's installed security upgrades, including the installation of military-grade communications equipment. We tracked the purchases and confirmed delivery.

ME

All circumstantial.

SF

I'm not done.

SF

Check the attachment. It details
documents we located by hacking into a
server the Moores own in Iceland. It's a
series of detailed technical documents
outlining infrastructure vulnerabilities,
time-stamped months before the
attacks. All written in Dorian's distinctive
technical style. That could never have
been his father, as Dorian is the
tech guy.

SF

We originally thought he was working
with his father, but if what you are saying
is true, he's executing this on his own or
with others within the alliance.

SF

And this isn't everything. Since 2015,
he's attended twenty-two conferences
with well-known cyber warfare experts.

ME

Pattern analysis 101—correlation isn't causation. We're building a narrative from disparate data points. What's our confidence level on the Iceland server attribution? Hedge fund managers always have complex trading positions. And cyber warfare conferences are industry standard for satellite companies.

I can hear the defensive tone in my response. Can she? But since the beginning, this investigation has been a series of throwing theories at a wall.

The analyst in me can't ignore the pattern, but something doesn't track. Why would someone controlling 80 percent of global satellite infrastructure need burner phones? And the technical documents—if they were really from Dorian, they'd be exponentially more sophisticated. He thinks in quantum computing terms, not infrastructure vulnerabilities.

SF

Are you back with him?

SF

Is your judgment skewed?

It was only a matter of time before she asked.

Is my judgment skewed? The CIA trained us to separate emotional attachments from analysis, but they also taught us to trust our instincts. And everything about this evidence feels too neat, too perfectly arranged—like intelligence crafted to tell a specific story rather than raw data pointing to a conclusion.

Dorian fills the doorframe, his dark eyes watching me. But this time, instead of girlish glee or lust, nerves erupt.

CHAPTER 23

CAROLINE

"What're you doing?"

His tone is icy. Or is that my imagination?

I close the lid on the laptop.

His gaze falls to my lap, then flits to my face.

Corded tension connects us, spanning the space between us like a deadly live wire.

Stop it. Your imagination is spinning out of control.

Sophia's grasping at straws. She's off base.

This is Dorian.

"I want you in my bedroom." He places his hands in his pockets.

A Langley trainer would say to be alert if the hands are hidden, but this is Dorian. What am I afraid of? That he's got a weapon shoved in his sweatpants pockets?

"Why are you in here?"

He scans the ceiling and then the windows. It's dark outside, pure black through the window now that the floodlights have clicked off.

His questions slowly filter through my conscience. He wants me in his bedroom. This isn't an inquisition. He didn't magically read my computer screen.

"Ah, this is where I had my things."

He rocks back on his heels. With those observant eyes, he reads me too well. He's picked up on my unease. That's the reason he's standing by the door, giving me space. My oxygen.

"When I said I want you in my bedroom, I meant it. Did you doubt me?"

He's focusing on the bedroom. And he'd only do that if he has no idea what accusations are being torpedoed his way.

Do you believe he's innocent? Because if you do, it's time to stop playing games and get the information you need to prove his innocence. Otherwise, Luke or others from Arrow are going to blast their way in to save you from the imagined monster.

With that thought, I flip open the laptop.

I'm logging off. Still staying the weekend.
I'll be in touch.

I scroll upwards, reviewing the messages and the evidence Arrow's tech team found.

"What's wrong?"

If I'm going to come clean, we shouldn't be in a bedroom.

"Can we talk?"

"Isn't that what—" He stops himself. His lips press together, and he angles his head to the side, as if there's a conversation going on in that head of his. "Yes. We can talk. We can talk about anything you want."

"Is there a place we can talk that's…not a bedroom?"

A barely there, sexy smirk flits across his face, but it passes so quickly I'm not positive it existed.

"Is this work-related?"

"Can we talk somewhere secure?" The CIA term slips out before I can stop it. In this world of quantum computing and satellite surveillance, 'secure' has layers of meaning, and in Dorian's house, those layers are particularly complex.

His head jerks back like I've slapped him.

"I already told you. No one is monitoring my home."

"You have a full security staff. They aren't in the house with you. How do they monitor to ensure you're safe?"

"The surveillance equipment is on the outside of the house and grounds." He's telling the truth about traditional security systems, but Zenith's quantum-encrypted communications network could theoretically turn any networked device into a listening post. It's the kind of capability that keeps counterintelligence analysts up at night. "No one could arrive at the house without being picked up. Physically impossible. There's no need for surveillance inside the house." His eyebrows close in over the bridge of his nose. "But it's not only my security team you're thinking about, is it?"

"Let's go to your office." Arrow will be listening. When I address what they are accusing him of, they'll hear him.

He steps back, gesturing to the hall. I lift my laptop, and cool air nips at my bare legs. His sweats I wore earlier are up in his bedroom. I shouldn't address the accusations against him without pants on.

"Can you give me a minute?" I ask, closing the laptop.

I run up the stairs, leaving a confused Dorian in my wake. I slip on the sweatpants and sweatshirt I wore earlier. Still his clothes, but they're better than his dress shirt.

What am I doing? What does it matter what I'm wearing? Why am I uneasy?

The answer is all too clear. There's a part of me that's worried he's guilty. That he's the one who has instigated these incidents around the globe. He wouldn't aim to usurp democracy. He's no made-for-television villain. But he's dedicated his career to building Zenith. Is he hoping to increase fears so more governments enter into contracts with Zenith? The assumption all along has been that these mini-attacks are tests of the systems in place for a larger-scale incursion. What if the mini-attacks are all he's planned? What if his ethical boundaries have shifted? His risk tolerance in business has increased since our marriage. The Dorian I knew would never have attempted to corner the global satellite market. But he did, and he succeeded. Where else might those boundaries have moved? In intelligence work, targets almost always believe they're serving a greater good.

Dorian would never aim to kill millions or destroy the world order, but he's susceptible to misguided notions. Perhaps he believes fear will drive nations to prioritize defense spending, and thus the world will be more secure.

"Should I come up there?" Footsteps sound on the steps.

"No. I'm coming."

I round the corner, and he smirks.

"No, unfortunately, you aren't. But we can fix that."

He climbs a step, but I point down the stairs.

"We're going to have that conversation."

The question is, do I really want Arrow to hear it?

The CIA trained me to compartmentalize, to separate personal feelings from professional judgment. But they also taught me to trust verified intelligence over circumstantial evidence. Arrow's data points to Dorian, but something feels orchestrated about it—too perfect, like a trail deliberately left for analysts to follow. The kind of false flag operation I used to brief senior officials about.

Where do my loyalties lie? With my employer or my ex-husband?

I need more information.

"Let's talk here in the kitchen."

CHAPTER 24

DORIAN

She pulls a seat out from the kitchen table and directs me to sit across from her. I do as she asks, and it occurs to me that I don't think I've ever sat at this table.

I always sit at the kitchen counter to eat. If I dine with my father, we eat at his house. I don't entertain. If it weren't for my father, I would vacation in Colorado, not live here. I built this house to have a space to retreat to when needed. Caring for my father can be challenging, even with a round-the-clock staff.

She opens her laptop, and I itch to flip it around to see if she's written up her points.

Did she see a therapist who listed our issues and recommended solutions?

"There are those who believe you're behind..." She avoids my gaze.

A cold dread spreads from my chest to my fingertips, numbing as it travels.

"Illegal activities."

Our serious conversation has nothing to do with us? I should've known.

"We've collected evidence."

"Who's we?"

Back straight, shoulders back, she's addressing me with a formality I recognize. I'm in my home, in sweats and a thermal, and she's addressing me like we're in a board meeting. Suddenly, Caroline's desire to change out of my shirt and talk in a common area makes a lot more sense.

"Arrow Tactical Security." She swallows and clears her throat. "And others."

"Who hired Arrow?"

My interruption to her presentation throws her, evident by her right eye's twitch.

"What?"

"Arrow. I'm familiar with the firm. Jack Sullivan is the primary investor. Countries hire the organization. Which country hired Arrow Tactical to investigate me?"

Come on, Caroline. You had to know I'd ask. Given they know she's here, they know I'm asking.

"Do you know Jack Sullivan?"

I raise an eyebrow and link my hands beneath the table, keeping my calm.

Jack and Liam Sullivan inherited Sullivan Arms, a leading gun manufacturer, but they've grown the business into a global weapons manufacturer. I'm told Liam Sullivan leads R&D, and rumor has it, he's expanded into weapons of mass destruction and drones. From what I gathered, Jack Sullivan is an investor in Arrow Tactical and has nothing to do with day-to-day operations.

"This project is a joint effort by intelligence agencies around the world." She slides the laptop a couple of inches to the side but keeps it within easy striking distance. She must have something on there to show me.

Intelligence agencies. International investigation. My fingers drum the tabletop. I hold government contracts all over the world. I'm investigated all the time.

"Don't keep me waiting. Please, share the details of the investigation."

If she's here, and there's an international investigation, we're not talking about minor regulatory violations or accounting malpractice.

"What do you think I've done?"

"I don't..." She stops herself, and her lips press together. When she lifts her gaze to mine, I sense her determination. "Over the past year, minor attacks have been occurring around the world."

She has to be fucking kidding. That's what this is?

"Baltic Sea wire cutting, attacks on electrical substations, an EMP attack—"

"That EMP attack cost me forty next-gen satellites and upwards of a billion dollars in classified government contracts. It's the kind of loss that makes the Pentagon nervous." My jaw clenches.

"Covered by insurance."

Unfuckingbelievable. "Insurance doesn't cover the strategic implications of losing military-grade orbital infrastructure."

She turns the computer around. On the screen, I read through an exchange between CS and SF.

"Caroline Scott? Using your maiden name at work?"

She hasn't legally changed her last name from Moore. If she'd done so, I would've been notified.

"Are you innocent?"

Way to bypass the question, *Scott*. "Of attacking the world?" I scrub my hands through my hair, aiming to corral my thoughts.

She believes this bullshit. And if she can believe this, she doesn't know me. Definitely doesn't love me. This weekend hasn't been about us working things out or even closing things out. It's been a ploy.

I push up from the table. I can't sit there.

The screen on the mobile lights up. I don't give a shit who's contacting me, but I'm on autopilot and head to the counter.

> ALERT: Explosion at Orange County
> Utility Leads to Extended Blackout

I flash the phone screen to Caroline. "Do you think I did this, too?"

I can't deal with this. I need space.

"Where are you going?"

I don't bother answering.

With one loud slam of the door, I'm out, charging away.

I'm halfway to the winding path when it occurs to me she can take an Uber into Denver.

Let her.

Leaves crunch beneath the thin layer of snow, and a biting cold slices through to my skin.

What the fuck is wrong with you?

I spin around, returning home.

Within seconds, I fling the door open right as my phone lights up.

GEOFFREY CROMWELL

Your father wants me to inquire if you made the requested changes to your portfolio.

Isn't Dad drugged?

The drugs probably made him just lucid enough to fall into his worry track on whether I'm taking his investment advice. *Fuck me.*

Through the open doorway, I shout, "I'll be back. Don't go anywhere." Leaving will probably piss her off, but she's got to understand. "I need to calm down, but I will return."

There. That's mature.

I've never been to a therapist, but I have to believe that's what he'd tell me to say.

The door slams with an earsplitting loud bang.

I didn't quite mean to slam it, but it's a heavy fucking door.

The walk to my father's house passes in a blur. By the time his house comes into view, I've got some ideas on how to prove to Caroline that the accusations are meritless. She's going to feel like shit once I prove I'm not the asshole she believes me to be. Or will she?

Maybe this is all one big work project. She didn't plan on spending the weekend.

Of course, Nick also mentioned the attacks. Is he the entity funding Arrow's investigation? He told me to keep Caroline here.

Is more going on than I read in those messages between Caroline and SF?

I've always assumed Putin was behind the crap going on around the world. He's the worst kind of greedy because what he wants more than anything is power and for history to see him as one of Russia's great leaders, which in his mind requires expansion, treating the world like a Risk board for megalomaniacs. China's Xi isn't much better, but Europe doesn't fit into his near-term or even mid-term goals.

My father's house is quiet as I enter. It's always quiet. He has plenty of staff, but they're relegated to other sections of the house.

A light glows below the door to my father's office suite. I rap against the door and push it open without waiting for a response.

My father reclines in his chaise lounge, eyes closed. Geoffrey sits behind his desk, tapping away on a keyboard.

He starts at my entrance. He's in a suit, like always. The lamplight reflects on the gray strands, swept back and styled. With one quick scan of the room, I confirm the absence of nursing staff.

"Are you here because of my text?" He looks genuinely surprised, which is fair, because he didn't ask me to come over. Typically, when he texts, I respond in kind.

"Wanted to check on Dad." *And for the thousandth time, my investment portfolios are not your concern, Geoffrey.* "Have you seen his nurse?"

I'd like to find out how much they had to give him for him

to settle down. If I'd known seeing Caroline would disrupt his day so significantly, I wouldn't have brought her around.

My shoulder muscles burn, and I stretch my neck to the right, kneading the tight muscle. Dad's eyelids flicker, like he's waking. Or maybe he's in REM.

"Why did you send me that text?" Clearly, Dad has been sleeping.

"Going through my to-do list. Like I said, I didn't expect an immediate response."

That's fair. I often leave it to my assistant to respond to Geoffrey.

"I've been checking in with you on your—" I hold up a hand to stop him from continuing.

"I know." *I'm sorry*, is on the tip of my tongue, but I bite it back, because Geoffrey's still not in the right here. He's fully aware he could back off and not bother me every time Dad tells him to, and Dad wouldn't register if it was done or not. He'd probably love to manage part of my portfolio, but it's not gonna happen. Unlike my father, I only hire the best, especially when it comes to portfolio management.

"Why is Caroline back?"

Does he remember her? Did he come to our wedding? Probably. Dad's invitation list numbered in the hundreds.

"Does she want something?" Geoffrey's question strikes me as intrusive, but depending on what he overheard Dad saying this afternoon, maybe it's not. "Did she tell you why she's here?"

"What did Dad say to you?"

"Dorian." There's a rattle in Dad's throat.

"Are you thirsty?" I step to a bar cart that's over to the side. Top-shelf alcohol bottles still adorn the bottom, but the pitchers on top are now water and orange juice. I pour Dad a highball glass of water and bring it to him with a straw, sitting on the edge of the chaise. Alcohol isn't recommended, and whereas I thought we'd fight forever on that point, in the last year or so, it's almost as if he's forgotten to argue over his beverage choice.

His hand trembles as he reaches for the glass, so I keep hold of it as he sips.

A shadow falls over the rug, and I look up to find Geoffrey standing over us.

"Has he been sleeping long?"

"No," Geoffrey answers.

"My two sons," Dad says, bringing my attention back to him.

"What?"

These days, Dad rambles about the strangest things.

"I'm glad you're both here. With me. My sons."

Geoffrey sits sideways on the chaise across from me, hands together in a prayer pose, elbows on his thighs.

"Do you know what medication they gave him? Has he been rambling…"

Geoffrey's professional pose remains, his expression reminiscent of when I reviewed Dad's financial reports. Impatient and condescending.

To Geoffrey, Dad isn't rambling. If anything, he's annoyed I'm slow on the uptake.

"Dad, is Geoffrey your son?"

"Bastard child," Dad says, lifting a shaky hand for more of the water I'm holding.

Slowly, I turn to Geoffrey. He's at least twenty years older than me.

"He had you when he was fifty-two," Geoffrey says. "Did you really think you were his only child?"

Well, yes, because that's what he told me.

"You're my brother?" He straightens his tie. "And you said nothing?"

"Half-brother," he answers. "Your knowing wouldn't have changed anything."

Maybe it would have. I insisted he not join Bedrock and stay focused on Dad's portfolios. I'd seen him as an important staff member for Dad.

"Why did Dad keep it a secret?"

Dad opens his mouth and closes it, eyes glazed. Is he following the conversation?

"Halston didn't want people to know he sired a child with a prostitute."

I study Geoffrey. I've disregarded the suit-wearing kiss-up for so long, but I mean, he's so much older than me. We were never friends.

"Wow." This news takes the bite out of Caroline's accusations. The anger I felt coming over here has been completely replaced by...I'm not sure...confusion? Bewilderment? "Well, I'd say welcome to the family, but you've been with us all along."

I can't remember him not being there. And always in a suit.

"I wouldn't say that."

"You're closer to Dad than I am." It's an honest assessment. He's the guy Dad calls for everything. I manage the staff and ensure others are in place to handle his calls and requests.

"You're taking this news better than I thought you would," he says, studying me with the same analytical gaze I've seen across negotiating tables. I maintain the composed demeanor that's served me well in hostile takeovers and congressional hearings; there will be time to process the emotional implications later.

"Why didn't you ever tell me? Why keep it a secret all these years?"

"I signed an NDA. It was a condition for him covering my college tuition. My mother signed one before that."

Holy shit.

"But he looked out for you?"

He raises a shoulder, and the movement exposes a glint of his gold Rolex. "I've done well."

"Of course, he did well," Dad says. "Moore blood. And I looked out for him. Pushed him. Pushed both of you."

There's clear pride in his tone, pride that, at least with me, he doesn't deserve. Gloria Hawkins raised me. She put up with unreasonable demands from my father to remain in my life.

A sense of unease sets in. "Do I know your mother?"

Please tell me it's not Gloria. How old is Gloria? Would the math even work?

"You never met her. He insisted she keep her distance. The same way he kept your mother away."

My mother left us, but maybe Geoffrey's mother left Dad, too. His wives always left him, eventually.

A vision of Caroline flashes. *Like father, like son.*

There's a knock on the door, and the weekend help files in.

A woman dressed in leggings and a zippered sweatshirt, presumably his personal trainer, asks, "Mr. Moore, do you think you might be up for a walk before bedtime?"

"It snowed," he says.

"We won't go outside. We'll walk around the indoor pool. Or, if you'd like, you can swim."

She looks to us for direction.

"Since he's up, some movement would be good. He'll sleep

better," I say, standing and backing away, giving her the all-clear.

She helps him up, and he slowly shuffles out of the room, back hunched slightly, his hand on the nurse's arm for balance.

Geoffrey moves to the desk, opens the briefcase he always carries, and gathers his things.

Now it makes sense. Geoffrey's always around, even on the weekends, because he's watching out for his ailing father. I'd thought he was always trailing Dad because it's what Dad expected from his employee, or because maybe he aimed for inclusion in Dad's will. But no, they've been functioning as father and son.

"If you'd told me—"

"NDA," Geoffrey snaps.

"Should we… Do you want to…get dinner sometime?"

Geoffrey cocks his head. The light reflects off his spectacles.

"There's no need to force a relationship where one doesn't exist."

Right.

"Did you shift to a conservative mix?" he asks.

"My investment strategy?" *Is he really going there?* "I'm covered."

I'm on the fucking board of one of the world's largest financial investment firms and, together with my father, own a majority stake. I have the world's brightest geniuses managing my portfolios. That's really what he wants to ask me about?

He gives a curt nod and moves to leave.

"Geoffrey—"

"This changes nothing between us. I could be your father. We're too old to feign closeness."

"You really don't like me, do you?" On some level, I've

always known he doesn't, but I chalked it up to him seeing me as his boss's son and of no importance to him.

"It's not that." He shoves a hand into his trouser pocket and rolls his lower lip. For the first time, I recognize the habit as similar to Dad. "If you want, let's have dinner next week. I'll have my assistant coordinate with yours."

With that, he exits.

What the hell just happened? It doesn't even matter. I'm over here in my father's house, and my focus should be on Caroline.

CHAPTER 25

CAROLINE

"It's done."

"What's that?" Sophia asks. "What did you do?"

"I told him everything."

"And?"

"He denied it."

"As expected. That's why we need surveillance. Give us time to listen. You didn't—"

"No, I didn't tell him, although he suspects."

"Wait…where are you?"

"In his house."

"Where is he?"

"He left to calm down. When he returns, we'll continue talking."

"We didn't pick up a conversation. Are the mics—"

"We talked in the kitchen."

"While he's gone, activate a listening device in his kitchen."

"Sophia." My gaze rolls to the ceiling.

"What? That area of the house needs to be bugged, too."

I pull out a stool and sit, hit by a wave of exhaustion as the adrenaline declines. I set the phone to speaker and set it flat on the countertop.

"There was another attack." Sophia's voice sounds hollow in the vast great room.

"I've been with Dorian. It wasn't him."

"We both know someone with his resources would be the architect, not the trigger man. Satellite networks, quantum computing, global reach—he has the perfect infrastructure for coordinating disparate events while maintaining plausible deniability."

"And we have no evidence he's funding terrorists."

"Simply because we haven't identified the funding mechanism doesn't mean it doesn't exist, especially given a funding mechanism has to exist."

She's right. But why would someone finance domestic terrorism? As an analyst, we're taught to study terrorist profiles and motivations. At the moment, we're at a disadvantage because we're guessing. We don't know if it's a country, a group, or a highly influential whale. Sophia believes it's the latter.

Others are exploring scarier possibilities: Russia, China, North Korea, extremist groups.

Arrow wants me to vet Dorian as a conceivable whale. If I focus solely on my role—vetting Dorian—I should start with the basics. I should consider his biography. What socializing experiences does he have, and what personality traits affect his decision-making and leadership style? In short, I need to understand his rationale to best predict his future behavior.

He stormed out because he didn't like being accused, but is he also guilty?

"Let me send a car for you," Sophia says.

"No. I need to hear him out."

"I don't like this. If he's guilty, you're not in a safe place. Men like him don't react well when cornered."

"Can you ask the team to look into his satellite contracts? I've been thinking about the why. He's got contracts the world over. Zenith is Dorian's baby. A company he founded as opposed to inherited. Can you see if there's any connection between these random events and Zenith contracts being granted?"

"You're thinking it's coming down to money?"

No, he has more than he can spend in a lifetime. But for some, acquisition becomes an addiction.

But this is Dorian.

"It wouldn't just be money. That's what I want to understand."

Motivation is the key to understanding the human mind. The words from a Langley instructor tell me I've been approaching this all wrong.

"Power, perhaps? See if you can access the contracts. What information does Zenith collect? What restrictions do the contracts place on them? See if there are any significant variances between countries in those contracts. Do you get where I'm going?"

"I'll get a team on it. See what they can uncover. It'll take some time."

"Also, look to see who benefits if Dorian is framed." A

thought comes to mind. "You told me you couldn't tell me your source, but–"

"Our initial source has determined it's not Dorian."

"And you don't find that suspicious?"

"We do. Do you remember that list of names we showed you in the briefing?"

"Yes."

"Our source is one of the unlisted names. Nicholas Ivanov. British national, Russian descent."

"You're still researching Dorian because you haven't decided if you trust Nick." Her silence confirms my assumption. Nick's reputation is less than sterling. "I know Nick, by the way. He was in our wedding." But I understand why they didn't leverage my relationship with Nick for information. I recently debriefed a deep undercover operative who worked closely with Nick for years. If the team needed an expert to weigh in on Nick Ivanov, they'd go to that source.

"Caroline, we're still pursuing this angle because he remains a person of interest. In the meantime, I'm sending a team to the gate."

"I'm staying." What I'm not sharing is that I need to stay for reasons that have nothing to do with Project Unity.

"Luke's pushing hard for you to return. He's concerned for your safety." Her voice drops an octave. "I know you said you're not interested, but all signs here point to a spark on his side. And a highly protective streak."

Zero chemistry existed between Luke and me. I sigh loudly so she'll back off.

"Tell Luke there's no need to worry, and I'll see him when I'm back."

"Do you want to tell him yourself?"

"Negative."

"Someone's been hanging out with the Arrow Tactical guys."

I can hear her smile.

"Your fault."

"Be safe."

The call ends, and I glance around the sparse living area.

They want evidence.

Little of Dorian is in this house. He's not someone to hold on to sentimental items.

He has your photos hanging on his office walls.

With that thought, I return to his office.

———

"Cara!"

The shout echoes through the hall with an urgency that sends me running.

"What happened?"

Dorian appears, face flushed, beads of sweat along his brow.

He bends over, breathing through his mouth, but his gaze stays on me, as if he's confirming I'm real.

"You thought I'd left."

He nods at my statement, hands on his waist, scanning the space.

"Are you digging through my stuff?"

"Yes."

His hands fall to his side, and he arches his spine to breathe deeply.

"Why are you out of breath? You're in good shape."

He gives me a look that says he'd like to smack my bottom.

"I ran all around the house looking for you. Up and down the stairs." His gaze falls to the files stacked on his desk.

"Did you find anything useful?"

"No."

He exhales a loud huff. "All right. Let's do this."

"What?"

"Point by point. I'm going to prove my innocence."

He swipes his brow, sits down on the sofa, and slings an ankle over his knee. With one arm slung on the armrest and one over the back of the couch, he's the quintessential relaxed man. However, I'd wager he's anything but.

"You mentioned the Baltic Sea wire cutting, attacks on electrical substations, and an EMP attack. Let's tackle them one by one. Russian fishing boats were observed in the area. Only, the fishers onboard those boats were seen doing calisthenics each morning. They weren't fishermen; they were Russian military. The world recognizes Russia is responsible. They're testing and learning."

"Right. No one suspects you're behind those."

"A beautiful thing."

I roll my eyes, grin, and then focus. "The attacks on the United States electrical substations have been ongoing. Current theory places the blame on white supremacists or other small terrorist groups."

"If you're thinking I'd hire someone to take a shotgun and shoot up a substation, you're wrong. And frankly, it hurts for you, of all people, to believe I'd do something like that. And why in the bloody hell do you think I'd allow an EMP attack that takes out my satellites? What's the logic?"

"For the record, I don't believe you're guilty. I suspected your father." Our eyes lock, and his gaze softens. "But not you."

It could be my mind playing tricks, but I feel like his demeanor visibly calms with my admission. "At the moment, we've divided efforts to investigate persons and countries of interest."

"And they assigned you to investigate me." His dry, clipped words tell me exactly how he feels about that. *Fair.*

"I volunteered."

His index finger taps a steady beat on the leather armrest.

"Because I believe you're innocent. The more suspects we eliminate, the closer we come to figuring out how to stop further attacks or..." It sounds surreal to say this... "Avoid a world war."

"Nick made a cryptic comment. Told me to keep you here, to keep you safe."

"Did he?" I pick up my phone and tap out a quick note to remember to discuss this with Sophia, now that I know he's the source who originally named Dorian.

When I set my phone back down, I meet his gaze once again. I could join him on the sofa, but it's better to keep the desk between us.

"We have confirmation that you met with arms dealers and government leaders on the terrorist watch list."

He shrugs. "I'm sure I have. As a matter of practice, I don't scrub my meetings with the terrorist watch list. To be honest, I don't know that I've ever obtained the list. Why would I? Without having seen your list, I'd bet those meetings pitched Zenith. Or it's possible they're Bedrock clients. Now"—he holds up an index finger—"we do our research to ensure we minimize our exposure for funding terrorism. So if those meetings had something to do with a Bedrock connection, that would be an error of due diligence within the firm, and I'd appreciate knowing who we shouldn't be taking on as an investment client. But," he waves a hand in the air, "I shouldn't have mentioned that. As a board member, it's rare that I meet with a Bedrock client. That would likely be a coincidence with us taking part in the same conference or symposium."

That's exactly what I assumed.

"You've also been hedging complex derivative trades and shorting positions before events."

"I have?" His eyelids lower, and his lips purse. "It might surprise you, but I leave my investments to the experts. If you recall, I don't get the same thrill from investing as my father." It had been a sore point between them. Halston hadn't been keen at all for him to leave Bedrock and launch a new venture. "Can you get me a list of those trades?"

"Yes." I add it to my list to request from Sophia.

"Although, I'll tell you, many trades are based on complex algorithms these days. Our systems could pick up on activities within markets that might appear prescient but are actually reactive."

"That's fair."

"What else?"

"The team identified encrypted communications sent at odd hours from your father's accounts. Conversations with known extremists and Russian sympathizers. Calls to burner phones where the attacks occurred. The frequency of those calls has been increasing, not declining."

He leans forward, intrigued. "Phone records show this?"

I nod.

"Can you see the content of the communications?"

"No, I don't believe so. But for encrypted written communications, my bet is we'll see it shortly."

"Right. If you can't, I'll ask Nick. He's got the best in the world."

"Arrow has some talent, too." He's definitely not acting like someone who has anything to hide. And we're in his office, which means Arrow is listening. "What're you thinking?"

"That my father might be reaching out to old contacts. I didn't think he did much of that, but I could be wrong. I would imagine his communications are erratic, nonsensical, but..."

"Maybe they aren't?"

"AI could help him craft communications. On the phone, I think he'd ramble. Weave. There would be more evidence of dementia on the phone than in writing." He focuses on a far-off spot on the floor. "If this is true, I fucked up, leaving him with a phone and email. I just didn't think..." His foot taps the floor with three quick beats. "He might've had conversations with old friends, but he's not the mastermind behind anything. I've been watching him deteriorate for the last several years. His short-term memory is weak. He repeats conversations, doesn't remember anything from the day prior. He forgets words or mispronounces them. He's erratic."

"I concur," I say loudly, hoping that whatever team is listening to us hears my conviction. "When I met him, I had the same conclusion."

My phone lights, and I read the incoming message.

SF

Technical documents outlining
infrastructure vulnerabilities, Dorian's
technical style.

"Anything else?" he asks, possibly reading into my facial reaction. Years may have passed, but he can still read me.

I click to log into our secure site to access an attachment I haven't yet read.

"The team hacked into servers Zenith owns. Somewhere in Iceland." I tap away, using the authenticator code to log in. "They found a series of detailed technical documents outlining infrastructure vulnerabilities, time-stamped months before the attacks. They claim they're written in your technical style. I haven't yet assessed these, but is this document yours?"

He pushes off the couch and reaches for my phone. He pinches the bridge of his nose, then points at a drawer. "Can you get my readers?"

I pull out a long, narrow drawer and find four readers neatly placed in a row.

"You use readers?"

"Shut it. Not a word."

"Dorian, if you need glasses, that can make your migraines worse."

"I read little on the phone."

"That's a lie."

He slips his readers on and focuses on the screen, disregarding me. Classic Dorian, struggling with reading because vanity dictates he can't look weak.

"These are my team's documents. Wrote them for a consortium of tech leaders—people who control everything from fiber optic networks to quantum computing cores. The infrastructure vulnerability assessment was meant to strengthen global systems, not provide a blueprint for attacks." He removes his readers, rubbing his temples. "You know how quantum encryption works; once information is observed, it's changed. These documents were meant to stay within a trusted circle."

"Who did you share them with?"

"The syndicate. Nine men. They may have shared it with others within their circles."

He hands my phone back to me. "Like I've already told you, it's a group my father founded fifteen, twenty years ago. Leaders in specific sectors around the world. Representation on every continent. He pulled me in around the time you left me."

I involuntarily flinch.

"Nick's in it." He's thoughtful. "He's been a member longer than I have. You think these documents provided the framework being used?"

"Our tech team does."

"The syndicate fractured. We haven't reconvened since Nick was ousted. This is a document… I meant for it to be shared as protection, but…once a document is shared, you lose control." He strides to the window and crosses his arms looking across the expanse of trees. "Jiang Tu has been missing for months. If, as we suspect, Xi has him, the Chinese government would have everything of his. Or at least anything he didn't successfully conceal."

Jiang Tu is a billionaire Chinese businessman, and he was on the list Ryan reviewed in the briefing. If he's the source, then that would mean China is behind it all. Chinese businessmen don't typically work independently from the Chinese government. Weakening democratic countries could fit with a One China strategy. It's not inconceivable.

"We'll need to look at the timeline," I say, hoping Sophia is listening.

"Is my office bugged?"

I still, knowing the team is listening, and my answer will be heard.

He shakes his head with amusement. "You're a little obvious. It's cute, but clearly, you're aiming to talk to someone other than me."

I don't bother mentioning the conferences he's attended that also placed him on a person of interest list. It overlaps with his interest in Zenith.

"Is that it?" he asks.

"Yes."

"You getting hungry? Can we go back into the house?"

He's pale. On instinct, I move to him and brush my hand across his forehead while studying his pupils. "Is another migraine coming on?"

I say it softly, as much in hopes to keep the question between us and not those listening in, as to ensure the volume of my voice doesn't hurt.

His fingers wrap around my wrist, and he brings my palms to his lips. His dark eyes meet mine, and he shakes his head slightly. "Shouldn't happen again for a few days."

I hate that he suffers this way. "Let's get you something to eat."

The team can wait. It's been a long day, and we can regroup in the morning.

If China is behind recent events, we're looking at a new kind of warfare—one where satellite infrastructure and global communications are the battlefield. With Zenith's reach, it's likely he'll have clients at odds which each other, opposing countries, which makes his position even more precarious. The intelligence community will need him, but they'd never fully trust him.

Downstairs in the kitchen, I open the refrigerator and search through lidded food compartments, settling on smoked salmon and cold sesame noodles, set it out on one plate, and grab two forks. I pour each of us a glass of filtered water. If I weren't worried about a recurring migraine, I might get him wine, but instead, I'm going to ensure he's hydrated.

There's warmth in his eyes, but also maybe amusement.

"Do you want me to split it on two plates?" I suppose it is presumptive of me to assume we'd share.

"No, not at all." He moves the barstool near him, patting it for me to take a seat. "I've missed this. You taking care of me."

"Please." I roll my eyes and nudge him to eat. "You've got a full staff taking care of you."

"Not like you. It never feels the same. They're doing their jobs. You're doing it because you care. In spite of everything, you care about me." He sips his water and sets it down. "I think I could be penniless and you'd still care."

"That's true," I say, meeting his gaze head-on.

He snorts. "You liked me more when I was a penniless grad student."

"Please. You were never penniless."

"You thought I was."

I narrow my eyes. He has no concept of penniless.

He becomes solemn, and his focus falls to the plate, but I recognize that faraway look. He's gone somewhere, lost in thought. I let him eat, knowing that regardless of what he says, if he doesn't take care of his body, he'll pay the price in pain. If not today, soon.

When there's not much left on the plate, he sets his fork down.

"The rest is yours."

"I'm done," I say.

"No." His lips are set in a firm line. "Eat more."

I'm ready to insist he eats more, when he snaps his fingers, hops off the stool, and strides to the pantry, coming out with a gold foil wrapper and my favorite chocolate.

"I know you'll eat this."

He's right. I will.

As I take a piece, he lifts his fork to finish off the noodles. I knew he'd eat more.

"Do you remember that time Nick boiled lobster?"

"Stunk up the whole flat," Dorian says with a smile.

"I haven't eaten lobster since," I admit.

Nick, Dorian, and I spent a lot of time together that spring. He functioned as my biggest advocate, and, as Dorian tells it, it was Nick who pushed Dorian out the door when I'd been sick back home in Boston. Nick told him to take care of me, which is why he showed up at my door with tissues and cold medicine.

"How is Nick doing these days?"

I actually know far more about our old friend Nick Ivanov than I can let on to Dorian since I debriefed an undercover operative tasked with working for Nick. Due to close ties in the operation, Arrow had been given an opportunity to debrief the operative after his faked death and before he returned to civilian life.

"Nick's Nick." Dorian says, scooting the stool away and lifting our plate to take it to the dishwasher.

"Does he still frequent those clubs?"

The undercover operative mentioned a few as meeting locations, but I didn't dig deep into Nick's personal life. That wasn't my objective at the time of the debrief. It was before Nick was targeted and a hit placed on him, so our questions centered on Nick's businesses, specifically the arms deals he brokered.

Dorian answers, his back to me, sleeves pushed up, as he rinses our dishes. That's got to be my favorite look of his, cleaning in the kitchen. He hasn't put his watch back on, and his forearms flex as he moves the plate under the stream of water.

"I don't know." He opens the dishwater and sets a plate inside. "Well, that's not true. On one of my last trips, he went." He turns, making a point of looking me in the eye. "He invited me. I declined."

You could have gone is on the tip of my tongue, but I bite it back. He obviously knows he could have gone.

"But he's in a serious relationship now."

"Seriously?"

"Yes."

Sophia and Fisher went abroad and assisted Nick when he was attacked. I wasn't on the project team. It was a rescue operation, and I was aware of it, but it all happened quickly. Sophia handled the reporting, and to my knowledge, there was no debrief.

If asked to join the project, I'd been prepared to remind Sophia that I have a personal connection to Nicholas Ivanov. I did include the information on the debrief report when meeting with the undercover operative, code name: Saint.

But now I suspect Sophia had been well-aware. She obviously hadn't forgotten I'd been married to Dorian Moore, and she took care to bring me onto Project Unity without blind-siding me.

"Maybe one day we can visit him. Go back to our old stomping grounds."

I grin. "Wasn't that long ago, but it feels like a lifetime, right?"

Dishes rattle as he closes the dishwasher.

"I'm surprised you didn't leave the dishes for the cleaning service."

"If I'd done that, you would've cleaned." He rests his hands on the counter opposite me, a smile playing across his lips. The effect lightens the exhaustion haunting his dark eyes.

"My assignment is to evaluate all alternatives. If it's not you, your father, or Nick, who else could it be?"

"How long would you say this strategy has been in play?"

"Years. It's been in the works for years."

"Are you asking me about other syndicate members?"

I shrug. "I'm not looking into them. Others are. Just curious on your take."

"On my take." He exhales. "I'm curious about this company of yours."

"Oh?"

"You know those clubs you were asking me about?"

Nick spoke about them once. That's the only reason I know about them... That and the undercover operative mentioned them in the debrief.

When Nick tried to get me and Dorian to join him one night in London, Dorian shut him down. And Nick was absolutely joyous. "Now I know she's the one. I want to be your best man. You hear me!" he'd shouted. We'd only been together for a month, maybe two. He'd come across like a lunatic.

In retrospect, he'd been prescient. Dorian proposed weeks later. I'd gone home at the end of my semester and had gotten sick on the flight. He showed up at my door with chicken soup and insisted he didn't care if he got the flu; he simply wanted to take care of me.

"Those clubs…" he prompts, bringing me back to the topic at hand.

"Yeah?"

"Your boss's brother is a frequent visitor."

"Ryan? He doesn't have a brother."

"I don't know a Ryan. Jack Sullivan. His brother, Liam, from what I understand, is a fixture on the scene. Lives in Houston, but he travels."

"Jack's not my boss."

"He owns your company. Doesn't that make him your boss?"

"Technically." I hold up a hand. "I don't want to hear about Sophia's father's sex life."

"Not her father, her uncle."

"Same," I say. "None of this is material."

"Maybe," he says.

"What does that mean?"

"Just that maybe you should broaden your scope."

"That reminds me. Can you get me a list of your father's staff? Everyone who works with him?"

He sighs like he's tired, and I can understand why he is, why I keep coming back to him. But he is my assignment, and I need to focus and clear him. There's a sadness to Dorian's expression, and I sense he's about to say more when my phone lights up.

SF

We need you back here tomorrow. A car
will pick you up at 9.

. . .

Is she still on about my safety? No, they heard everything Dorian said. He shouldn't be a suspect—not anymore. My assignment must be changing. Dorian reads the message on my screen, and I lift my shoulders, shrugging because I learned at the same time he did.

"You can't stay the weekend?" He's incredulous, and I don't blame him. I said I'd stay the weekend.

"Can we not argue? Can we just go to bed?"

His entire expression changes, and the next thing I know, I'm in the air, legs around his waist, being hoisted up the stairs.

"What're you doing?" I shriek, laughing.

"Fulfilling your wishes, because I thought you'd never ask."

CHAPTER 26

DORIAN

Last night, I slept better than I have in years. Yes, the day had been exhausting and the sex fulfilling. But it was more than that. She's the missing piece, and my soul isn't at peace unless she's near. The thought is hokey and cheesy, but it's the only explanation I have.

Yes, last night cradled in my arms, she accused me of only wanting what I can't get. She did that years ago, too. Shortly after I proposed, a story broke about her stealing a friend's boyfriend in high school and also in college. The story implied she was conniving and a woman leveraging relationships for connections and social upward mobility. I made the mistake of assuming it to be true and asked her about it. She took off her engagement ring and walked out of the restaurant. It took me two months to win her back. I had to propose three times before she said yes again. There was a time when I suspected she might have been right, that I fell hard and fast for the one woman who was willing to walk away. But it's deeper than that. When she's with me, I can breathe.

What I've got to figure out is how to ensure that when I'm with her, she can, too.

She types away at her laptop, absorbed in a discussion with her colleagues.

She's mentally vacated, lost in her world.

This morning when I woke, mindful of her early planned departure, I came down to get her coffee and discovered her cleaned clothes had been delivered and left in the entry. I brought everything to her, she showered, packed, and opened her laptop.

I sent her the list of employees, everyone with access to my father's office. She'll investigate, but it won't go anywhere. If these events are coordinated, it's not being done by someone serving as an employee or advisor. No, only someone with a narcissistic personality and alpha drive could plan to destabilize the free world, and that personality wouldn't survive serving others.

Our syndicate was filled with the kinds of personalities that conceivably could play Prophet. Nick floated that word a few times, implying my father wanted to play that role. Someone so powerful they could see the future, which of course, in the modern world, means mold the future as one planned. I don't believe it's any of the men in our group. We all wanted market stability. Were we willing to play in the sandbox with criminal organizations and bend a few rules? Certainly. But destabilization is directly counter to market stability.

She's way off. Both on my father's employees and on the syndicate. But I'll let her discover that on her own. I once treated her as if her job didn't matter, and I won't make that mistake again. This time around, I'm going to support her. Although, I can't say that I love that she's working for the Sullivans. She may not believe that an investor plays an active role, but if an investor wishes to play an active role, he does. And I'm not certain those brothers are trustworthy. I'll have to touch base with Nick. He's still searching for the person who put a hit out on him, and like everyone else, I'm sure he still believes it's conceivable I'm guilty. But I wonder…what does he think of these Sullivan brothers?

He's the one who told me to keep Caroline here, to keep her safe. What does he know?

Caroline closes her laptop and announces that it's time.

Resigned to her departure, I wheel her luggage to the door, leading her to the outside. As if underscoring how much has changed since she arrived, instead of an unseasonably warm fall day, the temperatures shifted with a brutal cold front, and snow covers the leaves from yesterday.

Given it's cold, I set her luggage in the SUV, opting for warmth over the golf cart experience. She closes the door as I crank the heat. There's a deadness in the air that I can't shake. There are no similarities to when she left me last time, yet I feel like I've done this before. Back then, she hailed a yellow taxi, and I watched her drive away from the dining room window and later through the security video. Back then, it had meant the end of our marriage.

She taps away on her phone as I reverse out of the garage, creating fresh tracks in the freshly fallen snow. After she leaves, I'll call Nick. His guys might be better positioned to monitor darker trades, those done through multiple shell accounts to avoid detection. If it's an individual, a group, or a country doing this, for certain, they've positioned their holdings to benefit. That's what we should be searching for. In every downturn, someone benefits. And you had better believe if the downturn is planned, the planner will benefit.

"How was your father?" The question sounds like small talk meant to fill the silence.

The younger version of myself would have answered fine and left it there. But...I'm not that same person. "He's the same. I learned something while I was there, actually."

I could've told her last night, but I needed to clear her name, and then she suggested the bedroom and nothing else felt relevant. I loved holding her in my arms as our conversation waned and she slipped into sleep.

"What?" She flips her phone on her lap, screen side down, giving me her full attention, at least until we're at the gate.

"I've got a brother."

"What?"

I half-laugh at her incredulous expression, a perfect mirror to my reaction.

"Yeah. I mean, he's like twenty years older. Different mothers, obviously. But I've known him my whole life. Dad had him sign an NDA. Can you believe that?"

The guardhouse and gate come into view, and I lighten the pressure on the accelerator to slow her departure.

"Who is it?"

"Geoffrey Cromwell."

"His financial advisor?"

"The one and only. He knows you. I assume he was at our wedding."

"He's the man I saw from the helicopter. He was talking on

the phone. I didn't get a good look at him. Does he look anything like you? Is there a family resemblance?"

"No." It's funny she thinks about things like that. It never crossed my mind. "I assume he looks like his mother." I refrain from sharing that his mother was a prostitute. That feels like private, irrelevant information. "Of course, he's mostly grey now, in his sixties, so I'm guessing it would be hard to see any family resemblance on either side."

"When did you find this out?"

"Yesterday. Dad wasn't doing well. That's why I went over." That, and because I needed to calm down, but there's no point in rehashing that. "Geoffrey was in the room with him. Dad rambled in that way he does. Incoherent thoughts. But he mentioned both his sons being in the same room." I lift a shoulder —half-shrugging, half-steering the car. There's not much to share. "We talked. He said he never said anything because of an NDA." I release my frustration with a sigh. "Dad loves his NDAs."

"How'd you take it?"

I come to a stop in front of the guardhouse. A uniformed man I don't recognize steps outside, and I wave him away, signaling I want more time.

"Did you get angry?"

That's what she would assume. "I offered to go to dinner with him. Get to know him."

"But you said you've known him for decades."

"As one of my father's employees. Not as…" I let it trail. Not as a person. Definitely not as a sibling. "He didn't seem interested, but then he changed his mind. We'll go to dinner next week."

"Wow."

"Precisely. And now I'm wondering how many children Dad might have."

"Seriously?"

"It's possible, right? That he's got a slew of kids with NDAs threatening trust funds if they speak up? It's conceivable. In retrospect, it's surprising he didn't force me to sign an NDA."

"No, only your wife."

She's bitter. Interesting. She never seemed angry before about the NDA.

Her hand covers the door handle. One foot out the door, so to speak. Understandably. The Moore family has baggage.

"Geoffrey seemed incredulous that I never questioned if a man like my father hadn't fathered more children. Perhaps I was naïve. Did you ever suspect?"

"I don't think…" Her head shakes slightly. "That wouldn't be a normal thought process."

"He's a known philanderer. He said my mother left us, but I assumed she left because he cheated."

"I'm surprised you've never reached out to her."

Caroline wanted me to reach out to her, probably in the hope I had one parent she could warm to. But the woman left me with him…

"You know, her lawyers probably didn't stand a chance against his." That's a point Caroline has made multiple times.

My mother took a payment for giving up custody. Caroline knows this. It's immaterial. And it's an old, long-buried circular disagreement that doesn't need to be unearthed.

I pop open the custom-fitted compartment in the armored SUV and remove one of our proprietary tracking devices— similar to an Airtag but with military-grade encryption and direct satellite uplink.

"Will you do me a favor?"

She studies the silver disc.

"Will you carry this? It's like an air tag."

"You keep a stash in your car?"

"I throw them in bags, just in case someone tries to nab a laptop. It's… I keep spares in my vehicles."

"You want to track me?"

"It's a precaution. Nick said to keep you here. It's…probably entirely unnecessary. As you said, countries the world over have teams working to prevent a major attack. But if one occurs…"

"If there's a blackout, you won't be able to find me."

"You forget, I control the most sophisticated network of tracking satellites ever built. Our quantum mesh network has redundancies even the Pentagon doesn't know about. I'll find you." The words come out more possessive than intended, but when you've built a reliable global communications infrastructure, it's hard to be casual about its capabilities.

"All right." I watch as she tucks the silver disk into her handbag.

"Here's another one to keep on your person." Her eyes widen. "It's too easy to forget to move it from a handbag. Take two. It'll make you more cognizant."

She's thinking about saying no, but I stop that by tugging her to me and covering her lips with mine. She softens and arches closer. I love how her body responds to mine. I always have.

"Next week, can I take you on a date?"

"I might be working a lot."

"That's fair. When this dies down, can I take you on a date?"

"Are we really going to do this?"

Those blue eyes swim with unnecessary questions. I will win her back. I'll earn her love.

"Yes." I caress the soft curve of her cheek. "Please? I'm not above begging."

"Okay, then."

"Excellent." I'll get Jay to research restaurants.

She smiles. "I assume you'll get the crash investigation results…"

She's right. I need to oversee that. Ensure that we figure out what happened. "I'll come out to my place in California as soon as I can. Montecito isn't far from Santa Barbara. I'll stay there. We can take our time."

"What about your dad?"

"He's got a full staff, the best neurologists money can buy. If he continues to decline, I'll have the entire medical team relocated to California. We're here because he prefers the mountains, but if he continues to decline, it won't matter where he is."

"Dorian, I don't—"

"I know. You don't want a life in politics. Or the limelight." I smile, remembering how she used to say that phrase over and over, and I chose not to hear her. "I don't need it. I need you."

"Dorian…" All of her hesitations come through the one utterance of my name.

"Give me a chance, Cara. We'll take it slow." That's a lie. We won't. She and I don't do slow, but if that's what she needs to hear, I'll say it. "Letting you walk away was the single biggest mistake of my life."

"I needed to leave."

"I know, and I understand. Perhaps I should amend my statement. Making you feel less than or, to use your words, depriving you of oxygen, is my biggest regret. I won't repeat my mistake. Please. Give me a second chance."

The backseat passenger of the black Chevrolet SUV parked outside the gate exits and stares directly at our vehicle. He's wearing reflective sunglasses, black slacks, and a black sweater. I'd peg him as security, but he's probably an Arrow colleague.

She presses her lips to mine and exits the car. "Call me later."

"You'll answer?"

"Always. You'd know that if you ever picked up the phone before."

A sting right to the chest. I bite back telling her I was advised to leave all communications to our lawyers. After all, it would be a childish lie. She's my singular case study of refusing legal advice. I refused a lot of things back then.

I exit the car. This time, I won't sit behind glass and passively watch her leave.

CHAPTER 27

CAROLINE

Luke leans against the SUV with folded arms and a stern expression. If I didn't know better, I'd interpret his stance as giving off jealous boyfriend vibes. But I do know better, and Mr. Alpha is fulfilling his protector role.

I don't see a weapon on his waist, but he's on guard.

I catch my reflection in his sunglasses as I approach the vehicle. Distorted in the reflection, I appear small and childlike, with flat blonde hair and an egg-shaped face.

Behind me, Dorian stands in front of the open gate. I wiggle three fingers in a stilted wave. Dorian stands straight, arms at his side, his expression unreadable, the elusive titan guarding his estate.

I don't recognize the driver of the SUV. There's an Uber sticker on the front windshield. Is it really an Uber, or is the flannel-wearing driver one of Arrow's and the black Chevrolet Tahoe a clandestine façade?

Luke puts my luggage in the back and comes around to the open door. I expect him to close it, or say something, but he stands there with a blank expression.

What is his deal? We went on two dates, and one of those was in a coffee shop. He gestures, and it hits me. He's not riding up front.

I slide across the bench seat, buckle my seat belt, and whip out my work phone. Dorian remains at the gate. One of his security men stands by his side now, but they don't appear to be talking. As we drive away, I twist in my seat and watch him standing there, watching us drive away.

"So, you're back with him?" Luke asks.

Direct. I'll give him that.

"It's complicated." That hasn't changed.

"Explain."

I look to the front of the vehicle. The driver has earpods in his ears, which means nothing. He could use them as hearing aids.

"Is he moving to California?" Luke asks.

I scope Luke from head to bent knee, evaluating my colleague. We aren't in the relationship space where his questions are remotely warranted.

"Are you moving to Colorado?"

With a fast flick, my phone comes to life. "Like I said, it's complicated." With a pointed look, I add, "And personal."

I can feel his accusatory gaze while I peruse headlines. I set the phone down on my thigh. I should've known better than to date a colleague. *Damn, Stella.* "You're looking at me like you are an injured party."

With that comment, his scowl breaks, and he shifts in his seat. "I get it," he says, voice lower than mine, presumably so the driver doesn't hear. "We weren't an item. It was casual. But I don't feel you've been honest with me. It's a sore spot."

During dinner, he shared that his ex cheated. My actions played into his insecurities. I grit my teeth in frustration. I should've never agreed to a date.

"I'm sorry." Dammit. This is on me. "Yes, you're correct. There's still something between Dorian and me. It's quite possible there always will be. We were married. I don't know what will happen, but yes, we've agreed to see each other and see where things go."

My head swirls with the admission, and I press back against the headrest, settling the dizzy sensation. When I flew here, I came to clear Dorian's name, and I held the expectation it might be the last time we were in the same space. Three days later, I haven't cleared his name, but I've alleviated some suspicion, and I've agreed to date him.

We ride in silence for the duration of the trip to the airport. I'm tempted to send a personal text to Sophia, but I refrain. Luke is sitting too close, and it's too likely he'd read the screen.

So instead, I fill the time reading through project updates. China, Russia, and North Korea all deny involvement. Privately, they've each offered to assist in the investigation. Publicly, leaders from each country have stated the United States is falsely casting blame and disseminating false information.

It's the perfect subterfuge and the expected play. Time and again, we have possessed irrefutable proof of their attempts at infiltration and hacks, and they've always denied culpability.

This idea that it's one or two people orchestrating it all is a wild card. It doesn't make sense.

The SUV pulls up to a small private airport.

"What's this?" I ask.

"We're flying back on a private plane. Seems we've hit the big leagues," Luke answers, sounding slightly less disgruntled.

The awaiting jet is small, and Telluride isn't my favorite place to fly in and out of. Personally, I'd prefer Denver, especially after the helicopter incident, but no one asked me.

Luke retrieves my luggage and a black duffel. He takes both items and charges up the steps to the aircraft. A uniformed pilot smiles. He's an older man with thin white hair and kind eyes. I'd bet he's semi-retired, and flying these private planes is as much a hobby as a job.

"Welcome. Do you have any special needs?"

"No, I don't. How's the weather?" I haven't checked, although if I'd known about the small plane plan, I would've studied it closely.

"Should be smooth flying all the way to Santa Barbara," he answers. "Ah, here's Sheryl."

A woman speed-walking along the tarmac in a tight navy skirt and matching crewneck sweater approaches.

"We pulled this together on short notice," he explains. "Not a problem at all, of course. Happy to do it. If you need anything during the flight, anything at all, you let Sheryl know. It's a well-stocked plane. Chances are, she can meet your needs."

Sheryl, Bob, the pilot, and I exchange pleasantries, then climb the few steps onto the plane. Unlike some private planes I've been on, this one is a standard configuration with a row of wide leather seats on each side of a standard aisle.

Luke claimed the seat furthest to the back. It's likely part of his training, positioning himself where he can observe everything. Unlike me, he didn't meet and greet before boarding.

I take a seat in the second row, and Sheryl and Bob disappear behind a walnut door.

Luke can't possibly read my screens, so I remove the phone I've been using since the crash. There's a text from Dorian.

MY EX

Who is that guy?

I grin.

ME

A colleague.

MY EX

If he's security, he needs to be replaced.
He was looking at you, not me.

ME

Might that be in your head?

MY EX

No.

ME

BS. He wore reflective shades.

Sheryl enters the cabin and returns my smile, but I'm smiling at my phone, not her.

MY EX

Trust me.

I request sparkling water and return to my screen. I'm intrigued by his newfound brother. It's curious that his father never mentioned him. I can understand why he'd avoid scandal when he was an up-and-coming business magnate. But now? Few remember him, and those who do wouldn't be surprised. While he might have wanted to avoid scandal, he didn't succeed. His father was never plagued with the Epstein variety scandal, but affairs, often with married women, were par for the course.

Is that why his father kept his brother a secret? Is Geoffrey's mother still alive? Is there a husband out there who believes Geoffrey Cromwell is his son?

Dorian was born some twenty years after Geoffrey. Does

Dorian's mother know the truth? For so many years, I begged Dorian to visit his mother, but he always refused. He said he had no desire to meet a woman who chose money over her son.

I've always doubted that story. Halston forced her away, I'm certain of it. I once researched his mother with little success. I found her *New York Times* engagement and wedding announcements and an article in *Town and Country* with photographs of the wedding, but little else. Unlike Halston's other wives, Dorian's mother shied away from the spotlight.

MY EX

Still there?

ME

Y

MY EX

Leaving from Telluride?

I roll my eyes.

ME

Tracking me?

. . .

MY EX

With your permission.

I waffle with my response. If I'm honest, I like that he cares.

MY EX

It's important. If you need something,
call me.

MY EX

Trust your instincts.

ME

I always do.

MY EX

I still love you, you know...

I type out a warning message… *We're taking things slow,*
remember? But then delete before hitting send. Instead, I high-
light his message and hit the heart key.

I don't know what I'm doing.

I text Sophia to check in with her.

ME

Homeward bound. Luke???

SF

He requested the assignment.

SF

Insisted.

ME

The assignment? I wasn't in danger. I
could've gotten myself to the airport.
You knew that.

SF

Have you taken off yet?

I snap a photo of the snowy mountains through the airplane window and send it to her.

SF

We needed to get you out of the compound. We've triangulated too many communications with his IP address.

She isn't thinking this through.

ME

He's a tech guy. If he were breaking the law, you'd be tracing those communications to Iceland.

The second I hit send, awareness alights. She should be suspicious. A kernel of suspicion formulated last night, but in the light of day, I'm positive.

ME

He's being set up.

SF

Or you refuse to see the truth.

.   .   .

No, he's definitely being set up. And given Halston's state, it's someone who has access to Halston's office. Possibly someone on his medical staff. They could jump on his computer. Any passwords that were needed, they could get by using his biometric readings. Halston's so easily confused, it might not even register that someone is holding a phone up to his face.

But why set Halston up? If an investigation opens, Halston will easily be cleared. No, the purpose isn't to set him up. It's only to use his accounts. His access.

It might appear Dorian is to blame, but just like Dorian easily deflected accusations when I spoke with him, I'd bet he can easily prove his innocence in a court of law.

I switch back to my exchange with Dorian.

ME

Have you done background checks on the staff at your father's home?

MY EX

Of course.

ME

Can you send them to me?

. . .

MY EX

?

ME

Someone with access to your father's
office is setting you both up. It's the only
explanation.

MY EX

You going to share with your team?

ME

Y

MY EX

Check your email. There's a Dropbox
link. Keep in mind, that's every employee
with grounds access over the last twelve
months. I have a responsibility to protect
their privacy.

I switch back to my exchange with Sophia.

> **ME**
>
> I'm sending you a link with background reports to every person with access to the Moores' Colorado property. Will you have the team cross-check? Any one of these people could pretend to be Halston Moore. They all have access.

> **SF**
>
> On it.

I scan through the files, noting the metadata: upload dates, file sizes, modification timestamps.

There's one name without a background report. And from what Dorian said, he is an employee, or at least a vendor. His half-brother has access, whether he's an advisor or an employee. And it's conceivable he has motive. If he hates his father.

There's a problem with the theory. If it were the case of an estranged child seeking revenge, he could've transferred funds to his name and left the country ages ago. Dorian said Geoffrey moved to Colorado when Halston's dementia symptoms were noticeable, to be closer to his father. That's a prime time to rob him blind.

Could there be another connection? Additional children?

There's one person I've always wanted to meet, and she might have information we'll never find in a database.

———

It takes me a little over an hour to reach Manteca, California, the town north of Santa Barbara, where Aurora Calloway lives. I landed at the Santa Barbara airport, threw my bags into my car, and drove.

When Luke asked if I was headed to the office, I told him I needed a break. I didn't lie. I am looking for a break.

Dorian told me to trust my instincts, and that's what I'm doing. When we were married, I sensed that his absent mother haunted him, and possibly us. The string of divorces he witnessed didn't set a great example, but his refusal to reach out to his mother never sat right with me. If he had agreed to see a couple's therapist, his mother was a topic I planned to bring up.

So now, am I using this case as an excuse to finally meet his mother? Or might she know something useful? Did she know Geoffrey Cromwell existed? Had she met him? Why did Halston insist on keeping his son a secret? Are there any other children out there? Are any of them working for Halston in some capacity? Anyone out there who might attempt to frame their father and the favored sibling?

Of course, it's more likely that someone with ties to Russia or China was hired as a caretaker with the purpose of infiltrating Halston's network by pretending to be him. But if that's the case, the Arrow team will make the connection. Or one of the intelligence agencies will.

With this logic, I enter a fifty-five-plus community with a neighborhood entrance that proudly proclaims *The Collective*, with flags flapping in the wind, advertising model units available for touring.

There's a community pool and pickleball courts. Newly planted palm trees line the streets, and small bushes planted in orderly rows decorate the front of the one-story homes. The neighborhood is nice, but not what one would expect from a woman who walked away with a large sum from a billionaire ex-husband.

My navigation highlights the path around a circular center until I turn off the loop and arrive at a one-story new construction home with a short driveway, a manicured lawn with a mulched bed stretching across the front, a two-car garage, and light blue batten board over a cream stucco base. The sound of wind chimes is carried on the breeze, although none are visible.

I park on the street and disconnect my phone from the charger. A message flashes on the screen.

MY EX

Where are you?

ME

Landed. I'm safe.

MY EX

You aren't home.

·   ·   ·

Does he know where his mother lives? It was easy enough to find her new address, but I had her old address. Has Dorian kept up with her over the years?

ME

I'll call you in a little while.

I debate leaving the phone in the car but opt to keep my work phone with me in case I want to take any photos or notes.

An older man walking a small dog approaches. I wave, but he doesn't seem to see me. Indeed, as I knock on the door, he never glances my way as he shuffles by.

The door opens, and a beautiful woman with mostly gray hair and brown eyes opens the door. Her eyebrows are salt and pepper, and wrinkles line her sun-kissed skin, but she exudes a friendly warmth that belies her age.

"Hello," she says, scanning my body, no doubt checking to see if I'm selling something.

"Hi." I falter, unprepared.

"You look familiar. How do I know you?" She peers down the line of houses. "Are you a neighbor?" She asks, but then shakes her head. "No, you wouldn't be. You're not nearly old enough."

"Ah, I might be familiar because I was married to your son."

I watch her microexpressions carefully. The slight widening

of her eyes and the infinitesimal pause before responding tell me more than her words will.

With notable caution, she asks, "Who do you think I am?"

CHAPTER 28

DORIAN

What the hell is she doing?

I double-check her location.

Our trackers ping her location with military-grade precision. A quick check through Zenith's DMV integration confirms the vehicle registration, one of countless data streams we process daily.

This is the license plate registered with the California Department of Motor Vehicles in her name. But what is this place? A fifty-five-plus neighborhood? She said her parents are still in Connecticut. Does she have a relative who lives in California? Or is this somehow work-related?

GEOFFREY CROMWELL

Why are you in California? Did
something happen?

The message notification fades from my screen.

When I left to follow Caroline, I didn't take any steps to hide my travel, but it's annoying that Geoffrey has the information. He probably called Jay. And now that I know he's my half-brother, he may feel justified in inquiring.

Are there other half-siblings with NDAs swearing them to secrecy? I'd bank on it.

Dammit, Dad.

The small new construction home piques my curiosity more than Geoffrey's nosiness. The man has always been too interested in my affairs for my taste. Now, at least I understand why.

A woman pushing a dog in a stroller waves at me, and I wave back. She's probably wondering why I'm sitting in a parked car.

This isn't Caroline's home address. An hour away from Santa Barbara, it wouldn't be the address of someone she's dating, would it? She said she's not dating anyone.

How annoyed will she be to learn I followed her here? When she drove away, I spiraled into a free fall. It felt like I was watching her leave all over again. I packed a duffel, jumped into my SUV, and drove to a small private airport where I store my plane in an on-site hangar. By my estimation, I tailed her by an hour. Seven years ago, I watched her leave and did nothing. I'm not repeating that mistake.

Besides, Nick's warning repeatedly flashes like a red stock

alert. If she's safest with me, and she wants to be in California, then I'll come to her.

I enter the address into Google, but there's no owner associated with the information that populates the screen.

I call my assistant.

"Mr. Moore."

"Jay, pull up the title owner for this address."

I recite the address to him on the phone.

"Just give me a second."

Clicks sound through the receiver.

"By the way, did Geoffrey Cromwell call you today?"

"No, sir."

Interesting. How did he know I left Colorado?

"Okay. I have it. The property is owned by Aurora Skye Calloway. Closed on the property about three months ago."

I stare at the house, my mind eerily quiet.

"Mr. Moore, do you need anything else?"

"No, thank you, Jay."

What the hell is she doing at my mother's home? This isn't research. She landed and came straight here.

Why?

I won't find out unless I ask. I could wait to see if she tells me what she's doing, but we're past games.

The late-morning sun glints off the roofs of the homes on the west side of the street, casting a golden glow, while a young Hispanic teen pushes a lawn mower two houses down. These yards are postage-stamp size, but it's surprising to see so much grass. I thought with all the water restrictions there wouldn't be so much green.

Not that any of that matters. I exit the car and stand on the sidewalk. What to do now?

I've no memory of Aurora Calloway and no wish to meet her. I've explained this to Caroline more than once.

Did Caroline know I'd follow her? Is this her way of winning an old argument? Of forcing my hand?

No. I shake my head, having a conversation with myself on the sidewalk.

If Caroline is here, it's with my best interest at heart. She's never worked against me, only with me.

The door opens. A woman with long, straight steel-gray hair and a colorful, patterned skirt and Birkenstocks steps onto the front stoop. She hugs someone inside the house. Blonde hair comes into view. My peripheral vision blurs as I home in on the two women.

Caroline steps outside. She stops and holds a hand over her eyes as if confirming that the sun isn't playing tricks on her.

Yes, Caroline, I'm here. Why are you?

Caroline holds Aurora's hand, saying something to her that I can't hear. She steps off the porch, and I sense Caroline approaching, but my sight remains locked on my mother, standing still in the doorway.

I don't know what I expected Aurora Calloway to look like, but bohemian hippy isn't it.

"Dorian," Caroline says. "You followed me."

My gaze remains locked on Aurora. The tank top she's wearing reveals lean arms one would expect from an active lifestyle. Casting aside her hair color, she appears younger than her sixty-some years. Like all of my father's wives, she's undeniably attractive. I'd accuse her of being as vacuous as his other wives, except she'd look more at home at a pro-choice rally than Neiman Marcus.

The world sees me as a business titan, a man who can buy

anything or anyone. But standing here, I feel like that abandoned kid again. The difference is now I understand power; real power isn't about money, it's about control. And this situation—my mother, Caroline's presence—none of it is under my control.

"She goes by Rory." Caroline touches my arm, and I flinch. "Would you like to meet her?"

"Are you friends with her?"

How long has this been going on? Anger unexpectedly stirs, and I clench my hands, seeking control.

Caroline's rapid blinks and wide eyes tell me she didn't expect my anger. Neither did I. But it's here.

"Your mother knows your father's history. I came here to—"

"To what? Meet the woman I said I never wanted to meet?"

"To learn more about your father's background. To find out if you have more siblings. How often he used to travel out of the country, because we don't have the records from back then. To learn if there are any missing pieces of the puzzle that we should be aware of."

"You want me to believe you came here as part of the investigation?"

"It's the truth."

"Didn't you just tell me you believe I'm being set up?"

"Yes. And this is part of that investigation."

I study her light blue irises. Her posture and poise convey an elegance that the media painted as aloof and snobby, but they got her wrong. She's intelligent and passionate. Driven. The anger lessens. Perhaps it stems from desperation, but I believe her.

She should've worked with me on this, but I understand.

"What did you learn?"

"A day hasn't gone by that she hasn't thought of you. Your father threatened her and forced her hand. His lawyers fabricated evidence that she'd been an unfit mother. She didn't have the resources to fight his claims, and his attorneys had connections with the judge."

"None of that clears my name."

She glowers.

With a huff, I give in. If this is the topic she wants to cover, fine. "Did she share how much he paid her?"

"Only what was in the prenup. Not a dollar more. And she had to wait years for that."

That actually tracks. Not the threatening of an unfit mother, but limiting the payout to contractual obligations. I always imagined the payout to be one that she perceived to be massive. To some, a million is a life-altering figure. To others, it's a weekend getaway.

"The prenuptial agreement granted her two million dollars. She used the money to buy a home in Los Angeles, and she remarried. They had a happy marriage and two children together. He passed away about eighteen months ago. She sold their home and retired here. She has one daughter who lives in San Francisco and one who lives in Chicago. You have two sisters."

She sounds hopeful. What is there to be hopeful about?

"I can tell..." She flattens her palm against my chest, like I'm a dog she's trying to calm. "We'll talk about it later."

Will we?

"Your mother didn't know about Geoffrey. She thought you were his first child, and he did nothing that made her suspect otherwise. But your mother always wondered about you. She has a search on Google that notifies her every time your name appears in an article."

"Would you quit calling her my mother?"

"Fine. Rory. She was twenty-five when she married your father. Said the age difference caused quite a stir, as he was twice as old. She'd worked as a personal trainer at the gym he attended. The trainer your father hired had been sick and asked her to fill in for him. She says it was love at first sight." Caroline waffles her head slightly. "Until it wasn't."

Until someone else caught my father's attention. That fits the pattern.

"You should meet her. She said she's written to you, but she never received a response."

I recall a couple of letters. I tossed them, assuming she wanted a handout. Instructed Jay that he should recycle any correspondence from Aurora Calloway.

"I think you'll like her. She worked as a physical therapist but recently retired. She has a garden in her backyard, and she's building a—"

"Caroline. Stop." The woman remains on the front step. The yard is so small, she may hear us.

"I'm not ready." It's the most honest I've been with Caroline. In all those years of her pushing me, I wasn't ready. "I don't know if I'll ever—"

"She didn't leave you willingly. Put yourself in her shoes. She had no money. He cut off her credit cards and accounts. His lawyers played nasty. She didn't see a way to beat your father in a broken justice system that caters to wealth."

A slight dizziness hits, and a familiar warning pain pulses behind my temples. I have Vicodin in my bag, but I don't need it. Breathe. Focus.

"Did you learn anything useful?"

A buzzing in her handbag catches her attention, and she pulls her phone out.

Her mouth opens slightly, and her eyebrows lift.

"What is it?"

"There's been an explosion. Five simultaneous detonations across the country."

A terrorist event will kickstart emergency protocols. Futures are going to nosedive.

"Dorian, we're under attack."

CHAPTER 29

CAROLINE

Sophia picks up on the first ring. "Where are you?"

"About an hour north of the office. Research," I add, answering the question before she can ask.

"Get to the office. Keep your phone on. Blackouts in the top five metro areas. The military is en route to protect remaining substations."

Dorian says, "I'll drive. You can have your hands free."

It's a good suggestion, so I head to his car.

"Is this a rental? Do you want to take mine?" But he's already in the driver's seat.

"Is everything okay?" Rory calls from the stoop.

"I'm going to leave my car here. I'll be back to get it."

Dorian rolls down the passenger window and says, "Tell her to stay home. If there's an escalation, we'll be back to get her."

"Depending on what happens, we might not be able to get back here."

Doomsday scenarios mean freeways turn into parking lots. Any travel completed by foot. An hour by car is a lot longer walking, and it would be dangerous.

"Trust me," he says, reading my thoughts. "If we have to fly by helicopter, we will." I need to remember that I'm with a billionaire. There's no scenario that he believes he can't manage. A scenario where his wealth doesn't work for him is unthinkable.

"Stay here," I shout across the yard. "We'll be back. You have my number." It's not a question. We exchanged contact information before I left.

"Should I tell her to watch the news? Pack a bag?"

"Caroline, get in the car."

I swing the door open and do as he says. Dorian hits the accelerator, and I wave goodbye to a concerned Rory.

"Caroline, who are you with?" Sophia's voice reminds me she's still on the line.

"I'm with Dorian, and I have you on speaker. We just left his mother's house."

I don't miss the flex of his jaw, but it's not a point of debate. She is his mother.

"Haven't turned onto the freeway yet. How's traffic?"

"You should be fine getting here. The cities with blackouts are under control. Still daylight."

Daytime attacks are unusual, suggesting either desperation or a larger strategy we're not seeing yet. Coordinated infrastructure hits usually come at night.

"Are you expecting an EMP attack?" Dorian asks.

"Worried about your satellites?" Sophia responds through the speakerphone.

"You should be, too," he answers.

"It's on our list of concerns," Sophia admits.

A male voice shouts Sophia's name.

"I've got to run. Come straight here."

The call ends.

Dorian turns onto a major thoroughfare.

"I don't know where I am. Can you use your phone for navigation? I need to make a phone call."

"Maybe I should be driving."

"Not the time to be a smartass."

I glance up from the phone screen, expecting a glare, but there's a hint of a smile.

"This car has nav, but it's tied into the rental, and it's not great."

"No problem."

I set my phone down so he can see the display and pick up his phone.

"Siri, call Nick Ivanov."

"Calling Nick Ivanov." Siri's voice sounds eerily familiar.

"Did you use my voice for your Siri?"

He shrugs.

"I didn't know you could do that."

"You can't," he answers with a shy grin.

The line rings on speaker.

"Hey, mate," Nick answers in his recognizable British accent. "I likely don't know more than you."

"I'm away from my computer. Driving Caroline to her office in California."

"Ah, she's with you?"

"Hi, Nick."

"Hello, love. Is he holding you at gunpoint?"

"Not funny," Dorian quips.

"Yeah, well, fair question. As you know, I've had two different teams tracking communications. And trades."

"And?" Dorian asks.

"Your father. The person behind all of this is your old man. And I know, you told me, he's got dementia. If you're straight up, then it's someone playing at him. I'm waiting for a helicopter, and I'll be headed to London. I'm going over everything with MI6 and Interpol."

Dorian reaches the freeway. Surprisingly, traffic is light. He floors the vehicle.

"I'm not sure how far back his decline goes, but he's been messaging me," Nick says. "Not too recently, but not that far back. When you gave me the news, it got me thinking. I went back and confirmed. Over the last two years, he's messaged regularly."

"I have his messaging app set up to interact with an AI assistant."

"You do?" Why didn't he mention that?

"He gets too flustered if he can't send and receive messages. But they're cocked. So, to protect him, I created an app. Uploaded his message history and email history to give his friends and colleagues some authenticity in responses, but really, it was probably unnecessary. He's mostly nonsensical."

"Sometimes his messages do feel cocked, but not AI cocked," Nick says. "Any chance someone's got access to his accounts?"

"I'm not sure. I'd tell you to trace it, but our current bet is someone on staff has been entering his office." Dorian side-eyes me. "Actually, I learned that I have a half-brother. He doesn't live with my father, but he's frequently present. Can you have your team see what they can find about Geoffrey Cromwell?"

"Why is that name familiar?"

"You've probably met him. He's my father's primary financial advisor."

"He's not with Bedrock?"

"No, but he oversees the team at Bedrock that handles my father's investments."

"We're also researching the medical staff," I add, wondering why Dorian would suspect the worst from his newly discovered brother. Although, in all fairness, Geoffrey Cromwell is now on my mental person-of-interest list, and I plan to request a background report on him.

"Who's doing that research?" Nick asks.

"The company I work for. It's called Arrow Tactical."

"I'm familiar," Nick responds.

"I don't know who is pretending to be my father, but his symptoms began about three years ago. About two years ago, I brought in full-time staff. Minimized his interactions. It might've been eighteen months ago. I'd need to check my records."

"And never said a word? How are there not at least rumors?"

"He's ninety-two," Dorian says, exasperated. "Most people assumed he retired and was taking a step back. And he was making a lot of gaffes. I think he knew it, which is why he agreed to move to Colorado."

"I had wondered," Nick answers.

"Well, whoever is acting as your father, if they speak, we'll get clued in fast," I say.

Dorian grins. "You bugged Dad's office?"

"It was the assignment."

"Well, all my communications with your dear father have been in writing," Nick says. "Nothing on the phone. I assumed he might've a hard time hearing, so he preferred messaging. Assumed that given his age, he wasn't as wary of the risks."

"Can you send a note to our contacts, letting them know that Halston Moore has been compromised and not to trust any communications from him?" Dorian asks.

"Certainly. What about your father's accounts? Does he still have access?"

"Geoffrey obviously knows his condition. He has full control of his financial accounts. I changed the password on accounts I was aware of, but if someone is in his office…"

"Nothing would prevent them from gaining access to everything."

"Right."

"What about your satellites?"

"That's my company. Halston never touched it."

The separation between Zenith and Halston's empire could be crucial for tracking the source of the attacks. Classic intelligence work: follow the access points.

"So he'd have no access," Nick clarifies.

"None. If someone contacted one of my employees claiming to be Halston, they wouldn't get far. I'd get notified."

"And that hasn't happened?"

"No."

I pick up my phone. "You're good on nav, right?"

Signs are pointing us to Santa Barbara.

I don't wait for his agreement but shoot a note to Sophia.

ME

Geoffrey Cromwell is a person of
interest.

The message feels cold, clinical, reducing Dorian's newly
discovered brother to a data point in an investigation. But
emotional distance is crucial when the stakes are this high.
Even if it means treating your husband's family as potential
national security threats.

SF

FBI en route. To both Halston Moore's
and Geoffrey Cromwell's addresses.

CHAPTER 30

DORIAN

Traffic gets heavier the closer we get to Santa Barbara, but it's moving. Reports are coming in that traffic in Los Angeles is at a standstill, partially from traffic lights being out and intersections off the freeways getting clogged. If they can't get power restored by nightfall, there's a possibility of a curfew. On the East Coast, nightfall will occur shortly.

If the plan was to rock the world with a sudden multitiered attack, it seems the plan isn't being executed correctly.

"Sophia says a fringe white supremacist group out of Texas has taken credit for the attacks on US soil."

I glance at Caroline and the phone in her hand.

"Are they buying it?"

If true, then there's no tie to my father. Although these guys may not buy that. They've already accused him of funding fringe groups, dismissing the fact that he funds both parties to cover his bases. For as long as I can remember, my father has viewed politicians as toll keepers. If you want to avoid court or have a favorable policy outcome, pay the toll. Want legislation that hurts your competitor? Pay the toll. Want legislation that allows your business to grow? Lower taxes? Lessen restrictions? Pay the toll.

"No one's buying it. It's a grab-the-limelight ploy."

"Are you headed to Texas?" If she is, I'll go with her. I should have my security detail with us, but I left them back at the compound.

"FBI and Homeland Security will handle." Caroline sets the phone down and looks out the window at a sprawling neighborhood set off to the right, far too close to a freeway. "I'd bet this group has been on a watch list for years."

"They being dismissed outright?" I ask.

"Not in the media, but...reading between the lines, they already know the players and don't believe they have the capacity or funding to pull this off."

Up ahead, a sign informs us we're eighteen miles from Santa Barbara.

"We have a solid twenty minutes before we're at the office," I say. "What did you learn from Aurora Calloway?"

I don't miss the hope in her eyes. It's misguided. I'm not open to a relationship with a woman who walked away from her child. I get that my father can be intimidating, but if she cared, she wouldn't have given up.

"She has two framed photographs of you. One when you were in the hospital, in her arms. Another when you were learning to walk. You were holding both of her hands. You were a chubby child."

"Did you learn anything useful?"

Her silence draws my attention. Her lips are scrunched together as if she's struggling to keep from saying something.

"Caroline, just say it."

"She had no choice when she left you. She didn't stand a chance against your father's wealth."

That's what Caroline has always believed. But for the moment, that's not relevant.

"Did you find anything useful for the situation at hand? That's why you went to her house, right?"

"Possibly. She said your father frequented gentlemen's clubs."

"That's hardly news. Much of his generation did. And like we discussed last night, your boss's brother does, too. As does Nick."

Or he did. Maybe he won't now that he has a new girlfriend. Last I saw him, he was into the redhead, so into her he was willing to throw away his membership in the syndicate to keep her in his protection when the mafia wanted her.

"But there was one your father frequented that was associated with the Kremlin."

"In what way?"

"It was before Rory's time. She said that he'd been remorseful. But he told her that there were photos of him and other friends of his. Used for blackmail."

"Infamous Russian trick. It's not surprising. It clearly didn't harm him."

"No, but her theory is that if he had any other children, they came from that period in his life."

"So her theory is that Geoffrey Cromwell is Russian?"

"Raised by a Russian."

"What would make her say that?"

"Because your father seemed protective of his past."

"But nothing ever came of it? To her knowledge?"

"No. She walked in on him with the au pair, who was seventeen at the time."

"She was a fool to marry my father. What I've never understood is why he didn't opt for an open marriage."

"She said your father always gets what he wants. He wanted her until he tired of her."

She's still looking out the window.

"You know I never tired of you, right?"

"I wasn't trying to insinuate you did."

"I never cheated on you, either."

"I know."

Her knee bounces up and down, and she resumes scrolling on her phone screen. "For the record, what happened between your parents has nothing to do with us."

"I'm always compared to my father."

"Yes, but I don't compare you to him."

"No, you don't." Perhaps I should apologize for insinuating she did. When Caroline fell for me, I was an unknown to her, and once she learned about my family, she wished I didn't have that baggage. She's always seen the real me. The person, not the heritage.

The GPS announces that we should take the exit in half a mile.

Once we reach the Arrow Tactical office, people will surround us. Her colleagues, bosses. People who see me as a person of interest—code for suspect.

Caroline's attention fluctuates between her phone and the window.

"I shouldn't have accused you of comparing me to my father," I say, as that's probably what she wants to hear.

Her head tilts, and she leans forward. "Is that your idea of an apology?"

That was an apology. I open my mouth to argue, but then I catch her smile and the shake of her head.

"You're unbelievable."

"What do I need to apologize for? You're the one who went to my mother's house."

"And I might have uncovered an interesting angle."

I flick the turn signal to exit the freeway, following the directions laid out on her phone.

"If Geoffrey's mother is a Russian immigrant, or if there are any other ties, Nick will uncover it."

The navigation directs us through the streets, leading us to the tourist area of Santa Barbara.

Palm trees sway against crisp, cloudless blue skies. Given what's going on with the world, there's a surreal quality to the setting.

Caroline directs me to underground parking, but I see an open spot on the street and nab it. I don't live in Santa Barbara, but I've been here often enough, I understand the fortuity of street parking.

We exit the car in tandem and cross the street.

To one side is a brightly painted front for a shoe company. The nondescript door Caroline opens is part of a larger building that could be mistaken for the side of a parking garage. But when we enter, the small reception desk in front of a black glass wall has a different feel entirely. A black security camera hangs prominently from one corner, the placement making it clear they want everyone to be aware of the device.

A woman with black, short-cropped hair and an athletic build sits behind the desk. She clocks us both head to toe. She and Caroline exchange hellos, and the woman asks for my identification.

"Seriously?" The word comes out sharper than intended, but isn't time of the essence?

"He's with me," Caroline says. "They're expecting him upstairs."

"I'm aware," the woman says. "I'd still like to see your identification."

Grudgingly, I withdraw my wallet and pass her my Colorado driver's license.

"I'm surprised you haven't relocated to Florida, given the absence of a state income tax," Caroline says as the receptionist scans my license in a machine.

"Unlike some of my friends, I'm not petty enough to give a damn about taxes." My gaze roams the walls and ceiling of the diminutive space. "And clearly, neither are you or your friends, given you're in California."

My quip earns a slight smile. The receptionist returns my license, and Caroline pulls on a doorknob. We enter a narrow vestibule, and she presses a button for an elevator. Two additional doors line the hall. Presumably, one of those doors goes to a stairwell.

I glance over Caroline's shoulder and see that she's messaged we're here. The message is likely entirely unnecessary, given that I'm certain we were observed when we entered.

The elevator climbs one floor, and the doors open into a vast room of cubicles with offices lining the exterior. The setup is typical Silicon Valley—glass walls and open concept, though I note the military-grade security features subtly integrated throughout. Different from the quantum-encrypted fortress I maintain in Colorado, but effective in its own way.

A door on the opposite wall opens, and the woman I recognize from photographs exits.

She waves Caroline in, gesturing for her to enter the room. Unlike the other offices with clear glass, smoky glass forms the walls of this room, and as we approach, I recognize the glass as switchable glass, meaning it can become opaque with the touch of a button.

"Geoffrey Cromwell has exited the country," Sophia says as we approach.

Interesting.

"Do you know how?" I ask.

"By plane."

"Private?"

"Yes, why?"

"Because he knew I'd left Colorado. I wasn't sure how he knew, but I wouldn't be surprised if he flew out of the same location I did. He probably spoke to someone who told him I left."

"Right." Caroline's friend holds the door for us and closes it behind us as soon as we step inside. "Dorian Moore, I'm Sophia Fisher."

"It's nice to meet you."

She gives a curt nod and makes no move to offer her hand, so I lower the one I've extended.

Four other men sit at a long conference table. I recognize only one of them—the jackass who picked Caroline up earlier this morning.

Interestingly, he averts his gaze, focusing on the laptop in front of him.

"Do you mind, Dorian? We need to confer with Caroline privately."

"Not at all. Do you have an office I can use?"

"Do you need a computer?"

"No, I have my laptop." I pat the shoulder strap of the bag I'm carrying.

"He can use my cubicle," Caroline offers.

"I'd prefer more privacy, if you have it." The issue with cubicles is that anyone can see what's on your screen. An outfit like this, it's quite possible they have temporary staff doing recon.

"He can use my office," the man at the end of the conference table says.

Based on Sophia's reaction, she doesn't like that idea at all. "It's secure," he says to Sophia. To me, he adds, "I'm Ryan Wolfgang, CEO of Arrow Tactical."

"Ah, you work with Jack Sullivan."

"Do you know Jack?"

"I know of him. We've attended some of the same conferences over the years. Friends in common with his brother, Liam, as well. They both hold an interest in satellites." Satellite surveillance, actually, but I sense Ryan is informed.

With a polite nod, I follow Sophia out of the conference room and into an adjacent corner office. Through the glass, beyond the buildings and the street, a sliver of the Pacific Ocean shows.

"If you need anything, just knock on the conference room door."

The door closes before I can respond. I scan the ceiling. There's no visible camera, but I assume anything I do or say will be recorded. Still, I prefer the dignity of an office over a cubicle surrounded by strangers.

I power up my laptop and dial Nick. The desk is clean. Void of all items, save ports to plug chargers and connections. There's not even a pen holder. Three monitors but no laptop. I suppose this is what he meant by his office being secure.

The setup is bare but efficient—exactly what you'd expect from someone who understands digital security. I connect through my own quantum-encrypted VPN. I'm taking no chances with data security.

Nick answers on the fourth ring.

"Where are you?"

"Santa Barbara. Arrow Tactical offices."

"I'm in London. At my flat. How are things there? People worried?"

"When we parked, I saw two surfers lugging surfboards down to the ocean and a line at the coffee shop down the street. But it's LA that has the blackout. We're about two and a half hours away. What're you hearing?"

"I have a reputable source claiming that Five Eyes has been infiltrated."

"Infiltrated how? Hacked?"

"An employee. A leak."

"Working for who? Russia?"

There's no way. Those employees are thoroughly vetted.

"Awaiting details. Interesting that you bring up Russia. Your father's financial adviser, Geoffrey Cromwell, is Russian. Did you know that?"

"Does he have dual citizenship?"

"No, nothing that obvious. His mother."

Look at that. Rory's hunch was right.

"I'll shut down my dad's accounts."

"If Cromwell is involved, he would've transferred funds before this went down."

"I'll get someone to check." I shoot off a note to Jay to request a full account report from Bedrock on my father's accounts.

The geopolitical implications hit me. With Zenith's control over global communications infrastructure, any state actor would see us as both a threat and an opportunity. The satellite network I built could be the ultimate prize. But no—Zenith is out of Geoffrey's reach.

"Another option would be that your half-brother is setting up your father for treason. The question is, if he wanted him dead, why not just kill him? Or kill you, for that matter? The math's not working on that one either."

"Well, he may have attempted to kill me. My helicopter may have been sabotaged. Hydraulic lines. Cause yet to be determined."

"Why would he aim to kill you and not your father?"

"Maybe Geoffrey's not in the will? If I die, he'd be added?"

"Come now. The bloke's controlled your dad's finances for ages. He could've robbed him blind and spent his twilight years sunning on a beach off the grid."

"You think he's working for Putin?"

"Or he's looking to hurt your dad where it will hurt him most—his reputation. But Halston's not of sound mind, right?"

"And Geoffrey's aware. Maybe Dad's dementia forced him to alter his plan. It's been a gradual decline. Perhaps he went from someone who could be easily manipulated to someone who wouldn't comprehend what had been done to him. I don't know. Investigators have yet to visit the crash site. It's not easily accessible, and a storm system came through late yesterday. I'm guessing there, too. Could've just as easily been a mechanical malfunction."

"How old's your bird?"

"Latest model."

"Get your head out of your arse. It's sabotage."

"Would my staff be in on it?" My question is as much to myself as to Nick. In my rush, I didn't bring anyone with me, but I've got a hefty payroll back in Colorado.

"That, I can't say. But one thing is certain. Someone out there has infiltrated the syndicate, and that someone fakes your father well. You've got to let everyone know the truth about your Dad. Not just the syndicate. Anyone with weight that he influences."

CHAPTER 31

CAROLINE

As the door closes behind me, Ryan's stern expression underscores the seriousness of the moment.

Trevor, Luke, Fisher, and two men I don't recognize gather around the end of a conference table, reading updates streaming in from a source.

Ryan follows my gaze to the men at the end of the room.

"We boarded the ship. It's ours," Trevor says. "Getting the lay of the land. It'll be deposed shortly."

He's talking about the ship they mentioned during my Project Unity debrief. The US and allied partners tracked it for weeks. In my opinion, they should've taken it out when they first located the stolen chemical weapons.

If Trevor's sharing an update… "Is Arrow going—"

"No," Ryan answers. "Stolen chemical weapon cargo. Justifiable action. If what we learn implicates an American…" His head shifts, and those ice-blue eyes question, judging my character? No, assessing my performance.

"It's not Dorian. You believe me, right?"

I glance back at the other men, but their attention is trained on Trevor's laptop.

"Let's talk privately," Ryan says, leading me back to the conference door.

As we exit, Luke's attention breaks, and with Ryan's back turned, the look he gives me is pure venom. Damn. He's pissed.

Because Dorian's here? Because I didn't come straight to the office like he asked? Because I'm the second woman he's dated who has chosen her ex over him?

I can't worry about his reasoning. I breathe in deeply, blinking away the ridiculous situation.

"Caroline, let's use Stella's office," Ryan says, leading the way.

As I follow him along the hallway, I listen to the subdued chatter and keys. The tension in the air has lessened, yet here I am, following my boss for a private discussion. This is feeling like I'm in for a reprimand.

When he enters Stella's office, he leans against the front of the desk, half-sitting, half-standing.

"Close the door."

"Is everything okay?"

"Our military and allies have things under control. At the moment."

"Stella and Trevor's son? He's safe?"

"He's deployed." Ryan crosses his arms over his chest, making it clear he won't share more, and I understand. There isn't more he can say. "Sophia's kept us informed."

I expected as much.

"In a mission, we all play a role. From Arrow's perspective, you played a vital role in our assignment. Our government and our allies are counting on us to provide accurate intel."

"Do you have a question?"

The overhead light reflects on the gray hairs sprinkled throughout his short-cropped black hair. His eyes narrow.

"Can we trust you?"

"Absolutely."

"Don't be offended by my question. I understand how loyalty can be tested. If someone asked me to choose between my wife and my country...I'll hold my head up high and stand by my wife."

"Ryan, you have my word. I'm not lying. I'm not even bending the truth. Dorian Moore isn't behind this. And Halston..." I shrug. "He's unreliable. He alternates between lucid and..." I press my lips together, at a loss for the right word. "In all probability, someone is accessing his accounts and leveraging his network. It's highly unlikely someone in his deteriorating state could pull this off. I won't say it's impossible, but at the very least, people he hired are executing."

"And you believe that person is his financial advisor? This Geoffrey Cromwell?"

"It's conceivable." I already relayed all of this to Sophia. I haven't written it up in a report, but... "Sophia said he exited the country."

"There's a flight plan," he says.

"But no sighting?"

Ryan nods. "If he's behind this, he's in the wind."

"What's the next step? What do you need me to do?"

"Right now? NSA has their people doing a background on

Cromwell, business associations, and Halston Moore's contacts. The president has asked that he receive a full report."

"Dorian has nothing to hide."

"That's what I needed."

"What?"

"Your confidence. As for what we do…we wait. We did our part. We narrowed the persons of interest list. Now we wait for additional assignments."

"Is what I read correct? The National Guard has been deployed?"

"Marines and National Guard are deployed to protect the electrical grid. The news has that right."

"What do they have wrong?"

"Let's just say it's a busy day for the world's military. If Russia is behind this, this may be their waking the beast moment."

"Do you think we'll go to war?"

His lips purse. "If they're behind this, they're watching our movements. Seeing how and where the US and our allies are deploying troops. They'll stand down. Wait for a less cohesive and aligned resistance." He stands, signaling the end of our meeting. "As for you, when your husband finishes his call, why don't you head home? We'll call you if you're needed."

What he's telling me is that I'm not needed. It's in the hands of others now. These guys may still be following the investigation, but I'm not needed. Actually, they probably want me to take Dorian away from here.

"As soon as we leave, you're going to listen to the audio from your office?"

He grins. "I already have someone doing that. Deciphering anything he types might take more time."

I shouldn't grin in response, but I do. It's not personal.

"That's not to say I don't trust you," Ryan emphasizes. "It's a precaution. The fact that no one has interrupted us means you're safe to head home with him."

We'll head back home. Perhaps return to Rory's house to get my car. She's got to be worried.

"Are you back with him?" Ryan's question is unexpected, but I suppose it's understandable he'd inquire. We entered the office together. He referred to him as my husband.

"For how long?" I shrug slightly and give my boss a half-hearted smile. "That's the question."

"My advice?"

I study the founder of our company, wisdom etched in the corners of his eyes, in his weathered skin and rough-hewn hands. The man has had a storied career, and he garners the respect of all in his employ.

"Please."

"I've never been divorced, by the grace of god. But I've witnessed divorce. Some couples bring out the worst in each other. And divorce is a blessing. But sometimes—and I expect this is rare—time apart, time to grow, that's all that was needed. I had a buddy—I won't use his name, as you know him—whose divorce wrecked him. He wanted her back." Ryan's eyes grow cloudy, reflective. He inhales as if snapping himself back from the past. "Looked like it might happen, too, but there was a car wreck. He never got his second chance. Not a real one. Not with her. I'm not saying all this to be morbid. I'm just saying... we're not guaranteed tomorrow. Do the important stuff today."

Sophia's mother died in a car wreck, and I can't help but wonder if Ryan is referring to Jack Sullivan, Sophia's father. Her mother died a long time ago. To my knowledge, her step-mother, Ava Sullivan, has been in her life for ages, since long before I met Sophia.

Ryan claps me on the shoulder and directs me out of the office.

About half of the cubicles now sit empty.

"Is the blackout over?" I ask, pulling out my phone for updates.

"No, but we believe it's under control. Our part's done for the moment. We've been working nonstop for weeks. We're sending folks home to rest up and be with their families. It is Saturday, after all."

"And if the blackout extends here—"

"Stock up on water," Ryan says. "Actually, if you need anything, you come here. We take care of our own. We're prepped. But we're not expecting the blackout to spread. Government agencies, the Pentagon, they're all over this. Let's take the break while we can."

Through Ryan's office door, I see Dorian with a phone held out in front of his mouth, his back to me, as he takes in the view from Ryan's corner office.

Luke steps up. "Do you have a minute?" he asks, glancing between me and Ryan. "I thought we could clear the air."

Clear the air? He had to choose those words? I thought we cleared the air on the ride from the airport, but I have no choice but to agree, given we're standing in front of our boss.

"Certainly. Do you want some tea?" I ask, slightly thirsty.

"What do you say we take a step outside?" Luke counters. "I've been cooped up indoors too long."

Dorian appears to be in an intense conversation, one I'm certain an Arrow team member is listening to, and I'm just as certain Dorian knows this and has determined his conversation doesn't require privacy.

"Yeah. Let's step across the street." I'll bring back something for Dorian, and then I'll take Ryan up on his offer to call it a day. I'm tired. I woke up in an earlier time zone.

Luke asks one of the guys I don't know if he wants anything and ends up jotting down a couple of drink orders, which feels unnecessary, since most of us have been told to call it a day. But, a lot of the Arrow guys are former military, and while we may not be active participants in the mission at this juncture, I understand the desire to get the updates and stay, just in case.

We step through the reception area. The desk sits empty.

Something feels off. The empty reception desk breaks standard security protocol, the building too quiet for an active crisis situation, even if some have been sent home. Perhaps it's no longer an active crisis situation.

"What—"

A blunt, hard metal object presses into my ribs. Based on the pressure point and angle, likely a Glock 19, standard issue for private security.

"Keep walking. You fight me, and we go to Plan B."

"Luke." I draw his name out, buying time to catch up.

"Plan B involves you, dead. And a remote detonator blowing the Arrow Tactical building sky high."

CHAPTER 32

DORIAN

I wrap up my calls and exit Ryan Wolfgang's office. There's no doubt his team listened to my business calls. I hope they were suitably bored.

The conference room is ajar, and I rap my knuckles against the frame, pushing it slightly, scanning the room for Caroline.

A couple of men sit around a laptop.

I nod my apology for interrupting, but their attention quickly returns to the screen.

Sophia Sullivan Fisher, Caroline's friend and a woman I've loosely monitored ever since I received a photograph of the two of them at a DC restaurant, spots me across the office.

As Sophia approaches, I recall the file I have on her. After we split, Caroline lived with her parents for several months. When she moved out, I waited for the press to do their job. The absence of news troubled me. I envisioned her having a torrid affair with one of my more reclusive friends and hired a PI.

The PI sent a slew of photographs but pulled herself from the assignment about a week into it. Said she'd been spotted. But in that one week, I learned enough.

Sophia might be the daughter of a billionaire and a member of a highly respected Texas family, but from what I can tell, she's a dedicated public servant. Given our current situation in a privately held office partially owned by her father, it seems the CIA officer takes on side projects, too.

Regardless, it's easy to see how Caroline and Sophia became close. Like Sophia, Caroline chose to work. Our prenuptial agreement entitled her to enough that she wouldn't have to work another day in her life. But she never pursued a dollar of those funds. She never hired legal counsel. Of course, Caroline's background with two school teachers as parents is far more provincial than Sophia's.

"Dorian, before you head out of here, do you mind if I ask you some questions?"

Sophia's direct, I'll give her that.

"Shoot." I scan the cubicles. "Where's Caroline?"

One guy at the conference room table hears my question and answers. "She and Luke went on a coffee run."

Luke. That's the guy who couldn't take his eyes off her.

"There's nothing going on there," Sophia says.

Mind-reading must be one of the skills they teach at the Central Intelligence Agency.

"What do you need to ask me?" If she's direct, I can be, too.

"There's an APB out on Geoffrey Cromwell. We suspect he's left the country. Do you have any idea where he might go?"

I suppose she means other than Russia. I scrub my fingers through my hair, exhaustion infiltrating after the long day.

"I've known Geoffrey Cromwell most of my life. But we've never been close. I've never been to his home. In Colorado or New York. I couldn't even tell you if he's married or single, straight or gay. Our relationship has been strictly professional. I suppose Caroline told you that, until yesterday, I had no idea that he's my brother. Well, half-brother."

A dull pain surfaces along my brow. *Dammit.* The last thing I need is for a migraine to surface.

"But he's been to your home?"

Geoffrey spends most of his time at my father's home. I thought of him as one of the cronies who orbit my dad, kissing his ass.

"Many times. He lives somewhere nearby." I lived with Dad when I was building the house. Geoffrey asked lots of questions during the process. "Geoffrey built his home in Colorado around the same time I built my house. We used the same builder. I actually hired my builder, per his recommendation." In retrospect, that was a fuckup. I'll need a team to sweep the house. "But you say he's not in Colorado?"

She shakes her head. "Do you know any of his friends? Assistants?"

I lean against the wall, racking my brain. My friends aren't friends with Geoffrey. Our professional circles overlapped, but those are all acquaintances.

"When Geoffrey moved to Colorado, he retired. Semi-retired. He kept my father's account. To my knowledge, he let his employees go. You could ask my assistant, Jay Colston, if he knew any of Geoffrey's employees. He always dealt with Geoffrey for me."

I hear my uselessness and hate it. How could I have been so inattentive? But in all fairness, suits circled my dad. At a young age, I began weeding through those I needed to pay attention to and those I could completely disregard.

"How can I reach Jay Colston?"

I pull out my phone and send her a text with Jay's contact info.

"How do you have my number?" Sophia asks.

I release a sigh that holds a mix of exhaustion and dismay. "I've had it for a long time, Sophia." She tilts her head, silently questioning. I shouldn't have to explain to her that phone numbers aren't exactly hard to come by. "You were my wife's close friend. Of course, I had it."

"Ex-wife."

"Separated," I counter.

"You didn't sign the papers?"

And I'm not going to. "We're taking things slow, but I'm hopeful."

I stare straight into her eyes and notice they're blue, like Caroline's. A deeper blue, whereas Caroline's are ethereal.

"Where is Caroline?" I'm ready to call this day. "Where's this coffee shop?"

"Come on. I'll come with you. I'll ask questions while we walk."

"I'm not holding anything back."

"Didn't say you were. It's the little things that can be useful. Like your builder. Can you share his contact info?"

I fumble with my phone, sending her the requested contact card. I could argue, but hell, maybe he has something useful on Geoffrey. Especially if Geoffrey bribed him to do anything funky to my house. Although my security team would've caught anything out of the ordinary.

After I share the builder's contact, I shoot off a message to Jay, giving him a heads-up that he'll be hearing from Sophia.

I did a background check on my builder. Standard protocol for anyone touching my infrastructure. It's four years old but archived on our network. I jot a note to myself to check it when I'm logged in on the portal.

Sophia's already down the stairs at the exit door, and I hustle to catch up with her.

One flight, I don't know why they bother with an elevator.

Sophia's right hand rises. "Shh."

I slow, attempting to peer over her head through the exit door.

"Stay here," she says, stepping through.

I snatch the knob just before the door closes.

A quick scan reveals nothing out of place. But I've seen this foyer exactly once.

She turns the corner.

Her voice projects loudly. "Cam? Why isn't anyone at reception? Who's on-site surveillance?"

I round the corner.

She's got a phone pressed to her ear. It's a landline that's connected to reception.

"What do you mean Luke said it's covered?"

My heart stutters.

"Where's the coffee shop?"

She ignores me, flustered, her focus on the phone.

"Sophia!"

That gets her attention.

"Coffee shop."

She points. "Across the street."

I've got to find Caroline.

I charge across the street, scanning the coffee shop with open windows and doors.

Fuck. Where is Caroline?

I pull out my phone and press the tracking app.

Two quantum-encrypted tracking signals, military-grade precision. One signal originates within fifteen feet of my position.

I spin on the sidewalk, holding the phone out.

I am on the dot.

A trash can inside the door of the coffee shop snags my attention.

Fucking hell.

I shove the swinging trash can top aside.

Caroline's purse.

I dig it out of the trash and flip it open.

Her phone.

Dammit. Fucking hell!

Someone has her.

Luke. Does that bastard work for Geoffrey?

Please let her still have the other tracker on her body. I press to locate it and sprint across the street with her handbag.

I sling the door open to Arrow's offices. Ryan, Sophia, and two others are standing in the reception area.

"He's got Caroline. Found her handbag in the trash. But she's got another tracker on her he doesn't seem to know about."

I pull up our satellite command interface on my phone.

Within seconds, I have eyes on the area from three different orbital positions. He—or they—might be able to dodge street cameras, but they can't hide from my network.

I thrust my phone screen in Ryan's face.

"They're on the move."

CHAPTER 33

CAROLINE

Establish dialogue, build rapport, gather intel.

"What do you want with me?"

"I told you—quiet."

Details tell a story: his tight grip on the weapon, microexpressions, vocal stress patterns. Luke's at ease, focused, and there's no internal conflict.

The driver rounds the bend. We're in a limousine with black tinted windows. Luke's handgun remains trained on me.

If elimination was the goal, he had cleaner options at the office. This is about leverage, which means I'm worth more alive than dead. Classic strategic play: target the asset that provides maximum tactical advantage.

"Who do you work for?"

"Quiet. I'm not telling you again."

The driver's wearing sunglasses and black leather gloves. I've never seen him before, but I suspect he's watching me in the rearview.

The limousine is a good choice. The blacked-out windows fit, and no one will suspect the vehicle holds a kidnap victim.

But why me?

Geoffrey Cromwell and I met only once.

That I remember.

Perhaps that makes it less likely Cromwell is the one who hired Luke to abduct me. It could be someone else. Someone who's not even on our list.

But Cromwell's one of the few who knows Dorian and I never legally divorced. If he suspects Dorian still has feelings for me, then I'd be a bargaining chip. That would mean it could be Cromwell.

But a bargaining chip for what? He's been in control of Halston's finances for ages.

Inheritance?

I can't imagine it comes down to greed. Control of Bedrock? Cromwell couldn't simply step into the chairman of the board role through blackmail. Neither could anyone else. It's a public company.

The satellites. Zenith. Halston has zero involvement in Zenith. It's a private company with independent infrastructure. But with me as leverage… I remember briefing scenarios like this at Langley: Find the pressure point that bypasses all the technical safeguards.

Zenith owns 80 percent of the satellites orbiting Earth. If Geoffrey is behind this, he could be counting on me being the one thing to force Dorian's hand. But for what? He can't expect Dorian would just hand over his company as ransom.

And Dorian must have fail-safes in place. He had to have thought about this risk. Not only someone blackmailing him, but blackmailing any of his employees.

"This won't work, Luke. Fail-safes are in place. Terrorist threats won't work."

The ice in Luke's gaze is that of a stranger. The friendly face, the kind words, it was all an act. The man holding a gun at me is a cold-blooded mercenary.

How did he get past Arrow's background checks?

A reference. They didn't look hard at me. Didn't dig into my marriage. Who vouched for Luke?

"Who said anything about terrorists?"

"What do you call it?"

He looks to the front of the car as we slow to a stop. Through the windshield, I can see a helicopter sitting on a concrete tarmac. It's a private helipad, but we're not alone. There are other cars parked nearby.

"It's funny. You're sitting here, all high and mighty, believing you're smart. You've had all of what…ten minutes to put the pieces together. This plan has been in place for years. Just shut up and do what I say. If you don't, your friends at Arrow Tactical…" He makes an explosion image with his fingers splayed and a boom sound.

I have no way of knowing if he's full of shit or if he's wired the place. He had access. He's been working…

"How long have you worked for Arrow Tactical?"

The driver exits the car, buttoning his suit coat as he stands. Luke and I both watch as he enters a small building off to the side.

"Now you're asking the right questions. Five months. Joined shortly after you did."

"But Dorian and I hadn't talked in years."

"You're not divorced, though, are you?"

"I'm not the only piece in play, am I?"

Whoever is behind this thought of all the angles. The plan included putting resources on wild cards, like me. A long game. Sleeper agents.

"Are you working for Geoffrey Cromwell or Russia?"

His gaze flicks between me and the building. He's waiting for a sign.

"We're going on a little trip. Getting in the helicopter. Don't get any wild ideas. No one here is going to help you. We all work for the same team."

I don't believe him. He's keeping me hidden with a gun trained on me. His driver went to clear our flight. The driver might be the pilot.

Luke never mentioned a pilot's license. If the background he supplied Arrow is accurate, which it probably is—closest to the truth is always best—he wasn't in Naval Aviation, and he hasn't been out long enough to pursue a license in his free time.

Luke's got at least sixty pounds on me, with a special ops background. But he's expecting compliance—standard protective services mindset. The element of surprise might be my only advantage.

Can I overpower Luke? There's no doubt he's stronger, bigger, better trained. But I'm more agile. I wish I were wearing stilettos and not these square heels.

I scan the adjacent parking lot. Three empty vehicles. The sun's glare shields the interior of two vehicles. That's a minimum of five individuals on-site, somewhere in this vicinity.

We're close to the coast. Is he flying me to a ship in international waters?

When the driver comes back, can I take out two men? I've got to try.

If I get on that helicopter, I'll never be seen again.

CHAPTER 34

DORIAN

My attention remains locked on the transponder signal, a precise GPS coordinate moving across my tablet's topographical display. The Mark IV tracking system has a ten-foot margin of error—not perfect, but enough. Even with my hands steady, my blood pulses through my fingers strongly enough that I'm aware of the rapid flow as I grip the phone.

I swear, my heart might pound out of my chest.

Ryan insisted on driving.

There are two SUVs behind us, loaded with armed men. Fisher's in the backseat.

Do I wish I had my security team with me? Hell yes.

If my arrogance and desire for privacy get Caroline killed… I've built a business on controlling every variable, anticipating every threat to my infrastructure. But I never imagined she'd become collateral damage in someone else's power play. I too often refused to be trailed by security, insisting I was safe.

My throat constricts at the thought of her in danger because of me. Cold sweat beads at my temples as images flash through my mind—Caroline hurt, afraid, alone.

Even when Caroline and I were together, and the press hounded us, hoping for photos of my new bride, I refused security. I thought I was protecting our privacy, our sanctuary. Now that choice haunts me with crystal clarity. If my arrogance gets her killed...I won't survive it. Not this time. The universe is giving me a second chance with her, and I'm watching it slip through my fingers like sand. The weight of dread sits heavy in my chest, a physical ache that makes it hard to breathe.

"Nick checked in," Fisher says from the back seat. "He's got a team on this, but so far, no leads."

Trevor stayed behind, dealing with the emergency team and securing the office. I don't know the others with us. Names were shared, but they didn't stick.

Thanks to my satellite footage, we know where she is. The dot hasn't moved, and we're minutes away.

A helipad comes into view up ahead on the hillside.

Fucking hell.

"Can you go faster?"

Stop-and-go traffic slowed us down, but we're out of the city, and the speedometer reads ninety-two.

Every second counts.

"If the chopper takes off, we'll track it."

That's not the answer I want.

"Tracking is exactly what he expects—what he may want," I say, stating the obvious.

"We've got a team researching Luke. May lead to some clues," Fisher offers up, I'm sure in an attempt to be helpful.

I stare at the dot.

"How did he get by your security check?" I don't know a ton about Arrow Tactical, but when all this is over, I'm sure as hell raining fire down on them until they root out the incompetence or Caroline walks away from the outfit.

"We're looking into that," Ryan clips.

There's something about the way he says it, how he won't look me in the eye.

"Are there others? In Arrow?" I remember the empty reception area. He's staring straight ahead…

"Ryan, this is my wife." For emphasis, I growl the words again. "My wife. What's going on?"

"He came in through a recommendation from an investor's brother."

It clicks.

"Liam Sullivan."

"You know him?"

"He knows Geoffrey Cromwell."

Ryan says, "Fisher, you hear that? Communicate it back."

"You're close. It's up ahead," I tell the car.

"Fisher, tell the others to hang back, surround the vicinity on foot. If shots are fired, call the local PD," Ryan says.

"Shouldn't we involve the FBI?" It's not the first time I've asked.

"They'll slow things down," Ryan says. "We'll bring them in when they're useful."

My ankle jerks up and down. The rapid tapping grates on my nerves, but I can't stop it.

Ryan slows as we pull into the facility.

A Sikorsky waits on the pad, rotors already spinning, tail number covered. The exhaust pattern suggests they've been ready to fly for at least twenty minutes. The Sikorsky's rotor wash creates invisible heat waves above the pad, distorting my view of the facility entrance. The Mark IV's signal pulses on my screen—steady, unwavering—unlike my hands.

"Stay in the vehicle," Ryan commands.

The second the wheels stop rolling, I'm out of the car.

The door to the building opens. A man dressed in black steps onto the tarmac. He's wearing a dark suit, and the protrusion at his waist signals he's carrying.

"Mr. Moore. I've been waiting for you."

"Where is she?"

"I've reserved a meeting room. Please come with me." The man looks past me to Ryan and the others. "Only Mr. Moore."

Ryan and I exchange a glance. I don't know any of the Arrow team well, but I sense these men see Caroline as one of their own, and they'll act accordingly to protect her. At least, they'd better fucking act to protect her.

"You'll need to give me your phone," the man says.

"Why would I do that?"

"I was told you'd be difficult. Listen first, then act—if you want her alive. We're progressing through a precarious part of the plan with diverse possible outcomes."

The barrel of Ryan's handgun enters my peripheral view.

"Hold your fire," the man says. There's no recognizable accent. "You're going to want to hear me out. And see what I have to show you."

He holds a phone out, like it's a bargaining chip. To hell with waiting. I snatch the phone from the man's hand.

My vision blurs.

Ryan crowds me.

"Please. Enter the meeting room."

I hear the man, but my focus and everything in me goes to the nightmare playing out on screen.

My vision blurs as I stare into the device. Caroline—bound with duct tape, a gash across her eyebrow, half her blonde hair darkened with blood.

The man shoves Ryan away. "That's not for you to see."

Her hands and ankles are bound.

I blink to clear the image.

Mother of god.

There's a bomb strapped to her abdomen.

"What is it?" Ryan asks.

"They've got Caroline."

The suit stretches his arms wide. "There's no detonator. Video is rolling. You kill me, she dies. Ryan shoots me, they see, she dies. Any snipers? They get trigger-happy, and she dies. You get the gist?"

"What do you want?"

"Thank you, Mr. Moore. I was told you would be amenable after receiving the right information. The meeting room, please. Mr. Wolfgang won't be needed."

"I'll wait," Ryan says, eyes locked on mine.

Message received. He's here if needed. He'll marshal resources. Nick. Anyone he believes he can bring on without putting Caroline in danger. When I did research on Arrow Tactical, I learned that hostage situations are an area of expertise. He'll know what to do.

I follow the man into a small, windowless room with a table, four chairs, and a monitor on the wall. The antiseptic smell of the facility hits me as we enter. Fluorescent lights buzz overhead, casting hard shadows across the man's face. My footsteps echo against polished concrete floors—each step bringing me closer to Caroline.

"May I have your phone?"

Reluctantly, I hand the device over. I'd like to shoot off a text to Nick, but that's not an option.

If this man is indeed carrying, the suit doesn't feel it's necessary to show me his weapon.

The door clicks closed, and the screen on the wall flicks to life.

Caroline's bloody face comes into view.

Her eyes…watery.

Something's off.

The tears aren't from fear.

No, there's something about the way she's looking at the camera.

At the person holding the camera.

Who is it?

Geoffrey?

My father?

It wouldn't be my father.

It couldn't be.

But as I study her eyes, the horrifying truth begins to dawn. She's not looking at her captor with fear.

She's looking with recognition.

CHAPTER 35

CAROLINE

The yacht pitches beneath my feet as I face my captor, squinting into the sun.

"Why are you doing this? Who's paying you?"

Luke stares back through mirrored sunglasses, unmoved. The same silence he's maintained since forcing me onto the helicopter at gunpoint.

He's assumed the role of mercenary. How did he fool Arrow into hiring him?

Hours ago, I was at Arrow Tactical. Now, I'm in the middle of the ocean with a colleague I trusted, who turns out to be a mercenary. I check the bruises on my wrists where he bound me for the helicopter ride—evidence this isn't some elaborate misunderstanding.

I feel sick thinking about our coffee dates, our conversations at Arrow. Every interaction now reframes as calculation

—him studying me, gathering intelligence, seeking opportunities. And everyone at Arrow encouraged it, thinking he was good for me. My instincts were right, but for all the wrong reasons.

"Whose yacht is this?"

After a heavy object came down hard on my head, I came to, strapped into a helicopter seat.

If I put up a fight, he'll likely knock me out again.

But what the hell am I supposed to do? Sit here and wait?

Salt spray occasionally mists over the railing as we cut through deep blue water. No land in sight—just endless horizon in every direction.

Jumping into the ocean is not a viable option. We're not alone on this yacht, though. A ship this size has a crew somewhere. Are they all mercenaries?

"Who else is on the boat?" I ask, fully aware that chances are great Luke will remain silent or tell me to be quiet.

Can I win him over? Create a sense of regret for agreeing to be a part of this plan? I doubt it. He's cold. Determined. Self-righteous. His orders are likely to remain silent, but also to keep an eye on me.

A door slides open, and the silhouette of a man appears against the glare. As he steps forward, my stomach drops.

"Ms. Moore, thank you for joining me." Geoffrey Cromwell exits into the sun. It's the first time I've heard his voice. The accent is American but void of any regional notations.

"You're behind this?" My voice rises despite my determination to stay calm.

He adjusts his cufflinks, unperturbed. "Forgive me, but you'll need to be more specific."

"Abduction. How's that for specificity?"

"That's an ugly word, Caroline. I prefer *strongly encouraged you to attend a meeting.*"

"A meeting?"

"Yes, right this way."

He gestures for me to enter the cabin, and I do as requested.

"It's better to view the video outside of the sun's harsh glare."

I squint into the interior. Black and yellow spots mingle as my eyes adjust from the transition of bright to dim lighting.

A black screen flicks to life.

"Have a seat," Geoffrey encourages as the yacht rolls over a wave. My knees are locked, and I can withstand the roll of the boat easily, but I comply, taking the seat as instructed.

Luke remains at my back, although he holsters his gun.

Dorian appears on the screen, standing before a podium. His Adam's apple appears abnormally large at this angle, or maybe it's how the collar hits his throat. There's something off about the image, but I can't trust my perception when I might be suffering from a concussion.

"Oh, the sound's not working," Geoffrey says, and he clicks a button on a remote.

Dorian's deep voice fills the cabin.

"It is a great honor to accept the position of chief of staff."

My fingers dig into the leather armrests as Dorian's face fills the screen. He looks different—polished, distant, wearing a bespoke custom suit. The man on screen bears little resemblance to the one I just saw at Ryan's office. His hair is shorter, as if he had a trim, and a make-up artist worked to give him color under the harsh spotlight.

As he speaks about accepting the chief of staff position, my chest tightens. This can't be right. The timeline doesn't make sense.

"In light of recent domestic attacks, I will move to assume the role as quickly as possible. The first action I will take is to step away from any business investments that may represent a conflict of interest. Effective immediately, I will set my investments into a trust and step down from my board seats in Bedrock and Zenith. Times of uncertainty require strong leadership, and this is what I intend to provide for our country. May we all stand united in the face of our enemies. God bless the United States of America."

The video ends.

"Would you care to read his social posts?"

"Social posts?"

"His statements on X, Truth Social, and BlueSky."

"Dorian doesn't tweet." Although, he does employ a PR firm. I suppose they could have a slew of posts and press releases on the ready for an event such as this.

But I just saw him. None of this makes sense. He was in Ryan's office as recently as a few hours ago. How is any of this possible?

"Caroline, when faced with a choice, we all knew what Dorian would choose. You aren't surprised, are you, dear?"

I stare at Geoffrey, mind racing. The Dorian I just saw in Colorado was struggling with migraines, fighting to keep his company afloat amid mysterious attacks. The man in this video looks healthier, confident, almost like a different person altogether.

Either this video is old, or it's not really Dorian. Or worse—everything he shared with me was a lie.

CHAPTER 36

DORIAN

The windowless room feels like a trap closing around me. I'm acutely aware of the armed suit by the door—the only barrier between me and finding Caroline.

The screen flickers to life. Geoffrey appears with snow-capped mountains behind him—the view from our father's Colorado office. But something's off. The edges around his figure shimmer slightly against the background. He's using a filter to disguise his actual location.

"Hello, little brother," he says with a smile that doesn't reach his eyes.

"Do you have Caroline?"

"I do." Static crosses over the video before fading to black. "Please put the headset on."

The suit, gun still trained on me, fingers my ears, checking for a device, then passes me a wireless headset with earpieces that will cover my ears entirely.

"It's a safety precaution," Geoffrey says.

He wants privacy. The man holding a gun on me is trusted to kill me, but not to hear Geoffrey's threats.

I slip the headset on, and Geoffrey's voice continues. Which means he's watching from somewhere. There's a video feed to this room.

"Seven years and you never divorced her." His voice carries a note of genuine curiosity. "I had theories, of course. Never imagined she'd become the perfect asset."

"What do you want with her?"

"Isn't it obvious? She's collateral. Money isn't sufficient incentive when someone has more money than he can spend in a lifetime. Am I right?"

My hands clench at my sides. The headset suddenly feels too tight, the leather sticky. Each word from Geoffrey slides like a blade between my ribs, the pain so terrible it awakens terror. He's found my one true vulnerability.

"What do you want?"

This situation is why the loved ones of any powerful or influential person need security.

"I want you to listen."

The man with the suit has backed up to the door. I'm not sure if he's giving me the semblance of privacy or listening for activity on the other side.

"I'm listening," I say.

"I doubt it," Geoffrey says in that same ingratiating tone he uses when counseling me. "You spent your life blind and deaf to everything going on around you. You blindly pledged your allegiance to our father while he held you at arm's length. Never questioned if all he told you about your mother might be inaccurate. Never sought her out. You assumed the worst in the woman while never questioning the man. A man who, time and time again, cut business deals that favored him, bulldozed laws, a man whose sole purpose was to build a legacy in name and fortune. And you worshiped at his feet."

"You sound angry."

"Do I?" Silence follows Geoffrey's question, as if he's giving the question merit.

I circle the room, pacing, passing the one exit and the man with a gun.

"Anger is not an emotion I feel. You know, I've spent a lifetime watching you from afar."

I wish I could say the same. I haven't paid nearly enough attention to Geoffrey. He was just one of many circling Dad's orbit. At least until Dad's gravitational force weakened, and I moved him to Colorado permanently, all to protect his integrity and reputation.

"I also watched our mothers. Of course, my mother raised me. She loved me. But I was curious. I wondered if our father treated our mothers equally. If you're curious, he gave millions more to my mother. She was a bigger threat. He couldn't bear to let the world discover his penchant for prostitutes. Interestingly, the adultery claims never bothered him."

"They wouldn't," I hear myself say. "It bothered him endlessly that I didn't follow in his footsteps."

The press speculated about my faithfulness. Caroline's, too. We did our best to ignore the lies, but we wouldn't be human if, at times, doubt didn't fester. But I was faithful until long after the day she packed her bags.

"He believed you were too soft. He was right."

What about Geoffrey? How closely did he follow in our father's footsteps?

"Did you marry?"

"You really know nothing about me, do you? You trusted me with our father, let me spend more time with him than anyone else, and yet you know so little about me."

"I grew up trusting you. I don't recall a time without your presence."

This fact won't win him over. But it's the truth. I didn't give him my portfolio to manage because I saw him as an extension of my father, and I wanted my independence.

"You shouldn't blindly trust anyone, Dorian," he says, still using the too-familiar tone that I hate. The one that conveys he's wiser.

Why is he doing this? Is this personal, or is our relationship immaterial?

"Was your mother Russian?" That's one theory, that she raised him to do this.

"I'm not here to tell you my life story."

"Fair enough." My gaze falls to the suit blocking the door. "What happens now?"

"I'm leaving you with a choice. I'm phrasing it as a choice, but I've always known what you will do, what actions you will take."

I pull out the chair to sit and listen, to learn what this sociopath has concocted. But my muscles are wound too tight to remain still, adrenaline crackling through my system like electricity. I shove the chair back under the desk and glare at the point where the wall meets the ceiling.

"Let's hear it. What do you want, Geoffrey?"

"When I started this, I wanted to take everything from you.

Everything you took from me by merely existing. I watched you grow up in the spotlight while I lived in the shadows. I watched you inherit the Moore name while I carried my mother's. I watched you build Zenith on connections that should have been mine by birth."

"You had the same connections. More so. You were always by his side."

"Are you willfully blind? Are you that ignorant of how the world works? That you think you and I had the same opportunities?"

"You believe our opportunities differed because the world didn't know you were his son?" He attended an Ivy League school. I don't remember which one, but he's had a stellar career.

"No one knows I'm his son. He didn't allow my mother to place his name on my birth certificate."

"You realize Dad was protecting you, right? The press would've been relentless. They would've researched your mother. You would've been known as the son of a prostitute who was only given a job because of the man who mistakenly fathered you. Wall Street would've accepted you, but when your back was turned, you would've been the butt of jokes."

"You're such a fool," he snarls. "That man never performed a selfless action in his life. He's easy to read. It's easy to predict his actions. Why can't you see him for what he is?"

"Believe it or not, I—" The words die on my tongue. I never saw Dad as a good person, but I worked to please him and, most recently, strove to protect him. "My actions don't matter. You realize his legacy will remain intact, right? Whatever you've planned to hang on his head, the world will know you're the one responsible."

"An interesting perspective. I knew your thoughts would go there. How exactly will you inform the world? You'll admit that you've been pretending to be our father for years because of his deteriorating mental capacity? That you orchestrated TED Talks, filmed an entire MasterClass on risk management? Even if you tell the world about me, his unknown son, and that I've been acting in his stead, some out there won't believe you. After all, you're guilty, too. You've acted in his name. You have an entire board believing he's functioning and of sound mind and body. The board will wonder if you illegally controlled two board seats."

"He retired."

"They'll wonder. They'll ask when his mind deteriorated. When did you take over? What did he do?" Static and breathing cross the line in a pattern much like a winded chuckle.

"Conspiracy theories will abound. He weaves nonsensically when he talks, and his minions leave his office thinking he's a genius. A mastermind. Or his favorite word: prophet. Will world leaders believe you? Your clients? Will your precious syndicate? They already possess doubts about your integrity. Worse, about your loyalty."

"Who are you working with?" There's no way he's doing this all on his own.

"You assume I can't possibly pull it off without help from someone else. You see me as a worker bee, an employee taking orders. You would be wrong. While entry into the syndicate was handed to you, I formed my own network. But you see...or, no, you don't, do you? Willfully blind. I know you better than you know yourself, little brother. I've spent a lifetime watching you from the shadows, learning every little detail. How you take your coffee. How you make decisions under pressure. Who you call when you're worried. What medicine you take. The art you chose, the photographs you framed. You never noticed me, but I noticed everything about you."

"You do understand, you're twenty years older than me. I was a child when I met you."

"You're not a kid now, though, are you? I studied you for years—as a teen, college student, businessman. I knew Caroline was the one thing you truly loved—the one thing you couldn't replace. I'm not surprised you fell for her. She's so much like your mother. Willing to walk away from the money. Few are, you know?"

My teeth clamp down so hard they ache. If he were in the room with me, I'd attack. I've never been one to lose my cool, to throw fists, but if he were here...

"What do you want, Geoffrey?"

"A recalibration. A correction, if you will. And you get to play a role. I'm going to give you a choice." Geoffrey's expression evolves from twisted malevolence to matter-of-fact businessman. "Enter politics as planned—all the way to the White House. Or watch everything you care about burn."

I grip the edge of the table. "You engineered my nomination for chief of staff. How? Did you bribe the president?"

"Bribe? No, Dorian. We made a deal to ensure the future. Your future. The sky's the limit for you, little brother, just like Dad wanted. Of course, when you step into politics, you'll need to step away from conflicts of interest."

"Zenith? That's what this is about? You want Zenith?"

"Considered it. Seizing your highest accomplishment. But I weighed your choices and value system. Ultimately, I determined that acquiring your business under duress to be a high-risk maneuver with a low likelihood of a favorable outcome.

Zenith will remain yours, although your interest will be placed in a trust, and those who run the day-to-day of it will be like-minded and loyal to me. Zenith isn't just a company to you—it's proof you're more than just Halston Moore's son. That's why controlling it, not destroying it, is so much sweeter. What do you get? The presidency. You get to protect our father's legacy and the Moore name. I expect you'll choose wisely."

Geoffrey believes he's won. He's studied me. He believes he can predict what I will do and how I will behave.

He believes I'll play along to protect our father. To protect our family reputation. That I'll willingly step into a life of politics and continue growing our wealth. Perhaps he suspects I'll step in to help thwart whatever broader plan he's concocted. Maybe he has something planned to undermine my presidency, to humiliate me.

"I've already taken the first step for you. You've announced your transition plans to the world."

"You created an AI deep fake of me accepting the chief of staff position?"

"I have so much video and audio that I can create you doing anything. You don't actually need to live. I don't need you, Dorian. You can die today, and the world will believe you lived decades into the future. But I will allow you to act, to make choices that will save what you care most about: Caroline."

He's insane. Obsessive. A sociopath.

"You believe I'll play along because of Caroline. But how do I know that video of her isn't fake? I'm calling your bluff. If you can fake a video of me, you can fake one of her."

That's why there wasn't terror in her eyes. AI can recreate tears, but not terror.

"This is one scenario I considered. That you would require

further proof. You're also the type who would trust the judicial system and due process as an option to prevent me from moving forward. But consider this—if I get called into an investigation, or put on the defense, I possess evidence that will destroy you. Everything your precious syndicate was involved in, every illegal arms deal the group brokered, every deal that violated sanctions or pulled in favors, I possess evidence. Any evidence our father possesses, I possess."

There's no reason not to trust him on this point. He's had unfettered access to Dad's computer and files for years. He went so far as to pretend to be Dad in syndicate communications.

"I hoped Caroline would be enough to persuade you, but I also believe you love yourself more than her. When I combine it all—your future, your reputation, the Moore legacy, plus Caroline—now that's the winning hand. When you leave this room, you're going to get into the sedan, fly to a private airport, and return to Washington."

"And Caroline?"

"I'll send you videos. Over time, perhaps you'll earn visitation."

"You plan on using Caroline in perpetuity to ensure I behave as you wish. Have I got that right?" He's not a sociopath. He's a psychopath.

"You know what kept me going all these years? Have you taken a second to consider? I'll tell you. Watching our father sign documents that were slowly undermining you. Having him unknowingly approve transfers that would eventually be used against his golden boy. Each time he patted me on the back for a 'good investment decision,' I'd think about how that money would eventually help break you. That vision kept me going. A vision of your future with Caroline will keep you motivated. It's so easy to envision the future."

"Wouldn't it be easier to kill me?"

"Easier? That depends on the goal. And Dad taught us to think big. Shoot for the moon. Chief of staff is just the beginning. The world will see Dorian Moore, but I'll be pulling every string."

"If that's your grand plan, why sabotage my helicopter?"

"To slow you down. You were flying her home, and I'm tired of waiting. I had faith in your skills. I know the pilots who trained you."

"We could've easily died."

"It was a risk. Life is full of them."

"You got lucky."

"Don't discount me. This wasn't some hasty plan, Dorian. I've been preparing for decades. Moving money, building connections, studying you. When our father's mind began to slip, it was almost disappointing—too easy. But it gave me the final piece I needed: complete financial control. You used to do Dad's bidding. Now you'll do mine."

He's a lunatic.

"Caroline is your reward for good behavior." He checks his watch, and the movement causes the background to flicker. "Disobey, and her death will be the last thing you witness before your own. The world will read whatever story I choose to write. And remember, destroying our father's legacy will give me great joy if you force my hand."

He pauses, savoring the moment.

"The end is already determined, Dorian, but the immediate choice is yours. As chief of staff, you'll convince the president to enact martial law, giving you the opportunity to convince the fools in Washington that the only way to stop future attacks is to centralize our nation's critical infrastructure under one entity they believe they'll control: your company, ultimately my company, Zenith."

"You're out of your mind."

"You'll do as I ask, or Caroline's body washes ashore, cause of death to be determined. Possibly filmed for your later enjoyment."

The suit opens the door. Our time is up.

"There's an elegance to it, don't you think? Every dollar spent destroying you came from our father's accounts. The same fortune he denied me is funding your downfall. They won't come to your aid. I've been moving pieces of it for years —small enough amounts he'd never notice, investments he'd never question. The ultimate irony—Halston Moore paying for the destruction of his precious son."

CHAPTER 37

DORIAN

"I won't do anything until I see Caroline." My voice is steel, leaving no room for negotiation.

The screen flickers, a shift in scenery, to Caroline bound and gagged in dim light, a black box device with red letters straight out of a film strapped to her middle, but I shake my head.

"No. In person." I hold the suited man's gaze, unwavering.

There's no way in hell I'll comply with any of Geoffrey's requests, but one thing is certain: if I stand a chance of seeing Caroline again, this is the moment to fight.

He says he's willing to kill me, but he hopes for a pawn in the White House. And for that, he needs me to be amenable.

"I foresaw this scenario," Geoffrey states, sounding almost bored, his words muted through the headset. "When you exit the room, we will take you to see her. Instruct Ryan Wolfgang and his colleagues that you will no longer require their assistance."

I remove the headset and step out of the building to where Ryan and his team are waiting. While I hold up one hand to Ryan, acknowledging him and telling him to stay back, I tap out SOS in Morse code against my leg with the index finger of my other hand.

Ryan stills and gives an almost imperceptible nod.

He couldn't have heard anything Geoffrey said through the headphones, but he's aware that something occurred in the closed room. If he didn't correctly read my finger movements, someone going over the video after we've left will interpret them. There are security cameras on the eaves of the building, and if there are questions, Arrow will hack into the feed.

I step out onto the tarmac and climb into the awaiting S-76D helicopter.

The armed suit climbs in beside me. "When we return, you'll fly to DC."

I neither confirm nor refute his statement, instead shifting to stare out the window.

As expected, we set across the Pacific, leaving the United States behind. Through the window, the coastline disappears beneath us. No witnesses. No jurisdiction. Perfect for whatever Geoffrey has planned.

The suit beside me remains vigilant, his hand never far from his weapon. While I could overpower him and the pilot and take control of the helicopter myself, the image of Caroline with a bomb strapped to her body stops me cold. Knowing what I know now, I'm almost positive it's an altered video, perhaps entirely generated by AI, but for now, I play along.

But once I get to her, all bets are off.

Geoffrey may have studied me, but he's seriously underesti-mated me. He believes I've lived my life doing as Dad wished and that he can step into our father's shoes and force me to do his bidding. But he's wrong—on both counts.

We fly for approximately forty minutes. I track the time on my watch.

A Feadship mega yacht materializes through the marine haze, its 70-meter hull gleaming like a predator's smile. The Dutch engineering is unmistakable—clean, modern, and built for serious ocean capability. This isn't just luxury; it's a floating fortress designed for escape and evasion.

By the waterline mark, she's running light, maybe 60 percent fuel capacity—the sweet spot for both range and speed. Speed is a necessity to outrun coastal patrols.

If Caroline is on this ship, that video is definitely a deep fake. Detonating a bomb on a ship is suicide.

But what if she's not on this ship? What if this is another lie? That's the problem.

I have no reason to trust this bastard.

What if all of this comes down to a child who believes he was shunned now wanting power? The thing is, Dad didn't shun him. He kept him close to his side.

Did Geoffrey come up with this plan all on his own? He mentioned he's built a network of his own. How well-formed is his network? Is he the leader, or is he one of several, another group of men working together in an alliance like the syndi-cate? Is he being played? Being set up to be the fall guy, one piece in a broader, longer-term strategy?

At the end of the day, it doesn't matter who is leading whom. There's right and there's wrong. And Geoffrey chose wrong.

Stalin once said that death is the solution to all problems. No man, no problem. It's tempting to agree with him. But time has proven Stalin wrong. Good exists, even in man. It's a matter of valuing the good and exposing the evil.

The S-76D settles onto the yacht's helipad, its skids connecting with the deck's pressure sensors. Four pop-up security cameras track our landing: Axis Q6215-LE models, if I'm not mistaken. Military-grade surveillance.

At the armed suit's instruction, I release the five-point harness and exit, cataloging details. No visible crew. Two covered RHIBs mounted on the stern davits, the yacht's quick escape vessels. The SATCOM dome is a newer VS240, capable of maintaining broadband connection even in rough seas. Which means they've got real-time communications despite being well outside coastal range.

A hard object presses into my back, right below my shoulder blade.

"Walk."

The pilot remains strapped in the helicopter.

Is he flying away? Or on standby?

I'm in international waters. They could shoot me, throw me overboard, and proceed as they desire. He could've killed me already. Had me poisoned or killed in my home. I'm alive for a reason.

I grab the lacquered railing, leaning into the rolling motion of the vessel.

Spotless white. Clean lines. The pride of the ship's owner.

The stench of motor fumes blends with salty air.

"Keep walking," the suit directs. "Along the side."

He hasn't searched me. He has to know there's a tracker on me. Ryan and his team watched me leave. They have a plan.

But Geoffrey would know they have a plan. Does he have others positioned to eliminate pursuers?

I round the bend and enter a cabin.

Caroline sits on a pristine white leather sofa, her eyes widening at the sight of me, gray duct tape over her mouth.

My heart stutters. In two strides, I'm kneeling before her, fingers trembling as they trace the edge of the bruise darkening her eye, the dried blood from the gash above her eyebrow.

"My god, are you okay?" My voice breaks, relief and rage colliding in my chest.

She jerks at my touch.

Fuck. How deep is that scalp injury?

I grip the edge of the tape, the corner frayed and peeling off her skin.

"Uh-uh," a male voice says behind my back.

Recognizing the voice, I look over my shoulder and see Luke.

And he's not alone.

Geoffrey. In a suit. No gun.

"I'll let you remove the tape," Geoffrey says, his voice no different from any other day in Colorado. "But only if she promises to be quiet. I have the beginnings of a headache, and you know what that's like, right?"

I rip the tape off her mouth in one sweep.

She gasps, and I scan her body, searching for any other injuries. There's no bomb currently tied to her.

The video he showed before was definitely altered. But is a bomb somewhere else on the ship?

"If you speak, dear, the tape goes back on. I didn't plan to be so vulgar, but she's quite the little she-devil. Almost didn't get her here; isn't that right, Luke? Did you know that Luke dated your wife?"

Caroline's bright blue eyes ground me. There's no terror, no fear. She's searching mine, questioning, but she understands the most important element. I'm here for her, and we're going to get through this together.

My absence of a response to his goading must prompt Geoffrey to focus on his next steps. "Now, you've seen her. I'll give you five minutes. Then we depart."

"You're going with him?"

Disbelief etches the question. Her incredulity means she trusts me. And she should.

"Caroline, you don't know him at all, do you?" Geoffrey scoffs. "I know exactly what path he will choose. And deep down, you do, too. That's why you left him."

Geoffrey believes he's won. He's studied me. He believes he can predict what I will do and how I will behave.

He believes I'll play along to protect our father. To protect our family reputation. That I'll willingly step into a life of politics and continue growing our wealth. He truly believes he's a prophet, but he's blind to all that matters.

Luke holds his hand to his ear, listening.

"We need to go," he says to Geoffrey.

The suit who accompanied me heads out in the direction we came from.

Geoffrey nods. My gaze roams over him, tracking the gelled hair, the doughy, vein-riddled skin below his eyes, his slight paunch, and his hunched shoulders from years of poor posture. He doesn't appear to be carrying a gun, and if that's the case, he's reliant on the men he has hired.

Luke reaches for Caroline, and I slam into him, pinning his arm holding the gun against the side of the counter.

"Hands off my wife."

It's a growl and a declaration.

Luke pushes back, and I throw a left hook while gripping his wrist, knocking the gun from his grip. My knuckles connect with the solid ridge of his jaw, sending a shock of pain up my arm, but his head barely moves. Military training. This was a mistake.

Luke drives his knee into my ribs with crushing force. White-hot pain erupts through my side as I struggle to maintain my hold on his wrist. The metallic taste of blood fills my mouth.

"You're dead," he hisses, his breath hot against my face.

We circle each other, fists raised. My breath comes in ragged gasps. Luke bounces slightly on the balls of his feet, professionally balanced, while I desperately scan the boat for anything I can use as a weapon. A heavy vase. A knife. Anything.

Geoffrey backs away in the direction his guard went, his face a mask of clinical interest. He's watching us like we're a lab experiment.

Luke moves with trained precision, feinting left before launching himself at me. His weight crashes into my chest like a battering ram. We go down hard, the polished deck slamming against my spine. The impact forces air from my lungs in an agonizing rush.

I'm on my back, fists pummeling his sides, but it's like hitting concrete. He pins me with practiced ease, his weight immobilizing me as he draws back for a finishing blow. His eyes are cold, professional. This is just a job to him.

Time slows. I see Caroline behind him, Luke's gun gripped

in her hands. Her face pale but resolute, arms extended in a perfect shooter's stance.

The gunshot doesn't sound like in movies—it's sharper, more violent, a crack that seems to tear the air itself. My ears ring with sudden deafness.

Luke's expression changes in an instant—from focused rage to blank surprise. The tension in his body releases all at once. Something warm and wet sprays across my face. Metallic. Copper. Blood.

He collapses onto me, suddenly deadweight. The crushing pressure of a human body, no longer animated by consciousness. I feel his last breath exhale against my neck, warm then cooling.

I push him off with trembling hands. He rolls to the side, limbs loose like a discarded marionette. Bright red blood blooms across the pristine white flooring, expanding in a perfect circle. A small, neat hole has punctured his temple, almost surgically precise, with a trickle of blood flowing from the dark opening.

The silence that follows is deafening. Just the sound of waves against the hull and my own thundering heartbeat.

Caroline stands perfectly still, the gun now pointed at Geoffrey, her hands steady while mine shake uncontrollably. Her face is a professional mask, but her eyes are wide with the enormity of what she's just done.

Geoffrey's as ashen as I feel. He, like me, has probably never witnessed death outside a sanitized hospital room. This is different. Raw. Final.

"I'll go. For now," he says, taking a step back. "Nothing changes."

"No?" I'd say everything has changed. He can't threaten me

with an edited video, and we now have a gun trained on him. One of his hired guns is dead. He didn't think this through.

"I know which path you'll take. You'll protect your reputation." There's a notable tremor in his voice, and his backward movement weakens his meaning.

He didn't plan this. He didn't foresee it.

In truth, I didn't foresee this, either. Nausea churns, and there's a subtle tremble in my limbs. I swipe at my face, using my sleeve to clear the blood splatter.

Geoffrey could theoretically seek out the suit and instruct him to come for us. But he's off-kilter. We all are.

Slowly, almost in a daze, I follow Geoffrey up to the helipad, Caroline on my heels.

The pilot is strapped in, ready to go.

The armed suit, the one who flew with me out here, sits beside him.

Based on their expressions, they didn't see what happened with Luke.

The rotors are moving. The two men in the helicopter prepare for departure.

"Geoffrey, you need to give up. Turn yourself in," I shout above the wind and mechanical rotor noise.

"No. The plan's the same," he says. "Think about everything you have to lose. If you don't join me in DC, you'll face an investigation, trials. Zenith will lose clients. You've already lost the trust of your precious syndicate. They won't come to your aid."

"You're the one who set the bounty on Nick. You're the one who wanted to make it look like it was me."

It's a statement. Not a question.

There's no denial.

"Think my offer over. Discuss it with Caroline. You can have her with you. That piece changes. Perhaps holding her against her will was a miscalculation on my part. She'll make a wonderful first lady. Or you can spend years in court and then in prison. Once again, your choice."

Whatever damage Geoffrey believes he's inflicted, there's nothing that can't be undone. Yes, there's an AI-generated video out there, but it's easy enough to issue a press release and allow the press to handle disseminating messaging regarding a deep fake.

Perhaps a younger version of myself might have fallen for his ruse. For the false narrative that reputation, wealth, and power are everything.

But he's out of his mind. Our Dad didn't dictate my life, no matter what he believes, and I'm not about to let this lunatic dictate my future.

Geoffrey climbs into the helicopter and straps himself in, speaking into his headset, likely giving instructions to depart.

Caroline joins me, Luke's gun aimed down.

I see the moment the armed guard notices the gun in her hand. His mouth opens, speaking, and his hand goes to his waist, but just as quickly, he lowers his hand.

There's no point in a shootout. Geoffrey has to land somewhere. The authorities will find him and detain him.

The chopper lifts, and Caroline's golden strands fly around her, whipping every which way.

We both cower from the wind, and I try to protect her with my body until the worst has passed.

Geoffrey has to suspect there's a chance I won't do as he wishes. What will he do next?

As soon as the roar of the rotors quiets, the helicopter rising into the sky, I turn to Caroline.

"Are you okay?"

"I'm fine. There are others on this boat. I don't know where or how many."

"No, I mean, are you…" She shot a man.

"I'm fine." I'm not sure she is. "I'll be fine," she insists.

The helicopter swings right, heading off to what I presume is a southeast direction.

I take her hand, the one not holding a gun.

"Let's get one of the boats down," I say, pulling her toward the stern where I spotted the RHIBs earlier.

"You think that's safer?" She scans the upper deck.

"To your point, we don't know who else is on board. And Geoffrey's been threatening bombs. If there's one on this yacht—"

"We might not find it until it's too late," she finishes. "But I don't think he ever had a bomb. I never saw one. Luke made the same threats to me about a bomb at Arrow's offices."

The yacht remains eerily silent as I activate the davit system, which lowers the dinghy toward the rolling water below. Caroline stands guard, her stolen weapon tracking every shadow while my hands work the controls.

"Do you have Ryan's number?"

"I know Arrow's, but I don't have my phone."

I hand her mine, taking the gun from her hand while I watch the small boat descend slowly.

Her arm comes around my waist, and I hold her to me, bracing us against the railing. She said there are others on this boat, but I doubt it. If he had firepower on board, I suspect we'd be cowering about right now. He wouldn't have let us win so easily.

The lifeboat hits with a splash, and I drape a rope ladder with wooden slats over the side and urge Caroline down. She hands me my phone. It has satellite capabilities, and one glance at the screen shows the call is in process.

"This is Ryan," a deep voice barks.

"Ryan, it's me. I've got Caroline."

"Are you on a ship?"

"A yacht."

"We're on the way. Can you talk?"

"Geoffrey left in his helicopter. Two others are with him."

"Geoffrey plus two. Copy. We're tracking it. Didn't know if you were in on it."

"Stay on him."

"Copy. Can you get off that ship?"

"Disembarking into a dinghy."

Caroline's almost at the bottom of the ladder; two more rungs and her feet will be in the boat.

"Good. Push away. We believe he may have acquired a bomb. Might be on your ship."

"That's my fear. Caroline's off. I'm climbing down now. Others might be onboard. We haven't cleared it."

"Copy. Disembark and push off. Coast Guard is en route. So are we."

I end the call, and with one last scan of the deck, climb down the ladder to join Caroline.

"What did Ryan say?"

"They're on the way."

"Are they tracking Geoffrey?"

"Yep."

At this point, the Arrow team has pulled in full resources. Geoffrey may believe he's above the world's military and intelligence forces, but the world is growing smaller. Even if he changes to a different helicopter before we reach him, we'll find him. We can find anyone.

"Are you sure this is the best idea? It's possible we're the only ones on the yacht. Or those still onboard are crew and won't hurt us. This boat feels small."

She's not wrong about the size. Compared to the yacht, to the waves, it's tiny. "My gut's telling me we need to move." I flip the small outboard motor engine on, and we sputter away.

There might not be a bomb on the yacht, but there could be. There could be mercenaries too. Anyone on the boat was hired by Geoffrey, which means we can't trust them.

Caroline joins me on the bench seat, snuggling into my side as sea spray lashes every time our hull crashes into the crest of a wave. Clouds thicken into a steel-gray hue, blanketing the setting sun beneath a foggy shroud. For a brief moment, I second-guess myself and consider going back, but no, this is the smarter plan.

Seated on the bench, the dinghy feels impossibly small against the vastness of the Pacific. Gray clouds gather on the horizon, promising rougher seas ahead. Each wave lifts us high before dropping us into troughs that seem to swallow us whole. Salt spray stings my eyes as I grip the throttle, pushing us further from the yacht with every surge.

"The video of you," she says. "So real. It's scary they can do that."

"I agree. The video of you with a bomb terrified me. Jesus, Caroline." I shake my head, hoping to shake the image. "If there were any AI markings, I didn't pick them up." The terror damaged my objectivity. I'd like to go back, study the video again, and take the time to find the markers. They have to be there.

"What happens now?"

At this very second, I'm hoping we're clearing enough distance that we'll be safe from the blast radius if there's a bomb on the yacht, but she's asking a bigger question.

"I'll call in every favor. Geoffrey won't have any pull, even if he tries to impersonate my father. Or me. I'll make sure the evidence reaches every major intelligence agency simultaneously." My father's legacy may be shattered, but he'll never need to know. "The Arrow team will track down Geoffrey. If whoever he's working with pulls off some bigger plan, my company won't be used to further their goals. He must've truly hated me to misjudge me so greatly."

With greater distance between us and the yacht, I loosen my grip on the engine handle, slowing our speed, and pull back to inspect her injuries. "Are you sure you're okay?"

"I'm fine." She brushes my hand away, but she can't see the gash on her forehead. "Dorian, what was he talking about? Have you broken laws? Are you–"

I stop her with a light press of my finger to her lips. "I'm not perfect. I've arranged deals with questionable enterprises. Worked with people you wouldn't approve of."

"Criminals?"

"For the most part, no one who's been convicted of a crime." It's a weak defense, but in a global economy, crime is a multifaceted concept. "I followed in my father's footsteps. But Geoffrey misjudged me. Power isn't something I crave."

"That's easy to say when you've always had it."

"Caroline, for all of his studying me, one thing he didn't

grasp is that I'd give it all up for you." In all fairness to Geoffrey, I'm not sure I understood that about myself until this weekend. He clearly understood that I love Caroline, but he didn't understand the depths of my feelings. I'd give up my life before I let anything happen to her. I'd give up everything for her. Or maybe, come to think of it, maybe he did understand.

"What he said about an investigation...are you going to cover this up? You could, you know. There's no reason for any of what you or your father have done to be exposed." There's an earnestness to her words that tells me she'd help me.

"Kill the investigation?" I meet her gaze directly. "Not an option. The lies, the deceit. That wouldn't work out well for me in the long run. I couldn't win you back if I did that. No. I'll work with the authorities. And I'll do what I need to do to ensure nothing like this happens again."

She studies me for a long moment. "The Dorian I left would've chosen differently."

"I'm not that man anymore." We're far enough from the yacht, and I kill the engine, letting the boat roll with the waves. When the rescue team approaches, we want to be easily found.

I gently lift her chin. "I thought power and legacy were what mattered. But living without you—" My voice catches. "Those were empty years."

The boat rocks beneath us as I carefully touch the wound on her forehead. "When I thought I might lose you today... I realized there's only one legacy I care about building."

"And what's that?" Her voice is barely above a whisper.

"A life with you. If you'll give me that chance." I take her hands in mine. "I'm dismantling the Moore empire, piece by piece if I have to. The satellites, the companies—they'll serve the world, not profit from it. That's my choice, and it's one Geoffrey never foresaw."

A smile—the first real one I've seen since this nightmare began—spreads across her face. She leans into me, and this time when our lips meet, there's no goodbye in it.

"I've missed you," she whispers against my mouth.

An explosion rips through the air, catching us by surprise. Bright orange flames and black fumes strike a surreal image against the horizon. I scan the ship, but don't see anyone jumping from it. Perhaps there was no crew. Debris litters the ocean, and the yacht falls on its side.

"You were right," Caroline says under her breath.

Off in the distance, a Coast Guard chopper appears on the horizon, and I hold Caroline close against the wind and spray.

"I was blind for so long," I say, my words blending with the wind. "To what really mattered. To what was coming. No more."

"No one can see everything," she counters. "There's always a different angle. Always."

She's comforting me, standing by me, even as the world burns from my blindness.

I kiss her as the helicopter descends, lights beaming over the murky ocean, its rotors scattering the mist around us like a veil that's finally been lifted from my eyes.

CHAPTER 38

CAROLINE

Five days later

The last week has been a whirlwind of activity.

Geoffrey Cromwell was detained by an Arrow team when he landed in Mexico and was handed over to the FBI.

Working with Nick Ivanov's team, Interpol, and intelligence agencies from around the world, we've been gathering evidence against him. It's a challenging task. He had broad access to all of Halston's accounts, and it's impossible to know what he did versus what Halston did. There are no cameras in Halston's office, and even if there were, unless we had a view of the computer screen, Geoffrey's presence in Halston's office proves nothing.

The news has been flooded with recaps of the attacks by a

domestic terrorist group on US soil, and the connection to Halston Moore and his unknown financial advisor have been picked up on only detailed, extensive articles covering the event, and even then, all mentions were caveated with words such as "alleged" and "suspected."

Financial donations and investments through shell companies are being tracked to better understand Cromwell's connections to extremist groups and foreign governments.

The president informed Dorian that he didn't believe it was a good time for him to step into the public spotlight, and Dorian agreed. Three other names are currently being rumored for consideration as the next chief of staff.

Geoffrey never distributed the AI-generated video of Dorian accepting the chief of staff position, so there's no cleanup in that regard, but I'm certain there are law enforcement and intelligence groups investigating Geoffrey's connections to the president.

The syndicate, a group of men Dorian's father worked to coalesce, disbanded. Dorian said that Geoffrey's attempt to assume a leadership position, posing as his father, awakened the group of industry titans to the weakness in the group's structure. None of the sector leaders desired a boss, and yet in the face of chaos, the egalitarian structure proved ineffective. Dorian doesn't seem bothered. He says he'll maintain his relationships during annual conferences and events, and that if he ever needs to lean on any of the members, he's confident they'll come through, or at the very least, negotiate a mutually beneficial deal. He also believes that when the group began working with criminal organizations to maximize global influence, they lost legitimacy, and if not legitimacy, integrity.

Dorian has spent most of the week between Colorado, overseeing the helicopter recovery, and in DC, meeting with senators who were debating opening a congressional investigation. While he welcomes an inquiry, he doesn't believe a public inquisition will occur. He's convinced that Geoffrey was working with other players who have yet to be uncovered, and he also suspects some of the individuals within the US political sphere are complicit.

He also believes that if the FBI, or any other intelligence agency, uncovers evidence tying Geoffrey to anyone within other countries, they may choose to classify the information, ensuring only those with the highest security clearance will ever know the truth.

Dorian is suspicious of Liam Sullivan because he's the one who recommended Luke to Arrow Tactical and because he also has connections to Geoffrey Cromwell, but so far, all of those connections appear to be based on frequenting some of the same social clubs.

At this point, the Arrow team believes Liam's connections are coincidental. Jack Sullivan informed Ryan that he supported all efforts into the investigation, but that he thinks his brother is innocent, even if he's too trusting of those he meets and takes a liking to. The story Liam's telling is that he met Luke at a bar in Hawaii. They hit it off, kept in touch, and when he needed work, he recommended him, completely unaware that he had any connections to Geoffrey Cromwell. And, in truth, there's nothing in Luke's background report that would have red-flagged him. However, we found payments from a shell company to Luke going back years, and I've been told they traced the shell company to Geoffrey, which means Luke has been working for Geoffrey since he left the military. We can't ever fully know Luke's motives, but it is conceivable that his motives were entirely monetary.

DORIAN

I have some bad news.

It's Friday evening, and I'm at home, waiting for Dorian's estimated arrival time so I can pick him up from the airport. A sinking feeling hits, and I'm almost certain I know what he's going to say.

ME

?

DORIAN

Winter storm tracking across the country. It's looking like I won't make it in.

There's no denying the disappointment that knocks my euphoria down a notch. While this week has been an incredibly busy work week, the regular texts and calls from Dorian have extended a buzz that's both exhilarating and unnerving. I suppose it's fitting that reality would step in to remind me what life is like with a high-profile executive.

ME
Tomorrow?

DORIAN
First thing.

ME
☺

Yes, I'm smiling again. Carrying my phone, I walk to the back of the house to change into pajamas. I'd planned on ordering in, depending on what time he got in this evening and what he was in the mood for. I'm not that hungry after snacking at the office. Perhaps I'll eat cereal.

ME
Any update from Bedrock?

DORIAN

It's been suggested that I step down
from the chairman role during the
investigation. I plan to comply.

ME

You okay with that?

While the mass media may not have picked up on all the
nuances of recent events, those in the financial world are quite
aware, and, as Cromwell intended, the reports inflicted damage
to the Moore name and reputation.

DORIAN

I am. My time has recently become more
valuable.

I grin and set the phone down on the bed. I change into a silk
chemise and pull on a silk robe, then slip on fuzzy slippers.
Maybe I'll curl up with a good book and a glass of wine.

Light flashes on my phone screen, and I step back to the bed
to read the screen.

DORIAN

I miss you.

. . .

I pick up the phone, smiling from a happiness that emanates from deep within, bursting through with the warmth of the sun on a summer day.

ME
Miss you, too.

I pause, staring at the screen, my finger hovering over the send button. I take a deep breath and type.

ME
I love you.

DORIAN
Go to your front door.

I grin and head down the hallway, approaching the front door that opens directly into the living area.

What did he send? Flowers?

He sent flowers this week to the office and to my home address. The silk chemise I'm wearing is one he sent, along with a small circular framed selfie of us in Boston. We'd taken the photo right after he proposed, and I said yes. The photo now sits on my desk at the office, and, while I'll always treasure the memory, the radiating joy that somehow comes through in our smiles is contagious.

I swing the wooden door open.

"Dorian!"

"Surprise." He grins, quite pleased with himself.

My heart practically stops, then races to catch up. For a moment, I can't move, can't speak—the sight of him standing there hits me with startling intensity.

His hair is slightly ruffled, and there's a hint of shadow below his eyes, which I'm not surprised by, given the hoops he's jumped through this week. He's in jeans, a button-down, and sneakers that fit with a suit, the kind that are all the rage with the tech world these days. He's gorgeous, but it's the heat in his eyes, a raw hunger, that has me entranced. His gaze tracks from my face, down my body, and to the robe fallen open to my sides.

"That's what you wear to open the door?"

His near growl amps up the tension to a tangible, viscous level.

He steps forward, and I step back. He wheels in a large suitcase and kicks the door shut.

"Fuck, Cara." He grabs me and pulls me against him, pressing his lips to mine, his tongue in my mouth, ravenous. His hands slide over my back, gliding over the silk, and lower, around my curves, until he can go no lower.

He breaks the kiss, sucking in air, his fingers tugging at the hem.

"Take it off."

My fingers toy with his collar as I eye the buttons on his shirt, equally breathless, skin vibrating, thighs shaky.

"Take it off, Cara. Now."

Eyes locked on him, I lift the chemise over my body and let it drop to the floor. I step out of my fuzzy slippers, backing away toward the bedroom.

"It's been a week. I've been away from you for a week. And you open the door like this."

He follows, his steps faster, crazed with lust. It's a look I haven't seen from him in a long time. Stripping off his shirt, he stalks forward until the backs of my thighs hit the mattress.

"Off," he says again, and his gaze drops to my lace panties. He toes off his shoes, and his jeans and briefs drop to the floor.

I expect him to kiss me again, but he stands there, soaking me in, his fingers around his thick, hard shaft, stroking.

"That's better. I can see you now. And my god, you are exquisite."

And then he's on me, desperate, like a starving man. His hands cup my bottom, and he lifts me up. My legs spread, welcoming him. His finger swipes my seam, and he sucks his skin.

"You're so fucking wet."

I love this side of Dorian. The unleashed, uncontrolled side.

And then he's over me, pushing in. I revel in the shock, the ecstasy.

"Tell me again."

He thrusts, filling me with him, with love, with life.

"Tell me." His low growl vibrates near my ear.

"What?" I gasp, my fingers clawing at his back.

"You love me."

"I do. I love you so much."

And then, I lose the ability to speak. To breathe.

His movements, his words, just him.

"So beautiful. Made for me."

"Yes." It's all I can get out.

"You're mine."

I've always been his. And always will be.

CHAPTER 39

CAROLINE

I stretch in bed, luxuriating in the warmth, the spent feeling in my muscles, and the faint scent of coffee. Light streams through the seams in the closed white plantation shutters, and the high-pitched melody of chirping birds seeps through the walls.

Footsteps approach, a soft thud telling me he's barefoot. The door eases open, and there he is: my husband, bare-chested in low-slung pajama bottoms, holding two steaming coffee mugs. His hair is tousled from sleep, eyes still carrying that vulnerable softness from our night together. Surreal, but not a dream.

"You found my coffee machine."

"You like coffee when you wake. I made some." He shrugs like it's nothing. "Your refrigerator is sparse, though. Reminds me of mine back in college. We'll need to head out for breakfast."

"We don't all have a staff to shop for us and keep the refrigerator stocked." I don't add the part about a chef to stock fresh, easy-to-heat meals.

"Well, you could if you wanted." The mattress sinks with his weight, and I push up, positioning the pillows behind my back so I can better accept the coffee. After I take the mug, his free hand immediately falls to my thigh, covered by sheets and a light coverlet, yet his warmth still penetrates my skin. "My place in Montecito isn't far away. But I like your place, too."

"You like my house?" I mean, I like my home. It's a restored cottage close to a walkable district filled with cafés and boutique shops. "The rooms are smaller than your closets."

"I like the feel of this place. It feels like you." He eyes me over the rim of his mug. I watch his throat as he swallows. "It feels like home."

"It almost feels like you're asking to move in with me."

"I know you want to go slow, but technically, we're still married. We're sleeping together." He looks pointedly at me.

He's right. And if I get my way, we'll have countless repeats of last night.

"My work requires travel. You won't have to put up with me all the time."

"You say that like it's a good thing." I'm mocking him with my tone, but I understand what he's saying. When we grew apart before, his travel was partially to blame. The media frenzy made my career impractical. I still remember the isolation I experienced when all of my friends were busy during the day, pursuing their dreams, and I was stuck in our Manhattan townhouse, fearing photographers if I dared to leave.

The memory is enough for me to restate a point I've already made this week. "I'm not giving up my job."

"I wouldn't want you to." He stands and cracks open the

shutters, peering out at what can only be the bushes separating my lot from my neighbors. "If you like the work you're doing, you could consider opening your own firm. You don't need to be an employee."

"Why would I want to do that?"

"Why wouldn't you?"

"We aren't all entrepreneurs."

"If you wanted. I'm not pushing you. I'm mentioning the possibilities."

"Speaking of possibilities, you know, you could still change your mind on a political future." I'd absolutely hate it, but it is a possibility. If he were to choose to run, he'd need to begin work on a campaign immediately. "There's been so much attention on the bigger events at play...your connection has been lost. None of the headlines mentions your name. Or your father's, for that matter."

His eyes narrow, and he returns to the bed.

"No."

"You could do good. You won't be beholden to anyone. If deals were struck to get you into consideration for chief of staff, you didn't strike the deals. You don't need to honor them."

"The chief of staff door closed. You know that. And I wouldn't change it if I could. Caroline, more than anything, I want you back in my life. And you don't care for DC. Or for the paparazzi or for the security detail I would force on you."

"I don't want you to give up a potential presidential run for me. It's a chance to follow in your uncle's footsteps and to refurbish the Moore legacy."

"Technically, I'm not giving anything up. The path was a pipedream and one that was never guaranteed."

"Don't give me that." He's the party's dream. Relatively

young, charismatic, well-spoken. And thanks to all of his satellites, he probably has kompromat, to use the Russian word for dirt, on anyone standing in the way of his initiatives.

"Telling you the truth." He crosses one ankle over the other, relaxing on the comforter. "I love my work at Zenith. That's enough for me. I'm fortunate. A digital nomad lifestyle is easily within my grasp. But…"

"You'll need to travel."

"Yes."

"How about we compromise?"

"Are you listening? You don't need to compromise. Tell me what you want. I'll make it happen."

"Do you not understand the definition of compromise?"

"What is there to compromise over? I'm offering you—"

"If you want me to move in…"

"Oh." He straightens as understanding registers. "I guess I did assume we were on the same page about that."

"See…that's where we get into trouble."

His grin is devious. "All right. So tell me. What compromise has this insightful brain of yours cooked up?"

"During the week, we'll stay at my place. Meaning, we'll spend the night here. You can work wherever you'd like during the day. I haven't seen your new place in Montecito, but I imagine it's probably a preferable place to work."

"I can find office space down here. Keep going."

"And on the weekends, we stay in Montecito or wherever you want to go."

"You don't work on the weekends?"

"Not normally."

"So you're saying yes to moving back in together, but…"

"I'm saying I'm not willing to give up my place yet. I'm

saying last time, we moved too quickly, and I gave up a lot right from the get-go."

"You don't need to give up anything."

He's so sincere. But he's also wrong.

"That's part of being a couple. But I'm not ready yet. And we need time. Time to see if we fall back into old habits, and if we do, how we break them. If we can, that is."

"Whatever you want, whatever it takes. You name it, I'll do it."

"Well, first, why don't we throw on some clothes and grab breakfast? I'll take you to my favorite place."

"Sounds like a plan."

"Then we can maybe go for a walk down by the beach. And then there's the holiday office party this evening. You want to join me?"

"Absolutely."

"So we'll need to get you clothes."

"If you'll ride with me to Montecito, I can pack a bag. What are you doing for the holiday?"

"The Arrow offices close between Christmas and New Year's. I've already told my parents I'm coming home." I hesitate, searching his face. "Would you have any interest in coming with me?"

His entire being lights up, reminding me of the young man I fell for years ago, before the world got between us.

"I can't imagine anything I would prefer more," he says softly.

"You've never been excited about visiting my parents before."

He takes my hand, his thumb tracing circles on my palm.

"You're giving me a second chance. With you. With them. With everything that matters."

———

Snow might be absent from the California coast, but holiday magic fills the air as we arrive at the party. The estate of a prominent actor—coincidentally adjacent to Dorian's Montecito property—glows with thousands of twinkling lights, transforming the palm trees into something from a fantasy.

Jack and Ava Sullivan stand at the entrance, greeting each employee with the warmth of family rather than bosses. They're a stunning couple, Jack with peppered gray hair swept back, spectacles, and a well-tailored suit that communicates understated wealth, and Ava in a deep red velvet sleeveless dress with tattoos lining her arms and thick bangs that crown her enormous, deep-set dark eyes. They live in San Diego, but I haven't met Ava Sullivan before. She's as beautiful as she is approachable and warm.

Jack takes my hand and introduces me to his wife.

"Ava, this is Caroline, the one I've mentioned so often this past week." I smile at the skillful absence of a last name, given my no-longer estranged husband is at my side. "And this is Dorian Moore."

Dorian and Jack exchange firm handshakes.

"It's wonderful to meet you," Ava says, her attention focused solely on me and not the tall, attention-grabbing man at my side. "I understand we're indebted to you."

"Well, the investigation is still ongoing," I answer, although her statement makes me wonder what exactly her husband has shared.

"I've been assured that the FBI is confident in their case against Cromwell. This has been a good year. Arrow's done good work," Jack says.

I tilt my head, curious about his statement, not certain I agree it's been a good year.

The US media had focused on the extremist groups responsible for the domestic attacks, but by the end of the week, the leading headlines shifted to stock rebounds and holiday sales forecasts. The international media headlines have shifted to international cooperation and calls for increased security initiatives.

In our last briefing, the FBI and NSA were both working on procuring evidence of links between Cromwell and the extremist groups he co-opted for his purpose. The prosecution team didn't share their strategy, nor will they, as they are in the initial stages of processing the case, but it's widely expected they will pursue individual prosecutions, which means Cromwell's case will not depend on the prosecution of any other involved members.

"You don't look like you agree," Ava comments thoughtfully.

"No, I do," I say, as it's a holiday party, and I don't wish to dwell on dark subjects, like my concerns surrounding current events and if we can truly say it's been a good year. But with Dorian at my side, and given I might not get the opportunity again, I ask Jack, "Did you determine if your brother had any involvement?"

There's no sign of discomfort or annoyance with my question. If anything, I sense respect in his steely gaze.

"Other than being susceptible to a friendship struck in a bar, and recommending Luke to Arrow, he had no involvement."

I want to ask if that's been officially determined, if the

investigation has officially concluded Liam Sullivan had no involvement, but I sense Dorian's hand at my back, and the tips of his fingers dig into my waist.

"Your friend, Nick Ivanov, has proven a great ally," Jack says.

Jack and Dorian are nearly the same height, and it feels as if the conversation is now between the two of them, with Ava and me as spectators.

"Surprising, isn't it? Given his connections?" Dorian answers.

"It is," Jack says. "Are you still in touch with your other friends?"

Dorian's lips spread into a smile, and it's then that I realize he no longer appears bound by societal or business expectations. That smile is one that says he's truly done with climbing or cloak-and-dagger charades.

"The alliance disbanded. As I'm sure you're aware."

"Are there any negative implications for you?"

"No, none at all, actually," Dorian answers. "The friendships remain. The connections. Zenith maintained security in stressful times, and if anything, has retained respect and confidence from clients."

"See? A good year," Jack answers. "Have you heard from Jiang Tu?"

The Chinese national went missing months ago.

"Word on the street is he went golfing. Should be home before the new year."

They both exchange knowing smiles, and Dorian, ever mindful of all of those surrounding him, directs a question to Ava. "And how has the year been for you? I understand you opened up a new rehabilitation center? One in Arizona?"

"Yes." Ava beams. She runs a successful nonprofit drug rehabilitation center with a focus on transition from rehabilitation into society. "And I must thank you for your donation."

I expect to see surprise on Dorian's face, as he employs someone on staff who manages his charitable trust, but that's not what I see. No, what I see is gracious acknowledgment, and a shared understanding passes between Dorian and Jack.

Sophia sees me across the room and approaches with a smile. "Dad, you're supposed to greet the guests. Not monopolize them." She takes my arm to pull me away, then, as if spotting Dorian for the first time, says, "Dorian, it's good to see you."

"Is it?"

My gaze darts to him, but I relax when I see his soft smile. She's my friend, and while she led the charge in placing him on a person of interest list, he doesn't hold it against her. After all, if she hadn't given me a reason, I might never have shown up at his gate. He's brokering a truce and finding ground for friendship.

"It's definitely good to see you," she says. "Come with me. Let's get you both drinks."

As we step away, Ryan and Trevor join Jack, and Dorian squeezes my hand, saying, "I'll catch up with you."

He wishes to speak with the bosses. Of course, he does. There may be more to discuss. He may be hoping for more information. Geoffrey Cromwell remains in custody on kidnapping charges, but they've been working on getting information from him all week. The investigation is far from over.

"So..." Sophia says the second we're out of earshot.

"So," I counter.

"You're back with him? It's a done deal?"

"We're taking it…" I bite back the overly simplistic, taking-it-slow description. "We're being intentional."

"You ready for DC?" She's challenging me. That's fair. She's a good friend.

"He's not pursuing a political career."

She's skeptical, but instead of voicing her doubts, she raises one eyebrow and smirks.

"He knows that's not the life I want. I've pushed him on it, actually, but no, he's insistent on staying away from politics."

"Good. I'm glad he's accepted that's not the life you want." Before, it wasn't that he didn't accept that I didn't flourish in the spotlight, he just didn't know what to do about it. At the time, leaving New York didn't feel like an option. "Are children on the horizon? Is that the life you want?"

"One day." I breathe deeply to steady myself. A month ago, I was dating other men. I need to give myself time. "Getting pregnant in our first month, even our first year back together, has bad idea written all over it. We need to find our grounding. I need to figure out how to be with him without something as unsettling as a child in the mix. Does that make sense?"

"It does. Children are…" Her eyes widen for dramatic emphasis. "Yeah."

"Are you and Fisher?"

"Not yet. But it's something I've been thinking about."

"Didn't you tell me one night years ago that you didn't want kids?"

"Things change."

"While it's just us…does it bother you at all that there's no investigation into Liam Sullivan?"

I don't call him her uncle, as I know that she's not particularly close to him. Liam has a son, her cousin she hasn't spoken to in years, who is constantly in and out of the tabloids. Her cousin lives in Los Angeles, and Liam lives in Houston, and neither of those cities are ones she travels to regularly. She's spent more time abroad than anywhere in recent years.

"I don't think he broke any laws." She slows her steps and looks at me. "He was played. That's all."

"Perhaps, but everyone in the defense industry will gain from the renewed defense priorities. I can't help but think it's worth investigating."

"There's no investigation, that I'm aware of into Dorian's involvement."

"It's not a tit-for-tat situation," I answer. "And that's not exactly true. The Bedrock board will hold an internal investigation." From what I understand, the investigation is more to review all communications from Halston, as they may have been compromised, but an investigation will occur. "And I believe the NSA is still…"

I leave the sentence unfinished. No one knows exactly what the NSA will do, but this strikes me as a situation they will not close until a comprehensive review has been completed.

"Why don't you let it go tonight? Enjoy the holiday party."

She's right. I should let it go. But this idea that the wealthy and connected aren't investigated doesn't sit well with me, especially when they have the propensity to be far more dangerous to national security and welfare than the ordinary citizen.

We reach the bar and both order the signature party cocktail, a red concoction with maraschino cherries speared with an Arrow. She taps my glass and says, "You'll drive yourself mad if you can't step away from it all and enjoy those around you.

There will never be a shortage of crises, and the one constant is change."

She nods her head in Dorian's direction. He's talking with Fisher, her husband, but was clearly headed in our direction before getting waylaid.

"Case in point," she says. "Dorian went from suspect to friend overnight."

"That he did." I absentmindedly touch my thumb to my ringless ring finger. Changes indeed. "Speaking of changes..." Sophia and Fisher have been staying in Santa Barbara in an Arrow condominium for weeks. "Are you leaving the CIA?"

"No. The line on projects between Arrow and the CIA can blur, given Arrow occasionally takes on projects from them and, you know, my father's role, but we'll be heading back east after the holidays."

Actually, I'm not clear about Jack's role within the CIA, but I'm certain it's a need-to-know arrangement.

"But I do want children. One day," Sophia says wistfully. "When I transition out of the field."

"Wow. I had this vision of you working in the field past retirement age." She grins. "You know, gray hair, knitting on a park bench."

"Nothing's set in stone. It's an idea."

"A Christmas miracle."

Still grinning, she clinks her glass against mine.

"Do you ever see Sydney?" The three of us finished in the same class at Langley. Whereas Sophia got a plum assignment pretty quickly, Sydney and I suffered for years under the same asshole. Sydney finally got her chance in the field, but last I heard, she'd been relegated back to DC, working for the same jerk.

"I hardly ever see her. You know what it's like. When Fish and I are home, we don't go out as much anymore. Getting older, I guess." Sophia shrugs her shoulder. "When we return, I'll call her. It's been a while since we got together. Too long."

"I should reach out, too. Last I spoke to her, she put in for a transfer."

"Oh, really? What does she want to do?"

"Anything outside of Flanagan's domain."

Sophia nods her head, all too knowingly. "He's such an asshole."

"Misogynist fuckwad."

She tips my glass with hers. "But you escaped."

As our glasses clink once again, I send a wish to the universe for Sydney to find something better.

"Don't look now, but Ethan's headed over."

I narrow my eyes in warning. I put up with her pushing me about Luke, but now she knows I'm with Dorian.

The tall man approaching is familiar, but only through the photographs on Stella's desk. Ethan's sandy blonde hair is longer than I would've expected from someone in the military, but he's fit. The bear hug he gives Sophia has her giggling, and her feet lift off the floor.

I watch their reunion for a moment, remembering how Sophia had described their friendship—comfortable and uncomplicated. Something warm and slightly envious twists in my chest. Before I can analyze the feeling, a familiar presence appears at my side, the subtle scent of sandalwood announcing his return before his voice does.

"Sorry about that," Dorian says, pulling me to his side. "What are you drinking?"

"It's the holiday cocktail on the menu. It's a little sweet for your taste. The snowflake martini might be more to your liking. Or you can choose your poison."

He lifts the cocktail from my hand and sips. His nose wrinkles.

"Not to your liking?"

"No," he says.

"They may have a bourbon you like."

"In a minute. Would you like to meet someone from Interpol? Actually, his wife is here, too, and she's also with Interpol. London office."

"How do you know them?" It's a silly question. Dorian seems to know everyone.

"He became friends with our old buddy, Nick. He introduced himself. I told him I'd loop back to him once I caught up with my wife." He winks, grinning proudly at the use of my descriptor.

"What do they do for Interpol?"

"I doubt his official role is listed on LinkedIn. Come to think of it, an alias is likely listed."

"Understandable. I still tell people I work for a bank." He frowns, and I sense he wants to pick at that thread, but Sophia's voice draws our attention.

"Caroline. Dorian," Sophia interjects, "I'd like to introduce you to Ethan. He's Stella and Trevor's son."

"The infamous Ethan," I say, taking his hand with a smile. "It's nice to meet you."

"Same. And I've heard a lot about you."

A familiar touch warms the curve of my spine.

"And I'm Dorian. Caroline's husband."

Our eyes lock, and an unspoken conversation flashes between us. Will I argue with him over this point? No, I accept he's territorial, but we agreed to take things day by day, and he's not sounding like he's holding to our agreement.

"How long are you in town for?" I ask Ethan

"I'm on leave through New Year's. I'll probably stay in town through Christmas and then head home."

"That's nice. I know Stella loves having you home."

Trevor steps up behind Ethan and slaps a hand on his shoulder. "We both love it when this guy makes it home. We're hitting the canyon on Monday. Mountain bikes. If you want to join us."

I hesitate a second, uncertain why he would invite me mountain biking, then it hits, he's not. He's talking to Dorian.

"Rain check? We're flying out to visit Caroline's parents for the holiday. But I'd like to take you up on that."

"You're in Colorado, right?" Trevor asks, his tone casual despite the detailed file on Dorian's properties that I know exists in Arrow's databases.

"I have a place there. As you know." Dorian's voice remains even, acknowledging the game without playing it.

"Right, I do." Trevor's gaze shifts to me, then back. "So you'll be sticking around with this one?"

The protective intent behind the question hangs in the air. Dorian's hand finds mine.

"I'll do my best to do just that," Dorian answers, a simple truth carrying the weight of promise.

With a wide grin, Ethan scratches his jaw and says, "Always so protective." He slaps his dad on his back and steps away, saying, "Nice to meet you, Caroline. Dorian."

We all watch as he joins Stella and Ava.

"He didn't bring a date?" Sophia asks Trevor.

Trevor shakes his head, grinning. "No. He got corralled last minute into coming. But he's spent years with these guys. They're like family."

"Ryan and Alex have kids too, right?"

"They do. College. They're too busy these days when they're home on break to come to something like this."

"It's a nice holiday party," Dorian says, clearly making small talk.

"It's smaller than normal. The guys from up north stayed up there this year."

"Up north?" Dorian asks.

"Napa area," Trevor says. "They've got family up there, so it's hard to get away. A lot of our team works remotely. We also have team members based in North Carolina, but one of those guys just had a baby. They're not here tonight either."

"You're talking about Knox, right?" I ask, and he grins with a nod. "The way Stella shares Knox's daughter's baby photos around the office, you'd think she's the grandmother."

"Have you worked with Knox?" Trevor asks.

"Not Knox, but I debriefed Sam." I feel like I know him now. "He's on sabbatical, right?"

"Well-deserved. He's a good guy. On call if we need him, but hopefully, we won't."

The risk level has de-escalated. Our allies are working with us to assess the situation and enact appropriate prevention protocols. And it's the holidays. The world feels calmer during festive periods.

"Let me know if there's ever anything I can do," Dorian says. He's undoubtedly referring to his satellite network.

"For now, let's hope we can all relax and enjoy the holidays," Trevor says. "You know, we're talking about taking a summer vacation. Bringing all of us together on Jack's island at a time of year when it's easier for everyone to get away. If we do it, you'll get to see everyone. Knox and his baby included. The island's fantastic. Stella and I have a place there. We get away every chance we get."

"Stella mentioned it," I say, remembering her office photo of Trevor windsurfing.

"Yeah, we've been talking about it for a while, but it'll happen. Stella's determined. If we do it, I hope you both can join us." Trevor gives Dorian a firm handshake and steps away.

"Ethan was correct. Trevor is protective of you," Dorian says.

"It's just how he is. I'm in the office a lot, and since his office is in another building, he floats around, talking to everybody when he comes over. He's gotten to know me, and he looks out for his team."

"They know you left me, right?"

"You left emotionally before I left physically." I point a finger at him with enough of a smile that it's clear I'm not looking to start a world war, but I won't bear the fallout of our marriage alone.

He nods. There's a conversation going on behind those dark eyes of his again, and I'd push him to hear his thoughts, but we aren't in the right place. Still, I'm done repeating past mistakes.

"Here's what we're going to do," I tell him. "We're going to say hello to Ryan, and I'll introduce you to his wife, Alex. There's more for us to discuss, but we won't do it here. Tomorrow, we have a long flight on a private plane and nothing to interrupt us. I want to hear everything going on inside that head of yours. Got it?"

I reach up to tap his temple lightly with my index finger, and he circles my wrist and presses his lips to my palm.

"I like this side of you."

"You do?"

"Taking charge. Speaking your thoughts."

"Yeah, well, that goes both ways. Unless you say what you're thinking, I can't possibly know."

"True." His gaze roams the festive decorations and the lighted trees clustered in corners. Outside, lights wrap the palm trees. "Why don't you have any decorations up in your house?"

"Didn't feel it this season." In truth, I haven't decorated since I left our decorations behind in our townhouse. But those decorations weren't on display in his home. "You didn't decorate either."

"No. My house manager offered, but I told her not to bother."

"Do you still have our decorations?"

"I do. Found the boxes after moving to Colorado."

"You found them?"

"Well, the packers found them. Asked me what to do with the boxes."

"You worked with the packers?"

"No. The house manager did. She asked me."

I grin, rolling my eyes.

We navigate the rest of the party, Dorian's hand rarely leaving mine. As he charms Ryan's wife with a story about satellite launches, I find myself watching him—this man I once left, now returned to me somehow both changed and the same —and still evolving.

Later, as we walk back along the moonlit path toward the cars, glittering string lights marking our way, he pulls me close against the evening chill.

"I never put up those decorations after you left," he confesses quietly. "Couldn't bear to see them without you."

I stop, turning to face him. "I never bought new ones. Didn't have the desire to replace what we had. Christmas kind of lost its sparkle."

His smile reaches his eyes, crinkling the corners in that way that always makes my heart skip. "Next Christmas."

"Next Christmas," I echo, the simple phrase containing a universe of promises.

He brushes a strand of hair from my face, his touch lingering. "Maybe we could start a new tradition. Something just for us."

"Like what?"

"I don't know. Maybe we each choose one new ornament every year. Something that represents the year we had together."

I smile, leaning into him. "What would this year's be?"

"A helicopter," he suggests with a laugh. "Or maybe a yacht."

"Or maybe just a key," I say softly. "For second chances and new beginnings."

He pulls me close, his lips brushing my forehead. "I like that. The key to everything that matters."

Around us, the holiday lights twinkle like stars brought down to earth, illuminating not just the path before us, but all the possibilities that lie ahead. Not a perfect ending, but a perfect beginning—again

CHAPTER 40

DORIAN

The car service pulls up in front of the familiar two-story brick colonial in Old Greenwich, Connecticut. Snow dusts the lawn like powdered sugar, and Christmas wreaths with red velvet ribbons hang in each window. Even in daylight, the Christmas tree positioned behind the picture window glows with warm white lights—clearly lit in anticipation of their daughter's arrival.

I take a deep breath, my stomach tightening. Last time I stood on this doorstep, I was delivering Caroline's childhood possessions after she left me.

The front door opens, and her parents crowd the stoop. Her

father stands patiently behind his wife, and surprisingly, his focus appears to be on his daughter, not on the man he instructed to "take care of her."

Anne, Caroline's mother, releases her daughter and turns to me. Her smile isn't as warm as the one she gave Caroline, but it's more than I expected. "Dorian. It's good to see you again."

Take care of her.

Those four words her father spoke on our wedding day echo in my head. Words I failed to honor.

On the way over, I asked Caroline what she'd told her parents. She said that she'd told her mom we were seeing each other again. That we're taking things day by day.

Then I asked what she'd told them when we separated. "I told them I wasn't happy and that it was better if we split." She held my hand to soften the truth, but it still sliced. The pain didn't make the fact any less true.

Take care of her.

I let her father down.

If she had ever needed money, I most certainly would've given it to her. I chose not to follow my father's precedent. I never canceled her credit cards or closed down access to her bank accounts. I told my lawyer I wanted a fair prenuptial agreement, not that she ever saw a cent of that because we never filed for divorce. Neither of us did. But she didn't need the money. Or if she did, she never asked for any. But her father wasn't telling me to provide for her.

Where I failed is in taking care of his daughter's heart. I dragged her into a harsh world filled with scrutiny and didn't protect her. I left her to fend off the vultures while I pursued my dreams and familial responsibilities.

She said that she was suffocating. I should've been the one to give her oxygen, but instead, I allowed my world to smother her.

Anne Scott's hug is quick, nothing like the long embrace she gave Caroline, but I'm off-kilter from her unexpected touch. When she steps back, her husband offers his hand.

"Dorian. Good to see you again, son."

My throat tightens and doesn't ease until Caroline's fingers slip into my hand.

"Come on inside. It's chilly," Mrs. Scott says.

It's actually warmer than in Telluride, but compared to Santa Barbara, the low forties here in Connecticut are chilly.

We crowd the foyer beneath an antique chandelier that's hung there since Caroline was a child. The scent of cinnamon and pine mingles with something baking—cookies, maybe— creating that unmistakable fragrance of a family Christmas that I never experienced in my own childhood home.

"Oh, Mom, I love the decorations." Our gazes connect, and an unspoken promise crosses between us.

Next year, we'll have our own.

Mr. Scott bends for a suitcase handle, and I'm quick to jump in. "I can take these."

Her father is in good shape, but he's in his late seventies and doesn't need to be hauling our luggage up the stairs.

"Oh, I have Caroline in her room," Mrs. Scott calls up to my retreating back. "And…um…you can take the room across the hall."

"Mom," I hear Caroline say, and I'm glad my back is to them so they can't see my grin. While it's ludicrous that at forty-one I'd be sleeping across the hall from my wife, the rules are heart-warming in a way. Their insistence on following the rules they themselves grew up with makes me feel like I'm part of something—not just something, their family.

As I open my mouth to say it's fine, Caroline's voice rings out, "Mom, we're still technically married. We never divorced."

"I don't see rings," Mr. Scott says.

A touch of mirth coats his words, but nevertheless, when I reach the landing, I dutifully deposit Caroline's suitcase in what was once her childhood bedroom. The lavender walls and daisy curtains I remember from our engagement visit are gone, replaced by tasteful beige and navy. Her collection of worn paperbacks and academic trophies, the physical evidence of who she was before me, is all packed away.

It strikes me how little I know about her formative years, how rarely I asked. Another failure to add to my list.

A creak on the stairs lets me know someone is coming.

"You know, they never come upstairs. This is just—"

"Caroline, it's fine." I press my lips to her temple. "Your father's right." I lift her hand, my thumb brushing across her bare ring finger. The absence feels significant in a way it never has before.

"Do you still have your rings?" I ask quietly.

"Yes." Her answer is immediate, certain.

I nod, studying her face. "I've never felt their absence quite so much."

"Are you okay?" The concern in her eyes reminds me how perceptive she's always been—perhaps why I fell into the habit of not speaking my thoughts. She seemed to understand without words.

I lift her hand and press a kiss to her ring finger. "One day," I say, meaning it as both a question and a promise.

"My rings are in my jewelry box back home."

"Mine is with my cufflinks in Colorado."

"We can—"

I stop her with a finger over her lips.

"We will. One day. I promised you we'll take it day by day, and I intend to fulfill my promise."

She flattens her fingers over my chest, smoothing the holiday plaid flannel shirt she picked for me to wear today.

"I thought, maybe, we could give your mom a call?" Caroline's voice is gentle, tentative.

Something tightens in my chest. My mother. The woman I met for the first time just days ago, after a lifetime of believing she abandoned me.

"It's Christmas," she adds when I don't immediately respond. "We can call her together."

"She has her own family. I'm sure she's busy with them." The excuse sounds hollow even to my ears.

"She'd love for us to call. I told her we might."

"Caroline…" I start to protest, but those pleading blue eyes make resistance futile.

"We don't have a relationship." It's the truth, but saying it aloud feels like admitting defeat.

"No, but that's the funny thing about relationships. They build over time. And they start with a conversation." Her fingers brush my cheek. "She never stopped loving you, even when she couldn't reach you."

The words shouldn't hit, but they do. I pull Caroline tight against me, grateful for her solidity while everything else in my world has shifted.

"You really want this, don't you?"

She nods, with her upper teeth sinking into her lower lip. It's a look I've never said no to.

"All right. Let's do it."

"Mom has a list of cookies we need to make to give to the neighbors. Why don't we do that, and after we finish, we'll call. I'll text your mom to coordinate a time."

"Okay. Make sure she doesn't feel obligated. She shouldn't miss out on time with her family."

"Dorian. You're her family, too. You're her son. She loves you. And she always will."

Man, saying it like that stirs emotions I'm too old to feel.

"We can call your dad, too."

"Nah, we'll see him on our way back." I can't stand the confusion he so often exhibits when we have a video call. Even though video calls were coming into use before he slowed his time at the office, he never warmed to them. And now, they just seem to increase his confusion.

"I didn't ask…when you saw him in Colorado, how was he?"

"He misses Geoffrey. I think he keeps expecting him. But Dad's doing okay. The staff is good with him. They're good at redirecting him."

"When we go back, do you think I can go through his files?"

"Of course. Whatever you want. These days, most everything is electronic, but Dad's from a different generation. There's no telling what you might find in his files."

"That's what I'm thinking."

The authorities likely have access to all his electronic files, but my father has decades of paper files. She can dig as much as she likes. I won't hide anything from my wife.

She links her fingers with mine.

"Are you ready to brave the parentals?" Caroline asks, squeezing my hand.

I smile at the term she's always used. "Do you think our kids will refer to us as 'the parentals'?"

"No. I mean, we wouldn't force separate bedrooms—"

"Who says? If we have a daughter, absolutely."

She pinches my sides, and I twist away, laughing. "Ow!"

"We will treat any son or daughter equally."

"Are you two coming down?" Anne calls from the base of the stairs.

I pull Caroline against me, pressing my forehead to hers. "You know, I never imagined having this again—family, holidays, a future worth planning for."

Her eyes soften. "Is that what you want? A family?"

"With you? Yes." I brush my thumb across her cheek. "Once we've found our way back to each other properly."

She leans up and kisses me softly, but I don't take the kiss deeper; instead, I call down to Caroline's mother, "Yes, ma'am, we're coming!"

But instead of moving, I hold Caroline a moment longer.

This house, with its Christmas lights and cookie-scented air, represents everything I missed growing up—and everything I nearly lost forever. But as Caroline leads me down the stairs, her hand warm in mine, I realize it's not just her parents' home we're experiencing, but the promise of our own.

A home where promises will be kept. Where separate bedrooms are a quaint memory. Where perhaps someday, the patter of small feet will join ours on Christmas morning.

Not today, but someday. Day by day, just as we promised.

The End

Blind Prophet concludes the Arrow Tactical Series, but the

spirit continues, with visits from the Arrow world, in The Sinful State Series.

The first book, Only the Wicked, releases September, 2025.

When the meek inherit the world, the wicked shall rule it.

GRATITUDE

This is the NINTH book in the Arrow Tactical series. It's hard to believe this series is coming to an end. I'll miss these guys, but like I told my newsletter peeps, I expect cameos in my next series. I've got connections with those guys so I don't think they'll deny me.

Coincidentally, I wrapped this series up in the same month my daughter graduated from high school. One chapter closes, another opens. Bittersweet days.

Where to start with the gratitude?

On this one, I have to say, Mr. Jolie deserves HUGE thanks. He read the first draft and was like…"Oh no. You must make changes."

To my betas…thank you for your input. You read before it's polished and your insights are so, so valuable.

I kept going around this one (it's SO hard to end a series!)—to the point I sent revisions to my editor WHILE she was working on it. And…Karen…oh my. Your patience on this. And all of your effort. You're the best.

Then Jaime…during your move no less!…you went through and polished and corrected and found little words and phrases I just have wrong in my head!

To Damonza, the designer for the entire series, thank you

for your care and attention and for creating covers that I believe will work for this series for years and years to come.

To my advanced reader team, thank you so much for reading, reviewing, answering my questions, and sharing my books on the vast web and beyond. Every time someone asks to be on my ARC team I get so excited—it's an honor. You are the loveliest! Pure gold!

To my readers, thank you for taking a chance on me. There are millions of stories out there, and I'm grateful you chose to read mine.

ALSO BY ISABEL JOLIE

Sinful State Series

Only the Wicked - Releasing September, 2025

Only the Devil - Releasing November, 2025

Only the Lovely - Releasing March, 2026

Arrow Tactical Security Series

Better to See You (Wolf and Alexandria)

Sure of One (Jack and Ava)

Cloak of Red (Sophia and Fisher)

Stolen Beauty (Knox and Sage)

Savage Beauty (Max and Sloane)

Sinful Beauty (Tristan and Lucia)

Gilded Saint (Sam and Willow)

Scarlet Angel (Nick and Scarlet)

Blind Prophet (Dorian and Caroline)

The Twisted Vines Series

Crushed (Erik and Vivi)

Breathe (Kairi and David)

Savor (Trevor and Stella)

Haven Island Series

Rogue Wave (Tate and Luna)

Adrift (Gabe and Poppy)

First Light (Logan and Cali)

The West Side Series

Blurred Lines (Jackson and Anna)

Trust Me (Sam Duke and Olivia)

Finding Delilah (Delilah and Mason)

Forgetting Him (Jason and Maggie)

Chasing Frost (Chase and Sadie)

Misplaced Mistletoe (Ashton aka Dr. Bobby and Nora)

Standalone Romances

How to Survive a Holiday Fling (Oliver Duke and Kate)

Always Sunny (Ian Duke and Sandra)

The Romantics (Harrison and Zuri)

ABOUT THE AUTHOR

Isabel Jolie, aka Izzy, lives on a lake, loves dogs of all stripes, and if she's not working, she can be found reading, often with a glass of wine. In prior lives, Izzy worked in marketing and advertising, in a variety of industries, such as financial services, entertainment, and technology. In this life, she loves daydreaming and writing contemporary romances with real, flawed characters with inner strength.

Sign-up for Izzy's newsletter to keep up-to-date on new releases, promotions and giveaways. (**Pro-tip** - She offers a free book on her home page...just scroll down after arriving at her site.)

Buy ebooks and signed paperbacks direct from Isabel at www.isabeljoliebooks.com

Want to say hi? Email her through her website or reply to her newsletter...she loves to hear from readers.

www.ingramcontent.com/pod-product-compliance
Lightning Source LLC
Chambersburg PA
CBHW061545190726
48289CB00004B/1176